THE HERMIT
OF
LAMMAS WOOD

This book and any parts thereof may not be reproduced in any form, stored in any retrieval system, or transmitted in any manner except as authorized in writing by the author.

All characters, places, and events in this work are fiction or fictionalized. Any resemblance to actual people, places, or events is coincidental.

ISBN-13: 978-1-940575-07-0
ISBN-10: 1940575079
BISAC: Fiction / Fantasy / Historical

For more information, or to leave a comment about this book, please visit us at:
http://www.lammaswood.com

Copyright © 2013 Nathan Lowell, Greeley, CO

PRINTED IN THE UNITED STATES
First printing: January, 2014

To Debora Geary

who convinced me that happy endings

sometimes make good beginnings.

Also by Nathan Lowell

Quarter Share

Half Share

Full Share

Double Share

Captain's Share

Owner's Share

South Coast

Table of Contents

1. A New Beginning 1
2. Mother Oakton 7
3. A Misplaced Corpse 15
4. Bon Voyage 21
5. Plans Laid 25
6. The King's Own 31
7. Time To Go 41
8. Slipping The Leash 47
9. On The Trail 53
10. Flown 59
11. Followed 63
12. Ole Man 69
13. In The Black Rock 75
14. Canyon Dreams 81
15. A Touch Of Weather 87
16. Those Who Came Before 93
17. Valley Of A Thousand Smokes 99
18. A Stone Cottage 105
19. Cider 117
20. Tall Tales 125
21. A Lonely Mule 131
22. The Old Knowledge 139
23. Beginning Lessons 145

24. Terrible Gossips	153
25. Sticks And Stones	161
26. Going South	167
27. Into The Woods	173
28. More Lessons	179
29. Intruders	183
30. Strategic Retreat	193
31. A Mad Plan	199
32. Into The Hole	205
33. Chained	213
34. Some Outside Help	219
35. Punch Press	225
36. Break Out	233
37. Hide And Seek	241
38. Hunters And Hunted	249
39. Unlikely Ally	255
40. Bad News	261
41. Back Down	271
42. Trapped	279
43. New Plans	285
44. More Gossip	297

The Hermit of Lammas Wood

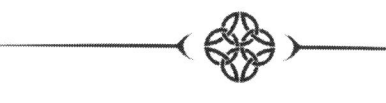

Nathan Lowell

Durandus

Chapter 1
A New Beginning

———◆———

The scent of pine and wood smoke drew Tanyth out of sleep. A watery light from the window hinted at a dawn not long past, and the quiet rumbles from below spoke volumes about early risers. Lifting her head, she glanced over to the empty cot where Rebecca should have been. The coverlet lay pulled up and smoothed.

Tanyth smiled and rolled herself out of the warm cocoon of blankets, shivering a bit across her arms at the sudden chill. She tugged on a woolen pullover before reaching for her trousers, then padded barefoot across the smooth wooden flooring to peer out the window.

The inn sat on a rise. The view from the second floor overlooked the narrow harbor and the Bight beyond. The sun's rays slashed across the water and stone piers. Beyond the headland, blue stretched to the horizon. One small craft beat its way out of the harbor, disappearing around the headland as she watched. *Zypheria's Call* rested beside the pier, her masts looking oddly naked without the canvas suit.

The clanking of cutlery and rumble of voices drew Tanyth back inside.

"Time's wastin'," she muttered.

She picked her way down the stairs to find the dining room bustling and a cheery fire in the huge stone hearth. Rebecca smiled at her and gave a little wave from a table near the fireplace.

"Good morning, mum," Rebecca said as Tanyth joined her.

"Good mornin'. Did you sleep well?" Tanyth helped herself to a mug of tea from the heavy china teapot on the table.

"Took me a while to get used to the bed not rocking." Rebecca gave a short laugh. "Funny the things you get used to, eh? Slept good after that." She pushed her mug toward Tanyth, who topped it off from the pot.

"Did seem strange not to have to brace myself to put my pants on," Tanyth said.

They shared knowing smiles and addressed their tea.

Amanda sailed out of the kitchen, baskets of bread stacked on a tray. She smiled at Tanyth and gave a little nod. "One minute, mum," she said. She made one pass around the room, delivering baskets in her wake to the other diners and ending at Tanyth's table where, with a flourish, she placed the last one.

"Good mornin', Amanda," Tanyth said, inhaling the yeasty aroma wafting out of the covered basket.

"Good morning, mum. Sleep well?"

"Oh, aye. That husband of yours brews a fine ale, and I found it quite relaxin'." She grinned and took a pull from the mug.

Amanda's smile broadened. "He does, but don't tell him that. He's already got enough of a head on him that gettin' him through the door is a challenge some days. You ladies want some breakfast this morning? Comes with the room."

"Yes, please," Rebecca said, lifting her nose into the air to take a deep breath. "Something smells wonderful."

"Perry's in there makin' griddle cakes like there's a room full of longshoremen out here."

A gnarled older man with ruddy cheeks and a stubbled jaw at the next table guffawed. "Wonder why he thinks that?" he said, slapping the table with his open hand.

Amanda cast her gaze around the room at all the burly men seated in the booths and at the tables. "Don't know where he gets these notions, Willum. Something in the wind, maybe," Amanda said, a wry smile pulling at the corner of her mouth.

Several men at nearby tables chuckled.

"Sounds lovely," Tanyth said.

The outer doors opened and a few more burly men stomped in.

"I better tell Perry he'll need a few more cakes," Amanda said. "You two want anything special this morning?"

"Griddle cakes sound good to me," Rebecca said, her lips curled in a smile.

"Comin' up." She disappeared back into the kitchen with a swirl of skirt.

Rebecca put her cup down and looked across at Tanyth. "So, what're you thinkin' we should do next, mum?"

"Visit the local healers. Check out the lay of the land."

"Think they know of the hermit?"

Tanyth lifted one shoulder in a shrug and let it fall. "Either way we'll learn somethin'."

Willum's rough, low voice interrupted them. "The hermit?"

Tanyth turned to find the man leaning away from his table to speak to them. "You know of the hermit? Willum, isn't it?"

"Yes'm. Willum Mayter."

Tanyth held out a hand. "Tanyth Fairport. Nice to meet you."

The man's shaggy eyebrows bobbed up and down a couple of times before he briefly grasped her hand. "Howdy," he said.

Tanyth felt the rough calluses on his hands and the strength in his grip. "Aye. We're looking for the hermit," she said. "You know of her?"

"Mum, ever'body knows of the hermit. Nasty piece of work. You really don't wanna be messin' around there."

Tanyth shared a brief glance at Rebecca before turning back to the man. "You've met her?"

Willum's eyebrows shot up but couldn't even approach the hairline that appeared to have gone out with some long-ago tide. "Hardly, mum. And the hermit ain't a she. He's a he."

"Must be two different hermits," Rebecca said. "Gertie Pinecrest? You know of her?"

Willum's eyebrows came back down, almost meeting in the middle as he frowned. "No," he said at last. "No, I don't believe I know that name."

The Hermit Of Lammas Wood

"She's supposed to be the hermit of Lammas Wood. I need to find her," Tanyth said.

"Well, good luck on that one, mum," Willum said. "Only hermit of Lammas Wood I know of is a crazy ole bugger lives on the far side of Notched Mountain up in the Valley of a Thousand Smokes."

"You've never met this hermit, then?" Tanyth asked again.

"Lord and Lady, no. I don't get that far out of town. The stories are bad enough." He shook his head and leaned closer. "You'd be wise to leave off right here and head back to Kleesport with Captain Groves."

Amanda burst from the kitchen then with platters of griddle cakes and small, fat sausages. "Who's hungry?" she called.

A great shout answered her along with much slapping of table tops.

Perry followed her out, and between the two of them they had the whole room served in nothing flat. The ambient chatter dropped to nearly nothing as hungry men dug into piles of cakes and sausages, all washed down with bottomless mugs of tea.

"This looks wonderful," Rebecca said, slathering her stack of cakes with butter.

Tanyth drizzled a bit of honey across the top of hers and nodded. "This'll get us off to a good start."

In less time than seemed possible, the men finished eating. The ambient noise in the room rose slowly until Willum pushed back his chair and stood.

"All right, you lot. Time to earn them griddle cakes." He jerked a thumb toward the door. "We got a ship to unload and reload. Time to git at it."

The gathered men all stood, queued more or less neatly, and moved through the doorway, heavy boots shuffling and the occasional taunt and chatter rippling through the crowd.

Amanda came out of the kitchen drying her hands on her apron hem. "That time already, Willum?"

Willum grinned. "Got 'em fed. Need to get 'em movin' before they start thinkin' it's time for a nap." He dug in his pocket, then tossed a gold coin onto the table. It clunked heavily on the wood and clattered a bit against the cutlery.

"That cover the damages, Amanda?"

"You know it's more than enough, Willum. Bring 'em back at lunch and we'll get 'em fed up again for the afternoon."

He gave her a salute with one meaty finger. "Thanks, Amanda. Gonna be a good season, I think."

"Hope so," she said. "We could use one."

"True enough." Willum pulled a heavy jacket from the peg on the wall and shrugged into it on the way to the door. He tugged a knit cap over his sparsely populated scalp before he disappeared out into the morning, the heavy doors at the front of the inn closing behind him with a heavy thunk.

Amanda crossed to the table and motioned at the teapot. "You need more tea, ladies?"

Tanyth hefted the pot and dribbled a bit into her mug. "We got plenty, I think. We'll be gettin' out of your way here in a few minutes ourselves."

"Big plans?" she asked, beginning to gather the used crockery and utensils from the next table.

"Gonna see the sights," Rebecca said, a wry grin curling her mouth on one side.

Amanda snorted. "That won't take long. Barely enough time to brew a fresh pot."

"Not much to see, then?" Tanyth asked.

"Well, you've seen the docks and walked past the warehouses. You've spent the night at the inn. Other than a few houses tucked back in the forest, that leaves only the King's Own garrison fort, a few shops, and a couple of taverns."

Tanyth glanced at Rebecca before turning back to Amanda. "That's it?"

"Well, the healers have offices in their houses. There's a lumber yard inland a bit. Maybe half an hour's walk." She paused and cocked her head to one side, her eyes focused elsewhere. "That's about it."

"You mentioned somethin' about the healers last night. All men from the King's College?"

Amanda stopped her bustling and straightened up with a glance at the kitchen door. "Yeah. Garrison troops and longshoremen take a lot of healin'. Most women in town won't visit them." She looked down, resting a hand on her belly.

"Any particular reason?" Rebecca asked.

Amanda's shoulders lifted and dropped in the tiniest of shrugs. "They're used to dealing with garrison troops and longshoremen," she said, as if that explained it all.

"Where do the women go? Town got a midwife?" Tanyth asked, toying with the mug of cooling tea on the table.

"Yeah. Mother Oakton. She's got a house on the next street up the hill. Most of the women see her when they've the need."

Tanyth gave Amanda a sideways glance. "Doctors don't take kindly to her, I take it."

Amanda sniffed and shook her head but before she could speak, Perry burst through the kitchen door, an empty bucket in one hand and a half-full one in the other. He flashed them a smile as he set to working along the wall of booths, stacking dirty dishes in the empty bucket and wiping down the tables with soapy water from the other.

Amanda gave Tanyth a small nod before returning to her chores.

"Right then," Tanyth said, pushing herself up from the table. "Lemme get my staff and hat, and we'll be off to see the sights."

Chapter 2
Mother Oakton

The sun shone brightly through the tops of the spruce trees by the time Rebecca and Tanyth stepped out of the inn. Tanyth pulled her wool coat closed around herself and buttoned a couple of buttons. Their breath steamed in the chill morning.

"Don't seem much like spring, eh, mum?" Rebecca said, buttoning her own coat and pulling her wool cap down over her ears.

"I 'spect it'll be warm enough by noon." She cast a smile in Rebecca's direction. "Sooner if we go visit them healers."

"Is there any point to that, mum? Sounds like Mother Oakton is our best bet."

"That's my thinkin'. Willum made me think the fewer people who know we're looking for the hermit, the fewer people we'll have tryin' to stop us."

"There's that."

They headed back to the main north-south road through town and turned up the hill. They passed a shop with worked wood in the small window–mostly carved items that might have been toys. Tanyth read the words "Andrew Carver – Cabinet Maker" painted on the glass in a neat hand. At the next intersection they stopped.

"Left or right, mum?"

Tanyth looked to the right. Several large buildings lined the road before it disappeared into the trees. A barrel hung suspended from a stout metal pole over the doors of one. "That must be the tavern."

"One of 'em, anyway," Rebecca said.

The Hermit Of Lammas Wood

Tanyth turned left and strolled down the hard-packed street. They passed small houses, some with stick fences around small garden plots–most just bare earth, still packed from winter snows. Near the end of the block, just before the street ended at a stand of twisted pine trees, they stopped in front of a neat two-story building. A pine-needle path traced a curving walkway from the street to the low porch. Other paths ran between and around patches of earth–some with brushy plants well established, others simple plots of fresh looking earth, and still others with mounds of leaf mulch clinging to them.

"Good morn, ladies. Can I help ye?" A young woman looking barely older than Rebecca came around the side of the house.

Tanyth pushed her hat back and leaned on her staff. "We're looking for Mother Oakton. Amanda said she lives on this street?"

A smile glowed against the woman's tanned face. "She does, indeed. In this very house, as it happens."

"We'd like to speak with her if that's possible," Rebecca said when it became clear the young woman had nothing to add.

"You are," she said and her smile got even broader. "You came on the *Call*, I take it?"

Tanyth answered the woman's smile with one of her own. "We did. I'm Tanyth Fairport and this is my traveling companion, Rebecca Marong."

Rebecca nodded in greeting.

"Well, neither of you seems to be with child. Why don't you come up on the porch and we'll chat about why you want to see me?" The woman followed one of the pine trails to the porch and tugged a couple of wooden chairs into the sun.

Rebecca and Tanyth shared a surprised glance as they joined the woman on her porch.

They settled even as the younger woman's smile graced them with her evident amusement.

"Most people who don't know me come looking for my mother," she said. "Dear soul passed these two winters back."

"And you took over the family business, I take it?" Tanyth

asked.

"Yeah. Such as it is." Her smile faded a bit as her focus turned to someplace in the middle distance. "Woulda wished she'd hung around a little longer. Woulda been nice to have her deliverin' her own grandbabies."

Tanyth saw Rebecca's eyebrows arch in surprise.

"Don't look so startled, dear," the woman said. "I reckon you're old enough to have a few of your own, and I've a few winters on you."

"Well, yes. Of course," Rebecca said. "Just...well...you don't look married." Her voice choked off and her face flushed red. "Or anything."

The woman threw back her head, musical peals of laughter echoing through the nearby wood. "Or anything. That's about it." She stopped laughing to bestow a friendly wink on the blushing woman. "Husband is helpful but most any man'll do. Just never found one I wanted to have around long enough to have kids with."

"Sorry," Rebecca said, looking at her hands where they clasped each other for support in her lap.

"Nothin' to be sorry about. Nothin' at all." She turned to Tanyth. "So, I'm Penny Oakton. Most people in town call me 'Mother Oakton' because it's what they called my mother. What can I do for you?"

"I need to find the hermit," Tanyth said.

Penny arched one eyebrow and pursed her lips. "Do ya now?"

"I do."

"Can I ask why?"

Tanyth paused for a moment. "You're not going to try to convince me that she's a he or that it's too dangerous?"

A hint of her previous smile returned. "No. I don't think so. I just wanna know why you think you need to see her."

Tanyth took a deep breath and let it out slowly through her nose.

"She thinks she's going mad," Rebecca said.

Tanyth shot a quelling look at Rebecca, who shook her head and threw her hands up in surrender.

"Well, madness. That's serious business," Penny said.

"You sure you wanna find the hermit? Lotta people 'round here think she's mad herself."

"So she's not a he?"

"Who told you that?" Penny asked, amusement adding a lilt to her voice.

"Willum Mayter."

She laughed again. "Anybody in pants is a man to dear Willum, and I'm sure he's never set foot more than two miles outside of this town since he's been here." She shook her head. "No, he's just repeatin' tales. Lotta folks have some strange ideas about old Gert."

"So you know her?" Rebecca asked.

"Well, I know of her," Penny said. "My mother knew her. Studied with her for a time, as I remember. Back when Papa was still with us."

"What can you tell us?" Tanyth said.

Penny's eyes squinted a little in the morning sun. She studied Tanyth—measuring her up and down–before spending several long moments gazing into her face. "I can tell you where to find her, but there's no guarantee she'll talk to you."

"I understand that."

After another short pause, Penny said, "So, tell me about this madness."

"She's not mad," Rebecca broke in.

Tanyth raised a hand, but Penny looked to the young woman.

"I said she thinks she's going mad."

"I get that a lot, too. Lots of people think they're going mad over the winters. Hard to get out. No place to go when ya do. Some of them actually do go around the bend a bit. Might be something I've seen myself." She paused and stared at Rebecca. "You care about her."

"I'm right here, you know," Tanyth said.

Penny reached over and patted Tanyth's forearm. "You are. And you're not mad. I wanna know why Rebecca thinks you are."

"I don't think she is," Rebecca said.

"But something's odd, right?"

Rebecca shot a quick glance at Tanyth before looking back

to Penny. "Yeah. Something's odd."

Penny turned back to Tanyth. "You're seeing things you shouldn't be seein'? Strange happenings around you sometimes."

"Well, seeing things I shouldn't be. Yeah."

"And strange things keep happening," Rebecca said.

Tanyth turned to her. "What strange things?"

"Storm? Poof? And then a new current? You don't call that strange?"

"You keep talking about that storm. I keep trying to tell you it was lightning."

"Tanyth? I was in the rigging. The storm was right there. I coulda touched it almost. You were on the deck under me? Remember?"

"Well, of course I remember. There's nothing wrong with my memory."

"And there's nothing wrong with my sight or my hearing. I watched you stamping that staff of yours on the deck and then keeling over like you'd been coshed. I'd have seen lightning if it hit ya. I'd at least have heard the thunder." Rebecca turned her gaze to Penny. "She was out for three days after that. Came to like nothin' happened."

"That's because nothing happened," Tanyth said. "You and the Groveses have been trying to convince me otherwise ever since."

Rebecca slumped back in her chair and waved dismissively.

"Seems to me that something happened," Penny said.

They turned to her. Tanyth opened her mouth to speak but Penny held up a hand.

"My turn to talk," she said. "You're not going mad. Strange things are happening." She cocked her head to the right, appraising Tanyth again. "You're what? Fifty-five winters?"

"Fifty-four."

"And she's been on the road for twenty of them," Rebecca said.

"That right?" Penny asked, turning to Tanyth.

"Yeah."

Penny shot Rebecca a wink. "Glad you're here. I'd never

get anything out of her otherwise."

Rebecca's eyes went wide with alarm. "I didn't mean—"

"Oh, shush," Penny said and turned back to Tanyth. "Your change started?"

"Last fall. Maybe a little before."

Penny nodded. "And this all started about the same time," she said. It was not a question.

"Yeah. About then."

"You need to see Gertie."

"That's what I thought," Tanyth said. "Think she can heal me?"

"No." The young woman gave her head a little shake. "There's nothin' wrong with you. You're just lucky enough to live longer than most. Nothin' Gertie can do about that—'cept kill ya, and that's not what you need her for."

"What do I need her for?"

"To explain what's goin' on."

"You seem to know something about it."

"I do. Something, but not enough. Someday, maybe. If I live long enough." Penny's happy smile took on a wistful air.

"Can you tell me what you know?" Tanyth said.

Penny took a deep breath through her nose and cast her gaze out to the dark pines at the end of the street. Eventually she spoke. "The All-Mother has a plan for all women. Just as the All-Father has a plan for all men. Her plan has three steps—maiden, mother, crone. When she takes away one gift, she gives another to take its place." Her focus returned to Tanyth's face. "You understand what I'm saying?"

"Yeah. I understand," Tanyth said.

"That's why you need to meet Gertie."

"Does she have the answers?" Tanyth asked.

Penny's smile spread slowly across her face. "Perhaps. But the answers are less important than the questions."

"You seem to know a lot about a woman you never met."

"I never said I didn't meet her. Just that I don't know her." Penny shook her head. "She's my grandmother. She moved out into the wood when I was but a wee girl. I remember her as a strong and vibrant woman who loved family and life."

"How can you say you don't know her, then?" Rebecca asked.

"People change. I've not talked to her since she took to the wood."

"Why not?" Tanyth asked. "Don't you know where she lives?"

"Oh, I know." Penny paused and gazed out at the trees again. "My mother showed me the way. I've made the trip several times. Each time, she's not there. Just a hot cup of tea and a fresh pastry on the sideboard." She shrugged and looked down at her hands. "I have no idea why. Maybe she's just bein' a hermit."

They sat there in silence for several long minutes. The sun beat down on them and Tanyth opened her coat to feel the warmth on her body. She tilted her head back, turning her face to the light like a flower might. Without opening her eyes, she asked, "Will you take us to her?"

"Audry McGilvry is due in a week. After she's done, we'll go." Penny's voice came low, barely audible over the rising sussuration of wind in the pine tops. "It'll take three, maybe four days, depending on how fast we can go. Can you do that on foot?"

Tanyth opened her eyes and turned her gaze to the young woman. "My dear, I've walked a thousand miles or more in the last twenty-odd winters. Three or four more days are a pittance."

Chapter 3
A Misplaced Corpse

Every passing day seemed a bit warmer, a bit more welcoming than the last. Within a pair of days, Saul and Benjamin Groves showed up at the inn and invited Rebecca and Tanyth to dine with them.

"We'll sail with the morning tide," Captain Groves said, raising his tankard of Perry's winter ale.

"To the morning tide," Benjamin added and held his own tankard up.

Rebecca and Tanyth clinked cups. "To the morning tide." They all drank.

Amanda served a huge platter of venison and roasted root crops. The four dug in while Perry and Amanda took care of the dining room around them.

When the initial flush of food wore off, Rebecca turned to the younger Groves. "So, did you get a good load for the return?"

His face split in a grin that showed his dimples to good effect. "Should be tolerable."

The elder Groves smacked the table and leaned in to speak quietly. "It's a darn sight better than 'tolerable,' you miserable whelp, and you know it." His wide, satisfied smile belied his gruff words.

"Yes, Father, I do–but I'd just as soon the rest of the town didn't."

Captain Groves laughed and clapped the younger man on the shoulder. "I'm pretty sure they already know, boy. They're the ones that loaded it for us."

Benjamin stopped chewing for a moment, cocking his head as if considering his father's statement. "Well, sure. Guess I wasn't thinking that through."

"You just haven't had enough ale yet," Captain Groves said. "Perry! More of that miserable swill over here if you can spare it!"

Perry's booming laughter joined that of the other diners as he brought a huge pitcher over to refill all the glasses at the table. "You only call it that because you love me," Perry said.

"He only calls it that so you'll keep pouring," Amanda said as she cleared away the mess of empty crockery and replaced it with a whole pie. Smiling at her husband, she nudged him away from the table with her hip. "Go pour some for the rest of our customers. I'm trying to serve, here."

He gave her a kiss on the cheek and hurried off, filling every tankard raised in his direction.

"Don't encourage him, Saul," she said with mock severity. "You'll have him back on your ship if you're not careful."

Saul's rumbling laugh made Tanyth smile in response. "He's got the best berth of his life right here, my dear," he said. "Nothing I can say or do would persuade him to give this up."

Amanda cocked an eyebrow at her husband's broad back. "Lucky for him," she said, her mouth twisting into a wry grin.

"Lucky for you, you mean," Saul said.

She gave a little shrug and smiled at him. "Yeah. That, too."

The other side of the dining room grew quiet all at once.

"Can we help you, lad?" Perry asked in the thickening silence.

A soldier wearing the uniform of the King's Own stood just inside the door. The boy, who couldn't have been more than eighteen winters, looked around the dining room before his gaze came to rest on Saul Groves.

"Message for Captain Groves from the base commander," the soldier said.

Perry nodded. "Well, he's right over there."

"Yes, sir. Thank you, sir." The soldier crossed the room,

clearly unused to being the center of attention. He pulled a folded piece of paper from his tunic pocket and handed it to the captain. "I'm to wait for a reply, sir."

Saul settled his tankard, wiped his mouth and beard with his napkin, then took the page and unfolded it. His face gave nothing away as he scanned the page a couple of times before passing it to his son.

"Tell the commandant we'll be there within the hour." He waved his hand to indicate the table. "We're almost done here."

Benjamin read the message and nodded without speaking.

"Thank you, sir." The soldier marched out of the inn, pulling the door closed behind him with a thunk.

Perry glanced at Saul, then poured a tankard for himself. "To the King's Own!" he said.

Saul raised his mug. "To the King's Own."

The rest of the diners slowly took up the toast, raising their mugs until all were held high to the King's Own. Then they drank.

Within a few moments the room had returned to something approximating normal of an evening, although Captain Groves collected more than his share of second and third looks as the meal ran its course.

Amanda brought a pot of tea and some fresh mugs to the table.

When Saul looked up at her, she shrugged one shoulder ever so slightly. "Wash the ale down before you meet with Prince Robert."

"Prince Robert?" Saul asked.

She gave him a faint smile. "That's just what we call him. With the airs he puts on, you'd think he was a prince."

Saul snorted as Amanda disappeared back into the kitchen.

"Trouble, Captain?" Rebecca asked.

"Not for us, I don't think." Captain Groves gave his head a small shake while he filled one of the heavy mugs with the strong tea.

"A garrison patrol found a body out on the road. They want us to take his effects back to Kleesport," Benjamin said.

"Was it somebody from Northport?" Tanyth asked.

The Hermit Of Lammas Wood

"Apparently not," the captain said with another shake of his head. "According to his papers, he was a sailor."

"Not one of yours," Rebecca said, her eyes wide with alarm.

"No."

"He used to be a longshoreman in Kleesport," Benjamin said, his knuckles turning white around the handle of his mug.

Captain Saul looked up at that. "You know him, Ben?"

Benjamin shook his head. "Not well, but I knew of him and his story. It was all over Kleesport just before we left."

"Wait," Tanyth said. "They were talking about something like this back at the Broken Gate. Is this the man who took a deckhand job because he was tired of being a longshoreman? His ship was lost on his first voyage?"

"That's him."

Rebecca looked from Tanyth to each of the Groveses in turn, her brow furrowed. "How can that be?"

Captain Groves lifted his mug in salute. "The very question I was thinking."

"Shipwrecked along the coast?" Tanyth asked.

"Possible, but the *Calliope* was bound for the eastern islands. They left Kleesport well before the Zypheria started blowing. They'd already been reported lost before you got to town," Benjamin said.

"And yet his body was found ten miles inland from here," Captain Groves said.

"How is that even possible?" Rebecca asked.

"That, my girl, is what the commandant wants us to explain."

"Can you?" asked Tanyth.

"Not with any degree of assurance," Captain Groves said, staring down into his tea. "But perhaps our extra cargo wasn't simply a message that we really needed insurance."

Benjamin frowned at his father and leaned over to speak quietly. "You think it was to keep us from discovering something?"

The elder Groves shrugged. "Maybe we were just supposed to be the diversion."

"Diversion? For what?"

"Now I think that's the question that Prince Robert should be asking, my boy." Captain Groves looked to his son. "Don't you?"

Chapter 4
Bon Voyage

The ship strained at her mooring lines as if eager to begin the voyage south. Tanyth raised one hand against the glaring sun to watch the sailors scampering through the rigging in preparation for setting sail.

"I think I'm going to miss that," Rebecca said.

Tanyth squinted sidelong to consider her companion. "It's not too late. You could prob'ly sign on again."

The young woman lowered her eyes to the stone pier and shook her head, a smile playing around the corners of her lips. "And miss meeting Gertie Pinecrest?"

Heavy footfalls on the boarding plank drew their attention. Benjamin Groves joined them.

"Forget somethin'?" Tanyth asked, with a sly glance at Rebecca.

Groves jerked his thumb toward the aft deck where his father stood at the rail, looking down. "Captain Groves sends his compliments, mum, and thanks you again for your help on the voyage out."

"Well, savin' my own hide was at least part of that, but you're welcome." She waved up to the captain.

"We'll be back in about six weeks. You've got a place aboard any time you want to go back to Kleesport." He glanced at Rebecca out of the corner of his eyes and kept his hands clasped behind his back as if trying to control them. "Both of you."

"Thank you, Mr. Groves. Thank your father for us," Tanyth said. "I'm not sure how long we'll be here, but we'll certainly be on the lookout for you."

He stood there for an awkward moment, his eyes alternating between the ship riding high on the tide beside the pier and the stonework at his feet.

"What'd you find out about that sailor?" Tanyth asked.

"Oh, yes." He paused to rub a palm across his lips as if to wipe away a bad taste. "'Twasn't pretty, mum. Not fit to talk about. Reggie White, right enough. I'd seen his face before—unloading the *Call*. Nobody can rightly say how he came to be back in the woods up here."

"How'd he die?" she asked.

Groves tossed his head in a dismissive gesture. "Near as anybody can guess, exposure. He wasn't dressed real warm, and he'd been beaten pretty recently." He glanced at Rebecca. "Nothing life-threatening. Only what you'd expect if he'd been in a bar fight or something."

"So somebody knows he was out there. And there hasta be somebody else out in the woods," Tanyth said.

Groves glanced once more at Rebecca. "Would seem likely since nobody'd seen him around town. Nobody who's come forward, anyway."

Tanyth held out her hand. "Fair winds and following seas, Benjamin."

A smile lit his face as he took her hand in both of his, his calloused palms rough against her skin. "Take care of yourself, mum."

"Thank you, Benjamin." She turned away and stepped toward the ship, tilting her head back to look up to where the white-haired captain stood at the rail. "Fair winds, Captain!" she shouted.

Captain Groves smiled down at her. "Following seas, mum. Don't let any bears eat you!" He raised a hand in salute and Tanyth waved in response.

She turned in time to see Rebecca stepping back from a surprised-looking Benjamin Groves, one hand lifted to his cheek. She stifled a grin.

With a final nod and wave, Benjamin turned back to the ship, striding up the boarding plank. "Single up the lines. Pull in that plank," he called. In a moment he appeared on the afterdeck beside his father, his eyes drawn to the crew aloft.

Tanyth and Rebecca stepped back from the edge of the pier while the lines flew through the air and two burly sailors pulled the boarding plank back aboard, securing it on deck. Several moments passed in silent anticipation before a quiet whisper started in the spruces behind them on the shore and tendrils of the morning wind played across Tanyth's face.

Captain Groves spoke quietly to his first mate and Benjamin's voice carried clearly on the fresh morning air. "Let go the lines."

The boatswain's rough bawl followed, and the heavy mooring lines began to snake back aboard the ship as she floated free of land once more.

"Set the foretop! Get that jib up!" Groves shouted.

White canvas blossomed as if by magic at the bow of the ship, pulling the craft out into the harbor as it stiffened and belled, catching the light breezes and riding them out to sea. As they gained way, more canvas blooms studded the yards and the heavily laden craft picked her way out into the bay.

Tanyth and Rebecca watched her go for several minutes. A figure on the afterdeck turned and waved one final time. Tanyth let Rebecca return the wave before facing the town and beginning the trek back up the pier.

They took several steps in silence, Tanyth casting small glances at her companion.

Rebecca's lips twitched as if a smile wanted to form on them. "Nothin' to say, mum?" she asked at last.

Tanyth's quiet laughter floated on the clear morning. "You coulda gone, my dear."

Rebecca cast a glance over her shoulder and shrugged. "They'll be back."

"You sound pretty certain. Life at sea isn't exactly free of danger."

Rebecca's laugh followed Tanyth's into the quiet morning. "And traveling with you is?"

Tanyth shrugged. "Well, that's a fair point. I guess nothin's exactly sure, is it."

They paced along in silence for a time before Rebecca gave

another long look over her shoulder. "Not exactly sure, no, mum," she said. "But maybe uncertainty is part of the plan."

Tanyth looked back at the ship in time to see it disappear around the headland. Glancing up at Rebecca, she saw the gleam in her eyes. "Maybe so, my dear. Maybe so."

"What do we do now?" Rebecca asked as they climbed the long hill toward the inn.

"Well, now we go back to the inn for a nice cup of tea and perhaps one of Amanda's scones."

Rebecca giggled. "No, mum, I mean what about the hermit?"

Tanyth raised and lowered one shoulder in a half-shrug. "That's up to the Lady and a baby. These things have their own timing."

"You haven't had any more visions since we've been here, have you, mum?" Rebecca asked after a few more steps.

Tanyth blew out a breath before answering. "No, but then I don't usually have 'em unless I need 'em, it seems." She glanced over at the young woman. "At least that seems to be how they're workin'."

"You can't...you know...just have them when you want them?"

"No," Tanyth said–then stopped herself, remembering a snowy morning far away when her need to know had outweighed her judgment.

"You don't sound that certain, mum. Pardon my sayin' so."

Tanyth chewed on her lower lip and didn't reply.

Chapter 5
Plans Laid

---◆---

Penny Oakton found Tanyth and Rebecca enjoying a mid-morning pot of tea at the inn three days later. Her steps sagged from fatigue, and blood smeared her simple tunic. However, her eyes shone brightly and a smile graced her lips.

"It's a boy," she said without preamble.

"That's wonderful," Tanyth said. "Would you like some tea? Something to eat?"

Amanda pushed through from the kitchen. "Gracious, Penny. You look ready to drop." She scooted another chair around and pressed her down into it. "You sit right there. I'll get a fresh mug."

"But I'm a mess," Penny said looking down at herself. She sniffed a couple of times. "And I smell."

Tanyth grinned at her. "Smells like a healthy newborn to me."

Rebecca waved a hand in front of her nose. "Is that what that is?" Then she laughed.

Penny grinned. "Well, I'm pretty sure part of it is me. I've been up for two days and young Master McGilvry took his sweet time."

"You look fairly done in," Rebecca said.

"I *feel* fairly done in, but I'll be right enough by tomorrow. More'n I can say about poor Audrey. Woman doesn't have the hips for childbearin', if ya ask me."

Amanda came back with a pair of mugs and some leftover breakfast sausages wrapped in fresh biscuits. She plunked it down on the table and pulled up a chair for herself. "You get on the outside of that, young woman. Can't have our only midwife keelin' over on our doorstep. Terrible for business." She grinned and poured hot tea into mugs all around. "Tough one, was he?"

"Fair. Not as bad as Melly Walters last winter, but Audrey really needs to pay attention to her cycles and keep current with her herb tea."

Amanda laughed. "Well, Melly didn't really get to choose when her girls would come and you're the only one who thought she'd have triplets."

"Triplets?" Rebecca asked, her eyes wide. "Mercy."

"Darkest night of winter and the Lady decides Melly should have triplets in the heart of the first bad snow of the season," Penny said. "When her Boris showed up at my door, his face pale as the snow on his parka, I knew we was in for it." She sipped her tea and leaned into the warm steam coming off the mug.

"Eat, dear. You need to keep your strength," Tanyth said.

Penny shook herself and reached for the sausage biscuit. "Was just trying to remember when I last ate. Sometime yesterday. I think."

"There's more where that came from, if you want it, Penny."

"Thank you, Amanda. Put it on my tab."

"Oh, go on. Your money's no good here."

Penny gave her a wan smile and nodded. "Thanks."

The four women sat in silence, sipping tea, while Penny made short work of the biscuit. She seemed surprised when the plate was empty.

"There's another in the warmin' oven, if ya want it," Amanda said.

Penny took a deep breath. Something seemed to unwind in her face, as some tension that Tanyth couldn't name relaxed. "I think I'm ready to get home and get some sleep." A heavy yawn almost caught her words, and they all laughed.

"Scoot, then. You've earned it," Amanda said. "I'll put up a couple of meat pies and some cookies for the McGilvrys. Perry can take it over."

Penny nodded, seeming distracted. "Yeah. Audrey's gonna be flat on her back for at least a day or two so that'd be good. Mickey'd poison himself trying to cook." She stood and pressed the fingertips of one hand to the table top to keep her balance. "Full belly, hot tea. Yeah. I'm ready for a nap."

"There's a bed upstairs, dearie." Amanda said.

Penny looked at the stairs for a long moment before shaking her head. "Mine's prob'ly just as close, and it's what I need right now. Thanks."

"We've got venison for tonight. Come back when you wake up. Our treat," Amanda said to her retreating back.

"I may take you up on that, unless I sleep through till morning," Penny said over her shoulder. "Right now, I need to get out of these smelly clothes and into a warm bed." She raised a hand and waved it without turning around.

The outer door closed with a quiet thump as she left.

"A boy," Amanda said. "Mickey'll be so pleased."

Rebecca hid a scowl behind her mug.

"Has a few daughters already, I take it?" Tanyth asked.

Amanda nodded. "How'd ya guess?"

"Something about Mother Oakton's comments. This wasn't her first little one, was it?"

"No. Her third. Two daughters who wrap that big lug of a daddy around their fingers. He dotes on 'em something terrible." Amanda paused to sip her tea. "But he'll have a son now to carry on the name. He'll be happy with that."

"Like daughters won't?" Rebecca asked.

Tanyth heard the bitterness in the girl's voice but Amanda gave no sign that she'd noticed.

"Oh, daughters are fine with Mickey McGilvry. Don't get me wrong." She sighed and took another sip of tea. "But daughters get married and leave. They're the treasures a father must share with the world. Sons, though–the work of the father is to leave a strong son. Sounds like Mickey'll have a chance to do that."

"So fathers don't owe daughters the same courtesy?" Rebecca asked, her brow furrowed in a scowl. "They just cast them off when it's handy?"

Amanda took a good look at Rebecca then, and smiled into the face of the storm. "Daughters are born strong, my dear. They have the magic in them to grant new life. That's something that fathers can never have, can never know. All they can do for daughters is love them enough to let 'em go when the time comes." She reached out and patted the young woman's hand where it lay on the table. "It's a hard thing for them, too."

Rebecca's eyes gleamed in the morning light but she blinked back whatever might have come next. With a sniff she buried her face in the mug and drained it. "Thanks for the tea. I should see to my pack and bow. We'll be heading for the hermit soon."

She stood and walked away from them, climbing the stairs with heavy steps and a ramrod in her spine.

Amanda watched her go and sighed when the door above them closed with a hollow smack.

"She's had a rough time of it, my dear. Don't take it to heart," Tanyth said.

Amanda gazed into Tanyth's face, her eyes moist but not leaking. "She's not alone in that. I wish I'd had sense enough to make up with my own da before I lost him."

Tanyth sighed. "Sometimes the Lady's gifts don't seem all that great," she said.

"You, too?"

She shook her head. "No, my father and I got along much better than I did with my mother. He passed over the year I was married, and my mother followed shortly after." She paused to look into her half-empty mug. "They weren't around to disapprove of me when I left him," she said, not looking up.

Amanda reached over and placed her smooth hand over Tanyth's wrinkled one, but didn't speak.

Tanyth patted it. "Thank you. It was a long time ago."

"No children?"

"One. A boy. In the beginning he was the apple of his father's eye. A strong lad, big for his age and just as stubborn and strong willed as his father. The two of them had some terrible fights." Tanyth felt a sad smile curling her mouth as she remembered those things she'd pushed aside for so long.

"What happened?" Amanda asked after a moment. "Sorry, mum," she said. "I didn't mean to pry."

Tanyth looked over into the younger woman's eyes. "No, nothin' to be sorry for." She patted her hand again and held it firmly in place. "In the end, Robert left home and joined the King's Own as soon as he was old enough. He disappeared into the military and I never heard from him again."

"He never wrote you? Ever?"

"Well, I never got any letter from him. I trusted that the King's Own would care for him. If not the way I would, then at least he'd be out of his father's reach."

"He just ran away?" Amanda's eyes started to brim again.

"It's not like that," Tanyth said, patting the woman's hand again. "He thought it would solve the problem. That with him gone, his father would become less angry. Less violent."

Amanda sighed. "But it didn't, did it?"

Tanyth shook her head. "No. With Robert gone, Roger had no other target for his anger. He climbed into a tankard of ale every night and when he stumbled home, I was the only one there. It wasn't too long afterwards that I left and started on the long, long path that's brought me here."

"He just let you go?" Amanda's eyes went wide astonishment.

Tanyth shook her head. "No, he came after me. The village healer had taken me in, and he found me there."

"What happened?"

Tanyth felt her mouth curl into a smile at the old, old memory. "She wouldn't let him in."

Amanda blinked. "She wouldn't let him in? How did she stop him?"

Tanyth shrugged a shoulder. "I have no idea. She stood in the doorway and wouldn't let him pass. He couldn't—or wouldn't—push past her. I just sat there in that old woman's kitchen while she blocked the door with her body." She paused, replaying the scene in her mind. "It's odd. She wasn't a big woman. Really rather a slip of a thing, and old. Lady, I thought of her as ancient. She'd lived in that same cottage for winter after winter, and she'd been old the first time I met her."

"But she turned your husband away?"

"Aye. That she did."

"Man doesn't usually let a woman do that to him," Amanda said, her voice low.

"She'd seen the bruises. She knew what he'd do to me." Tanyth took a deep breath and let it out slowly. "So did I, come to that."

"And she wouldn't let that happen again," Amanda said.

Tanyth's head bobbed in the smallest of nods.

"She must have been quite a woman."

"She was certainly more woman than I am," Tanyth said. "I couldn't stand up against Roger Oakhurst, but she did."

Amanda stiffened.

Tanyth glanced over to see the woman's eyes wide and staring. "What is it?"

"Oakhurst?"

"Yeah. Roger Oakhurst."

"And your son's name is Robert? Robert Oakhurst?"

Tanyth felt her face pinch into a frown. "Yes, what's the matter?"

"He joined the King's Own how long ago?"

"About twenty-three, twenty-four winters ago. Why?"

Her mouth opened and closed a couple of times before she found her voice. "The commandant. The one we call Prince Robert?"

"What about him?"

"He's Major Robert Oakhurst."

Chapter 6
The King's Own

Tanyth sat staring into the fire. "After all these winters, can it possibly be him?" she muttered.

"What're the odds, mum?" Rebecca asked.

"I have no idea. Two Robert Oakhursts? It's possible. Robert isn't that unusual a name and the Oakhurst clan is certainly wide spread."

"But twenty winters gone, mum? And him only a common enlistee?"

"I know. How could he be a major?" Tanyth shook her head, trying to dislodge the incongruity. "I've traveled all around Korlay," she said. "Of all the places he could have been? How can he be here?"

Amanda brought them a fresh pot of tea from the kitchen. "You still thinkin', mum?"

Tanyth looked up into a frowning face. "Yeah. I just can't believe it. It's crazy. It has to be some other Robert Oakhurst."

The heavy door at the front of the inn opened and closed as the first of the evening crowd came in for dinner.

Tanyth lifted the mug of tea to her lips and inhaled the savory fust, closing her eyes and letting the warm steam wash over her face.

"Would you know him if you saw him, mum?" Amanda asked, an odd tone in her voice.

"Lord and Lady, I have no idea. It's been over half my life since I saw him and he was just a boy at the time. Why do you ask?" She opened her eyes and glanced at Amanda.

The Hermit Of Lammas Wood

Amanda's gaze was fixed on the entry. Tanyth turned to see what was so interesting.

An officer of the King's Own stood there, the insignias and medals inscrutable to her, but the face that stared out from under the peaked cap was eerily familiar.

Tanyth wasn't aware that she'd moved at all until she stood in front of him, looking up into his face.

"You have your father's eyes," she said.

"And your chin," he said.

Her gaze flickered down to his chin, then back to his eyes. Oh yes, he *did* have his father's eyes. The same coldness, the same appraising look.

"It is you, isn't it, Mother?" he asked.

"If you're Roger's son, then yes, it's me." She tried to smile but the look in his eyes wouldn't let her.

"I'm his son." His voice growled out from his chest. "I thought I was an orphan."

She stepped back in astonishment. "An orphan? Who told you I was dead?"

"Father. Before he died."

Tanyth felt the floor shift under her feet for a moment. "You talked to your father? After you left?"

His head bobbed slowly in the affirmative. "When I'd completed my basic training, the quartermaster made me write home to tell my family where I would be posted. It—" His words choked off and he cleared his throat. "Our whole regiment was shipped off to the Eastern Isles, and they made us send the next-of-kin notices home in case we didn't come back."

"How long...?" she asked.

"Basic training lasted three months. We spent two winters in the Eastern Isles."

"I never saw your letters," she said. "I thought you'd escaped."

His eyes clouded for a moment. "So did I."

"But I was there then. It was only after you'd been shipped out..." Her voice tailed off as the realization struck her. "He knew."

"Yes, but I didn't. He told me you'd caught a fever right

after I left and died."

"But I didn't," she said.

"No, you didn't. You left him there alone instead." Ice wrapped his words and anger filled his eyes. "A sick man, one who could barely care for himself, and you just left him?"

"Who—? What—? Who told you such a thing?" she asked, her heart pounding in her chest.

"When he was dying, he wrote me. I had a chance to get home to visit before he passed."

"You went back there?"

"Of course, Mother. Where else would I go to visit my dying father?"

"When was this?"

He swept the cap from his head and ran a hand over his bristled scalp. "Ten winters ago? Twelve?" His gaze sought the rafters. "I'd been posted to the Southlands garrison, so it must have been ten winters. I spent three there and then moved up here to take over this Lord-forsaken and Lady-lost garrison. I've been here ever since." Heaving a sigh, he tossed his hat onto the nearby table. "I'll probably die here before they replace me."

"Ten winters ago? I was in the Southlands then myself. During the border raids?"

He blinked at her, his head cocked to one side as if she'd just spouted gibberish and he was trying to figure out what she'd actually meant to say. "You were where?"

"In the Southlands. About ten winters ago. On the borderlands with Barramor."

"During the raids?"

"Yes. During the raids. The King's Own were spread too thin; the raiders seemed to know where you'd be, and they'd strike while you were busy elsewhere."

"You couldn't have been."

"But I was. I stayed with Mother Ashbourne in Grentan from the time of the first raids until the beastly business with the infected cattle."

"You were in Grentan?" His voice carried his incredulity.

"Where were you?" she asked.

"Torland."

"Torland? That's where the infected cattle—" she stared up at him, the reality striking home. "You did that."

"Yes. We did that. We had to." His mouth pursed as if he'd tasted something bitter. "It ended the war."

"You killed thousands of Barramor's people."

"If you were there, you know. They were killing our people. They were destroying crops and disrupting trade." He stopped suddenly. "You were there," he said after a moment.

"I was," she said. "And I know."

"But you left Father to die on his own." His jaw tightened and his shoulders hunched forward.

"I left your father before he could kill me," she said, her voice tight and low. "The same reason you left to join the King's Own, unless you've forgotten that part."

He rocked back on his heels as if she'd slapped him.

Perry burst through the kitchen door. "Commandant, how nice to see you..." His words tapered off as his gaze swept the room.

Tanyth turned to see Rebecca sitting where she had left her, her hands clenched tightly over her mouth and her eyes red with unshed tears. Amanda stood rigid, one hand on the teapot, an empty mug forgotten in the other. Her wide eyes darted back and forth between Perry and the officer, her lips moving but no sound coming out.

Tanyth took a deep breath and turned back to Robert. "Perhaps we might have some tea and catch up? Shall we?"

The man blinked several times before tugging on his tunic as if to straighten it. He blew out a heavy breath. "Yes. A cup of tea would be excellent."

Tanyth turned to the assembled party. "Everyone, this is my son, Robert." Looking back at Robert, she said, "I think you already know Amanda and Perry. That young lady is my traveling companion, Rebecca Marong."

"Richard's daughter?" he asked, his voice practically squeaking with surprise.

Tanyth looked to Rebecca, whose eyes seemed two sizes bigger as she answered. "Yes. Why?" Rebecca asked.

"We've been looking for you since last summer. Your father's been burning up the backwoods trying to find you."

Rebecca looked from Robert to Tanyth and back. "That's ridiculous. He's known where I was for the last four winters."

"That's not what he's told the garrison here. He had us out sweeping the coastline half the summer."

Amanda clapped once, sharply. "Well, I think we all have a lot more to catch up on than we thought. Commandant? Did you leave your guardsmen outside?"

"Of course, Ms. Corbet."

"Perry, take them out some tea and pastry. I have a feeling we may be here a while."

Perry scooted back into the kitchen and emerged moments later, balancing a tray laden with mugs that looked more like tankards than teacups. He paused on his way past the commandant, who gave a small nod. "I'll have a cup of that tea, too, if I may?"

Perry grinned. "Of course, sir."

Amanda made an exasperated sound but said nothing, simply poured tea for the ladies and set about pulling extra chairs around the table. In a matter of minutes Amanda had finished, and Perry had returned with a tankard of ale for Robert and one for himself.

Amanda cuffed him on the shoulder and led him back to the kitchen by the arm. "Family business, dear. We've got a dinner to prepare, in case you've forgotten."

Robert stood until Tanyth had taken a seat, then lowered himself onto an empty chair as if afraid it might collapse. He offered her a tentative smile and Rebecca a polite nod. "Perhaps we've gotten off on the wrong foot," he said.

"That'll happen when you crowd your tongue with your toes like that," Rebecca said, a cheeky grin on her face.

Robert threw back his head and laughed. "You have me dead to rights, Miss Marong. My apologies."

"Don't apologize to me. She's the one you owe an apology to." Rebecca flourished her tea cup in Tanyth's direction.

Robert considered his mother for a moment and then looked down at his tankard. He took a deep breath, running a hand over his scalp again. "Yes. Of course. I'm sorry, Mother." He looked up at her from under a furrowed brow. "It was a shock to learn you were here."

The Hermit Of Lammas Wood

"No more of a shock than mine, Robert," she said, leaning forward to touch his forearm to reassure herself that he was real.

"How did you find out?" Rebecca asked.

"All ships file a manifest with the harbormaster. Eventually they get routed to my secretary and I happened to see this one. First ship of the season and all." He stopped speaking and looked down at his tankard. "And I wanted to see what the *Call* had brought by way of supplies."

"Was there anything good?" Tanyth asked.

He gave a little chuckle and took a swig of ale. "I don't know. I got to your name and felt like somebody'd hit me with a rock." He glanced over to Rebecca. "I should have read a little farther down the page."

"Where is my father?" Rebecca asked, lifting her mug of tea to hide her expression as she sipped.

"We're expecting him on the *Sea Rover* when she gets here. He went back to town for the winter."

"I wonder what he was looking for here," she said, brow furrowed in frown.

"He said he was looking for you," Robert said, the words dripping slowly from his lips one at a time.

"Yes, you said that, but he really did know that I was out at Ravenwood with William Mapleton's party. It's not like I was hiding from him." She looked up at the commandant with a small shrug. "He also knew I wouldn't likely be around up here because I was miles away in a village nobody'd heard of until we named it last fall."

"Your father did not strike me as somebody who wastes time on pointless exercises."

"He's not," Rebecca said. "And he'd be unlikely to spend anywhere near that amount of time looking for me, even if I were missing. So what was he looking for instead?"

"And why wouldn't he tell us what it was?" Robert said.

"Perhaps he'll tell you if you ask him," Rebecca said with a sly grin.

Robert answered her grin with one of his own. "You can ask him yourself. He'll be here in a few days. Fishing smack spotted the *Sea Rover* and *Red Wave* both beating into the wind coming up the Bight this afternoon. They should make port day after tomorrow."

Rebecca frowned at that. "I may not be here."

"Where would you be?" Robert asked.

"With her." Rebecca gestured to Tanyth with her mug again.

"Where are you going, Mother?"

"Inland. Lammas Wood," she said.

"Lammas Wood?" he looked back and forth between the two women. "There's nothing out there but bears and wolves."

"Well, there's also trappers and lumberjacks and miners, unless I've been misinformed," Tanyth said.

"And the hermit, too, but what truck can you possibly have with trappers and lumberjacks? You going into business?" he asked, a half-smile on his face as if he expected she was joking.

"You're right. I'm not going out to visit the lumberjacks and trappers," she said.

"Who, then? The hermit?"

Tanyth didn't answer, just gave a half shrug and tilted her mug up.

"No. Not the hermit," Robert said, looking to Rebecca.

Rebecca gave him a little nod.

"Really? You're going out to visit the hermit of Lammas Wood?" He slammed his tankard down on the table so he could brace himself with both hands.

"Well, I've been over twenty winters on the road to get here. Seems like kind of a waste if I get this close and don't finish it, don't ya think?" Tanyth said.

"But that's ridiculous," he said. "That's three—maybe four—days' travel through the back country. You wouldn't stand a chance out there on your own."

Tanyth shrugged and regarded her son through half-lidded eyes. "I've made it this far on my own. I suspect I can get a little bit farther."

"You don't understand, Mother. There's no law out there. My jurisdiction ends three miles past the tree line. After that it's anybody's. Trappers or hunters. Anybody you meet out there might be just as happy to kill you as look at you."

"Or worse, I suspect," Tanyth said, her expression not changing. "Lots of 'em have tried over the last twenty winters."

"None have succeeded, I hope," Robert said, his face turning red from the neck up.

Tanyth pursed her lips and shook her head. "No. None have succeeded." She paused as if thinking about it. "Most didn't survive."

Robert's eyes practically bugged out of his head. "Somebody killed them?"

"It's a dangerous life," she said. "Trust me when I say I know all about how dangerous it is."

"No, Mother. I don't believe you do. You can't go haring off into the back country alone."

"She's not going to be alone," Rebecca said. "I'll be with her."

"You can't go either," Robert said. "Your father will be here in a couple of days and he'll have my hide tacked to the wall if he learns you were here and I let you wander off."

"Your jurisdiction ends three miles past the treeline. You just got done telling us that," Rebecca said. "What are you going to do to stop us? Lock us up?"

Robert set his jaw and glared. "If I have to."

"Now, Robert," Tanyth said, reaching out to lay a hand on his forearm. "That won't be necessary. Of course we'll wait for the *Sea Rover*. I've waited this long, another few days won't matter."

Robert looked at her and then took another swig of his beer. He swallowed it and then placed the tankard on the table between them. "Good. I'm glad you've chosen to see reason, Mother." He smiled. "We've got a lot to catch up on. It'd be a shame to have to do it while you were behind bars."

She smiled back. "It would be," she agreed.

"All right then," he said, and stood. "I need to get back to the garrison before the dinner mess. Responsibilities, you know." He looked from one to the other of them and nodded. "I'll come back tomorrow afternoon and perhaps we can chat a bit more. What do you say?"

"That would be lovely, dear," Tanyth said. She turned to

Rebecca. "Won't that be lovely?"

Rebecca's glower practically scorched one or two of Robert's medals before she said, "Yeah. Lovely."

"Until tomorrow, then." He smiled and nodded to each of them before turning on his heel and marching toward the outer door. Grabbing his cap as he passed he settled it on his head, taking care to make sure it was level before he opened the door and stepped out into the late afternoon sun.

The door banged behind him.

Rebecca glowered at Tanyth.

"What is it, my dear?"

"You're not really going to wait until my father gets here, are you?"

"Of course not. We need to get word to Mother Oakton and be on the road by noon tomorrow at the latest. I want to be five miles into the woods before he discovers we're missing."

A bright smile split Rebecca's face.

"What? You think I spent twenty-odd winters on the road to avoid one Oakhurst male only to bow to the next one I find?" Tanyth made a rude noise with her tongue and lips.

Rebecca's expression turned serious again. "You sure you don't wanna visit with the long lost son?" she asked.

"I know where he works," she said. "I can always find him later, but I'm certainly not going to halt my trip just because he says so."

"How do we get word to Penny that we need to leave tomorrow?"

Amanda stuck her head through the open kitchen door. "She'll be here for dinner. You can plot to your heart's content then."

Tanyth looked up in surprise.

Amanda laughed. "Don't look so surprised. Sound carries from there, through the connected chimneys and directly to the kitchen. We heard every word."

"Eavesdropping?" Rebecca asked, her mouth sagging open in surprise.

Amanda grinned and nodded. "Entertainment's in short supply here. We'll take it where we can get it."

Rebecca's mouth clicked shut and she turned to Tanyth.

"Don't look at me. News will be all over town by morning anyway."

"Ha," Amanda said. "Try by sunset. It's a small place and news travels fast."

Chapter 7
Time To Go

The aroma of roasting venison must have flooded the village. By the time they started serving, Perry and Amanda had a full room. Perry even circulated tankards to the hungry diners waiting on the front stoop while Amanda kept tea and biscuits moving on the tables. The noise in the dining room went well beyond hubbub and into riotous territory.

Tanyth, Rebecca, and Penny held down a small table at the back of the dining room, almost under the stairs.

"You ladies'll be out of the way back here and can have a nice chat without anybody bein' the wiser," Amanda said, settling the latest in a long line of hot teapots on the table. "I'll be back with some food in a few minutes." She paused to survey the dining room. "If I don't get bushwacked between here and the kitchen."

"I keep tellin' you to hire some help," Penny said with a grin.

"Oh, tosh. Not hardly worth it for once a week," she said. "Besides, half these people just come in here sayin' it's for the food when they just wan' a good excuse to get together, drink beer, and gab. Waitin' an extra few minutes ain't gonna slow 'em down any." Amanda winked and rushed off to the kitchen, leaving the door swinging in her wake.

Tanyth warmed the cups with fresh tea and looked to Amanda. "So, he's goin' to try to stop us. Some misguided Oakhurst man stuck between thinkin' about protectin' the weaker sex and bein' the garrison commander when Rebecca's father starts askin' pointed questions, you know he's feelin' the pinch."

Penny nodded, her head barely rising and falling. She looked to Rebecca. "If your father knew where you were, what was he lookin' for here, then?"

"Dunno, but he most surely knew where I was. He yelled about it from Hunter's Moon to Flower and Lady alone knows how long after we left."

"Was he lookin' for that dead sailor?" Tanyth asked.

"Timin's wrong, I think," Penny said. "He had the garrison out all last summer and into the fall. Only gave up when the ice got so thick he risked wintering over if he didn't leave. He had to take a sledge out to the ice dock as it was. From what I hear, this dead guy had to have been lost sometime before the Zypheria this year."

Tanyth nodded. "They was mournin' the loss of ship and crew when we got to Kleesport. Had to have been sometime in early winter that they set sail. Woulda taken time for them to get where they were going, more time for them to be late, and even more time before word got back to Kleesport that they was lost."

"True," Penny said, her brow furrowed. "Might have been in the fall, even, but Marong was here at the Call last year. That woulda been before that ship got underway."

"What's an ice dock?" Rebecca asked. "You said my father had to take a sledge out to the ice dock."

"Oh, the sheltered places like bays and harbors tend to freeze first. They can get real thick before the open water beyond the headlands freezes. Generally when that happens the harbormaster builds a kind of floating dock just past the edge of the ice. It rides up and down with the ice and tide and lets us get a couple more weeks of trade in at the end of the season." She sipped her tea. "By midwinter the sea's too rough and winds too strong to use it and by Ice Moon, well...it's ice."

"Whatever it was, he didn't find it," Tanyth said, leaning into the table to be heard over the roar from the main part of the dining room. "He's comin' back."

"Yeah, but why the *Sea Rover*?" Penny asked looking back and forth between her companions. "Why didn't he book on the first ship out?"

"P'r'aps he wanted to *arrive*," Rebecca said, her mouth twisted into a bitter grimace.

"What's that mean?" Penny asked.

Tanyth shook her head. "We had a bit of trouble on the way out. Seems like somebody in Kleesport didn't want Captain Groves—or the ship—to be first to Northport. They put a bomb aboard. We found it before it went off."

"You mean you found it, mum."

Tanyth chuckled. "Well, a rat found it. I just helped her along a bit."

Penny's eyes grew round. "Somebody tried to sink the *Call*? That's dangerous knowledge to have."

"More dangerous to be sailing back when you wasn't supposed to arrive to begin with, I'm thinkin'," Tanyth said.

"Think he knew?" Rebecca asked with a sidelong glance at Tanyth.

"Who? Your father? Maybe," she said. "Maybe he just doesn't like Saul Groves."

"Maybe he made the arrangements last year thinking the *Sea Rover* would be first to answer the Call," Penny said. "This is all interestin' but it's not gettin' us out of town."

"We need to be out of here before noon tomorrow," Tanyth said. "And three miles out in the woods before he can catch us."

"Why tomorrow? You said he's coming to visit tomorrow afternoon?" Penny asked.

"Yeah. We didn't get as much time to catch up on old times as either of us wanted, but if he's goin' to be pig-headed like his father, we'll need to be well away before he figures out he needs to arrest us before we bolt."

"Arrest us?" Rebecca said sitting up straight. "For what?"

"Don't need much of a reason, far as that goes," Penny said with a half shrug. "Only needs to keep you here till the *Sea Rover* docks and your father arrives. After that, you're his problem."

"That might be the best solution," Tanyth said.

"He'll still try to keep you here," Rebecca said. "And my father isn't about to let me go harin' off into the back of beyond. He'd probably lock me up himself."

"No, but he'd have to explain what he's lookin' for or come up with another reason for searchin'," Tanyth said. "Which one you think he'd most likely do?"

Amanda interrupted their discussion with heavy platters of venison and roasted root crops. "You get on the outside of those and there's more in the kitchen. Any plans yet?"

"Still gettin' acquainted," Penny said. "I think we're gonna need to leave here around first light."

Amanda nodded. "That's what I'd do. And stick to the deer trails. A couple of the garrison are on the porch drinkin' Perry's ale and complaining about having to be on patrol on the north road by dawn."

Tanyth nodded. "He's plannin' ahead. Wouldn't be surprised if he shows up tomorrow with a couple of troopers to 'protect' us while we're in town."

"There's plenty of travel rations in the larder here, if you need 'em. More'n you'll need. You're welcome to 'em."

"Thanks, Amanda," Penny said. "I've got a good stock, too. Never know when I might need a fast meal between babies."

"So can you go in the morning?" Tanyth asked. "Nobody due?"

Penny smiled. "There's always somebody due. Audrey McGilvry was the last of the fall babies. There's another batch due in a few weeks, but things should be quiet until then."

"Oh, the blizzard we had just before Hunter's Moon?" Amanda asked.

"Yeah. Wasn't much to do with two feet of snow and winds blowing it more sideways than down. Charlene Noonan's gonna be next, I figure. Ed was just back from lumberin' when the storm hit."

The two women shared a knowing smirk.

Rebecca cast a glance at Tanyth.

"Don't start with that woodbox thing, again," Tanyth growled.

"Frank's a good man, mum. You know that," Rebecca said.

Amanda and Penny grinned at Tanyth's squirming in her chair.

"Something about a woodbox?" Penny said.

"Frank used to keep Mother Fairport's woodbox filled when she lived in Ravenwood last winter."

Tanyth addressed her venison with gusto and tried to ignore the grins all around the table.

"Is that what they call it now?" Penny said.

"Frank Crane is a good man," Tanyth said. "He looked out for me while I was helpin' out. That's all."

"Havin' a hot flash, mum?" Rebecca asked, flashing a cheeky grin as she sawed a morsel of venison from the pile on her plate.

Tanyth felt the heat flush across her neck and face for reasons that had nothing to do with a hot flash. "Waitin' for your father is soundin' more and more appealin'," she said.

"If you'd have asked, he'd have come with us," Rebecca said.

Tanyth took a deep breath and let it out, feeling her anger seep away to be replaced by something more like regret. "He's needed where he is and I couldn't wait," she said. She looked around at all the faces peering at her. "Some things just ain't meant to be."

Penny winked at her. "Some things just need time to grow before they can be."

Even Amanda nodded. "Good for you, mum." A shout from across the dining room made her scurry away without saying anything else.

"Sorry, mum. I didn't mean anythin' by it," Rebecca said, reaching over to place a hand on Tanyth's forearm.

Tanyth smiled and patted her hand. "I know, dear. Just..." she shrugged, unable to explain her reaction.

"Well, we'll need to get out of here without bein' seen in the mornin' and get to the deer trails by first light," Penny said. "No good thrashin' around out there in the dark, but from my place to the forest is a matter of yards. We can disappear there easily enough."

"How do we get to your place without bein' seen?" Rebecca asked. "We can't very well be hikin' up the main street and down your block."

Penny grinned. "The back gate to my place is just across the street here. There's an alley between the inn and old Murray's place next door. Perry uses it for deliveries to his brew house back there. You can slip out the back door of the kitchen and be across the street in nothing flat. Only eyes on you at that hour will be owls."

Tanyth snorted. "The owls are not what they seem."

Penny's plan rattled to a halt and she cocked her head to one side. "What?"

Tanyth shook her head and gave the younger woman a narrow smile. "I had a dream about an owl once. Nothin' important."

Penny looked to Rebecca who offered a shrug in return.

"All right then," Penny continued, with a last glance at Tanyth before picking up her utensils. "Eat up. This'll be the last hot meal like this until we get to Grandmother's house."

"She has a house?" Rebecca asked, a forkful of mashed potato halfway to her mouth.

"What? She's a hermit so she must live in a cave?" Penny asked, her lips curved into a lop-sided grin.

Rebecca just blinked her eyes several times. "Yeah. That's kinda what I thought, but...how do you get a house way out there in the woods?"

Penny shrugged. "Same way anybody does, I guess. Build it."

Tanyth grinned down at her plate and concentrated on fueling her body for the trek ahead.

Chapter 8
Slipping The Leash

The full Shearing Moon hung above the treetops, gleaming on the packed streets of the town. Somewhere not far away humans made man-noises. A cautious foray into the open often brought delicious rewards; her whiskered nose told her that food waited just beyond the building. Her kits needed milk; she needed food to make the milk. She knew the humans and relied on their food the year round. This place sometimes had softened grains and even cooked breads and vegetables. Her mouth watered at the thought but she hunkered down to wait. She could be patient until the humans went to their dens.

She had barely settled down when the big human came out and extinguished the lamp beside the entrance to their huge den. Darkness grew deeper, if not entirely black. The watching moon saw all. When the big human re-entered his den, she waited until she heard his heavy steps move away and waited a little longer. Haste carried more risk than reward.

When all was quiet and she smelled no fresh scents, she scuttled across the packed earth as quickly as her legs would carry her and disappeared into the shadows. Without winter's fat she moved quickly, her dugs swaying under her belly as she ran. She stopped and waited, listening and twitching her nose.

A scuffed step in the shadows nearly made her leap.

Two men in identical skins lurked just around the corner, her corner. Now that she knew they were there, her nose picked out their scents from the mess of odors that a mass of humans leaves behind. She'd nearly run into them in the dark.

Her heart beat fast and she backed away from them, exposing herself to the moon briefly before darting around the den to approach from the other side. There was food nearby and more than one way to get it. Her kits needed milk and she needed the food. Silly humans hiding in the dark could not be allowed to stop her.

☽○☾

Tanyth blinked herself awake but lay silently in her bed, listening to the night around them. A glance at the window showed her the silvery moonlight painting the treetops. "Well, that complicates things," she muttered.

"Wassat, mum?" Rebecca's sleepy murmur came from the shadowed cot across the small room.

"Nothin', dear. Go back to sleep. Mornin' comes before breakfast."

"Usually does," she said and rolled over again.

Tanyth slept fitfully until the rays of moonlight through the window told her that dawn was not far off. She heard the distant clatter of cooking coming from below and rolled out of her bed. "Rebecca. Time to go."

The younger woman rolled out of her cot almost immediately, weeks of working the deck of a sailing schooner training her to near-instant wakefulness. "Two shakes, mum," she murmured.

"We have a problem. There's soldiers in the alley."

Tanyth finished buckling her belt and pulling on her traveling coat. She looped a single strap of her heavy pack over one shoulder, settled her wide-brimmed hat on her head, and took up her staff.

"Meet me in the kitchen."

"You had a dream?" Rebecca asked, working quickly and quietly to gather her own traveling gear.

"Yeah." Tanyth slipped from the room and down the stairs, her worn boots making small scuff noises but otherwise silent in the quiet inn. The clanking of pots on the iron stove and the sound of a spoon stirring something drew her to the kitchen door.

"Morning, mum," Amanda said, when she stuck her nose into the kitchen.

Tanyth held a finger up to her lips and motioned Amanda out of the brightly lit kitchen.

Putting down the spoon, she followed Tanyth out to the dining room, a frown on her brow. "What is it?" she hissed.

"There's two soldiers in the alley, just around the corner from the front of the inn. I think they're watching the street and can prob'ly see into the kitchen."

"You're sure?"

"They were there at midnight when Perry turned out the lantern. Unless something's happened, they're prob'ly still there."

"Your son seems to be the cautious type," Amanda said.

"Being in the King's Own has taught him that, I suppose. Wasn't anything he learned at home."

Amanda's cheery smile shone in the dimness. "Well, we'll have to ask them in for breakfast, won't we?"

"What?"

"Stay here for a few more minutes. I've got the breads rising and the tea on. I figured you'd want something to eat before you hit the trail. Perry will be down in a couple of minutes; I'll get him to pull a pile of rations from the pantry and bring them out to you."

Rebecca joined them in the dark. "Mornin', Amanda. She told you?"

"About the guards? Yeah. It's under control, unless he's left some other little surprises. Sit tight. It'll only be a few minutes."

Perry clumped out of the back room and started when he found them all standing there in the near dark. "What the—?"

"Hush," Amanda said. "Come help me in the kitchen. We've got guests." With that, she pushed back through the door, Perry following without another word.

Tanyth and Amanda took refuge in the shadows beside the stairs and hunkered down to wait. In a few minutes, the kitchen door opened and Perry stomped in from the kitchen, headed to the hearth with a burlap sack in his hand. He spent several minutes laying out the wood and pulling kindling from the sack. A couple of quick scratches with flint and steel started the fire. He stood, dusting his hands together as the growing firelight illuminated more and more of the room, making the shadows by the stairs seem even darker.

Seemingly satisfied with his work, he picked up the bag and headed for the kitchen, dropping it at the foot of the stairs on his way. "Rations in there. Help yourselves," he muttered as he pushed through the door. "Fire's laid," he announced as the door swung shut behind him.

They heard Amanda say, "Good. Now take that pile of slops out of here and bring me back some fresh eggs, would you?"

"Of course, m' dear."

Tanyth snaked the sack back from the firelight. The two women added half a dozen wrapped travel rations to each of their packs.

"Think that's enough?" Rebecca whispered.

"Should be more'n enough. Penny'll have her own and this is enough for nearly a week of travelin'. Might get borin' but it'll keep us movin'."

"If you say so."

They didn't have long to wait before they heard male voices in the kitchen.

"Ma'am, we really need to be out front."

"Oh, please, you two are near to frozen and don't tell me a hot cuppa tea is against orders."

"But, ma'am—"

"Don't 'but ma'am' me, soldier," she said. "Perry, go open up the front doors and see if anybody's comin'."

"Yes, dear," he said and his burly frame bounced through the kitchen door. He marched loudly to the front of the inn and waved to Tanyth and Rebecca to follow. They dodged to the shadows beside the entry as he made way too much noise fiddling with the front door and sticking his head out. After a quick look, he held the door and waved them through it, pointing to a break in the fence diagonally across the narrow street. "Through there. Quick. Take you right to Penny's place."

They scampered down the steps and across the street even as they heard Perry's booming voice carry on the morning air. "Nobody out here. Who were you lookin' for again?"

The front door to the inn bumped closed as they scurried up the narrow trail and onto the pine-needle paths that led to Penny Oakton's door.

Chapter 9
On The Trail

Penny opened her door on the first soft tap. "You ready?" she asked. "The moon will set when the sun rises and we should have plenty of light to see by."

"Robert posted garrison troops to guard the inn," Tanyth said. "Sooner we get out of his reach, the happier I'll be."

"He what?"

"Tell you when we break for lunch—miles from here, I hope."

Penny nodded and grabbed her coat from the peg beside the door. Shucking into it, she pulled a knit cap from the pocket that she snugged down on her head. Her pack waited beside the door and she stepped out on the stoop with it in her hand. She closed the door and flipped a sign to read "In the woods" in rough-carved letters.

Rebecca snorted. "You do this often, I take it?"

Penny grinned, her smile bright in the dim light of the setting moon. "Often enough. People 'round here know enough to go to one of the king's healers if it's serious and they can pay."

"What if it is and they can't?" Tanyth asked.

Penny's smile disappeared. "Generally, they die. Let's go before the guards wise up." She pushed past Tanyth and headed for the woods at the end of the road, shouldering her pack as she went.

Tanyth followed, with Rebecca bringing up the rear.

The path that Penny led them down turned from a proper one to something more appropriately called a deer trail. Gaps in the canopy let in enough moonlight that they didn't trip on too many roots or run into any low-hanging limbs. Penny stopped after about fifteen minutes and leaned her pack against the bole of a tree beside the trail.

When she spoke, she kept her voice low. "Voices carry. Speak softly when you have to speak at all. Not talking until we get past Four Mile Creek is best. The sun'll be up in about half an hour, and that means the moon's going down. Light's gonna get bad so we'll have to go slower."

Tanyth and Rebecca nodded.

"You both doin' all right?" Penny asked.

Tanyth nodded. "I'm fine. Pro'bly be sore tomorrow, but good enough for now."

"Me, too," Rebecca added. "I got a lot more exercise on the way to Kleesport than she did, and I was huntin' on trails like this for the last four winters."

"All right, then." Penny's grin showed white against the darkness behind her. "We're going to be crossing the main north road in a few minutes. We'll keep an eye out for patrols but we'll prob'ly hear them before we see them."

She pushed herself off from the tree and walked down the trail again, moving more slowly and deliberately. Tanyth and Rebecca followed.

Within a few minutes, Penny halted on the trail and held up a hand for them to stop. They listened but only heard the faint whisper of the morning breeze in the pine tops. After a moment an owl's hoot echoed through the pre-dawn.

Penny stepped forward and they found themselves beside a road of packed gravel. Directly across from them a dark tunnel led off between two heavy trees. Penny pointed to it. Tanyth nodded.

Penny pointed at Tanyth and then at the tunnel across the road again.

Tanyth moved. The gravel crunched under her boots, loud against the morning's quiet, but she slipped into the mouth of the tunnel without incident. She took a couple of paces down the trail and turned to look back.

The gathering light seemed almost bright from her vantage point. She could see Rebecca and Penny clearly against the dark woods behind them.

Penny sent Rebecca ahead.

Rebecca's boots also crunched briefly but she, too, made it across without incident to join Tanyth under the trees.

"What was that?" A man's voice sounded loud even though he was speaking softly.

"What?" a second man said.

"I thought I heard footsteps."

"You been hearin' things all night."

Penny stepped back into the woods, fading into the darkness rather than stepping out onto the road.

"Well, there was a bear."

"Yeah, so you say, but shut up. You think this patrol is just for fun?"

"I got no idea. All I know is I'm cold and tired, and this is stupid."

"Dumb ass. Commandant says jump. We say how high."

"It's still stupid."

"Just shut your gob. Thomas and Ervin will be along any minute to relieve us and we can get back for a warm meal and some shut-eye."

Rebecca and Tanyth lowered themselves to the ground and watched.

As if from far away they heard a woman's voice. She hummed a lullaby, occasionally changing up the humming with la-la-las. It grew nearer and in a moment, Penny stepped out from the trees across the road and started walking away from town, singing away and scuffing her feet in the gravel.

"Halt!"

Penny squeaked and spun around. "Who's there?" she called.

"That's my line, lady. Who are you, and what are you doing here?"

"Martin? Martin Gluckman? Is that you?"

A voice muttered "what the—?" and two garrison soldiers walked noisily up the road. "Mother Oakton?"

"It is you. What are you two doing out here this time of day? Commandant punishing you for drinking again?"

"Naw, we're on patrol. Bunch of us out here."

The Hermit Of Lammas Wood

"Shut up, you idiot," the second voice said.

Penny held her hands high over her head. "Well, you caught me. Now what? You have to march me back to town or something?" She giggled a little.

"No, put your hands down. We're just on patrol because we're supposed to be looking for somebody trying to sneak out of town."

"Me?"

"No, ma'am. Not you. Some newcomers just came on the ship. Commandant said to make sure these two ladies didn't get into any trouble out here in the backwoods, and to bring 'em back if we find 'em trying to leave town."

"Well, I never," Penny said. "Why would two women be wanderin' around out here in the woods in the middle of the night?"

"That's what I bin sayin'," the first voice said.

"Oh, shut up, already," the second voice said.

"Well, if you're not going to stop me, can I put my arms down and go?"

"Where are you going, mum? If you don't mind me askin'."

"Spring mushrooms down around Four Mile Creek. Good for women's problems, and I can only get them early in the season. Now that Audry McGilvry's had her baby, I can get away for a bit and gather in peace."

"What'd she have?" the first voice asked.

"Little boy. Spittin' image of Ed."

"Aw. That's great. Ain't that great, Marty?"

"For cryin' out loud, we're supposed to be on patrol, not yappin' about babies and women's problems."

"I'm just sayin'—" The voice cut off with a meaty thump. "Ow."

"Speakin' of babies, stop bein' one, all right?"

The sound of marching feet came from somewhere down the road, along with the jangle and squeal of tack. "That'll be our relief," the second voice said.

"Well, good luck to you on your patrol. Sounds like you're heading back to town soon?"

"Yes'm. We get the dark and the cold and that—ow. Why'd you hit me for that time?"

"Shut up," the man's voice practically hissed with frustration. "Sorry, Mother Oakton. You're free to go. Don't get too close to the creek. It's still running pretty high."

"Thank you, Martin. You boys have a good day."

The two soldiers tramped past the opening again, going in the other direction. Neither of them so much as glanced in Tanyth's direction. In a few moments their footsteps began to merge with the sound of the oncoming patrol, and Penny ducked between the two trees.

"Come on before somebody with a brain shows up," she whispered and pushed past them down the trail.

Chapter 10
Flown

At mid-morning Penny called a halt. She slipped her pack off and sat down on the ground at the base of a spruce, bracing her back and stretching her legs. "Water, small snack. We'll take a proper break at lunch."

Tanyth followed her example and found a tree to lean on while Rebecca simply flopped on the ground after dropping her pack beside the trail.

"We more than three miles from town?" Tanyth asked.

"More like five or six," Penny said. "We came across Four Mile Creek about an hour back."

Rebecca looked over at her. "Really? I don't remember crossing any creek."

Penny fished a bar of pressed grain from her pack and gnawed at the end. "Remember that soggy swale? The one where you slipped in the mud?"

"Yeah."

"That was it."

"Really? I thought it was running high."

"We're at the headwater. You'd be surprised how big it gets about a mile to the south of us."

Tanyth fished an apple out of her pack and chewed on the juicy flesh. It lacked the crisp bite of a fall apple, but the sweet juice felt good rolling down her throat.

"You doin' all right, mum?" Penny asked, concern writ large on her face.

"Oh, my goodness, yes." Tanyth took another bite. "This is just a warm-up."

Penny snickered. "You may be more right than you know. We're goin' to be on the trail for the next three days."

"Yeah, but tomorrow morning, we won't have garrison troops trying to stop us from leavin'," Rebecca said.

"Well, that's prob'ly true, although I wouldn't wanna be Prince Robert when your father comes ashore and finds out you've been there and gone."

Rebecca snorted a short laugh and pulled a canteen from her pack. "I'd almost like to be a fly on that wall." She took a single deep swig and strapped the canteen back onto her pack.

Penny scrambled to her feet and brushed the seat of her trousers off with her hands. "All right, then. Daylight's burning. Time to move."

They struck off down the path once more. Tanyth noted they moved generally north and west as the path wound around hillock and through valleys. At midday they broke out on an alpine parkland. Craggy mountains bounded them on the north horizon, their rocky slopes still showing patches of snow on the lower elevations and solid snow fields toward the peaks. Far to the south, the shimmer of ocean illuminated the horizon while treetops ran nearly as far as they could see.

Tanyth felt the land under her feet, the swelling power of it. "It's lovely," she said, her eyes trying to drink it all in at once.

"I've never seen anything like it," Rebecca said.

"Wait'll you see the pretty stuff," Penny said with a sideways grin. "Come on, let's stop makin' targets of ourselves and get off this ridgeline. There's a campsite just down here. We can put our feet up for a bit."

She led them down a narrow ravine cut into the side of the ridge. A heavy stone upright stained with soot marked a fire pit lined with small rocks. Several slightly larger ones made handy seats.

"Can we make a fire for tea?" Tanyth asked.

Penny looked at the sky and seemed to sniff the air. "Prob'ly keep a cold camp here. I'm not sure who's out and about right now."

"Problems?" Tanyth asked.

"Prob'ly not, but why risk it? We'll have a fire tonight and a hot meal then. Best we move as fast and light as we can right now."

They settled around the cold fire pit and dug out travel rations of pressed oats and dried fruits. The tangy smell of pines offered the only condiment besides their hunger. Cold water from canteens helped moisten the dried fruit in their mouths.

"Rabbits?" Rebecca asked as she licked the sticky remains of the travel bar from her fingers.

"What about 'em?" Penny asked.

"I've my bow. If we see some, can we take them?"

Penny eyed her with new respect. "You can hit a rabbit with that thing?"

"Well, of course. Not much sense carryin' it all this way if I didn't know how to use it."

Penny looked to Tanyth, who nodded in confirmation. "She's really rather good with it."

"Well, sure then. Although we're likely to see more grouse than rabbits. Ever hit a bird on the wing?"

Rebecca shook her head.

"Rabbits'll be a bit lean after the winter, but we can stew 'em if you can take 'em."

"Fair enough," Rebecca said and took another long pull from her canteen.

"What about water?" Tanyth asked. "We're goin' through what we got pretty fast."

"And you're right to do so," Penny said. "We're gettin' up there and the altitude will dry you out a lot faster than you'd think. There's plenty of water around. Prob'ly too much in places."

Tanyth took a final swig from her own canteen and stood, strapping it back on her pack. "Well, in that case, we best get movin'. Robert knows we're heading for the hermit. He might take it in his head to follow and try to catch us."

Penny laughed and stood, shouldering her own back. "He might if he knew where she was."

That stopped Tanyth and made her cock her head to one side. "He doesn't know where she is? I thought everybody up here knew about her."

Penny shook her head and sucked in a deep breath. She held it for a moment before blowing it out. "Everybody knows about the hermit of Lammas Wood. She's almost a legend. My gran is only the latest one. There's been a hermit up here as long as there's been people."

"How's that work?" Rebecca asked.

"I don't know," Penny said with a shrug. "Granny Gert has been the hermit as long as I've been alive. I don't know who was hermit before her or how she came to be. All I know is, she's the hermit."

"And you know where she lives," Tanyth said.

"And I know where her cottage is," Penny corrected.

"Close enough," Tanyth said.

Penny shrugged. "Might be. Point is, not a lot of people know that. Almost all of them live out here in the backcountry. Trappers, hunters, lumberjacks. There's prob'ly fifty or a hundred of them that know. Few of them even visit town. Them that do haven't a lot to do with the garrison."

"So Robert doesn't know," Tanyth said.

"No way to know for sure, but it's not likely. He'll know generally, but there's a whole lot of nothing out here but woods and mountains and trees. It'd take a long time to find her unless you knew where to look."

"We're leavin' a pretty plain trail," Rebecca said, pointing to their footprints in the soft earth around the campsite.

Penny grinned. "Looks like it, don't it?"

"Yeah, it does."

"We'll be heading out across that parkland we saw from the ridge. There'll be a lot less trail to follow when we get to the other side."

Tanyth nodded. "Grass doesn't stay bent over very long."

"Not as wet as the ground is here," Penny said, nodding in agreement.

"Well, let's get on with it," Tanyth said. "Sooner we make camp, sooner I get my tea."

Penny grinned and headed back up the trail.

Chapter 11
Followed

---◈---

The silvery light of the waning moon limned the snow fields. They almost glowed against the dark sky. Across the park the male hooted once, a territorial call that made her shift her talons in frustration. The noise might warn her prey to danger and she hungered. The cold time had not been kind. She needed warm meat.

A rustling in the grass below alerted her to prey. A small, dark gray shadow moved among the dried stalks and then froze. She waited until it moved again, the faint whisper of stalk against stalk helping her focus on her meal's location in the grasses below her perch.

There!

She launched—wide, heavy wings made no sound as they carved the air toward her meal.

At the last moment the noisy male hooted again, his territory warning loud in the still night. The meal disappeared down a hole a split second before her talons could reach it. She nearly hooted in frustration, but silently flipped her tail feathers and tilted her wings to sail back up away from the ground and into the clear night sky.

She leveled off after she cleared the treetops. Another park lay just beyond the next ridge. Perhaps it was far enough away from that ridiculous male and his bragging calls that she could find a meal worthy of the name.

A glimmer of fire shone through the trees, and she saw the pillar of smoke rising from the ground. A faint breeze at altitude clipped the plume at an angle, sending it toward the big water far away. She changed course to fly nearer. She was no scavenger, but perhaps a meal might appear in the light.

In moments she came to rest on a limb overlooking a small clearing tucked into a ravine. Blackened stone and a glowing fire dominated the view, but patience paid off when a man moved in the shadows. He crossed to the fire and dropped a piece of wood onto the coals, sending a shower of sparks upward into the night. It smoldered, and then flames began to lick the edges.

In the additional light, more shadows resolved themselves into more men stretched out on the ground. One shifted, rolling from one side to the other. Not dead, then. Sleeping. She found it interesting but hunger drove her. Perhaps they would leave something to draw prey. She would have to return to see, but later. She needed something to fill the hollow in her belly and she'd need it soon.

She launched into the treetops and drifted over the ridge. In the far distance, the male hooted again. He would not be feeding very well making that much noise. Perhaps he had already fed, so could afford to brag. She clicked her talons, flexed them as if sinking them deep into a rabbit. Yes, a young rabbit or one of the larger ground squirrels would be an excellent meal.

Clearing the ridge, she drifted along the treeline on silent wings. Her eyes scanned the ground, but her ears would find her prey first.

☽○☾

Tanyth clawed her way to consciousness. The same moon shone through the spruce tops above her. The small fire had burned down to a few glowing coals in a bed of ash. Across the fire pit, Rebecca's tousled hair showed above the edge of her blankets. Penny lay curled in a ball on her side, knit cap still on her head and her face down in her bedroll.

She ran her tongue around her mouth, tasting the sourness of night breath even as she tried to recall the images of her dream. Soldiers slept in the same camp they'd had lunch in. At least four, perhaps more lost in the shadows.

"Bother," she muttered and rolled over, pulling her blanket over her face against the chill night airs. The pad of blankets protected her from most of the lumps under her, but the cold seeped through in places. She shifted to try to find the warmest spots, then let sleep claim her once more.

☽○☾

"Rise and shine, campers. The day awaits," Penny's cheerful voice made Tanyth smile as she crawled up from slumber.

"You gonna be all cheerful in the morning every day?" Rebecca asked.

"Prob'ly, but cheer up. Only three more mornings and we'll be at Gran's cottage."

Tanyth crawled out of her bedroll and stretched her back, arching it and then bending left and right to try to release the crick. She fished in the blankets and came up with her boots, sitting on the padded ground to slide them on.

Rebecca eyed her blearily, then cast her gaze to where her own boots stood next to the pack that served as pillow. "Why didn't I remember to do that?" she muttered.

"Outta practice?" Tanyth asked.

"At least."

Penny snorted and pushed a few more twigs onto the growing fire. "Tea will be ready shortly."

"Don't build that too big," Tanyth said. "Soldiers camped in our lunch spot last night."

Penny gave her a startled look, her eyes wide. "The campsite in the ravine?"

Tanyth ran her fingers through her hair in an effort to get some of the sleep-tangles out. "I think so. Any other places with a big, smoke-stained rock like that around here?"

Penny stared into the fire for a moment before shaking her head. "Not that I know of. There could be."

"Then we got soldiers on our back trail."

Penny stuffed another handful of twigs into the fire and watched the smoke puff upward and dissipate against the overhanging ledge above them. "How do you know that, mum?"

"She had a dream," Rebecca said. "Didn't ya, mum?"

"Yeah."

"'Nother raccoon?"

"Owl."

Penny's gaze went back and forth between the two women. "An owl." It was a statement more than a question.

"Yeah. Female and hungry. Looking for a bit of warm meat, but the big male on the next ridge kept hooting and spoiling her hunt." Tanyth's gaze stayed fixed on the fire but her focus was miles away. "She spotted the glow of the fire and went to look."

"And you dreamed this?"

Tanyth glanced at Penny. "Well, sorta. I was asleep. It felt like a dream, but I was seein' through her eyes. Feelin' the wind in her feathers and the hunger in her belly."

Penny looked at Rebecca who watched the midwife with a silly grin on her face. "Odd, huh?" Rebecca said.

"It's mad," Penny said.

"That's what I been sayin'," Tanyth said. "But the truth is I saw them guards outside the inn with the help of a raccoon, and those soldiers should be coming through the park in an hour or so."

"How do you know they're followin' us?" Penny asked.

Tanyth shook her head. "Don't. But what else would they be doin' out here?"

Rebecca jumped out of her bedroll and stuffed her feet into the frost-rimed boots, sucking her breath through her teeth. "Lady, that's cold," she said, sitting back down on her bedroll and pulling her jacket around her shoulders.

Penny looked at her with a smile curling her lips. "You coulda held them over the fire for a bit. Woulda taken the worst of the chill out."

Rebecca looked at Penny, then at Tanyth, and then down at the small fire. She hung her head forward, bouncing it on her neck a couple of times. "Coulda, shoulda, woulda," she said. "Next time."

"Next time take 'em to bed with ya and you won't hafta," Tanyth said.

"That, too," Rebecca said, not looking up.

The water in the small pot began to simmer against the thin metal and soon bubbled in a full boil. Penny tossed a handful of tea into it and pulled it back from the fire to steep.

Tanyth dug in her pack and pulled out a travel ration.

"Oatmeal tomorrow mornin'," she said.

Penny glanced at her. "You brought oatmeal?"

Tanyth nodded. "I always bring oatmeal. Good food when nothin' else is handy. Light to carry and stays with ya for a while. Besides..." She held up the travel ration. "Toss a couple of these in a pot next to the fire at night and we'll have mush by morning. Easier than gnawing on 'em." She smiled.

"We'll have rabbit stew tonight," Rebecca said.

Penny frowned at her. "We can't be stoppin' to hunt if them soldiers are comin' after us."

"Who said anythin' about stoppin'. I saw two easy shots yesterday afternoon but didn't have my bow out. That's not gonna happen today." She held out her tin cup.

Penny picked up the hot pot using a folded cloth from her pack and drizzled some into Rebecca's cup, then into Tanyth's, and finally her own. "We wanna make another pot?" she asked, staring into the lees.

Tanyth dunked the hard travel ration into the steaming liquid and shook her head. "With troops half a day back, we prob'ly should get movin'."

Penny nodded and upended the soggy mass into the fire, sending up an alarming amount of steam that disappeared almost as quickly as it formed. She stirred the fire apart with a stick and let the twigs burn a bit more while she sipped her tea and chewed her ration.

"What d'you suppose is out here?" Tanyth said. Her hands cupped around the mug for warmth and her eyes focused somewhere in the distant woods.

"Besides trees, rocks, bears, and the odd trapper, you mean?" Penny asked.

"Yeah. Rebecca's father isn't one to waste a lot of time chasin' down a lost cow."

"So I'm a cow now?" Rebecca said, a half smile on her face.

"Well, he wasn't lookin' for you. We know that because we know for certain he knew where you really were. He had to be usin' that story to cover what he was really lookin' for."

"Could he have been lookin' for Gran?" Penny asked frownin' into her own tea.

"Can't imagine what for," Tanyth said.

"Two things move my father," Rebecca said, eyes half-lidded and her face hard. "Money and power. If he was lookin' for something here in the woods, alone, it's one of them two things."

"Well, he wasn't exactly alone," Penny said. "He always had a couple of his own men with him and, generally, a couple of troopers as well."

"Wonder if he told Robert what he was really looking for," Tanyth mused.

"Not likely, mum," Rebecca said.

"Whyzzat?" Tanyth asked looking across the fire.

"Robert was surprised to find me at the inn. That wasn't the surprise of a man who was busy lookin' for something last year that wasn't really me. He seemed pretty adamant that Father was looking for me. Why else would he want to keep us there until he arrived?"

Penny said, "Maybe he didn't want us findin' whatever it is."

"And keepin' us in town until Richard arrived was his way of seein' that we didn't?" Tanyth asked.

Penny shrugged. "Possible."

Tanyth sighed. "Lots of stuff is possible. Wish I knew which was most probable."

Penny snorted. "You and me, too, mum." She stirred herself and clambered to her feet, kicking dirt over their dying fire. "Time to move. If we can make it into the next valley without bein' spotted, we'll be home free."

"Whyzzat?" Tanyth asked.

Penny just smiled and started rolling up her bedding. "You'll see."

Chapter 12
Ole Man

The trail led them deeper into the mountains as they climbed northwestward up a long north-south running ridge. The spruces were noticeably more stunted the farther the women hiked, until they broke out of the trees and stood at the foot of an unbroken ridge that ran straight up to the side of a massive snow-capped peak towering above them.

"We're not gonna climb that, I hope," Rebecca said, her head tilted back for a good look at the snow-crusted rock.

Penny laughed. "Not hardly. That's Ole Man. You can see his snowy head for a hundred miles."

"Don't look like a head much," Rebecca said.

"That's 'cause we're too close. By tomorrow you'll be able to look back and see it better."

Tanyth scanned the ridge line and then glanced over her shoulder at the scrubby trees. "Seems kinda exposed up here."

Penny nodded and shaded her eyes, gazing back down along the path they'd taken. "Yeah. We won't wanna stay here very long. Come on. Let's get over the crest of the ridge."

They followed the edge of the tree line across the lichen-covered rocks. When they reached the top, the vista stopped Tanyth in her tracks.

"Don't stop here, mum," Penny said. "Get off the ridge line and we'll take a water break so you can gawk. It's worth lookin' at."

They stumbled along until Penny found a couple of boulders they could shelter behind. Dropping her pack on the ground, she pulled out her canteen. "Drink up. There's a spring just down the trail a bit." She fished out a ration bar and plunked herself on the ground, using her pack as backrest.

Tanyth stood there for a moment drinking in the view before following suit, nudging Rebecca to do likewise.

Below them a wide valley stretched between tall cliffs. Instead of the smoothly curved ground covered with trees that she expected to see, Tanyth saw a broken patchwork of pillars and mounds, most of naked rock but some with tufts of vegetation on them like unruly haircuts on skinny children. Here and there water gleamed between them. The valley curved up and around Ole Man to the north, disappearing around his flank. To the south it widened and flattened. The broken land seemed to go on for miles.

"That's Black Rock Canyon," Penny said. "Once we get down there, nobody can follow."

"Is that a river?" Rebecca asked.

"Yeah, Black Rock River." Penny shrugged. "Not very imaginative but you'll see why when we get down there."

"We have to cross that?" Rebecca's gaze kept sweeping back and forth, her head turning one way then the other as she scanned.

"Oh, yeah. It's worse than it looks, but there's cover all the way across."

"We won't leave footprints?" Tanyth asked.

"There's a reason it's called Black Rock Canyon, mum. Most of the ground is covered in black rock scales and, when you get down in there, it's practically a maze. It's not someplace you go unless you know where you're going."

"And you do?"

"I do," Penny said. She turned to Rebecca. "Keep your bow handy. Might find dinner on the way."

"Well, let's get to it," Tanyth said, taking a final pull from her canteen. "Sooner started, sooner done."

Penny chuckled and stood, pulling her pack up and onto her shoulders. "Off we go then, the spring's just down here and then we'll climb down to the valley."

"Climb?" Tanyth asked.

"Trail. Lotsa switchbacks. That's the last bottleneck between here and Gran's." She strode off down the trail with

Tanyth and Rebecca following. "It's the only way up or down on this side of the canyon for ten, twenty miles in either direction."

"Does Robert know that?" Tanyth asked.

Penny paused and looked back at Tanyth. "Maybe. That's why we need to get down first. If he's ahead of us, that's where he'll be."

Tanyth nodded.

Penny started back down the trail. After a brief stop to fill their canteens from a clean, moss-lined spring, they began the long trek down the side of the valley.

The sun rode high in the southern sky by the time they reached the valley floor. Penny called a halt. "Lunch break. They're not here and we'll hear them coming down the trail if they start."

Rebecca immediately stripped off her pack and plunked down beside it on the ground, brushing away the dust-crusted sweat from her eyes. "That's gonna be a pain to get back up. Tell me it's not like that on the far side," she said.

Penny laughed. "No. The other climb's up a smooth grade. There's a campsite just on the other side of the valley. We'll stop there tonight and cross the ridge tomorrow."

Tanyth placed her pack on the ground, pulling out another travel ration and her canteen. "These are gettin' old," she muttered.

"I don't usually notice when I'm out here by myself," Penny said. "Funny you should mention it."

"Well, I didn't get my oatmeal with my mornin' tea," Tanyth said. "I miss it."

"And not like Amanda didn't serve big breakfasts," Rebecca said. She eyed the ration bar for a moment as if debating whether or not to eat it, before she started chewing on it.

"Oh, I've had worse," Tanyth said. "Made worse, to be honest."

"We'll have oatmeal for breakfast and something fresh for dinner, if we've any luck and Rebecca is as good with that bow as you say."

"That sounds like a challenge to me," Rebecca said, a wide

grin stretching her mouth.

Penny shrugged. "We'll see," she said, then laughed.

Their meager lunch soon behind them, they packed up and followed Penny out onto the valley floor. A line of black stones with regular sides stretched along the valley floor, some taller, some shorter but all with similar joins of five or six faces.

"What made these?" Rebecca asked as they hiked along the line of curious stones.

"Lady only knows," Penny said. "They're funny rock, though. Sometimes it's reddish like it's rusting. Places where it's underwater all the time it's almost always black. If you manage to break a chunk off, it's black on the inside. It's been here as long as we have."

"Longer, I suspect," Tanyth said. "This is old, old country here."

"Why'd you say that?" Penny asked.

"This river musta carved this whole valley down. I bet you dig into them pillars and piles, you'll find more of this black rock at the core. Dirt washed away faster than the rock."

Penny nodded. "Yeah. You're right. There's more'n one that's a solid block of rock with dirt on top and grass growing up there."

"Takes a long time to wear away that much dirt," Tanyth said. "Must be nearly as old as the mountains."

"Where's the river go?" Rebecca asked.

"There's a bay off that way about twenty, thirty miles," Penny said, waving her hand toward the south. "It dumps into that."

"No town there?" Tanyth asked.

Penny shook her head. "Nah. No beach. Cliffs straight down to the water. At least that's what the trappers say. Never been there myself."

"Must be pretty," Rebecca said.

"What?" asked Penny.

"The river running off the cliff and fallin' into the bay."

Penny stopped and looked back at her. Her mouth opened and closed a couple of times. "I never thought of it, but you're right. Must be." With a shrug she continued along the path of black stones, Tanyth and Rebecca following in her wake.

Tanyth eyed the sun and watched the rocks. Didn't seem like a place to take fresh game, but she followed along and tried to keep track of the path with lots of glances over her shoulder to gauge the position of Ole Man and the trail that led back to civilization–such as it was.

Chapter 13
In The Black Rock

———⟨✦⟩———

Penny led them around the piles of rock and dirt, always walking on the fractured black stone surfaces. The traveling was easy but nerve-wracking as the sound of rushing water grew with nearly every step. The sun angled into their eyes as they moved more and more directly west. By mid-afternoon they came to the main channel.

The muddy water boiled between the banks, which looked about half a mile across from where they stood. The noise echoing off the canyon walls made Tanyth's head pound.

"How are we going to cross that?" Tanyth shouted to Penny, to be heard over the rushing water as they paused a few feet from the bank.

Penny pointed up-stream. A rope bridge spanned the gap between two of the tall stone pillars.

Rebecca's eyes grew round.

Penny waved dismissively and started along the riverbank to the base of the black rock pillar. When they got there, what had looked like a straight column of rock turned out to be cleverly carved and chipped away to allow relatively easy access to the top. In a moment they stood above the roiling waters, staring across the swaying walkway to the other bank.

Flat planks with rope threaded through holes in either end made up the bridge decking, but instead of a handrail down either side there was only one rather hefty line strung above the bridge to serve as a handhold.

Penny motioned Rebecca and Tanyth to the end of the bridge. She pointed to the rope above. "Hold that," she shouted. "I'll help you keep your balance. It looks scarier than it is, just don't stop. Keep moving across. I'll go first and show you how."

With a cheery wave, she turned and wrapped both hands around the rope above her head, then walked out onto the planks. She moved steadily along, pausing halfway across to turn and look back. She motioned with her head several times.

Tanyth looked at Rebecca. "Just like workin' aloft in the riggin', huh?"

The thought seemed to please the younger woman. She grinned and nodded. "After you. I'll push you if you freeze up," she shouted.

Tanyth eyed her and then shrugged. "Not gonna cross standin' here, are ya, old woman," she muttered. She reached up and grabbed the rope, walking along the wet planking and concentrating on her hands rather than her feet.

"What?" Rebecca yelled.

Tanyth shook her head and kept going.

After a relatively long three minutes she arrived safely on the other side and lowered her arms. They objected, and she had to shake the cramps out of them. Penny hugged her, pulling her away from the end of the bridge to make way for Rebecca, who crossed with a smile on her face and only one hand hooked over the rope.

Tanyth felt her eyes all but bug out of her head in alarm, but before she could say anything, Rebecca stepped off the end of the bridge like she was stepping off a sidewalk in town.

"One hand for me, one hand for the ship, mum. It's what I learned," she shouted.

Penny pointed at the path down off the pinnacle. They soon found themselves walking on black rock paths between quiet pools with sandy bottoms. Within a dozen yards the sound of the rushing river faded to a dull roar, and they could speak almost normally.

"Get your bow strung," Penny said without preamble. "Dinner should be here somewhere."

Rebecca looked around but did as Penny asked. "What am I gonna shoot at? Geese or something?"

Penny shook her head. "Or something. Come on." She led them along the paths between the pools, pausing at each one to scan the water before moving on. At the fourth pool she stopped and held up a hand. She pointed to a dark shape on the sandy bottom.

Tanyth looked hard, but it was a few moments before she realized she was seeing the shadow of a decent-sized fish lazing in the clean, still waters. As she looked, she noticed several more shadows but had to study to find the fish above them.

Penny leaned her head over to Rebecca. "Can you hit one of them? They're not moving, but you'll have to aim low."

"How low?" Rebecca asked, squinting against the glare.

Penny pointed out a particular shadow. "You see the fish above the shadow there?"

"Just barely."

"Aim for the far edge of his shadow. It'll look like you're gonna shoot under him, but the water does funny things."

Rebecca shrugged and nodded. She nocked a barbed arrow and pulled the bow back until her thumb nearly touched her ear. The tip of her arrow tracked downward a bit and in an instant it was gone as if by magic, only the vibrating bow string indicating that it had been there at all.

Across the pool, the fletching shuddered above the water and then became still, sticking up at an angle from the surface. A cloud of silt and sand obscured the business end of the arrow under the water. All the other shadows in the pool had disappeared.

Penny patted Rebecca on the shoulder and scampered around to the far side of the pool. She splashed into the knee-deep water, reached down, and pulled up a fat trout by the gills. Rebecca's arrow had pierced the side of its head. "Nice shot," Penny called, then turned to clamber out of the pool.

Rebecca and Tanyth joined her as she freed the arrow and handed it to Rebecca. "Dinner," she said, holding up the fish. "You like trout?"

Rebecca nodded.

"I usually catch my own, but that's faster," Tanyth said.

Penny pulled a small knife from her belt and gutted the

The Hermit Of Lammas Wood

fish right there on the bank, leaving the entrails for the small scavengers to find before standing and heading down the path once more. "Half a mile more and we'll stop for the night. We'll wanna be fresh for tomorrow," she said.

Tanyth snorted. "I wanted to be fresh for today. Not sure I'm up to tomorrow."

Rebecca laughed at her mutterings and waved her ahead.

True to her word, Penny led them to a sheltered bend in the canyon. An undercut bank provided a bit of cover over them, and a sand bank deposited by some long-gone flood gave them padding against the seemingly endless black rock. Somebody had scraped a fire pit in the sand; the remains of the last fire lay in the shallow hole. The surrounding banks and mounds sheltered them from the worst of the noise from the river.

Penny shed her pack in the shade of the bank. Tanyth and Rebecca followed suit.

"We need to find firewood before dark," she said. "There's a stand of trees just over this rise." She pointed to the bank above their heads. "Should be enough blowdowns up there."

Tanyth and Rebecca followed the young woman up and into a stand of trees. The spring was still too new for them to have grown full leaves; most limbs sported little more than catkins. The smell of fresh forest went a long way toward flushing the scent of mud and stone from their noses.

It took only a few minutes for them to each gather a goodly armload of wood and return to their campsite. As they hunkered down to the business of lighting a fire and making tea, Tanyth eyed Penny.

"What is it, mum?" the young woman asked.

"Back in town you said you'd come out to visit your grandmother a few times over the years."

"Aye, and I have."

"You seem pretty familiar with the path," she said. "How to get down the canyon face. How to cross the river. Even where to find dinner." She jutted her chin in the direction of the fish laid out on the sand. "How often to do you get out here?"

Penny grinned. "This is my first trip this spring. I came

out a couple of times this winter. Snow shoes work really well once the snows get packed down by the wind a bit."

"What do you do out here?" Rebecca asked. "And in the winter?"

"Winter, mostly just to get away from town. There's some caves up ahead. We'll be staying in them tomorrow night before we drop down into the Valley of a Thousand Smokes. They're right snug and warm in winter." She looked up at the mountains around them, so tall they seemed to be peeking down into their modest camp. "It's beautiful out here. That's reason enough."

Tanyth squinted at her. "That's not the only reason, is it?"

Penny grinned and shook her head. A spark caught in the bit of fluff as she worked, and she leaned down to blow it gently into flame before thrusting it into the pyramid of small twigs she'd laid. "Midwife don't make much," she said without looking up. She puffed another bit of life into the fire. "Most folks in town that need my help can't pay much for the service. I get some of what I need in barter, but..." Her voice trailed off. She didn't look away from the fire.

"What's out here?" Tanyth asked.

"Gold."

"Gold?" Rebecca asked, her voice rising in surprise.

Penny looked at her and gave a half-smile. "Yeah. I come out here and poke around a few times a year. I usually find enough to pay for the things I can't get from customers. Like the taxes on my house."

"How can you hide somethin' like that in a place as small as Northport?" Tanyth asked, hunkering down beside the fire.

"I couldn't and I don't. I package the nuggets up and send them to my agent in Kleesport a few times a year. I get cash back in the return post." She pushed a few more twigs onto the fire, building it slowly. "I was hopin' Captain Groves would have something for me, but one of the other ships prob'ly has the mail contract for the season."

"How do you know they're not cheatin' ya?" Rebecca asked.

"I expect they are," Penny said. "But as long as I get

enough back to keep payin' my bills, I don't really care." She looked up at the mountains surrounding them. "Bein' out here is glorious. I'd prob'ly come out anyway, but this way I get a little icin' on my cake."

Tanyth felt the thrum of the earth under her feet. She stood and looked to the north, visualizing a prayer in her mind as she faced—quite literally—the guardians of the north. She turned and looked to the east, and a gust of spruce-scented air blew into her lungs. Turning to the south, she had an uninterrupted view of a distant band of clouds painted in golden fire by the setting sun. Looking westward, the evening sky looked almost as translucent as the water in the pools they'd crossed that afternoon. The blue unsullied by cloud or sun, the high bank cast their campsite in shadow and blocking Tanyth's view of the horizon. She turned north again, feeling the rightness around her. Sensing the flow of life surrounding them. Feeling her tiredness leeching down into the dirt beneath her feet as if in exchange for strength drawn from the rocks themselves.

"Mum?" Rebecca asked. "You all right?"

Tanyth blinked and looked down into their two faces. "Yes, my dear. Why do you ask?"

Rebecca shook her head. "No reason. Just—you seemed far away all of a sudden."

Penny's eyes showed white all around as she stared at Tanyth. "You've got power, mum," she whispered, then shook her head as a giggle escaped her lips. "I mean, I shoulda guessed it with all the talk of owls and such, but you're touched by the Lord and Lady, no question."

"Oh, tosh," Tanyth said with a wave of her hand. "I'm an old fool pokin' around the backwoods where I prob'ly don't belong."

But she looked back to the mountains—the solid earth beneath her feet, the spruce-scent-laden air in her nose—and knew that she was exactly where she belonged.

Chapter 14
Canyon Dreams

Night crept across the canyon, the floor growing nearly dark while the snow-capped crest of Ole Man still glowed in ruddy sunset. The roar of the river seemed quieter somehow as the day's light faded into night. Eventually even the mountain became little more than a dark shadow blotting out the starry sky. Tanyth set a pot of oatmeal to cook after their meal of fish and camp bread.

"What'll we run into tomorrow?" Rebecca asked with a sidelong glance at Penny.

"Nothin' special. We've had most of our fun," she said. "Day after we'll get into Thousand Smokes. That's pretty but won't do much to hold us up. Gran's cottage is up the valley a bit, tucked up against the roots of Crater Mountain."

Rebecca glanced at Tanyth and gave a half-smile. "Fun, she calls it."

"Well, 'tweren't borin'," Tanyth said, pushing the oatmeal a little closer to the coals.

"I'll give you that," Rebecca said. "Wonder what happened to them soldiers."

Penny tossed a bit of twig into the fire. "That's the real question, I'm thinkin'. We didn't see hide nor hair all day."

"Were you lookin'?" Rebecca asked, looking up from the fire in surprise.

"Oh, yeah. There was a couple places we'd have seen 'em if they were on our trail. Didn't spot anything."

Tanyth shrugged. "Might be they was just being cagey."

"Can you get your owl to look tonight?" Penny asked,

looking over to Tanyth.

"Well, she's not my owl, and I don't gen'rally get to pick. Sometimes yeah, sometimes no." She shrugged. "I don't usually know until after it's done."

Penny stared hard at her for a moment. "Gen'rally," she said.

"Yeah."

"Mum, you got a gift," the younger woman said when Tanyth didn't offer any more.

"Maybe. That's why I need to meet your gran. I can't think of anybody else who'd be able to help me."

Penny's eyes drifted back to the fire's glow. "Yeah. If she'll talk to ya. She is a hermit, ya know."

"I knew the risk before I left," Tanyth said.

"Should we set a watch?" Rebecca asked.

Penny looked at her, then up at the sky. "We could. I've never had a problem, but then I'd prob'ly not survive the first one."

"What about bears?" Tanyth asked.

"Never run into one. I seen 'em off and on, but they tend to shy away from smoke, fires, and people. Their hides fetch a pretty good price, and they're not stupid beasts."

"Two-legged varmints?" Tanyth asked.

Penny smiled. "Never had a problem with any of them, either. Out here, most everybody's alone. Trappers don't wanna share their traplines. Lumberjacks don't cross the canyon. It's too tough to get the lumber back to town, and there's more'n enough trees closer in. Hunters are hunters. They don't usually run in packs and when they do, they make enough noise to rouse ya. Anybody out walkin' around in the dark of night in the mountains gen'rally don't do it more than once or twice."

After a moment, Rebecca asked, "So, that's no?"

Penny grinned at her, her teeth white against the darkness behind her. "Yeah. That's a no." She tossed another small branch onto the coals and stood, brushing ash and dirt off her pants. "I'm gonna get some sleep. Morning'll be chilly and I'm lookin' forward to that oatmeal."

With that she grabbed her pack, moved up under the overhanging bank, and laid out her bedroll to settle in for the night.

Tanyth and Rebecca shared a glance and a shrug, then followed her lead.

Tanyth laid her bedroll out, taking care to pick all the sticks and rocks out of the soil. There weren't many. In moments she had her boots off, tucked into her bedroll, and found herself curled up in a snug ball. The glowing fire outside painted the rocks in flickering light but not so bright that it obscured the brilliant display of stars in the sky. The top edge of the moon rose over the ridge on the far side of the canyon as Tanyth slid over the brink into sleep.

☽○☾

The humans had gone, leaving only the scent of their scat and a drift of smoke where they'd had a fire. She sat quietly on the broken spruce and watched, listening for the rustle that meant food. The warmth she'd gained from the small meal she'd had was already a fading memory; she needed more food.

A faint stirring in the grass below drew her attention. Something moved almost silently among the longer grasses. Her eyes picked out a darker patch of shadow, but she held. It wouldn't do to move too quickly. Best be sure.

The shadow moved ever so slightly, the rustling sound drifting on the night breeze.

She leaned forward and let momentum carry her off the limb, releasing the scabby bark from her talons and swinging them forward as she fell toward the dinner that awaited her.

The shock of her landing broke the mouse's back. He died soundlessly. She reached down with her bill and flipped him down her throat, working the small carcass into her gullet where it could digest slowly over time. The warm meat filled her again, and she scanned the area to see if any other meal might be lurking.

Seeing nothing, she launched herself into the dark sky once more. Four powerful beats of her rounded wings lifted her high enough to soar out of the small ravine and across the parkland beyond. Far away that big male hooted again. Perhaps he'd be a suitable mate for her brood this season. His persistent call spoke of a strong protector with a good hunting ground.

The Hermit Of Lammas Wood

She caught an updraft and let it throw her up into the sky, the bowl of the park cupped under her. She circled once, twice...looking for the group of men. They would have a fire. She scanned for the light as she drifted north and west, the rising moon giving her more than enough light to see the forests below. As she neared the ridge line there was still no sign of the humans.

She twisted her wings and swung around to fly along the length of the ridge, heading toward the big water far away. She'd been there once. Food was plentiful there in the summer, she remembered.

She felt the warmth of the meal seeping into her belly and her wings found joy in the night's wind—cold though it was. She soared along the ridge, looking for a suitable roost. She might hunt again before morning, but a cozy roost would protect her from the cold. She dropped closer to the treetops and saw a likely branch. As she flew in a circle around it, a red glow caught her eye and she changed course.

On silent wings she soared through the pines and spruces, over-flying the humans as they lay huddled around their glowing fire. She fetched up in the dense top of a gnarled pine. It would be a good place to shelter from the wind for the night and to seek protection from the sunlight when the day came again.

Besides. The humans might leave more food behind that called fat mice to her dinner.

She preened her primaries and fluffed her feathers a bit before huddling down on the broad pine limb and gripping firmly with her talons. She set herself to wait and watch.

☽○☾

"Well, they ain't followin'," Tanyth muttered to the moon. She edged out of her bedroll and padded to the fire pit. Hunkering down, she held her chilly fingers to the glowing coals, taking a moment to add another small branch.

A step in the sand behind her gave her warning before Rebecca spoke. "You all right, mum?"

"Aye. I'm fine. Our garrison friends seem to have gone south instead of followin' us."

"You had a dream?"

"Indeed I did."

"Well, I'm glad they're not followin' us," she said.

"Me, too."

After a moment, Rebecca asked, "What'll you do when you get to Gertie Pinecrest's place?"

Tanyth gave a half-shrug without looking up from the fire. "Depends on what she does, I s'pect. If she's as elusive as Penny says, it may take a while to get through to her."

"But you don't think she's gonna be?"

"Nope. If she's really the teacher I need to find out about all this dreaming and visions and all, I'd guess she already knows we're comin'."

"How?"

Tanyth gave a quiet chuckle. "Who knows? Maybe she's got an owl of her own. Or a raccoon. Maybe she talks to the trees, and they whisper their secrets to her on the wind."

Rebecca's eyes turned to the stand of spruces above them on the bank. "They do kinda sound like whispers," she said.

Tanyth grinned at her. "You'll be hearin' 'em next," she said and turned her face up to the moon high in the sky overhead. "I think I'm gonna try to get some more sleep."

Rebecca dropped another small bit of wood on the fire and followed her back under the bank.

Chapter 15
A Touch Of Weather

---◆---

The morning dawned gray and overcast. The wind blew up the valley, and the air lay heavy and moist. Tanyth stirred the oatmeal in the pot and stoked up the fire.

"We gonna get wet now?" she asked, looking to Penny.

Penny stood sniffing the wind and eyeing the scudding clouds. "This could be nasty if we're out in it."

"Rain?" Tanyth asked. "Or snow?"

Penny shook her head. "Can't really tell. Storms like this blow up outa nothin'. This time a'year? Rain's possible. Snow's possible. Things are too warm for freezin' rain, but it'll be cold enough you'll *think* it's freezin'."

Rebecca huddled next to the fire. "So? Is it better to stay here another night and wait it out? Or keep goin' and hope we can find shelter when we get there?"

"Well, if we can make it to the caves by tonight, we'll be comfortable enough."

"And if we can't?" Rebecca asked.

"Could get wet. Could get dead. Could just have a blustery day on the trail," Penny said. "Can't really tell until it hits, and then we'll know."

"So we could sit here all day and just have it be like this? Threatenin' but not actually doin' anything?"

"Yep. That's about the size of it."

"My vote is eat up and head out. If it gets too bad, we'll have to hunker down," Tanyth said. "There pines and spruces the whole way?"

"Not the whole way, no. One exposed ridge is all."

Rebecca snorted. "If it's gonna storm, it'll happen then."

Tanyth laughed. "Prob'ly so. I still vote for going."

Penny nodded her head, slowly at first but with increasing conviction. "Yeah. I think that's the right choice. I don't really wanna be here in the canyon if there's much rain fallin' in the high country either."

"Whyzzat?" Rebecca asked.

"Rain gets concentrated in the valley. Couple inches in the mountains is a couple of feet down here," Penny said.

"Then I vote with Tanyth," Rebecca said. She ducked under the overhang to pack up her bedroll while Tanyth finished heating up the oatmeal.

In fewer minutes than it took them to decide, they'd eaten, packed, and broken camp.

Penny led the way along a path between tall spruces, the heavy canopy giving them some shelter from the wind. As they walked the wind's sighing in the treetops became moaning. They pressed hard through the morning, keeping an eye on the sky when they could see it through the trees. They stopped only briefly at noon to chew on travel rations washed down with cold water in the half-twilight of the cloud-shrouded canopy.

"We gonna make it?" Tanyth asked as they strapped their packs on once more.

"We're gonna make it," Penny said. "We may be soaked to the skin by the time we get there, but we'll make it." Her smile brightened the dark woods.

A few yards down the trail they broke out into the open.

"This is the ridge. We'll cross over the saddle here and then back down into the pines on the other side. We're more than halfway there already," Penny said. "We'll only be in the open a few minutes."

The words no sooner left her mouth than the sky opened up, and rain drenched them in noisy torrents.

"Long enough to get soaked," Tanyth shouted, thankful for her broad hat brim.

Penny grimaced and trudged away through the downpour, water already dripping from the back of her pack.

"Wet bedding. Lovely," Rebecca said and followed in

Penny's wake, leaving Tanyth to bring up the rear.

Tanyth just shook her head and kept walking.

Within a few yards the ground turned to mush. The firm soil of the forest gave way to loess-covered slopes on the ridge made loose and slippery by the rain. Tanyth had to watch her footing, once grabbing Rebecca's arm to steady her before she slid down the slope.

They gained the cover of the forest within half a mile, but by then everything was dripping wet. Odd breaks in the canopy gave them fresh water to deal with. They tramped on.

Tanyth felt the cold leeching her strength as they went. She eyed Rebecca, who walked huddled in on herself. Even Penny's energy seemed to be flagging.

"How much farther?" Tanyth shouted to be heard over the rain.

"Another mile. Maybe two," Penny shouted back. "Can you do it?"

Tanyth felt her teeth begin trying to chatter but she nodded and waved. "Go faster before we freeze."

Penny gave her a bedraggled smile and headed on up the trail, which took a turn into the base of the mountain a few feet farther along. Before they broke out of the trees again, the roar of the rain in the treetops vanished as fast as it had begun.

Somewhere in the distance Tanyth heard falling water–but it was a stream's sound, not the rain's.

"That's not good," Penny muttered as she picked up her pace a bit.

She led them to a narrow trail cut into the side of the mountain. The trail followed the curve of the terrain and disappeared around a jutting knee of rock just ahead. When they got around the rock, they found the origin of the running water sound. A heavy stream cascaded down the mountainside from high above and had carved the trail back to bedrock in its fall. The gap between here and there measured at least three feet, possibly four. There was nothing left to the trail except two ends separated by a long drop and flowing water.

"Ideas?" she asked, turning to Tanyth and Rebecca.

"I need warmth and shelter soon," Rebecca said.

"Do we have to cross there?" Tanyth asked.

"If not we have to go down, cross over, and then back up," Penny said.

Tanyth looked up at the falling water. "What about a bridge?"

"We'd have to go cut a tree for that. You got the strength for it?" she asked, looking first at Rebecca and then at Tanyth.

"Down and up, it is then," Tanyth said.

They scooted back around the rock and scrambled down the rain-slicked scree to reach the bottom of the slope. it looked a long way off from down here, but as her teeth started chattering, Tanyth moved along sharply to try to convince her body to stoke up the fire.

"This would be a good time for a hot flash," she muttered.

"You all right, mum?" Rebecca asked, turning around to look at her.

"Nothin'. Keep going. I'm fine."

Penny led them across the field of shattered rock and they waded through the wide, flat creek where the run-off spread across the rocky slope, cascading noisily down the mountain.

Halfway across Rebecca stopped, staring at her feet. She reached down and picked up something from the ground.

"What is it?" Tanyth asked, her jaw clenched against the shivers that threatened her.

She held up a smoothed, shining chunk of gold rock about the size of her thumb.

"Well, put it in your pocket, and let's keep movin' before I freeze out here," Tanyth said as she leaned heavily on her staff. Cold water slipped down the back of her neck, and she started shivering. She couldn't control it–couldn't breathe. The shakes pushed the air from her lungs and the darkness encroached at the edges of her vision.

"Penny!" Rebecca shouted and reached for Tanyth, grabbing her by the arm, supporting her body and pressing her own body against the older woman's. "Penny, we're in trouble here."

Tanyth's knees began to buckle, and that just was not acceptable to her. She twisted her staff into the ground, driving the iron shoe down through the loose rock—more by strength of will than of body. She felt the heat of the earth just beneath the surface. It called to her and offered her warmth.

She lacked the strength to call the full circle, but perhaps she had enough to call on the one guardian that mattered most. Staggering, she rotated around the staff, twisting it like a drill. She looked to the south, down-slope into the treetops still glistening with the morning's rain. The beauty of it reached into her and she closed her eyes, turning her face to the pale warmth of a sun half hidden by clouds.

"I call on the Guardian of the South, Fire of the Earth, Passion of the Heart," she muttered through a jaw that she could barely control, with breath she barely held. "Grant us warmth against the cold." She felt the earth under her shifting, the loose scree sliding a bit. "I ask in the name of the All-Mother." She didn't have the strength to stamp her staff on the ground but lowered her lips to the wet wood and kissed it. "So mote it be."

Under them the ground rumbled, no major movement. Not a large sound, but the stones began to steam and Tanyth felt the heat of the earth working through her boots and up her legs. With warmth came strength—up her legs from her feet, up through the iron shoe dug into the soil just inches below the rocks. Her lungs filled and emptied once, twice. Full breaths filled with the heat of a summer afternoon, warming her from the inside out. The quivering of her muscles slowed and ceased. With a final silent prayer of thanks, she opened her eyes and stared into the shocked face of Penny Oakton.

"Mum? Are you all right?" The woman's eyes showed white all around and her face held something that was either shock or fear. It might have been both.

Tanyth tested her breathing again before replying. "Yes, I think so." A yawn took her by surprise. "I could use a bit of a lie-down, I think. How far is it to your camp?"

Penny pointed. "About a mile that way. Twenty minutes if you're up to it."

Tanyth rested her forehead against her staff, silently offering another prayer of thanks. When she looked down, the rocks had stopped steaming. She stood in the middle of a

The Hermit Of Lammas Wood

circle of dry, white scree. She stared at it, her mind muzzy. Something about the dry rocks. Something important.

"Mum?" Rebecca said, taking her by the upper arm. "If you can walk now? We need to be going."

Tanyth nodded. "Of course, my dears. Lead on, Penny. You're the only one who knows the way."

Penny looked to Rebecca who nodded in return. She shuffled through the rest of the scree and led the way through a tight ravine of earth and trees at the base of the trail high above them. "It'll take us some doin' to get up to the caves, but I think we can get there if we take it slow," she said.

Tanyth let Rebecca lead her. The younger woman needed her support, after all. Soon they'd be safe and warm and dry in the cave.

The final mile took well over an hour, and the sun dipped too near the horizon for comfort but they eventually regained the high ground. Penny led them between two huge slabs of rock and into a hidden pocket.

Tanyth looked around at the walls' rough surface. "Not exactly what I'd call a cave," she muttered.

"No, mum. This is just the entry," Penny said and stepped through the rock face, disappearing.

Tanyth stared at the rock for a moment and looked to Rebecca. "Did she disappear?"

Penny's head emerged from the rock. "It's a crack in the rock. Come over on this side and you'll see it."

They shuffled around to the far side of the pocket and saw the narrow crack in the face of the mountain. Penny smiled at them. "Come on in. I'll get a fire going, and we can have a nice pot of tea."

"Tea. That would be lovely," Tanyth said, and turned sideways to slip through the crack.

Chapter 16
Those Who Came Before

Tanyth awoke, snug and dry in her bedroll with no recollection of having crawled into it, let alone laying it out. A ruddy glow illuminated one wall that arched up to a ceiling. A pile of wood lay against the back wall. When she turned her head, her face was just inches away from Rebecca's curly mop sticking out of a bedroll.

"Cozy," she murmured.

"Mum?" The hoarse whisper drew her attention to the shadows beyond the fire pit. Penny slipped from the darkness and leaned over her. "You feeling better now, mum?"

Tanyth blinked several times. "Better than what, my dear?"

"You remember bein' out in the rain? The trail?"

"Of course."

"You remember almost shiverin' to death out there in the scree?" Shadows made Penny's eyes into dark pools.

Tanyth remembered. "Yes, my dear. I remember."

"Do you know what you did, mum?"

"I know that I did something, and the earth warmed us enough to get here."

"You felt the heat of the earth?"

"Yes, my dear. I asked the Guardian for help. The Lady brought the heat a little closer to the surface."

"That's what you think, mum?"

Tanyth smiled at the serious look on the young woman's face. "That's what I know, my dear."

"Do you remember coming into the cave, then?"

"Well, of course. There's a narrow crack. We had to slip through it sideways."

"Do you remember having tea? Eating a travel ration bar?"

Tanyth stared at her for a moment. "When?"

"After we got into the cave."

Tanyth searched her memories. "I thought you had disappeared. One moment you were there. The next, gone. I remember sliding through the crack..." Her voice trailed off. "I don't remember anything after that."

"Mum, you're pretty weak still. The cold can take the starch out of old bones, and you were really cold. Your lips were blue. I don't know how you walked from the scree field all the way up here. I surely don't. I'm glad you done it because otherwise Rebecca and I woulda had to carry you, and that woulda been tough."

Tanyth smiled. "I'm glad, too."

"Whatever it was you did out there, it saved you, but it came near to killin' you, too. If we'd had to go another half mile, it mighta." Penny leaned down to kiss her on the cheek. "You go to sleep again, mum. It's just around midnight, and you need the rest."

Tanyth felt the truth of her words and simply nodded, pulling her blanket up around her chin and sinking below the surface of consciousness.

The dream, when it came, faded into her like a misty morning. All the women she'd shared the last twenty-plus winters with came to her and smiled on her. Agnes Dogwood led the procession and all her teachers followed along. The gray hairs. The gapped smiles. The laugh-lines on wrinkled cheeks. Each as precious as the last. Some were gone, others lived on. Even Alice Willowton, who distilled more than essential oils, and Mabel Elderberry, the last teacher who had pointed her north. A stooped and gnarled woman followed Mabel, her kindly face with high cheekbones and deep creases looking not the least familiar.

"Mother Alderton?" her dream voice asked.

The woman smiled and gave a small curtsey before moving on.

A dark shape followed her. Tall and straight, striding through the mists that had grown around her. He stepped into the shrinking clearing and smiled as well. His heart shone in his eyes; his familiar, precious mouth curled to one side in an endearing smile.

This was not right. The women had all been her teachers. People from whom she had learned and to whom she owed much.

Frank lifted a hand to tip his hat and gave her a cheeky wink before following the line of women into the mist and out of her sight. She turned to watch him go. He did not look back, just strode away fading into the void.

When she turned back, a new figure stood before her. Not a woman she knew. An old woman, perhaps the oldest she'd ever seen, her eyes milky with cataracts and her fingers knotted with arthritis. She stared at Tanyth with her white-sheathed eyes for several moments until a movement in her frizzy white hair drew Tanyth's gaze. A gray field mouse rested on the woman's head, his black eyes staring at Tanyth seeming to look into her soul.

"Well?" the woman said, her voice shaking with age and impatience. "Are you going to sleep or are you going to get here someday?"

"Mother Pinecrest?" Tanyth's dream voice said.

The old woman sighed, a soft huff of her breath. "Girl, you are the single most stubborn—. Never mind. We never had a lot of time, and what little we got left is running out. You need to get up."

"Well, of course, I do," Tanyth said.

"No, you need to get up now!" the woman said, reaching out to shake her by the shoulder.

"Mum? You need to get up now," Penny said, patting her shoulder again. "We need to get on the trail if you're up to it."

Tanyth blinked several times, trying to reconcile her mind to the reality it now perceived.

"Mother Fairport?" Penny said. "Are you feelin' all right?"

"Yes, yes." She pushed herself up on her elbows. "A bit stiff, but quite well."

"Mornin', mum." Rebecca grinned at her across the fire. "Tea's ready if you are. We even made some oatmeal."

Tanyth's stomach told her it had been too long since she'd last eaten. The inside of her mouth tasted like a gravel road on the summer solstice. She cleared her throat, trying to open her windpipe a bit. "Tea would be most welcome," she said at last.

She started to crawl out of her bedding, but Penny patted her back down. "You just rest there, mum. We'll fetch for you."

Tanyth nodded and pulled a deep breath into her lungs, blowing it out in something that wasn't quite a yawn and certainly not a sigh.

Rebecca handed her a tin cup full of tea, kneeling down beside her to look into her eyes. "Are you sure you're all right, mum?"

Tanyth held the cup up to her nose and inhaled the musky, spicy aroma. "Yes, dear. I'm fine, I think." She sipped with a slurp that sounded loud in the dead air of the cave. The tea nearly burned her tongue and she sucked in a mouthful of air to cool it. "Just had the strangest dream."

Rebecca smiled. "Another owl?"

Tanyth shook her head as Penny turned and leaned down. "Dream?"

"All my teachers were there. They just walked by me in a parade. They stepped out of the fog and smiled or nodded, and then walked on. One after the other."

"You sure it was a dream?" Rebecca asked.

Tanyth pursed her lips and thought. "Yeah. I'm pretty sure it was. It wasn't like one of my visions because I wasn't an animal. No owls. No rats."

"No raccoons?" Rebecca asked, her mouth twitching.

Tanyth chuckled once. "No, you cheeky thing. No raccoons. Just my teachers until the next to the last one, and I didn't recognize her." She paused, trying to see the woman's face again. "She was stooped over and gnarled as an old apple tree."

Rebecca's eyes narrowed.

"She had high cheekbones and deep creases on her forehead and around her mouth," Tanyth said.

"Mother Alderton?" Rebecca asked.

"That was my guess, but she didn't speak in my dream."

Rebecca rocked back on her heels. "What do you suppose it means?"

Penny snorted as she brought a small bowl filled with steaming oatmeal. "Means she's had a lot of influences on her life and that's her brain's way of sayin' 'thank you' to 'em. That's my guess."

"I saw Frank, too," Tanyth said, blowing on a spoonful of the hot oats before taking a nibble from the spoon's tip. "He didn't say anything, either."

Rebecca clapped her hands. "Well, if you had a line of teachers, only makes sense that Frank would be among 'em, don't it, mum?"

"Maybe they're not teachers," Penny said. "Could be just important people in your life."

Tanyth considered her words while she shoveled the cooling oatmeal into her very insistent belly. "Could be. That would make sense, except the last one was your granny."

"Granny Gert?" Penny asked, looking up from where she was rolling her bedding.

"That's what she said."

"What'd she look like?"

"Like an old woman with frizzy white hair. She had cataracts and her hands were all knotted up. She stood straight enough and looked me right in the eye. Told me to wake up and get movin'. That we're runnin' out of time."

Penny sat back on her heels. "Cataracts? How'd she look you in the eye?"

"She had a mouse in her hair."

Penny's face went blank and she cocked her head to one side. "A mouse?"

"Yeah, field mouse by the look. He sat in her hair and just looked at me."

"Huh." Penny shook her head. "Coulda been. What I remember of her, she had frizzy hair and the cold weather bothered her hands."

"Well, she was none too pleased with me."

Penny's eyes softened and she bit her lower lip. "Sounds about like the woman I remember."

"You haven't seen her in how long?"

Penny shook her head and focused on her bedroll. "Twenty-five? Thirty winters? She left when I was a wee thing. I couldn'ta' been more than five winters."

Rebecca looked at her. "Really? You don't look that old."

Penny and Tanyth both laughed.

"What?" Rebecca said, looking back and forth between them.

"Nothin'," Tanyth said. "Just struck me funny. Come on. Let's get packed up and get movin'. I'd kinda like to see this Valley of a Thousand Smokes I keep hearin' about."

Chapter 17
Valley Of A Thousand Smokes

The morning smelled clean. Stepping out onto the trail from between the huge slabs of rock, Tanyth looked out over the dark green spruce tops to the ocean gleaming on the horizon. She drank in the scent of spring as if the first time. Spring came late to the north country, it seemed, but it still smelled sweetly of promise and life.

"Huh," Rebecca leaned down and picked up a small pebble from the trail. "More gold?"

Penny tugged her pack straps snug and leaned over to look. "Yeah. Looks like it. Rain prob'ly exposed it." She grinned at the younger woman. "You found some before?"

Rebecca fished in her pocket and pulled out the other piece.

"Well, you're paying for your trip right enough. That's prob'ly worth a couple gold pieces by itself. Where'd you find it?"

"It was layin' on the rocks where the trail washed out."

"Runoff like that exposes a lot of it. I'll have to get my gear and see if I can find some. Winter's worth of runoff should be worth somethin'." She grinned and beckoned them with a head nod. "We better get goin' now or we won't make Gran's by nightfall."

"As many trappers and hunters as I keep hearin' about out here, why aren't these mountains crawling with miners?" Tanyth asked as the stepped along the trail.

"Prob'ly cause most trappers and hunters are lookin' for gold in skins and furs, not the ground," Penny said over her shoulder. "I s'pect if the word ever got out, Northport would come apart at the seams with all the people tryin' to get in there."

Tanyth snickered.

"It don't hurt that there's none of it on the other side of the Black Rock. I've only ever found it on this side."

"Well, somebody's comin' across the river often enough," Rebecca said from the back of the line.

"How ya figger?" Penny asked.

"Bridge. Somebody built it. They musta needed it, 'cause that's not just a put it up and forget it, one time kinda thing."

"Trappers need to get across the river with their furs," Penny said. "They have a couple of cabins down in the spruces where they set up for the season. Mostly late summer and fall. Bunch of 'em gather there. They'll run trap lines until the snow gets too much—or they run out of beer."

"How they get beer there?" Tanyth asked. "Long way back to town."

"They pack in the barley and yeast and make it. You ever get invited to try any? Pass."

Rebecca laughed and Tanyth put her head down and concentrated on walking. Something about the story sounded off. "You'd think somebody woulda tumbled on it before now," she muttered.

"What's that, mum?" Penny asked, turning her head back to look at Tanyth.

"Nothin', my dear. Old woman like me talks to herself to remember what she's thinkin'."

"Does it help?" she asked, a broad grin on her face.

"I don't know. I'm one of them people that it goes in one ear and out the other. I just can't convince me to shut up about it."

They all laughed and concentrated on following the narrow trail around the shoulder of the mountain.

By mid-morning, the fresh, green smell of the spruces took on the faint aroma of sulfur matches. They rounded one last outcropping of stone and stood at the top of a trail that led down into a forest of smoke plumes rising nearly straight up in the still morning air. The plumes seemed to go on forever.

Penny paused on the ledge so they could get a good look.

"Valley of a Thousand Smokes?" Tanyth asked.

"Yeah. Prob'ly more'n a thousand, though."

Tanyth let her gaze slide across the vista, not counting as much as taking it all in.

"Story is, one of the original trappers up here in the north country found this place and named it. I suspect a thousand was as high as he could count," Penny said.

"Prob'ly a bigger number than he ever needed," Rebecca said.

Tanyth looked at her. "You could be right."

"Well, you see that ridge that juts out about halfway up there?" Penny pointed at the far side of the long valley to a point where a cleared ridge extended into the valley floor.

"The one with the single spruce on the top of it?" Tanyth asked.

"Yep. Gran's house is just beyond that."

Tanyth measured the position of the sun in the southeastern sky and turned back to Penny. "We best get movin' then."

With a smile and nod, Penny led the way down the trail and into the valley.

As they worked their way down the side of the mountain, the temperature rose. Tanyth unbuttoned her coat to let the tails swing free. They passed several small pools where the very mud bubbled in soupy, gloppy glugs. Once they passed a cracked rock plate beside the trail and were startled when a plume of water hissed loudly into the air for nearly a minute before subsiding.

"What is this place?" Rebecca asked.

"The earth's heat is right under the surface here," Tanyth said. "It heats the water and cooks the land."

"She's right," Penny said. "Pay attention to where you're putting your feet or you'll find your boots smoldering under them."

"Why would she live here?" Rebecca asked. "And who made this trail?"

Penny shrugged. "Because this is where the hermit always lives, and not 'who' made the trail but 'what.'"

"All right," Rebecca said with a laugh in her voice. "What made this trail?"

They rounded a bend and came upon a grassy field. Dozens of elk stood looking at them. One of the bigger bulls trotted a few steps in their direction, putting himself between them and the cows.

"Oh," Rebecca said in a very small voice.

"Just keep walking and don't stare at them," Penny said, her voice barely audible over the noise of wind in their ears. "They come down out of the high country to winter over where there's water and heat," she said.

"Smart animals," Tanyth said, casting an admiring glance at the magnificent creatures feeding only a few yards away.

"Don't hunters come here for them?" Rebecca asked.

"Gran don't allow hunters in the valley."

Tanyth blinked. "I thought you never spoke with her."

Penny laughed quietly. "I don't."

"Then how...?"

"I talk to hunters," she said. "There are some ferocious tales about Gran out there in the world."

Rebecca's steps slowed and she fingered her bow. "Are they true?"

Penny glanced back at Rebecca. "Some are. Some aren't. Some are part true and some are part false. You are not a hunter. I'd be surprised if we even see her."

Tanyth snorted. "I hope you're wrong with that last bit."

Penny laughed again. "Come on. We've still got a long way to go."

They hiked up the valley floor, following the elk trail between bubbling pools and smelly mud pits. As they walked, the terrain changed from being mostly rock with a smattering of grasses to patches of rock in large clearings of alpine grasses and flowers. The farther they went the more the landscape became familiar, with a less-blasted feeling. By the time the sun sailed high in the southern sky, they could see the lone spruce standing on the ridgeline ahead.

"It's still a long hike," Penny said. "Let's grab some lunch and tea. Then we can go see if Granny Pinecrest is home."

"Tea?" Tanyth said. "You're goin' to start a fire?"

Penny shook her head and led the way to one of the exposed rock patches that dotted the landscape. She hunkered down and held her hand out over the rock, edging closer to the middle until she was standing in the center. "Too cool," she said and walked to the next patch a few yards away.

The grasses grew well back from the rocky scab on the ground. Penny didn't even bother to get close to the ground, just held her hand out at waist height. "Yeah. This'll do."

She stepped back onto the grass and the small party shucked their packs.

Tanyth dug out the teapot and a canteen. She filled the teapot with water and handed it to Penny, who walked back to the rocky patch and, with quick steps, went a few feet out onto the rock, placed the teapot on the ground and hurried back, scuffing her feet in the loose soil surrounding the rock.

"That's a bit warm," she said, lifting her feet to look at her boots. "Not scorched but they felt like it."

In less time than seemed possible the kettle started steaming and rattling around on the flat rock. Penny took a piece of folded cloth with her and scampered out on the rock to retrieve the kettle. "Lot faster than a fire," she said, setting the pot down so Tanyth could throw some tea into it.

"I could get used to this," Tanyth said. "Hot water on demand."

Rebecca eyed the flat rocky patch. "How could ya get a bath tub out there?"

Penny giggled. "Well, the tub would be pretty easy. Water would be difficult, and I think the problem would be keeping it cool enough. You saw how fast that pot boiled."

Rebecca frowned. "Still..."

"There're springs up in the foothills. They get fed cool water and aren't so hot to begin with. I'll show you one of these days. There's one near my cave."

The idea obviously interested Rebecca. Tanyth could practically see the thoughts roiling around behind the young woman's eyes.

They all dug out travel rations and dined in the sunshine, washing the dried fruit and grain down with luxurious gulps of hot tea.

"We got enough food to get back with?" Tanyth asked, peering into her pack.

Penny nodded. "I've got half a dozen bars left and there's dried fruit in the cave. Rebecca here can take all the fish we can eat at Black Rock Canyon. I'd guess you've got a trick or two yourself." She smiled at Tanyth.

Tanyth shrugged one shoulder. "Possible. Travel rations are a lot easier to deal with."

Penny split the remaining tea among their cups and then scuffed a hole in the soil. She dumped the dregs into it, pushing the dirt back with the side of her shoe. "Time to see if Gran's acceptin' callers," she said without looking up.

Tanyth accepted the empty pot and stuffed it back in her pack before climbing to her feet. "She is or she isn't. Either way, let's go see."

They shouldered their packs, and Penny led the way down the trail toward the ridge with the lone spruce on top.

Chapter 18
A Stone Cottage

By midafternoon they reached the ridge. Penny led them around the end of it into a pocket of forest in the shelter of the mountain. Some of the trees were bigger around than Tanyth. The rocky ground sported patches of grass, and—here and there—delicate wildflowers blossomed. The scent of lavender drifted on the afternoon breeze as they walked under the trees, toward the base of the mountain. Tanyth looked down to see drifts of it growing in the dappled sun. Their passage crushed the fragrant stems.

"This is beautiful," Rebecca whispered, her head turning this way and that as if on a spring.

"You should see it in summer," Penny said. "When the leaves fill in, it's even prettier."

They entered a grove of apple trees, the pale blossoms already showering from the limbs. The ancient trees felt healthy and cared for. Tanyth rested a hand on the mottled bark of one old-timer and gazed up through the lattice of limbs to a perfect blue sky above.

Penny and Rebecca stopped a few feet away.

"It's amazin'," Tanyth said. "It's almost magical."

Penny grinned at her. "I feel the same way every time I come here."

"Where's the house?" Rebecca asked.

Penny laughed. "Right there." She stretched an arm and pointed.

Not twenty feet away, a stone cottage nestled against the rocky feet of the mountain. The slanted roof sported sod instead of shakes and the walls were native stone so perfectly matched to the mountainside that the eye just slid right over it, unable to see the house among the rocks. A weathered wooden door and a few shutters on small windows were the only obvious sign that a building rested there.

Tanyth leaned against the tree and drank in the peace.

The door swung inward and the old woman with frizzy white hair from Tanyth's dream stepped out into the sun.

Time seemed to stop for Tanyth. She stood there for several long moments before stepping forward.

"Mother Pinecrest?" she said, her voice not much more than a croak.

"Fairport, isn't it?" the woman said. "Tanyth Fairport?"

"Yes. Mother—"

"I know who sent you. And when. You were supposed to be here last fall. Whatever possessed you...never mind. You're here now. Come in, come in." Her voice sounded strong and firm, even if her tone carried a certain level of exasperation. She stepped aside and waved a hand at the open door.

"Gran?" Penny stepped forward from the shadows, her face transfixed.

The old woman paused and her head turned back and forth as if trying to find the source of this new voice. "Penelope? Is that really you?"

"Yes, Gran. It's me."

"Who else is out there?"

"Good afternoon, mum. My name is Rebecca."

"Ah, the Marong girl. Good."

Tanyth saw Rebecca stop and blink her eyes.

"You know me, mum?"

"Well, not *know you* know you. I know *of* you, girl. Your father's been a pain in my side for decades now."

"I...don't know what to say."

"Then don't say anything, girl. Don't be a loon." The old woman's head scanned back and forth again as if searching and stopped facing her granddaughter. "Penelope, you and Rebecca here need to go back to your cave. You shouldn't be here. It's not time."

"But, Gran..." Penny stopped in mid-sentence, the sense of

loss plain on her face. "I've wanted to talk with you for...well, for ages. I've come to visit you half a dozen times and you are never here."

The old woman held out her arms. "Come here, my girl. Come closer."

Penny walked up to her grandmother, slowly and with halting steps.

When Penny got within reach, the old woman folded her in her arms and hugged her, rocking slowly and crooning as if she were rocking a baby while singing a lullaby.

"My dear child, I'm always here, but sometimes I...well, it's just the way things go. It's something I've had to get used to. I always knew when you visited. I thank you for the many warm and loving thoughts you've had of me."

The old woman pulled back and held Penny by the upper arms, easing her away slowly. Tanyth saw tears streaking down both women's faces.

"You are a wonderful healer, my dear. A talented healer. You have much to offer the world in your own place. It seems cruel, I know—Lady knows it feels cruel—but you and the Marong girl need to leave the valley."

"Why, Gran? Can't we stay the night?" Penny looked to where the sun was already beginning to disappear behind the mountain's rocky shoulder.

The old woman turned her face to the sun and then back to her granddaughter. "Yes, of course. Stay the night and leave at first light. Go back to your cave. Search for gold or mushrooms or fish. Go back to Northport, even. Whatever you wish, just..." the old woman bit her lower lip between her teeth for a moment. "Just promise me."

Penny looked at Rebecca, who looked at Tanyth.

Penny shrugged and nodded. "Of course, Grandmother, whatever you say."

The old woman's eyes crinkled as she smiled at Penny. "You make an old woman proud, girl. Surely, you do." She ushered them all into the cottage and closed the door behind them.

☽○☾

At first glance, the cottage seemed simple—a single large rectangular room with a stone hearth in one end, a low fire banked against the back wall. The back wall of the cottage, where it met the mountain, held cabinets and shelves. Artifacts of all kinds filled the shelves—books, bones, and rocks. Wooden carvings stood everywhere and as Tanyth's eyes got used to the dim light inside, she saw that almost every wooden surface in the cottage had been carved—even the exposed beams and rafters overhead. A low bed with a brightly colored blanket stretched its length along the wall near the hearth. Even the legs and headboard of that were carved. The only thing not carved was the table top—one single plank almost four feet across and perhaps six feet long mounted on legs carved in gentle curves with hooves at the feet that reminded Tanyth of goats.

Tucked in a corner at the back Tanyth spied a second door, also carved. Faces stared at her out of the wood and geometric patterns filled in the planes.

"This is amazing," Rebecca said, her gaze tracing the lines of carvings around the room.

Mother Pinecrest cackled. "Oh, yes. Amazing. Excellent word. This place is amazing. I've been amazed by something or other almost every day I've been here." She stopped in the middle of the room and twisted her head this way and that as if watching a pesky fly, or trying to tell where some elusive sound came from. "Tea? You didn't bring tea, did you?" For once her voice sounded wistful rather than querulous.

"Of course, Grandmother. We brought tea."

The old woman's eyes widened. "Well, would it be too much to trouble you for enough to make a pot of tea? I've missed tea more than anything."

"Of course," Penny said. "We've plenty."

The old woman clapped her hands together in a girlish gesture of delight. "Wonderful. Let's get a kettle going, shall we?"

In a few moments, the younger women had a pot of water cozied up to the fire. They spread their bedrolls out beside the hearth and each sat on the padded floor while the two older women drew their chairs closer to the cheery warmth.

As they waited for the water to come to a boil, Mother

Pinecrest turned to Tanyth. "Well, my girl, you've had a long and roundabout journey, eh?"

Tanyth smiled at the woman's turn of phrase. Being over fifty winters old and being called "my girl" by a woman who might well be old enough to be her mother gave her an odd, but comfortable, feeling. "Yes'm. I have indeed."

"So, now you're here, you ready to learn?" The old woman's pale blue eyes turned toward her.

Tanyth noticed the mouse hiding in her hair. "I'm not going mad, am I." A statement, not a question.

Mother Pinecrest's wrinkled lips curved upward into a bow. "No, dear girl. Not mad. You're one of the few of us who've lived long enough to receive the Lady's gifts." She reached over and patted Tanyth's knee. "But you didn't answer my question."

"If you're ready to teach me, I'd like to learn from you, Mother Pinecrest."

"Hush, girl. Call me Gertie. It's my name and we're going to be workin' close together. We can't be 'Motherin'' each other all the time or we'll never get nothin' done, eh?"

Tanyth found herself smiling back at the kindly, wrinkled face. "Gertie," she said.

"That's better. We've a lot to talk about, we two, but it'll wait until tomorrow. We have guests tonight." She turned to the women sitting beside the hearth. "Rebecca, have you found what you wanted on your grand adventure?"

Rebecca sat up, her eyes wide in surprise. "Mum?"

Gertie gave a little laugh. "Don't look so startled, girl. I don't need to be a mind reader to know a young girl's heart. You came with Mother Fairport to have a grand adventure, didn't ya?"

"Well, no, mum. That is, I suppose so, mum." Rebecca looked from Penny to Tanyth and back to Mother Pinecrest. "I suppose I was on a grand adventure."

"And was it everything you hoped it would be, girl?"

Rebecca pondered the question for several long moments. "It's been far different from anything I might have hoped for. I'm not sure I knew what I could hope for before we left. Now?" Her hands flipped up and down again. "I'm not ready

The Hermit Of Lammas Wood

for the adventure to end, I guess. There seems like so much more to do."

"That's my girl!" the old woman said. "Your father's right to be so proud of you. And you're right. Your adventure's just startin'." She turned to Penny. "How about you, girl? You ready for your adventure to end?"

"I'm not on an adventure, Grandmother. This is just life. Why would I want it to end?"

"Oh, you're on an adventure, daughter of my daughter. You've a few more paths to explore, I think." She cocked her head to one side to look at her. "Yes. A few more paths."

Tanyth heard the tea kettle start to boil just as Gertie said, "Who's ready for some tea? Besides me, that is?"

Penny pulled the kettle out of the fire and Rebecca tossed in a handful of leaves.

Gertie leaned down to inhale the aroma of fresh, steeping tea. Her eyes closed and she sat back in her chair, a beatific smile across her lips and her eyes closed as she savored the scent. "Oh, that's just what I've been needin'," she said.

She stood and walked over to the inside door. "Lemme get some proper mugs and we'll have a lovely chat, eh?"

She disappeared through the door, returning with four, gently rounded mugs with heavy ceramic handles. "These should do," she said, holding up the double handful of glassware. She placed the mugs on the table top and motioned for Penny to pour the tea.

"It's not quite steeped, Grandmother. Just a little longer."

The old woman tsked but nodded. "Of course. I'm just excited to have a real, fresh cuppa after all these years."

"Years, Grandmother?"

"Oh, yes. Nobody thinks to bring an old woman tea for barterin'. No, they don't." She threw her hands up in the air. "What's a body to do?"

"We've got tea to spare, Grandmother. Between what we brought and what Tanyth brought, you'll have enough tea to last until next spring, I wager."

The old woman smiled. "Oh, that would be lovely. It's so difficult to get supplies here."

"How do you get supplies here?" Tanyth asked.

"What we can't grow or harvest from the wild, we get from barter. Travelers sometimes call, even out here," she said. She resumed her seat at the table, her eyes fixed on the pot filled with steeping tea.

Tanyth heard something hard in her voice—some part of the story left untold.

"I come out several times a year, Gran," Penny said. "I usually only go as far as my cave, but if I knew what you needed, I could bring it."

Gertie's gaze shifted from the teapot to her granddaughter and back again. "Yes, yes. I appreciate the sentiment, dearie, but you did well to keep out of the valley."

"Why, Gran?" Penny asked, her eyes gleaming in the firelight.

The old woman held out her arms and folded them around her granddaughter. "It's not your time, dear one. When it is, you'll know."

Penny's arms wrapped around her grandmother and held on for several long moments before releasing her and stepping away, looking down at her boots and swiping her cheeks with her palms. "Tea should be ready," she said, a husky burr in her voice.

Tanyth reached for the pot and poured out four mugs' worth while Penny poked up the fire against the gathering night.

Gertie returned to the table, her head swinging side to side. She reached out her hand and Tanyth slipped the handle of a mug into it. Gertie lifted the cup and let the aromatic steam waft across her face. She closed her eyes and inhaled deeply. "Oh, my. That's heavenly," she said and sipped. "There's few things I miss more'n good tea."

Once more the younger women settled on their bedrolls beside the hearth while Tanyth and Gertie pulled their chairs closer.

"This is pleasant," Gertie said after a moment. "You young folks will have to pardon an old lady for not havin' proper guest manners. I get so few guests out here."

"Well if you were home to guests, perhaps you'd have more," Penny said, a cheeky grin curling her lips even as a bit of pique slipped into her voice.

Gertie chuckled to herself softly and nodded. "Well, that's true." She paused to sip from her mug. "Some things just are, I fear. May as well ask the mountains to bow down. They will, you know, eventually, but they do it in their own time."

An uneasy silence settled among them, only the snapping of the dried wood in the hearth marking the time.

"Mother Pinecrest?" Rebecca asked. "May I ask how you know my father?"

She turned her head to face Rebecca. "Never met the man myself," she said. "But I met your mother once. Lovely woman. A free spirit like you."

Rebecca's brow furrowed. "A while back you said he was proud of me."

"Oh, that he is, my dear. You can be sure of that." She nodded several times as if to assure the young woman. "You can be sure."

"If you never met him...?" Rebecca started to ask but the question died on her lips.

Gertie smiled. "You know Mother Fairport here has some peculiar dreams, yeah?"

Rebecca looked down into her mug then cast a glance at Tanyth. "Yes'm," she said.

Gertie wrinkled her nose and her eyebrows twitched as she leaned forward a little more. "So do I, my dear. Oh, my yes. So do I," she whispered. She sat back in her chair and took another sip of tea. "Who wants some dinner, eh?"

"We brought some rations with us, mum," Rebecca said.

"Oh, pish and tosh," Gertie said. "Dried twigs and tough fruit?"

Penny laughed. "They're not that bad, Gran."

"Well, I have something nicer than that and plenty to go around. You wait." She upended her mug, draining the last of the tea with a smile. "Oh, that's so good. You say there's enough for perhaps another pot?"

Penny laughed again. "I think we have enough to make tea all night, if you want, Gran."

"No, that's not necessary," she said. "Just another cup so I don't forget what it tastes like. We can switch to cider or water. There's plenty of both." She placed her cup on the table, well back from the edge, and stood. "Tanyth? Could I get you to help me for a bit?"

"Of course."

The old woman smiled her gap-toothed smile and led Tanyth through the carved door. Stopping just inside the room, Gertie stooped to pick up a lantern and held it high. The light barely touched the ceiling above them and a line of rough wooden boards marked a crude path deeper into the mountain.

Tanyth expected a store-room but the size of the space made her skip a step.

"Over here, Tanyth. There's a cold room..." Gertie clattered off along the path. "A bit bigger than what you expected, eh?"

"I expected a closet, not a cavern," Tanyth said.

The old woman laughed. "I remember when I first saw it. It's not changed much in the twenty-odd winters since I've been here." She took a left-turning branch and continued on under the roots of the mountain. "Not much call to change it, that I can see."

"Who built it?"

"Ah, Tanyth, there's been a hermit here since—well, since there's been people in Korlay, I suspect." She slapped a shelf as she walked by, the wood thumping under her bony fingers. "Back here, there's not much to make 'em rot. No sunlight. Not a lot of moisture...at least not here. The hot springs get damp and slimy, sometimes."

"Hot springs?"

"Oh, yes. You wait. You'll love 'em." She stopped in front of a door made of stout timbers hung on heavy iron hinges. "Here we are."

"Cold room?"

"Oh, yes. Ice room this time of year. Should be cold right up until fall and then the ice starts formin' again." Gertie slid the sturdy latch back and pulled on the door.

When they stepped in, Gertie's lantern picked out a wall of ice. The temperature dropped enough for Tanyth to see her breath. Shelves stacked with wooden crates lined the walls and several iron hooks hung from the stone ceiling.

"What you fancy after your long walk, eh?" Gertie said, her head cocked just a bit sideways as she looked at Tanyth.

"What are my choices?" she asked.

"Well, there's several bushels of potatoes and carrots left from fall's harvest. There's smoked fish and sausages in some of those crates. We don't have a lot of fresh foods yet, but plenty of dried, salted, and smoked. There's a couple of cheeses there, too. I love cheese but don't take the time to saw at the wheel much these days."

"Well, let's make a sausage soup," Tanyth said. "We can melt a little cheese on the top…"

"You gonna cook for me?"

"You gonna teach me what I need to know?"

The old woman smiled. "I'll teach you all I have time for, my dear. I'm feelin' old as these rocks and I still don't know all I need to know."

Tanyth laughed. "All right. Good enough for me."

"Sausages on that shelf. Deer and elk sausage in the first crate. Pork in the second." Gertie pointed with the hand holding the lantern. "Potatoes and carrots in those bins over there. Grab a couple of onions while you're in there."

"Where'd all this come from?"

Gertie waved her free hand dismissively. "Grew it, mostly. Where else?"

"You grew it?"

"Oh, yes. Traded for some. Grew some."

"Alone?"

"My Lady, no. At my age? Don't be silly. When I first came to the valley, I did most of it, to be sure, but now I have lots of help."

Tanyth's gaze went to the small gray mouse riding on the woman's head. "Like your little friend there?"

Gertie's free hand went up to her hair and a knotted finger stroked the rodent. "Oh, Squeek? Yes, he's my eyes, but no. Trappers and the occasional hunter come through. I barter for what I need, including some strong backs."

"Barter?"

"Yes, indeed. My cider draws trappers and hunters from

miles around." She waved a hand as if dispersing a small cloud. "But we'll have plenty of time to talk about that tomorrow after the girls are safely out of the valley. Now, we need to get what we need for dinner and get back before they try to come looking for us."

"Is that bad?"

"It is if they take the wrong turn in these caverns." Gertie's light and teasing tone carried a note of concern that resonated with Tanyth. "Grab that pot there on the shelf. Add whatever you want from the larder and we'll get back to them."

"I don't see any herbs here. Salt?"

"Oh, well, we'll talk about that later, too, but there's plenty of salt." She chuckled a little. "We got plenty of salt."

Tanyth pulled the heavy iron pot from the shelf and started gathering ingredients. If the hints that Gertie had given were any indication of the summer to come, it would be an interesting season indeed.

Chapter 19
Cider

Morning dawned crisp and clear. Tanyth strolled among the apple trees and lavender, a mug of hot tea cupped in her hands and faint rustlings above her as the breezes stirred the winter stripped branches just filling out with spring's leaves.

The door to Gertie's cottage swung open and she turned back. Rebecca and Penny dragged themselves out into the brilliant morning sun. Neither of them seemed eager to leave.

Gertie stood in the doorway and held out her arms. Each young woman took a turn being hugged and hugging back. The old woman had that air about her—a warmth and a welcome that Tanyth found at odds with a person known far and wide as the hermit of Lammas Wood.

They spoke among themselves but Tanyth only heard low, somber voices and not words. After a moment or two, the young women shambled along the path toward her.

"Mum? I don't like leavin' ya here like this," Rebecca said as they approached. "Why can't we stay?"

"Mother Pinecrest's house, her rules." Tanyth took her own turn to hug the young woman who'd come so far with her. "Not like you don't have plenty to do and you'll only be over the ridge there if you stay in the cave."

"We'll be staying there, at least for a while," Penny said. "I need to find some nuggets to pay for next winter's bills. Only way that'll happen is if we get them now so I can send them south and get paid for them before the ice comes again."

After an awkward silence, Rebecca asked, "Will you be all right here, mum?"

Tanyth sipped her cooling tea and cast her gaze around the orchard. "This feels right to me," she said at last. "I've come a long way to be here. I'm pretty sure the All-Mother didn't send me all this way just to plant me in the ground."

"What if she did?" Penny asked.

Tanyth barked a single laugh. "Well, then I'll be fertilizin' flowers and not much I can do about it, is there?"

"Still not sure why it's all so secret," Rebecca said, her voice carrying a slightly petulant tone.

"Age brings caution, my dear. Sometimes too much." Tanyth thrust her chin in the direction of the cottage where Gertie still stood in the open door. "She's far from the most secretive woman I've worked with. I think we'll have a productive summer. Who knows what fall will bring."

"Snow, if I'm any judge," Penny said with a grin.

"Well, that, too," Tanyth said, then held out her arms. "Give us a hug and get goin'. You've got a long road ahead to get back to town."

"We talked about it and we're not goin' back right away, mum," Rebecca said, wrapping Tanyth in a strong hug.

"We'll spend a day or two lookin' for rocks," Penny added. "If things don't work out here, you can always join us there."

Tanyth cast a glance at the cottage where Gertie Pinecrest still waited in the door. "It'll be fine, but good luck with your hunting and travel safe going back."

Penny accepted Tanyth's hug, after which the two young women turned their steps to southward and disappeared around a bend in the trail.

Tanyth drained her mug and walked back to the cottage.

"You ready to get to work?" Gertie asked as she drew near.

"Sooner started, sooner done."

Gertie snorted but a grin lifted the corner of her lips. "Well, I ain't never seen it done, but with two of us we can prob'ly beat it back a bit."

"What's first?" Tanyth asked.

"Cider." Gertie turned and disappeared into the cottage. "We gotta get the trade goods ready. We'll have company in a day or two. Best get ready for 'em."

"Company?"

"Nick Jacquard. He's a trapper keeps a camp two valleys to the west. He'll be here tomorrow or the next day lookin' for cider."

Tanyth followed Gertie into the tidy cottage and closed the door behind her. "He comes all that way just for cider?"

Gertie nodded. "Him and a dozen more. Good thing they do, too, or we'd have ta work a lot harder to keep body and soul together."

"Then why did the girls have to leave so soon?"

"Two reasons. The first bein' that Alden Jacquard will be here in a day or two. Two old crows like us don't have much to fear from him. Two youngsters like them?" She shook her head. "Just as soon not give him the temptation." Gertie headed into the caverns behind the house. "Come on, then. Let's get this over with and maybe we can make a pot of tea to celebrate."

Tanyth followed Gertie into the labyrinth and did her best to remember the paths.

"Should have a cask ready to bottle up. Might be a bit young yet but nobody'll complain."

"You age cider?" Tanyth asked, a suspicion growing.

Gertie cast a look over her shoulder, her eyes glinting with amusement in the faint glow of the lantern. "Why d'ya think these fine gentlemen come from miles around to trade with ole Gertie Pinecrest, eh? 'Taint for my medicinal potions and such."

Tanyth couldn't stop the delighted laugh from bubbling up. "I been meanin' to ask where your herbs are."

Gertie shook her head and took a right turn. "That's gonna be your job, I think. I've never been much for the herb lore. Oh, I know hyssop from verbena, but you're the expert there, my dear. All your teachers say so."

Tanyth felt her heart fall to her stomach.

Gertie pushed against a door and led them into a circular cavern. Dark, wooden barrels rested on rough shelves carved into the cavern walls. Small passages led off in various directions. Gertie used her lantern to ignite a brace of torches, and set them into hangers to light the room. The tangy aroma of

The Hermit Of Lammas Wood

old apples filled the air, along with something sharper that Tanyth couldn't name at first.

Gertie walked along the line of barrels and thumped the heads on several, cocking her head at each before moving down the line. She stopped in front of one and thumped it a second time. "Yeah. This is the one." She beckoned Tanyth closer and pointed into the shadowy space between the barrels. "You can see better in this light than Squeek can, I bet. Take a look in there and tell me what you see."

In the shadows Tanyth saw a wooden bucket with a hose running into it from the bung in the top of the barrel. "There's a hose and a bucket."

Gertie cackled. "Well, I'd hope so. Any foam in the bucket?"

Tanyth leaned in farther, trying to get a clear look. "Looks like clear water, but it's hard to tell in the dark."

"Clear water's what I expected. The foam'd show up plain enough."

"What is this, Gertie?"

"Hard cider, what else?"

"I figured that much. What's this set up? Hose in a bucket?"

"Keeps the cider from goin' off. While it's fermentin', the yeast in it bubbles and froths. Sometimes a little. Sometimes a lot. This trick lets the overflow out so the pressure don't hurt the barrel and keeps the air out of it because the end of the hose is under water. Nothin' can get back in."

"All right then. Now what?"

"Fish the hose out of the bucket and let it hang."

Tanyth did as she was told and stepped back.

Gertie held a tin cup under the spigot mounted in the end of the barrel and poured half a measure into it. She held the cup to her nose and took a deep whiff. She nodded and then took a careful sip. "Oh, my. Yes, this is ready." She offered the cup to Tanyth.

Tanyth took it and looked at the dark liquid within. The ripe aroma of apple and spice, along with the sharp edge that alcohol adds, drifted up from the cup. Her cautious sip transported her to fall's harvest and the crisp bite of warm days and frosty nights when an evening's fire was warmth as much as light. She let it roll on her tongue for several moments before swallowing. The sting of strong drink warmed her gullet and filled her center.

"Good, en't it?" Gertie said, breaking Tanyth's reverie.

Tanyth handed the cup back. "Now I understand why they come to barter."

Gertie laughed, her delight filling the dark cavern with joy. "Yes, indeed. Indeed they do," she said. "Now we need to put it in jugs and drag them up to the cottage."

Tanyth looked around the cavern. "Jugs?"

"This way." Gertie took a torch and stepped through the side passage.

Tanyth followed, feeling the temperature ratchet up the farther they went. At the end of the passage, Gertie pushed through another door into a low-ceilinged cave, where she lit a torch on the wall. The shuddering light revealed a tumble of brown jugs stacked on the ground around a stone basin filled with water. The air felt thick with moisture and hot as a summer day. A tiny trickle of water seeped down the far wall into the pool, while a notched overflow let the excess water drain out, down the edge of the stone basin where it disappeared into a narrow crevice in the floor.

"Hot spring," Gertie said by way of explanation. "We got a dozen or more of 'em in the caverns here. Later I'll show you my favorite one, but right now we need to wash enough of these jugs to empty that barrel."

"How many's that?"

"Start with twenty. Then we'll see where we are."

Tanyth crossed to the pile of jugs, some of them coated with dust, and picked up a couple by the looped handles at the top. "Where'd you get all these?"

"Oh, bartered for some. Made some. There's good clay for 'em not far off. Gettin' 'em glazed and fired was more trouble than it's worth to me. I get enough in trade to keep the pile growin'. You'll see by fall, I s'pect."

Tanyth took the jugs to the deep basin and started to lower the first jug into the water.

"Mind that water," Gertie said. "It's hot enough to cook

with."

Tanyth stopped and looked to the old woman. "You got a way of dealin' with this, don't ya?"

Gertie grinned. "Now you're learnin'. Lower 'em in so they sink. Tip 'em a bit so they fill with water but keep your fingers out. It's not exactly boilin' but it's plenty hot to the touch and you'll not like the burn. When they're heavy, let 'em go. There's enough sand in the bottom they won't break when they fall."

Tanyth lowered the first jug into the basin and felt the heat rising from the surface on her face and hands. She tilted the heavy crockery a bit, pushing the top against the buoyancy and letting some of the scalding liquid bubble into the narrow mouth. A few bubbles splashed onto her fingers, stinging them so she let go by reflex and the bottle sank with a glub. A trail of bubbles surfaced, then petered out.

"Well, that's good an' all, but how do I get it out?"

Gertie chuckled and pointed to a metal rod hanging from a peg on the wall. "Use that to hook 'em out by the handles when they've had a good soak." Gertie crossed the room, picked up a couple of the jugs, and slipped them into the water. "Put ten or so in there. Work across the front of the basin. By the time you get all the way around the front, start pulling them out in the same order they went in."

She crossed the cavern and came back with a small, wooden cart with iron-shod wheels. "Leave them full of water and put them on here. When we've got a load, we can roll it back to the cider room."

"How did you get all this stuff down here?"

Gertie just smiled. "Well, we're still at ground level here. One of my trapper friends made this cart and we just wheeled it in. It replaced one that was here when I came."

Tanyth continued sinking bottles in the steaming water. "And the barrels out there?"

"Rolled them in empty. Filled them here."

"How do you get them full?"

"There's a cider mill on the far side of the orchard. Apple grinder and press. Buckets of the stuff. I try to get a couple of my lumber jacks to help out before they head back to town in the fall."

"Do they?"

"Oh, yes. I pay them in last year's cider. No complaints yet," her smile gleamed in the dim light.

"So, why do you live alone?"

"That's a longer story and one that'll keep until we can settle in with cups of cider and a round of cheese."

"You have cows in a cavern somewhere?" Tanyth asked, picking up the hooked rod and fishing the hot jugs out of the water.

"No, but that's an interesting idea. I don't think I could feed a cow underground like that."

"Then how do you have cheese?"

"Goats."

"You have goats in here?" Tanyth straightened from her work to gaze at the old woman.

"Outside. They wander the valley and feed alongside the elk and deer."

"But you milk them and make cheese?"

"A small amount, yeah." Gertie shrugged. "There's a lot to do, but plenty o' time to sit and watch the trees grow. You'll see."

Tanyth lifted the last hot jug out of the water and placed it on the cart. She started loading fresh jugs into the pool while Gertie rolled the cart out the door and down the short tunnel. The hard iron rims grumbled on the wooden planks as they rolled.

In a few minutes Gertie was back with the cart. Tanyth loaded it again.

"That'll do it," Gertie said. "We'll fill these and see what's left."

"You do this often?" Tanyth asked as they rumbled the cart back down the corridor.

"What? Bottle up cider?"

"Well, make it, but yeah."

"This time o' year, lotsa trappers and lumberjacks comin' through. They know me and I know most of them by now. Long summer and lonely business. Long way to the nearest beer."

"Why don't you brew beer?"

"Cider's easier. Just need the apples and the All-Mother does the rest. I been doin' this longer than you been on the road. Just suits me, I guess."

It was a matter of less than an hour before they'd filled all the jugs. They poured the hot water out, set the jugs under the cask's spigot to fill them, and corked the tops. With the two of them working, it took no time at all. The jugs of cider filled the cart with a few left over.

Gertie picked up a pair of jubs. "If you'd drag that cart over to the cottage, I'll just slip these into the cold room and to chill. It'll be nice and cool by nightfall."

Tanyth took the handle and tugged on it, moving the cart easily despite its heavy cargo.

"Don't go too fast. That cart gets goin' and you'll have a hard time stoppin' it."

"Thanks for the warning," Tanyth said. Easing off on the handle, she trundled the laden cart through the stone halls to the broad storage area behind the cottage.

Chapter 20
Tall Tales

---◆---

With the cider jugs safely lined up two and three deep on the shelves beside the door, Tanyth moved the cart out of the way and stepped out into the cottage. Sunlight filtered through the treetops outside to paint the small windows with a flickering pattern of light and shadow, of green and gold. Crossing the room, she gazed out into the orchard, the sparse foliage allowing views of the peaks beyond the valley.

"It's lovely, isn't it?" Gertie said, joining her at the window.

"It is. I feel like I've come home."

"You have, dear girl. You have."

Something in the woman's tone made Tanyth turn to look at her. Gertie stood with her face turned to the light and her eyes closed. A small, dark gray nose peeked out of the woman's hair.

"Squeek shows you what you need to see?" Tanyth asked.

"Yes. Sometimes. He can be balky. Insists on looking at things that interest him and not necessarily what I need to see, but without him and his sisters and brothers I'd be blind."

"I have to be asleep to see."

"No. You're just more used to it. Sleep breaks the barrier easier. That's why you came, isn't it? Because of your visions?"

"Yes," Tanyth's voice was little more than a whisper in the stillness.

"You're not goin' mad, dearie." Gertie's voice held a gentle humor. "You're just gettin' old. But you knew that, didn't ya?"

Tanyth gave a small laugh. "Yeah, I know about the gettin' old part. My knees ain't exactly what they used to be."

"You're one of the rare ones. Touched by the Lady, they say."

"Is that what this is?" Tanyth leaned a shoulder against the narrow window frame and looked at the old woman. "These dreams where I see through somebody else's eyes."

"Yeah. That and healing your broken arm. Chasin' away that storm and changing the flow in the oceans." Gertie turned her face toward Tanyth; the small mouse seemed to gaze at her. "You almost killed yourself with that one, you know."

The words chilled Tanyth's core. "I what?"

Gertie's lips curled at the edges and the laugh lines at the corners of her eyes grew deeper. "I didn't think you knew about that."

"I don't understand."

"What part, dearie? The storm, the ocean, or killin' yourself?"

"My arm?"

"Oh, that. Yes, that, too. Didn't occur to you that it healed too fast?"

Tanyth's fingers sought the once-broken bone and danced along her skin as she remembered. "I had dreams."

"Pebbles in the stream?" Gertie asked.

"Yeah. Night time. The moon shining down on a stream and the pebbles clickin'."

"That was your body putting the stone back in your bone. You helped it along. Prob'ly took three, maybe four weeks off."

Tanyth tried to remember. "Mighta been. We were travelin' and I lost track of the days."

"You prob'ly slept good. Even on the ground," Gertie said. "Power takes power. Unless you know what you're doin', it all comes from you."

"The storm?"

"Knocked you out for a few days. Woulda killed a lesser woman. Woulda killed me," Gertie said, her words simple statements of fact with no particular emphasis.

Tanyth felt her jaw go slack.

"Say, you wouldn't mind makin' some tea, would ya?" Gertie asked. "Talkin' is thirsty work and we got a lot to talk about."

Tanyth felt her body go through the familiar motions of stoking the fire, filling the kettle, and settling it near the coals to heat. Her mind couldn't gather all the ideas that Gertie had strewn out like so much dandelion fluff in a summer breeze.

"The raven dreams..." Tanyth said.

"Which ones?" Gertie asked, propping herself up in one of the chairs and leaning her elbows on the smooth table top. "The nightmares?"

"Yeah. The ones where I couldn't change back."

Gertie snorted. "You didn't change to begin with. That's just your mind's way of telling you that somethin' ain't quite right."

"They seemed so real."

Gertie shrugged. "If they didn't, they wouldn't be so scary, now, would they?"

Tanyth blinked the older woman's face into focus. "No, I guess not."

"When you saw through the raven's eyes, you always knew it, didn't you?"

Tanyth shook her head. "Not in the beginning. I didn't know what it was."

"Well, sure. First time is always rough. I think Alice started up the still right after her first few times."

"Mother Willowton?"

"Yeah. Good woman, Alice. She made her peace and went back to the world."

"What's that mean? She went back to the world?"

"She came up here for a visit along about the time of her change. She has some gift but the All-Mother didn't so much touch her as blow a kiss in her direction. Was enough to scare the bloomers off her in the beginnin'." Gertie smiled a gentle smile. "Good woman, though. Made a darn smooth brandy."

"So she went home after visitin' you?"

"Most women do."

"Them that don't?"

"Well, most women don't come all the way up here to visit. Too many die first."

A grimace twisted Tanyth's mouth. "Sure, but we're not talkin' about those."

"So far, every woman who ever made the trip to learn from me went home again," Gertie said with a small slap of her open hand on the table between them. "I s'pect you already are home." She bestowed a gentle smile on Tanyth. "And I s'pect you already know that."

The kettle boiled over with a hiss of water against hearth. Tanyth busied herself with the homely task of setting tea to steep. "Wish I had my tea pot."

"We can get one," Gertie said.

"I got one I like. Just didn't bring it with me."

"'Fraid it'd break?"

"Yeah. I got it at Ravenwood and left it there on the mantel in my cottage."

"Ceramic's easy to replace here. Plenty of clay in the lower end of the valley. Plenty of heat to fire it."

Tanyth laughed. "That's a skill I never learned."

"You'll have time here, if you've a mind."

"What I've a mind for is findin' out what's happenin' to me." Tanyth took a deep breath and blew it out through her nose. "What'll happen next."

"Mostly that's up to you, dearie. The All-Mother's given you a gift. One I don't think we've seen in a couple of centuries. You're gonna be tested by it, sure as rain on a summer's afternoon. There's gonna be them that might be threatened by it, if they know of it."

Tanyth let the ideas sort themselves in her head. After months of living in fear and in motion, she felt thrown off-balance by the weight of her body in the chair, by her sense of stillness. It was the same feeling she got coming ashore in Northport after a couple of weeks at sea. She knew the ground lay unmoving beneath her boots, but her legs kept trying to compensate for the waves that never came. She focused on pouring tea to give her mind a chance to catch up.

"There's too many questions," she said after a sip of the hot tea. "Who's gonna be threatened? How'll they know?"

Gertie smacked her lips in appreciation for the tea. "Well, some know already. All them women you wintered with from Agnes Dogwood on. All them folks you left behind in Ravenwood. Every man jack on that ship. They all know."

"They feel threatened?"

Gertie shook her head and took another sip. "Naw. Most of 'em prob'ly don't even believe it. Your teachers all got some amount of the gift themselves, so they're gonna understand better'n most. You asked who knows. It's a bigger group than you might think. It's gonna get bigger, I s'pect. Once them sailors start spreadin' the word back in Kleesport."

"They prob'ly started in Northport already," Tanyth said, looking into her mug of tea.

"Prob'ly, but you got competition there."

"Competition?"

"The hermit. Fearsome stories goin' around about the hermit." A gleam danced in Gertie's eyes and the laugh lines on her cheeks deepened as she smiled. "Some strange happenin's out here in the Lammas Wood. Locals'll have stories of their own to tell."

Tanyth laughed in spite of herself. "I heard some o' them all the way down in Kleesport."

"What'd you hear?"

"The hermit breaks traps with her hands and releases the animals."

Gertie cackled loudly. "I been known to release a few animals. Trappers who should know better than trap in my valley. Course, they never mention that part, I bet."

"Naw. Always somewhere out in the woods."

"And I gen'rally use a rock to bust up the traps. Some of them are pretty rugged, too. Some I just drag back here. There's a box of 'em in the storage room." She took a sip of tea. "What else?"

"Oh, well. There was one story about a lumberjack who got chased away from the woods."

"I keep hearin' that one, too. Not me. Not enough lumber to attract them here. Nobody'll mess with my apple trees and there's little enough timber in the valley to tempt 'em. Barely enough for me to use for firewood these days."

Tanyth considered the wood stacked beside the hearth. "I didn't notice much stacked outside. Is that all you got?"

"There's some around the side of the cottage. There'll be more. The trapper who's comin' for the cider will bring some in for me. He's a regular. Knows what I need."

Tanyth sipped her tea and eyed the wood. "Must get cold up here come winter."

Gertie shrugged. "Not as cold as all that. Cold enough for the apple trees, but there's pools down in the lower valley that don't even freeze."

Tanyth snorted. "If they're hot as that pool I washed the jugs in, I can see why."

"Some're hotter. There's a couple that would boil dry without fresh water every day." Gertie nodded at the door leading back under the mountain. "There's some hot springs back there that're hot enough to cook in. The rocks around 'em can fry an egg if you'd a mind to do it."

"So if it gets too cold, you can just hole up back there?"

"Have and do. I gen'rally get plenty of notice when anybody comes callin'. I can decide if I wanna light a fire to greet 'em."

"How? The trees tell ya?" Tanyth asked.

Gertie's eyes sought the ceiling as she thought about it. "Trees, rabbits. Owls sometimes. Mostly mice. Don't know why but the little buggers like me."

Tanyth sipped her tea and listened to the fire crackle and snap in the hearth. She had a lot to think about.

Chapter 21
A Lonely Mule

Shortly after noon, Tanyth heard the sound of hooves outside.

"That'll be Nick and Sarah," Gertie said without getting up.

"Your trapper friend?"

"Friend might be too strong a word." Gertie shrugged. "He likes his cider and he always brings me wood. Sometimes cloth and flour."

"No furs?"

Gertie cast her a baleful look. "No furs."

After a few moments, a knock came on the door. "Hello? The hermit there?"

Gertie got up from her chair and opened the door. "Howdy, Nick."

Tanyth stood and peeked out the window at a pack-saddled mule with her head down, lipping at the scattered grasses.

"Afta'noon, mum. Brought back yer empties."

Gertie took the familiar-looking jugs from the man and placed them on the table. "Ah, thank ye, Nick. I can always use empties. How's Sarah doin'?" she asked.

"Funny you should ask, mum," Nick said. "She's been a bit off her feed lately."

"You ain't pushin' her too hard are ya?"

"Don't think so, mum."

Gertie stepped back out of the doorway and turned to Tanyth. "You feel like learnin' somethin'?"

"Always."

"Let's go look at Sarah. See what ya think."

The Hermit Of Lammas Wood

Tanyth felt her forehead wrinkle. "I don't know much about mules."

"You know enough," Gertie said. She nodded an invitation and stepped out of the cottage.

Tanyth followed and saw Nick for the first time.

His eyes went wide when she stepped out and he snatched the brimmed hat from his head. Looking down at his feet, he knuckled his sun-seamed brow in a respectful salute. "Howdy do, mum."

"Tanyth, that's Nick. Nick, Tanyth," Gertie said as she ambled across the stony ground toward the mule.

"Nice to meet ya, Nick."

"She'll be stayin' with me this summer," Gertie said.

Gertie stopped a few feet from the mule and just stood there.

Nick skittered across the yard to stand beside her. His wiry frame barely came up to the old woman's shoulder. "What ya think, mum?"

Gertie didn't say anything for a few moments. She waved Tanyth forward. "Do me a favor and give that girl a good lookin' at would ya, Tanyth?"

Tanyth crossed the yard and walked up to the mule.

The animal lifted her head and stared. Her left ear flicked two or three times and her long tail switched once. She shifted her weight on her hind legs, and Tanyth saw her nostrils flare a bit.

Tanyth reached out to let the mule smell her hand a moment before stroking back alongside the mule's muzzle, stopping to scratch behind her left ear. She worked her way down Sarah's left side, stroking the napped hair as she went. She stopped at her flank and patted her rump once, raising a cloud of horse-scented dust in the clear afternoon air.

"Somethin's not quite right," Tanyth said.

"Know what it is?" Gertie asked.

"Not yet."

She worked her way toward the mule's head again and walked down the right side, patting and speaking softly to her. She lifted Sarah's hind hoof, running her fingers around the tough edge and over the frog at the center of the underside.

Seeing nothing unusual, she let the hoof drop and worked her way forward again, stopping beside the mule's head. She reached out and scratched her behind the ear.

"Close yer eyes," Gertie said. "See what she'll tell ya if'n yer not lookin' at her."

Tanyth looked at Gertie. "Close my eyes?"

"Yeah. You're lettin' your eyes argue with what your brain already knows."

Nick's eyes looked big as saucers as he looked back and forth between the women.

With a shrug, Tanyth closed her eyes and leaned into the mule, wrapping an arm over Sarah's strong neck and resting her forehead against her jaw. They stood there for several moments, the two of them leaning against one another. It felt comforting in a way. A warm presence in a cold and lonely world.

Tanyth opened her eyes and stepped back, the realization startling her even as the mule heaved a huge sigh and blew it out through her wide nose. She turned to Gertie. "She's lonely?"

Gertie nodded. "That's what I thought, too."

Nick took a step back. "That's crazy. You two tryin' to tell me she's lonely?"

Gertie nodded her head and lifted a shoulder in a shrug. "Looks like."

"What? I need to get her a playmate or somethin'?" Nick's expression alternated between a cloud of disbelief and a half smile of amusement.

"You got another mule?" Gertie asked. "That'd be best."

Nick jammed his hat back on his head. "Ain't got another mule. Couldn't afford one if'n I did."

"You talk to her at all?" Tanyth asked.

"Well, course. Tell her what she needs to do all the time."

"No, not gee and haw and all that. Just talk to her."

Nick leaned forward, restin' his hands on the knees of his stained overalls. He wheezed out a few laughs before holding up his hand. "Sorry, ladies. Sorry. Jes' struck me humorous. That's what my wife used ta say all the time. 'Jes' talk ta me, Nick.'" He straightened up. "Di'n't know what ta say to her and I sure don' know what to say to Sarah here."

"Just scratch her ear and tell her she's a good girl. That'll do for a start." Gertie turned back to the cottage.

Nick watched her go, his mouth gaping open.

"Close yer mouth," Gertie said without turning around. "You'll catch flies that way. I'll get yer cider."

"We brung ya three good trunks," Nick said. "Left 'em out by the cider mill."

"That's fine," Gertie said and disappeared through the door, leaving Nick to look at Tanyth.

"You reckon she's right?" Nick asked, jerking his head toward the cottage. "Sarah's jes' lonely?"

"I'm not much of an expert on horse flesh, but there's nothin' wrong with her as I can see. Legs are strong, coat's in good shape. Feet been well tended." She smiled at Nick.

"Well, sure. I take good care of her." Nick's mouth screwed into a tight line for a moment. "That's why I asked if'n there was somethin' wrong. Get it fixed."

"How about a dog?" Tanyth asked.

Nick shook his head back and forth a couple of times. "A dog, mum?"

"Yeah. Seems like a dog would be helpful 'round the camp, and she'd have a friend." Tanyth patted the mule on her withers.

Nick scratched the side of his jaw with a couple of fingers. "Dog, huh? Might work, but where'm I gonna get a dog out here?"

Tanyth shook her head. "Can't say. Jus' think about it, and maybe next time you go back to Northport, you'll be able to get one."

Gertie came out of the cottage, a jug in each hand, her gnarled fingers hooked through the loop handles.

"Here ya go, Nick. Thanks for the wood." She handed the cider to Nick who stashed it in Sarah's packs.

"Thank ye kindly, mum. I'll look for a dog, I will."

"Come back around midsummer, and I'll have some more cider for ya," Gertie said.

"You need anythin' special?" Nick asked.

"Nope. Got all I need right here." She nodded at Tanyth.

Nick rubbed his fingers across his lips and nodded. "Well, we can bring you some more wood, I s'pose."

"That'd be fine, Nick," Gertie said. "We can always use wood."

Nick glanced up at the sun. "We best get movin'. Wanna be back in camp by sundown. Thank ya agin, mum."

Gertie raised a hand in blessing and Nick headed back down the trail, Sarah's lead in hand. Gertie completed her blessing, lips moving silently, just before he disappeared between the broad boles of the orchard.

"You knew he dropped off firewood," Tanyth said.

"Yep. Not exactly huge sticks but three goodly pieces jes' like he said. They're green and'll need some seasonin' before we can burn 'em, but good enough." She shrugged. "He'll be back when them jugs is empty."

Tanyth cocked her head and squinted at the old woman against the bright afternoon sun's glare in the stony yard.

Gertie gave her a short laugh. "How'd I know?"

"Yeah. Hard to see much from inside the cave."

"Depends on where yer eyes are, don't it?" Gertie asked. She jerked her head at the lone spruce high on the ridge. "Sparrow hawk sits in that tree up there. Good eyes. She's been watchin' Nick and Sarah off and on since they came over the west ridge draggin' the lumber."

Tanyth raised a hand to shade her eyes and looked up at the tree. "You don't need to be asleep to see?"

Gertie snorted.

Tanyth dropped her hand and shook her head. "'Course not. Sorry. Wasn't thinkin'."

"You can, too, ya know," Gertie said.

"Never been able to before."

Gertie shook her head. "You keep sayin' that but it ain't true."

They stood in the warm sun. Somewhere up in the treetops a bird tweeted a few times.

"It ain't," Gertie said again.

In her mind, Tanyth found the memory of pain and blood. She saw the weird, disjointed vision of herself in the snow and her raven sore and battered from doing battle with the last of Birchwood's thugs, alongside the other of Frank bursting through the snow-studded overgrowth, fear and anger in his eyes.

"It ain't," Tanyth said, her voice low.

"You got a gift. Time you started acceptin' that." Gertie smiled and waved a hand at the ridge. "See what you can see up there."

"See the most if I walk up there."

"And you'll be most of the afternoon gettin' up and back. It's a lot steeper than it looks from here and a lot farther away."

Tanyth turned her gaze toward the lone spruce again. She looked hard, trying to see the small falcon that Gertie said was there.

"Just reach for her. She's used to it by now," Gertie said.

"How? I never ..." A wintery morning ran a blizzard through her memory. Frank had been overdue and she had been near beside herself, fearing the worst. She glanced over at Gertie. "Maybe I have."

"Be surprisin' if you hadn't."

"But I was asleep."

"Make up your mind, woman. You either reached or you was asleep. Which was it?"

The words shocked down Tanyth's spine and seemed to fizzle in the rocks beneath her boot heels. She turned her face toward the ridge again and closed her eyes. The sun burned against her lids, making the dark pulse with red blood. Her hands felt heavy at her sides and her fingers flexed, reaching for the iron-shod staff she carried everywhere. The staff which stood inside the cottage. She drew a deep breath through parted lips and blew it out through her nose, willing her mind to follow the breath onto the wind and up the ridge to the spruce.

☽○☾

She blinked her eyes and puffed her feathers. The warm sun beat on her back but the wind still cut. Not a beetle stirred on the ground beneath her as she shifted her weight from foot to foot. Food would be important soon.

Far below a man and his beast made their slow way around the end of the ridge. She'd watched them enter the valley and might watch them go. She swiveled her head to the right, looking down the long valley with its ragged plumes of steam rising into the cold air. Perhaps the hunting would be better there. She looked to the left and down into the orchard that sheltered behind the ridge. The pale flowers and young leaves added texture to the valley floor. She turned a little farther and saw more humans standing in front of the cave that wasn't a cave. The white-haired one she recognized. A regular in her world. The other was new—

☽☉☾

Tanyth gasped and stepped back, her eyes snapping open and then closed again, dazzled by the afternoon sun.

Gertie cackled a bit. "Told ya," she said. "Now come on. We still got a lot of work to do today."

Chapter 22
The Old Knowledge

Inside the cluttered cottage, Gertie crossed to the hearth and tossed a couple of small sticks on the fire. She stood there, one arm resting on the mantel board, head bent as if gazing into the fire.

"Shall I make more tea?" Tanyth asked, stepping up beside her.

"No, not right now. A bit of bread and cheese wouldn't be amiss. And one of those chilled jugs of cider?" She didn't turn her head, just spoke into the fireplace. "Think you can find your way to the cold room?"

"Through the door, down the left path, second left, third door," Tanyth said.

"You were payin' attention," Gertie smiled at her then. "How're your legs?"

"I'm ready for food and drink, I think. They're a bit rubbery."

"That's the gift price. You used some of your own energy to reach the bird. Longer you stayed, the more it woulda cost ya." Gertie turned her face back to the fire. "You'll get stronger, I bet."

"I don't remember payin' that price before," Tanyth said.

"Most of the time you were already in bed, weren't ya?"

Tanyth shrugged one shoulder. "Yeah, I s'pose."

"Cheese is on the bottom shelf, next to the onions. Bread's just above it. We'll need to bake some more tomorrow."

Tanyth edged the stewpot closer to the fire with the toe of her boot. "Still a lot of stew left."

Gertie nodded, her head barely moving. "Been simmerin' there since last night. We'll have to throw a little liquid in it when you get back."

Tanyth took the hint and slipped through the carved door. When the door closed behind her, the light snuffed out and she stood alone in dark so thick it might have choked her. She reached with her right hand and found the lantern on the workbench there. A box of matches nearly skittered out of her grasp when she bumped it with questing fingers, but she managed to catch it, extract a match, and get it lit. After that, the lantern was easy.

Tanyth stuck off down the boardwalk and found the cold room without difficulty. While there, she took a quick inventory of goods. She found smoked meats and fish, net bags of root crops, and even boxes of apples and pears. The room itself was not terribly large, perhaps half the size of her hut back in Ravenwood. Packed sand made up the floor and the stone walls behind the shelving showed no tool marks except at the corners where the cavern had been squared off a bit. The one wall without shelves looked like layers of dirt and ice that extended from the floor to the ceiling. Her bare hand on it confirmed that it seemed to be one huge block of ice. She flecked a blackened stick from the ice face with her fingernail. The rough bark of a spruce tip, and a couple of the short, flattened spruce needles still hung on the twig.

With a shrug she grabbed a small log of the white goat cheese and a couple of the flattened loaves of bread. She also snatched a short hunk of sausage from one of the boxes, slicing the end off a link with her belt knife. Then taking up the stone lantern, she made her way back through the tunnels with her bounty cradled in one arm.

"Find anything interestin'?" Gertie asked from the hearth, apparently unmoved since Tanyth left her.

"Lots. I got a good look at the cold room. Where's that ice come from?"

"That's one of the big questions, ain't it?" Gertie grinned. "Cuttin' board over on the sideboard."

"I found a spruce twig embedded in it. It looks like layers of snow," Tanyth said, piling the food onto the cutting board and crossing to the table.

"I 'spect it was at one time." She jerked her head in the direction of the mountain. "My guess is there's some kinda crack or somethin' in the mountain up there. Snow falls into it in the winter and it's shaded from the midday sun in summer so it don't melt, then next year it gets more snow. After a few hundred years, I 'spect it builds up."

"Big crack," Tanyth said.

"Big mountain. Hard to understand just how big from down here."

"The bones of the earth," Tanyth said, her voice a quiet murmur against the crackling in the hearth.

"We got it all here," Gertie said. "Bones, breath, fire, and blood. All right here in this valley."

"Z'at why you live here?"

"Nope. Live here because nobody else does." Gertie turned and faced Tanyth. "Been a hermit here for hundreds of years. Sixty generations or so."

Tanyth looked around, the notion disconcerting. "Here?"

"Well, I 'spect most of the first ones lived in the cave. If you look around back there you'll see where there was fire pits and the like." She turned her face to the carved rafters and her face smoothed in a smile. "This cottage was built on the front about a hundred years ago. Furniture gets replaced pretty often–I built that table myself, as it happens. The chairs need replacin' but I haven't the will to do it anymore."

Tanyth sliced off a piece of bread and smeared some of the soft cheese on it, topping that with a thin slice of sausage. She offered it to Gertie.

"You remember the cider?" the older woman asked, taking a good bite from the bread.

"Oh, no. I forgot it. Got so wrapped up in the ice, it slipped my mind."

Gertie nodded and continued eating, standing on the hearth with her back to the fire. "No matter. We'll go back and I'll show ya the library, anyway. That might answer some of yer questions."

"Library?" Tanyth asked, folding her own bread and cheese around a slice of the spicy, dried sausage.

The Hermit Of Lammas Wood

"Yeah. That's what I call it." Gertie licked a stray bit of cheese from her finger and dusted her hands together over the hearth. "That was good, but now I'm thirsty."

Tanyth grabbed a couple of quick bites and followed Gertie back into the caverns. The ancient oil lamp flickered and flashed as Gertie clattered along the boards.

"There's a lot to see back here," she said. "Hope there's time to show you. If not, just remember: boards mean home. There's lotsa places where there's no boards. Don't go wanderin' down there unless you've got a string or a piece of chalk or somethin' to find your way back."

"Boards mean home," Tanyth said.

"Yeah, look at the boards."

Tanyth looked at the rough-hewn planks under her boots as she walked. "What about 'em? They look like boards to me. Old boards, some of them, but boards."

"About every fifth or sixth board? Right end's got a notch in it."

"All right." Tanyth spotted the notch in question. "How's that help?"

"Well, say you come to a branch in the tunnels," Gertie said holding up the lamp and turning back to face Tanyth. "How d'ya know which way is out?"

The meaning seemed obvious. "Put the notch on my left and keep walkin'."

"Yep. And if you got no light?"

Tanyth blinked. "No light?"

"Yeah. What if you dropped the lantern or it ran out of oil or somethin'. You gonna stand down here and yell and holler in the dark?"

"Crawl?" Tanyth asked. Just the image of crawling in the dark on her hands and knees made her back ache.

Gertie cackled a bit. "Well, that's one way, but if you just fumble around until you find the notch, you can put your hand against the wall and walk until the wall runs out. Like when it gets to a branch. Reach down and find the notches. Keep goin'. You'll be back at the cottage in no time."

Tanyth shook her head. "I can't imagine ever needin' to do that, but good to know just the same."

Gertie snorted. "Yeah, I couldn't imagine it either. Well, come on. Library's just around this bend."

The library proved to be a small cavern with a sand floor but without the cooling ice of the pantry or the warm rocks in the bottle room. What it had was shelves. Lots and lots of shelves. On two of the walls, the shelves were filled with books and parchments. Wooden spindles with parchment wound on them protruded here and there. There were even shelves around the door frame.

"What is this place?"

Gertie waved her hands at the loaded shelves. "That's all the old knowledge you came lookin' for. Journals and diaries of all the hermits that came before me."

"That's how you know how many generations?"

"Yeah. Not much to do most days but read. Not much to read but this stuff. Haven't been able to read much since my eyes went. Squeek here is good for basic stuff, but he balks at staring at spidery hand writin' for any length of time."

"How many books are there?"

"Dunno exactly. Every hermit left some writin' behind. Some left a single book or parchment. Most left a dozen or more. Journals, diaries. Even some pretty interestin' histories and such. I think some of them ain't exactly moored in the sea of sanity, but I never got bored readin' them. Or writin' them."

"You have books here?"

"Well, course." She pointed to a shelf that appeared only about half full. "I got one more book over in the cottage to finish, but there's my books, there. Nothin' much. What I learned about this place, mostly. Hot springs, rocks, geysers. I been up and down and across this valley a hundred times, I bet."

Tanyth gazed at all the works stacked neatly on the rough shelves. "When they called you the last keeper of the old knowledge, they weren't kiddin', were they?"

Gertie gave a shrug. "Well, I s'pose that's true. Not like one person could remember all that, but I know where the library is."

"Any herb lore in there?"

"Oh, yeah. One of the early ones. Should be a collection of scrolls bound together up on the shelf there." She pointed to the left side of the room. "Also, seems to me I remember one from about a century ago. That'd be about here." She placed her hand on one of the shelves at waist height.

"What else is there?" Tanyth asked, raking the shelves with her gaze, unwilling to disturb the works with her hands.

"Anything you can think of. One studied the stars and the sky. One worked on trees, another on birds. One studied the insides of animals and even people. Not sure where or how she managed that." Gertie shrugged. "If you can think of it, somebody in that pile already thought of it at least once."

"Geography?" Tanyth asked.

"Oh, yeah. Geography, politics, history. There's one who was a painter, but I don't know where her paintin's went. Another studied rocks. That's where I got the idea to study this valley. There's fire down there, you know. Sometimes it comes up to the surface."

"I felt it the other day comin' in."

"Yeah, saved your life by getting' warm and dry, but nearly killed you. Again."

Tanyth's heart beat a bit faster at that news. "Killed me? How?"

"Takes a lot of power to move the earth like that. Might be too much unless you're careful. You got lucky."

"I didn't know what I was doin'," Tanyth said.

"That's the first lesson," Gertie said, her gap-toothed grin gleaming in the light of the lamp. "Recognizin' that, you're gonna be better prepared to deal with whatever comes next."

"What does come next?" Tanyth asked.

"Next? We go get that cider and go back up to the hearth. I feel a gab comin' on and talkin' is thirsty work."

Chapter 23
Beginning Lessons

The questions swirled in Tanyth's head all the way back to the cottage. She didn't know where to start when they got settled with cold mugs and a warm hearth. A sip of the cider exploded in her mouth—rich with fall apple and peppery with alcohol. "You make a stiff cider," she said, rolling her tongue around in her mouth. "That's delicious."

"Thanks. Been doin' it awhile, but mostly I just follow the recipe and let the Lady do the rest."

"Recipe?"

"From one of the books," Gertie said, and tilted her own mug up, taking a good swallow.

"Of course," Tanyth tried another cautious sip and reached for some of the bread and cheese from their late lunch.

"Now's the time to ask, Tanyth. We're runnin' out of time and you'll wanna get as many answers as you can think of questions for."

"Who built this place?"

"The cottage? One of the hermits a century ago. Took nigh on fifteen years if I'm readin' it right. Most of us carved on it since."

"To build this?"

"Old woman and hard stone." Gertie shrugged. "Woulda taken longer but some trappers helped her a couple of summers. Not sure what they got in return. I s'pect they had some miners with 'em, too. Takes a lot to carve rock out of the ground and pile it up."

"The caves?"

The Hermit Of Lammas Wood

"Well, the Lord and Lady did most of it. The planking has to be replaced once in a while. Shelving units, too. Generally best to use a solid wood. Pine smells good but rots fast."

"Who chipped out the corners in the cold room?"

"Dunno," Gertie said and reached for some bread for herself. "Never read it in any of the books. Mighta been any one of them back along. Mighta been somethin' they hired done. Unless it's written down—or you done it yourself—kinda tough to say."

They sat in silence while the ideas swirled in Tanyth's head, too many to make a question out of even though the need to ask felt almost overwhelming.

"You knew I was comin'?" she asked.

"Oh, yeah. Been lookin' for you these last five winters. Just as glad you took your time, when it gets right down to it."

Tanyth blinked at her and took another bite of the goat cheese. "You knew I was comin' before I knew I was comin'."

Gertie's mouth shifted sideways in a grin. She shook her head. "I was pretty sure when Agnes Dogwood lemme know about you way back when. Then when I got the word from Alice Willowton, I knew it was only a matter of time. You impressed her, you did." Gertie nodded as if to herself and tossed back some more cool cider.

"Got the word?"

"Oh, aye. She sent word that you'd be along as soon as you got your other business squared away."

"How did she send word?" Tanyth asked. "You're not exactly gettin' mail and supplies delivered on a reg'lar basis, are ya?"

Gertie cackled. "You'll get it soon enough now, I'm bettin'."

"Get what?"

"What's happening," Gertie said. "You can already reach out and touch the hawk. You been messin' with the land, the sea, and the air. Hasn't killed ya, quite. At least not yet. Won't be long before the trees start talkin' to ya."

Tanyth laughed. "That's all I need. I already feel like I've gone about halfway round the bend."

Gertie just shrugged one shoulder and took another slug of cider.

"Wait," Tanyth said, looking across the table at the old woman. "That's not a figure of speech? The trees'll start talkin' to me?"

"Yeah. They ain't real chatty but you can hear the news on whisperin' winds if you've the knack."

"And you do?"

"Well, course. And so does—well, did—Mother Willowton."

"Did? Is she...?"

"Oh, aye. Been gone a couple winters now. Spoke about you often, when she was alive, though. The trees pass that kinda gossip along."

"That why you protect 'em?"

"What? Trees?"

"Yeah."

"I don't protect trees." Gertie's dark eyes stared at Tanyth from under her brows. "That's a couple times now you've mentioned it. Where's it comin' from?"

"Some of the stories down in Kleesport."

"Same stories like with the traps?"

"Seemed like. Lotta people who never met ya advised me to turn back."

Gertie snorted and slapped the table. "Like you could, huh?"

"Well, by the time I got to Kleesport with Rebecca, the dice were rolling and I knew they'd only stop spinning if I got here."

"What stories exactly?" Gertie asked, leaning in on the table with her elbows.

"Most of 'em talk about you running through the forest chasing trappers and lumberjacks. Lots of stories about lumberjacks and you tellin' them to git outa your woods."

Gertie twisted her head to the side. "That don't sound like me. Leastwise, not that I remember."

"Most of 'em think you're a man, too."

"Huh. I know a lot of 'em wanderin' around out there are just as blind as I am, but you'd think they'd be able to tell."

"I chalked it up to wearin' pants. Whole lotta menfolk out there think anything in a pair of pants is of the male persuasion."

Gertie looked down at her heavy trousers. "Only thing makes sense back here in the hinterlands."

"I agree with ya, but there's no accountin' for some folks' biases."

Gertie grinned. "And some just won't listen to reason."

"Met a few of them, too," Tanyth said. In her mind's eye she saw a single, shimmering drop of blood drip from the tip of a knife and fall slowly, slowly. She lifted her cup and took another sip of cider.

"Questions, woman. You was askin' 'em," Gertie said, lifting her own mug.

"I'm still tryin' to wrap my head around how you live out here."

Gertie smacked her lips a couple of times and turned her head to and fro. "Right comfy most of the time."

"Don't he crap on your head?" Tanyth blinked at the sound of her voice and leaned on the table. "Sorry," she muttered. "Not sure where that came from."

Gertie's laugh started as a chuckle in her chest and worked up to shake her shoulders. She put her hand up to her head and the mouse scampered onto it. Still laughing, she put the mouse on the table and he sat up, cleaning himself and not seeming at all distressed by people. Gertie rolled her head back and laughed and laughed. She'd almost get it under control and then start giggling.

"Good cider, huh?" Gertie said and was off again.

Tanyth couldn't resist and found herself chuckling and then laughing along.

Tears soon rolled down both sets of wrinkled cheeks. They leaned on the table with their elbows and laughed at the mouse. The mouse just groomed his ears as if nothing at all unusual was happening. After several long moments, the two women got the paroxysms under control.

Tanyth opened her mouth to speak but Gertie held up a hand in warning. "Wait," she said. "Lemme get my breath, woman." She closed her eyes tight and tilted her head down as if facing the floor. She sucked in a couple of huge breaths, blowing them out with great gusto each time. "All right. I think I'm good now."

"Sorry," Tanyth said, still fighting the odd chuckle. "Don't know why I asked that or why it was all so funny."

Gertie waved her hand in the air as if batting at a fly. "No, no. It's all right. I figure everybody ever come here...all the trappers, hunters, old ladies...I s'pect every single one of 'em prob'ly wondered the same thing and was too proper to ask."

"I never been accused of bein' too proper, but I usually mind my own business better'n that." Tanyth scrubbed her watery eyes with her fingers and shook her head.

"No, he doesn't," Gertie said. "Never has. They trade off a few times durin' the day." She reached out one gnarled finger and the mouse rubbed itself under the pad of it.

"How many are there?" Tanyth asked, looking around.

"Five or six. It varies by day and season. There's a nest of 'em under the stoop. Plenty warm in the winter. Plenty of food. Nothin' to bother them." Gertie combed her fingers through the white hairs on her scalp, and tilted her head back as if stretching her neck. "Oh, my. I haven't laughed that hard in ages."

Tanyth tried to remember the last time she'd laughed at all. She took another sip of the cider and then looked at the cup, a suspicion growing in her mind. "There's nothin' in this but cider, is there?"

Gertie shook her head. "Nope. It's just cider. Good cider and a bit of a kick. But nothing else."

Tanyth put fingers to her lips and nose. "Not tingly. I'm not drunk."

Gertie snorted. "I should hope not. You've had half a mug's worth and that jug's barely got a dent in it."

Tanyth reached for another piece of the tangy goat cheese and chased it with some of the bread, before taking another cautious sip. "Too much on an empty stomach, maybe."

Gertie shook her head again and leaned closer over the table. "No, there's nothin' wrong with you, my girl. Nothin' at all. You've finally gotten here and your body is smarter than your brain. It's relaxin' among friends. You been headin' somewhere for twenty-somethin' winters, and now you're here." She reached one wrinkled hand across the table to pat Tanyth's forearm. "Relax and enjoy it for a bit."

Tanyth sat very still in her chair and let the woman's words sink into her. The fire snapped once in the hearth but other than that, the cottage was so still she could hear Gertie's breathing as well as her own. The warm feeling of rightness started at her feet and worked up her legs as muscles tensed for travel unknotted. She took several deep, slow breaths and let the clamoring in her head and heart still. She was home.

"Why do you live alone?" Tanyth asked, her voice low, nearly a whisper in the silence.

Gertie sighed. "That's the price we pay for our gifts," she said, her voice almost as low as Tanyth's. "When the Lady takes our gift of fertility, she gives some of us new gifts. Those that want to take full advantage live apart from others—from the demands of individuals—in order to pay attention to the demands of all."

"That's why you sent Rebecca and Penny away?"

Gertie nodded. "Aye. People too close—they get in the way. It's harder to hear the wind. Harder to see the world around us. They shine so bright, it's like trying to see a match flame at noon on the summer solstice. You can't see anything but the brightest light."

"So you live in darkness?"

"No," Gertie said, her voice gentle as a kiss. "Twilight maybe, surrounded by the fireflies that jump and spin and swirl around us. You see so much more when you're not blinded by the light."

"That's why you're a hermit. To see?"

"It's a calling. The Lady calls one or two every generation to be mother to the world. I was lucky enough to be the one."

"At the expense of not knowing your granddaughter?"

Gertie's smile tilted. "I know her better than she knows, I think. I see her; even in Northport she's one of the brightest stars in the winter sky."

"But she doesn't see you."

Gertie's face drooped and she took another sip of her cider.

"No. She doesn't. She's paying the price for my gift, I'm afraid."

"It's not too late."

"P'r'aps." Gertie lifted and dropped one shoulder in shrug. "We still got a lot of work to do here, you and me. After that..." Her voice trailed off and she closed her eyes. "After that, we'll see."

"What work is that important?" Tanyth asked.

Gertie grinned. "You wanna hear the trees, don't cha?"

Tanyth's gaze went to the window. The afternoon light had already faded to near twilight as the sun took shelter behind the mountain to the west. An evening purple replaced the dappled gold and green. "I'm not sure."

Gertie sighed. "Can't say as I'm surprised." She sat back in her chair and cradled her cup between her two palms. "Well, let's get something to eat and you can ask more questions."

"I got one now," Tanyth said. "Where do you get the bread?"

"Make it."

"What about the flour?"

"Barter for it with the trappers. You met Nick. He usually brings me a fifty-pound bag every spring. He dropped off the fresh one just a couple weeks back."

"You're not an herbalist at all, are you?"

"Not really. I know stinging nettle from sage. Mint from rosemary, but no. I'm mostly a busy body." Her grin made Tanyth smile in return.

Chapter 24
Terrible Gossips

Tanyth found her bedroll next to the hearth and vowed to never try to drink along with Gertie Pinecrest ever again. The room swam around her. Only the sure knowledge that the stones could not move kept her from trying to grip the floor.

She lay there in the glow from the dying fire and gazed up at the oblongs of moonlight that marked the windows. A hundred winters seemed an incredible amount of time until she realized that it was only twice as long as her whole life. Less, really. Someone born when the cottage had been built might have been still alive when she started the long path that led her to it. Those who did the actual building were long gone, but time felt a bit more fluid to her—a bit more forgiving, somehow.

The night wind whispered in the eaves of the cottage. *A storm blows from the west, sweeping a bit of snow onto the peaks but dropping icy rain on the lowlands. Across the valley and over the next ridge, two women huddle in their bedrolls and stare at a meager fire. The scent of roasted rabbit wafts on the breeze. Far to the south, a dark blight festers in a notch on the coast.*

Tanyth sat upright in her bedroll and blinked her eyes wide in the dimness to wake herself. She found that she was not sleeping.

Gertie's chuckling interrupted the sound of the winds in the eaves. "Told ya," she said. "Terrible gossips, trees."

"You heard it?" Tanyth asked, lowering herself back onto

The Hermit Of Lammas Wood

the hard floor.

"Almost every night, there's a wind that blows up the valley. Surprisin' what you'll hear if you listen."

"Storm comin'?"

"Aye. 'spected as much. My hands ache somethin' awful when the weather changes. Trees not tellin' me what I don't know."

Tanyth rolled onto her side and cradled her head on an arm. "Never heard the like before."

"Never been far enough from people to hear before." The old woman sighed. "The price we pay for the gift."

"You're here."

"Aye, but only barely. The older you are, the less you're here until your body gives up and lets you move on."

Tanyth felt her eyes closing and sleep stealing over her. "That's why the girls had to leave," she said, her voice a low murmur.

"Aye. They're young and alive and very much there. The wind finds them and the trees see them clearly. Old sticks like me? Only barely here. Easy to overlook an old woman but even then I can't hear as well. See as much when you're here."

Tanyth heard the cot's ropes stretch and scrape as Gertie rolled over. If she was going to spend too many more nights here, she'd need to make a bed of her own. The stone floor offered scant comfort to old bones.

☽○☾

Breakfast brought griddle cakes and slices off a pork sausage along with a fresh pot of tea. Tanyth felt none of the aftermath from the cider. Perhaps a trifle bloated, but none of the headache or nausea she expected from an afternoon and evening spent imbibing strong drink.

"No chickens?" she asked while they waited for the griddle cakes to brown.

Gertie shook her head. "None since I been here. Thought about 'em often enough. Never felt the lack of poultry strong since I been here to do anything about it."

Tanyth reviewed the larder in her mind. "Fish, elk, venison...pork? Somebody keeps pigs around here?"

"The Lord and Lady raise boars all through the oak woods below the valley's foot." Gertie gave her a wry smile. "Easy to forget they always have the biggest farm."

Tanyth laughed along with her. "True. Something I thought I appreciated, but prob'ly need a few more lessons."

Gertie reached in with a wrap of cloth and grabbed the handle of the skillet, flipping the griddle cake in it with a practiced twitch of the wrist.

"You're pretty good at that."

Gertie grunted. "You'd be, too, if you done it for twenty-odd winters." She settled back in her chair with a low sigh.

"I can do that, you know."

Gertie gave her a shallow nod. "I know. Leave an old woman somethin' to do. Not like it's a great effort."

"So what'll we do today?" Tanyth asked after a few moments of silence.

"Hot springs. Calendar. Need a bath. Prob'ly show you the graveyard. I need to write in my journal, too. Prob'ly should do that right after breakfast."

"You don't have a garden?"

Gertie shook her head. "Never saw the need."

"What you do for greens?"

"Plenty of goosefoot and purslane. Reminds me, we should go down the valley and pick some fiddleheads." Gertie shrugged. "Never saw the need to grow it when I could just walk out and pick it."

The griddle cake began to send up small wisps of smoke so she flipped it out onto a plate. "There's honey if you've a sweet tooth."

"No maple syrup?" Tanyth grinned as she asked, expecting a sharp answer.

"No maple trees. They don't take to the altitude as well. There's a stand a few miles south, down toward the coast, but nothin' near enough here."

"You feelin' all right, Gertie?" Tanyth leaned over the table and looked at the woman closely.

"I'm fine. Fine. Not used to drinkin' with company, I guess."

Tanyth accepted the answer and topped off the old woman's

mug with hot tea before addressing her griddle cake. A bit of the creamy goat cheese added a savory bite to the otherwise bland flatbread.

"Where d'you get the baking powder?" Tanyth asked.

"What?"

Tanyth pointed to the griddle cake. "No eggs in this, but you put in flour, salt, baking powder and goat milk?"

"Oh, yeah. Get it from one of the hot springs. Grows in crystals. Kinda pretty. You can grind 'em up with a couple of rocks or a mortar and pestle. Like salt. Same place, actually."

"What about the goat milk?"

"They'll be around later this morning. They're here by midmorning almost every day."

"They?"

"You'll see." Gertie shrugged. "I'm so used to just going day to day, I don't think of it any more–just do it when it's time."

Tanyth finished off the griddle cake and sipped at her tea. "You don't find it borin'?"

Gertie smiled. "Never. There's always something to do, something to see. There's the trees and the animals. I get the odd visitor and then sometimes one of the old women makes the journey up to visit me, like you."

"Who was the last one?"

"Harriet Rockland. Fussy woman. Hated sleepin' on the stone but never thought to add an extra pad."

"What'd she come to learn?"

"She heard voices. One of 'em told her to come see me."

"Did she hear the trees?"

"No, poor woman just heard voices in her head."

"Did you help her?"

Gertie sighed. "Not really sure. She came, spent a couple of weeks here and went home again. From what she said, she hated every minute she was here and jumped at the chance to head back to Northport with a couple of lumberjacks goin' that way. The trees never speak of her."

"Supppose she made it back safely?"

Gertie sighed again. "I 'spect so. That kinda stuff, the trees talk about. Truth is most people out here are decent folk. They got the same temptations and desires as anybody, but most of 'em learn to control 'em or they don't last long."

"There are times I think this must be a hard life," Tanyth said, her gaze straying to the golden-green sunlight on the windows. "Other times it feels...well...it just feels right."

Gertie reached across and patted Tanyth's forearm. "People got hard lives wherever they are, if they think it's a hard life. Some have trouble findin' enough to eat. Some got no roof over their head. Some don't know about the Lord and Lady...or if they do, they don't trust 'em."

"Met a few of those," Tanyth said.

"Too many people think the Lord and Lady's just an excuse. That they'll just take care of a body if ya believe enough. They don't have enough sense to reach out a hand and pluck an apple."

Tanyth smiled. "You don't have to sell me. I've been living off the land for a long time. When yer needs are simple, there's plenty to go around."

"You're gonna like it here, Tanyth." Gertie smiled. "You gonna start your book now?"

"My book?"

"Yeah. The herb book? Wasn't that what you wanted? To find a quiet place to write your book?"

Tanyth felt the hair on her arms prickle. "Well, I was told you were the last keeper of the old knowledge. I started out to fill in the blanks on stuff I don't know."

"I'm the keeper, dear. Not the owner."

"The library," Tanyth said.

"Yeah. The hermit keeps the library safe and helps old women understand the All-Mother's gifts, such as they are."

"So, not every woman gets a gift like this?" Tanyth waved a hand around in the air, not exactly sure where to point.

"Most get something small. Some get more. Those with strong gifts have heavy responsibilities and you've met most of those women along your path over the last twenty winters. At least those here in Korlay. There are others in other lands. Some with gifts as strong or stronger, I imagine."

"You never met them?"

"They never came here." Gertie's mouth curved around in

a wry grin. "Sometimes the trees catch a wind from far away and they whisper tales. Terrible gossips, the trees."

"Heavy responsibilities?"

"They're the healers and midwives, quite often. Herb lore is prob'ly the most common but there's them that study the animals instead of the plants. There's lots to know about how to live. Me, I'm a gadfly. Flitterin' from one interest to another. I can tell you which rocks are salt and which mushrooms to pick. If your cow's sick, I can prob'ly tell ya why."

"If my mule's lonely?" Tanyth asked with a grin.

"That was good advice. A dog makes more sense than another mule. Easier to feed, and the mule'll appreciate the extra protection."

"You heard that?"

"Course."

"This is all real."

"Real as this cottage."

"Why isn't it common knowledge?"

"What makes you think it's not?"

"I thought I was goin' mad when I first started dreamin'."

"You're the only one who thought that."

A fragment of conversation wafted through her mind, a memory of a warm man who carried more wisdom than he knew. "Somebody else told me that once."

"You shoulda believed him."

"How d'you know it was a man?" Tanyth challenged.

"My eyes are clouded but Squeek sees really well."

Tanyth bit her lip and hid her face, pretending to sip from the empty cup.

"Well, I need to write a bit in my journal. Can you clean this up?"

"Fresh water?"

"There's a spring just the other side of the cold room. You can get a bit of that and then use the hot water from the bottling room to do dishes. Saves heatin' wash water."

"You mentioned a bath?"

"Oh, yeah. You're gonna love that."

"Well, let's get goin' then. Daylight's burning." Tanyth

stood and collected the dishes into a neat pile. "We're not expectin' visitors today are we?"

"Trees didn't mention it. You can check with the sparrow hawk. See if anybody's come into the valley."

"Later, maybe. I don't need to know that bad," Tanyth said.

"Practice, dearie. Practice."

"Yeah, well, you've had more'n thirty winters' practice. I'm still new at all this."

"You'll be surprised how fast you pick it up." Gertie lifted herself out of her chair, using her arms against the table to push.

"You sure you're all right?" Tanyth asked.

"Yeah. Slow startin' this mornin'. Don't have young'uns to impress and get movin' for today." She grimaced and glanced at the cider jug. "That don't help much right now, either."

Tanyth snorted. "I know what you mean, but it sure tasted good last night."

Gertie chortled a bit. "That it did. That it did." She crossed to the bookcase and pulled down a leather folder with papers stuffed inside. She slipped a quill behind her ear and grabbed a small bottle to take back to the table. "Don't just stand there, dearie. I'll be done here in a few minutes. You get them dishes done up and then we'll go take a walk outside."

Tanyth nodded and pushed through the door to the store room. A walk outside sounded like a very good idea.

Chapter 25
Sticks And Stones

The midmorning sun warmed the back of Tanyth's jacket. Being in the high country just felt colder most of the time. The Shear Moon would rise in a few nights and being bundled up in late spring seemed at odds with what she knew.

Gertie held her naked arms out to catch the sun's rays. "Feels good on the old bones."

"Don't know how you can go without at least a jacket," Tanyth said.

"Used to it. That's all." Gertie turned her face up and basked for a moment. "Well, let's take a little walk around, shall we?"

She headed north up the valley. A narrow trail of scattered rocks didn't so much mark the path as provide the clue that it existed at all. Only a lack of plant life set it apart from the loose scree at the foot of the mountain. A few dozen feet beyond the cottage's clearing, the apple trees gave way to an alpine meadow across the head of the valley. It spread a carpet of green grass and blossoms upward into the slopes before the stones of the mountains discouraged further adventures.

"It's lovely."

"Spring is my favorite time here," Gertie said. "The grass seems greener somehow. Or maybe it's just that Squeek sees it as greener after bein' cooped up all winter by the cold and the snow."

A sturdy frame building perched to one side, squared blocks keeping the wood from the ground, but no door hung in the door frame.

The Hermit Of Lammas Wood

"That the cider mill?" Tanyth asked.

"Yeah. Apples go in, and sweet cider comes out. The orchard provides plenty."

"You don't keep any apples?"

"Oh, yeah. A bushel or two. Prob'ly should keep more." Gertie grinned. "They taste so good, they're always gone by the winter solstice."

Tanyth stepped up into the building and eyed the grinder and press inside. "Seems like a lotta work for one person."

"Would be, but I usually have a trapper or two ta help in the fall."

"They lookin' to get an early lead on the new crop of cider?" Tanyth asked.

"I s'pect so. They always leave with a couple of jugs. Some take it sweet but others are happy to get a jug of barrel-aged hard cider when they go."

Tanyth rolled her tongue around in her mouth, recalling the crisp flavor of the cider. "Yeah. I can see that happening."

Gertie picked her way around the mill and into the meadow beyond. Hidden behind the building, Tanyth found a field of regular stones laid out in a rectangular pattern. "Oh."

"Yeah. Count the stones and you'll find out how many hermits have been here. Some of 'em go back hundreds of winters."

Tanyth counted over twenty stones. "Doesn't seem possible."

"What? So few stones? Or so many?"

"Looks like a lot spread out like that, but it's only—what? Twenty-five? Thirty?"

"Twenty-eight. Mine'll be number twenty-nine. I got a nice block picked out already." Gertie crossed the grass to the far edge of the field. A fresh square of stone about ten inches tall and nearly a foot long waited in the grass. Streaks of milky white quartz wrapped around the dark granite. "Nick and Sarah helped me drag it over a couple summers ago."

"It's...pretty." Tanyth looked at Gertie. "Did all the hermits pick out their own stones?"

Gertie's laugh echoed back from the mountainsides above them. "Lady only knows, dearie. Bein' a rock person myself, it seemed fittin' that I shouldn't leave that up to somebody comin' after. When I saw that piece had tumbled down out of the mountains over the winter, I thought it was just about perfect."

Tanyth knelt to run her fingers across the rough surface. "Yeah. I think you're right."

"I wonder where my girls are," Gertie said. She spun on her heel, looking out across the grassy hollow. "They usually come running when I'm out here."

A faint bleating came from the hillside. Tanyth looked up and saw a brindled goat with a head of heavy, curled horns standing on the face of the cliff. "How'd he get up there?"

"Him? He's always finding new and excitin' places to stand. Make you dizzy to watch him walk across nothin' at all on what looks like sheer rock faces. He got up on the cottage once. Thought it was great fun to eat my roof and leave his callin' cards behind."

Tanyth turned to see five goats trotting across the grass toward Gertie. Judging from the bags swaying under them, all were does. "No kids?"

"Should be some over on the far side of the meadow." Gertie held up a hand and pointed. "Squeek can't see so good that far away but you should be able to pick 'em out."

"Oh, yes. I thought they were rocks or something over there but one just got up and started eating."

"A yearling, prob'ly. The little ones are just layin' low. Give 'em a few minutes and they'll be eatin' grass and flowers and anything else that takes their fancy. Scamperin' around and buttin' each other. There's prob'ly twenty, maybe thirty goats over there. You just can't see 'em."

The does nuzzled up to Gertie, who stroked them all under their chins and alongside their necks. "My dears need a little relief, eh? Well, let's go find the buckets and a stool. Come along, dears, come along." The old woman turned and walked back around the cider mill toward the cottage, the does following in a single line. "You feel free to wander about, Tanyth. I'll just take care of my girls. You come back when you've stretched your legs a bit." She waved as she disappeared between the trunks of the ancient apple trees.

The Hermit Of Lammas Wood

The sound of the goats' delicate hooves on the stones faded into the whispering winds, leaving Tanyth blinking in the sun. She turned her gaze upward to the peaks on three sides. The cliff face above her ran bare up to where it curved away toward its peak. Even the ram had disappeared. She closed her eyes and focused on the lone spruce at the top of the ridge. From behind the orchard she couldn't see it, but she knew it was there. After several long moments she opened her eyes again.

"Foolish old woman," she said.

She started back along the path but stopped to gaze once more at the standing stones in the grass. Five hundred winters seemed too long a time to be accounted for by so few stones. Logically, it made perfect sense but something twisted in her gut. Five hundred years of old women living out their time in solitude, stripped of the lives they'd known for half a century. For the sake of a gift of what? Knowledge? An answer to strange dreams that came in the night and befuddled the dreamer?

The wind picked up and rustled the tree limbs in the orchard. It picked at her hair, blowing the loose strands past her face, swirling them around her head. For the first time in ages, she found herself outside without her hat. Her hands went to her head and she turned to see the gust of wind wave across the sward. *Change is coming. The blight far to the south festers. The two young women follow a path toward the black rock canyon.*

"I didn't ask you," Tanyth muttered.

Yet knowing that Rebecca and Penny had begun their trip back to Northport left her feeling relieved that they returned to the relative safety of town.

The wind gusted again, the whispers clambering for her attention.

"What is it now?"

Death comes on snow-white wings. The winds themselves died.

The goats clattered out of the orchard in a flurry, startling Tanyth out of her shocked stupor. "Gertie!" Her feet pounded in time with her heart as she raced through the grove. "Gertie!"

She burst into the clearing and found the old woman with a bucket in one hand and a small milking stool in the other. "Lady sakes, Tanyth. What is it?" she asked, turning from the open door, her face gone slack with alarm.

"You're all right?" Tanyth's breath huffed as she skidded to a stop in the scree.

"Well, of course, I'm all right. What else would I be?"

"The trees. Did you hear them?"

Gertie stopped and turned her face toward the branches. "I was milking," she said after a few moments. "I didn't hear anything."

Tanyth took a deep breath and blew it out through her nose, trying to calm her fluttering heart and control her breathing. The air was so thin. It made it hard to breathe.

"What did they say, dearie?"

"Change is coming."

Gertie laughed and pushed on into the cottage. "Change is always coming, dearie."

"Penny and Rebecca are on their way back to town."

"Excellent. They'll be more comfortable there than in that cave." Gertie dropped the milking stool inside the door and walked toward the back room. "Was there something else? What disturbed you so?"

"There's a blight in the south."

Gertie's steps slowed and then stopped. She rested one hand on the carved door. "A what?"

"A blight. It's festering in the south. That's what they said."

Gertie turned and cocked her head as if listening. "That's unusual."

"It's not the first time they told me."

Gertie put the bucket down with a heavy thump. "When?"

"Last night. It was one of the things they told me last night."

Gerties face clouded and one hand found her lips. The digits quivered.

"What does it mean?" Tanyth asked.

Gertie took a deep breath and let it out, her fingers swiping at her eyes. "I was listening last night. The trees didn't say anything to me."

"But what does it mean?"

"It means we have work to do."

"Work?"

"What? You thought being hermits meant we sit around drinkin' cider and milkin' goats?"

"What can two old ladies do?"

"Woman, get a grip. You walked ten thousand miles gettin' here. You killed a half dozen men who threatened you and yours along the way. You saved a ship and a crew from a bomb and blew away a storm with a prayer. You changed the ocean's currents and nearly killed yourself doin' it so you could be here. Now the Lady is tellin' us there's a problem. Don't ya think those things might all be related? Or do you think you're just here to write a book about herbs?"

Tanyth felt her jaw drop as Gertie—frail, funny, rock-studying Gertie—flayed her with her tongue.

"I'll just reload my pack," Tanyth said.

Gertie grinned. "Make sure you take some tea, dear. I'll grab some traveling food from the cold room and be right back."

Chapter 26
Going South

The sun had barely reached noon when a very determined Gertie Pinecrest led Tanyth Fairport out of the cottage. She'd come back from the cold room with a rucksack a quarter full of food, a canteen strapped to the side. Gertie folded the covers on her cot in on themselves and then rolled it from the foot. She'd grabbed an extra blanket from a cupboard and an oilcloth to wrap it all in, lashing the bundle together with some braided twine. She tossed some clothes and a length of rope in on top and pulled a poncho from another cupboard. Last she all but stirred the fire out of existence, leaving only a few coals resting harmlessly at the back of the hearth.

Tanyth lashed her own bedroll to the bottom of her pack and shrugged into her coat.

"Ready?" Gertie asked.

"You sure you should be traipsin' around the forest?"

"What? You think I'm too old?"

"No." Tanyth bit her tongue against the lie. "Who's gonna guard the library?"

"The Lord and Lady know it's there. Nothin'll happen to it." Gertie pulled the cottage door open. "Now, you ready?"

Tanyth grabbed her wide-brimmed hat from the peg and clapped it on her head before shrugging into the familiar weight of her pack. "Let's go."

Gertie led the way out into the sunshine. Tanyth grabbed her staff as she followed.

"Where we going?" Gertie asked as she pulled the door closed behind them.

"South."

Gertie turned a raised eyebrow. "Got anything more than 'south'? There's a lot of south out there."

"A notch in the coast."

"What? Like a bay?"

"How am I supposed to know? Yesterday this time I thought listening to the trees was a joke. All I got is a notch in the coast somewhere south."

Gertie snickered. "All right, dearie. Jes' askin'." She made sure the latch seated firmly by pushing on the door and then turned away.

"You're just gonna walk off and leave it?"

"Yep." Gertie started off on the trail around the ridge. "Come on, dearie. I've left that place any number of times and the worst that ever happened is I came back and found a big pile of goat turds on the step."

Tanyth shrugged and found she had to stretch her stride to catch up with Gertie. "They didn't like bein' left?"

"He thought it was a big joke."

"Goats have a sense of humor?"

"Dearie, if I looked like a goat, I'd really want a sense of humor, wouldn't you?"

Tanyth laughed and the two of them soon found their stride, wasting no more breath on talking.

By late afternoon they'd walked almost the length of the valley, passing the trail where Penny and Rebecca had gone to the east and the western path that Nick and Sarah had taken. The sulfur smell and bubbling ponds gave way to the spicy scent of spruce and the burble of icy snow-melt brooks. The forest seemed to close against them as they drew near. Rocky ground gave way to weeds in the scrabble and soon they found themselves in the cool, dark forest, walking almost silently between thick stands of spruce.

"How you holdin' up?" Gertie asked, a faint dew of perspiration on her brow and a spring in her step.

"I'm fine, but we should find a camp before it gets full dark. I don't fancy flailin' around in the woods in the dark."

"Half hour or so and we'll come to a pond. There's a campsite there." Gertie said.

Tanyth measured the sun's position through the trees and nodded.

Gertie led the way and, as promised, they came to a clearing in the trees. Cattails and bulrushes closed in one side, but the other sported a small sand beach and a stone fire ring between a pair of logs.

"Kinda exposed, ain't it?" Tanyth asked.

"If you count twenty miles of spruce trees all around you, yeah, I suppose." Gertie said. "Let's get some firewood and see if we can find something for dinner, shall we?"

Tanyth eyed the sky, already turning a rosy evening shade overhead. At least there were no clouds at the moment. She dumped her pack and staff beside one of the logs and set out to find some firewood. An old blow-down nearby provided all the wood she wanted, so she was soon back with a full armload.

Gertie came from the other direction with more, and they dumped their piles together beside the fire ring. "That'll get us started, I think," Gertie said. "Would you get it going? Squeek here doesn't like fire and it makes it tough not bein' able to see the sparks."

"How do you do it at the cottage?" Tanyth asked, more from idle curiosity than anything.

"Matches."

Tanyth looked up from stripping some soft, dry bark to see Gertie grinning down at her. "That was rather dumb, wasn't it?"

"Not really, dearie. You're doin' good for bein' tossed into the ragin' sea and bein' asked to serve tea instead of swim."

Tanyth coughed out a laugh as she struck the flint and steel into the nest of bark and grass. It caught, and by the time she had a small fire built, Gertie was back with another armload of wood. Tanyth pulled the kettle out of her pack and half filled it with water, setting it on one of the ring-rocks to begin warming.

Gertie pulled her own pack over, unrolled the oilcloth on the ground and spread out her bedroll on it, using the spare blanket as a pillow. "There, that'll be fine for tonight, I think."

Tanyth glanced upward again. "If it don't rain."

"Oh, it'll be a fine night. No rain. No snow."

"You sound pretty sure," Tanyth couldn't help but smile at the cheerful, smiling face across the fire from her.

Gertie held up her hands and flexed her fingers slightly. "My bones say there'll be no storm. They haven't been wrong in ten winters."

Tanyth shrugged and started stripping away the rocks and twigs from where she wanted to lay her bedroll. "What'll we do for dinner?"

"I thought you'd never ask." Gertie rummaged in her pack and pulled out a slab of bread, about a half pound of cheese, and a whole smoked trout wrapped in muslin.

"What? No cider?" Tanyth asked with a grin.

"After last night, do you really think that would be wise?" Gertie responded with a grin of her own.

Tanyth shrugged. "Prob'ly not."

Gertie pulled a tin cup from her pack and pulled the plug from her canteen. She poured the cup about half full and then offered the canteen to Tanyth.

"I got water," Tanyth said. "We'll have tea soon."

"I know, but I thought you wanted cider."

Tanyth's laugh echoed off the trees across the water and startled a pair of wading birds out of the reeds. She held out her cup and let Gertie slosh it half full of cider. She placed it by the fire and finished laying out her bedroll before sitting cross-legged on it and raising her cup in a toast. "You really know how to travel," she said.

"This is just the first night. Wait'll we been on the trail a while," Gertie said.

"Is that good or bad?" Tanyth asked, the heady scent of apple swirling through her nose.

"Yeah. Prob'ly some of each." Gertie took a sip of cider and leaned back against the log. "I don't know how far south we have to go before we find out what's happenin'. Then we'll need to figure out how to deal with it."

"You think it's bad?"

"Oh, it's bad. I just don't know if it's somethin' we can fix." She sighed and tipped her cup all the way up to get the last drops out of it. "No sense borrowing trouble today when we can get a full measure for free tomorrow."

Tanyth nodded and pulled the boiling kettle away from the fire. She tossed a few pinches of tea into the water and slipped it back toward the coals to keep warm. The tart bite of cider in her mouth left her wanting more but the tea would do, and water after that. Tomorrow promised to be a full day.

A breeze sighed through the tree tops and Tanyth strained to hear something, anything.

Gertie smiled at her across the tiny fire. "Sometimes, the trees are just trees. Like most gossips, they don't necessarily talk to ya when you like and gen'rally don't shut up when you don't."

Stars started blinking in the deepening dark above them, the spruces no more than dark shadows against the sky. White peaks gleamed to the north, still close enough and tall enough that the tallest spruces couldn't block them from peeking into the camp.

Somewhere in the distance an owl's hoot broke the stillness. A quiet splash from the pond told of a frog seeking shelter in the water. The fire snapped occasionally while Gertie speared chunks of bread smeared with the sweet goat cheese on long sticks. She handed one to Tanyth who fed their fire with one hand, toasting her bread with the other until the cheese bubbled a little.

They didn't speak. There was no need.

When the moon began sneaking above the treetops, the two women slipped out of their boots and crawled into their bedrolls. As her last waking act, Tanyth filled her small pot with fresh water and a measure of oatmeal and salt before pushing it close to the coals. She lay down and, propping her head on an arm, snuggled into the familiar bedroll with the musky scent of last year's spruce needles in her nose.

☽○☾

The moon sailed low in the sky but she knew it would soon give her more light than she needed to find food. She hooted once into the night to warn others away from her hunting ground. There would be mice to eat and perhaps voles with their pointed noses. The river gleamed in the moonlight as it raced toward the big water only to fall over the edge and drop down, down into the bay below. The distance muted the sound of its roaring to a quiet background hush, no louder than the burbling of a small brook. Certainly no obstacle to hearing a mouse in the weeds.

The stench of humans wafted on an updraft from below. It made her shift her feet and turn away from the wind. They were no threat, down below in their holes. She'd seen them as she soared above, riding the updrafts and searching the rocky cliffs for food. The seabirds did not appreciate her presence and soon mobbed her back into the forest, but she'd seen the humans.

A mouse rattled two stalks of dried grass almost under her feet and she dropped on it. Its final breath was a squeak that lost itself in the winds that funneled up the deep cut that led to the gleaming, open sea beyond. The mouse made a tasty morsel that promised a good night of hunting. She leaped into the sky and circled back to her perch at the top of a wind-blasted pine.

The moon continued its climb into the sky and she watched the shadows below, listening for the sound of her next meal.

☽○☾

Tanyth woke with her heart racing. People should not be there. A blight festering, the trees had said. The pungent smell of death seemed to cling to her nose, a memory gift from the owl. She sat up long enough to thrust another stick into the coals and watch the red sparks rise up to dance with the white ones above. The nearly full moon gleamed on the pond and, somewhere to the south, men died.

She pulled the bedroll up to her chin and curled up on her side. She closed her eyes once more and did her best to ignore the gossipy trees.

Chapter 27
Into The Woods

The smell of smoke woke her and she opened her eyes to see Gertie, her bedding draped over her shoulders, feeding the fire. A watery dawn sky hovered just above the tree tops. "Morning."

"Yes, dearie. It is. The trees have been full of news this morning, but nothing about whatever's going on to the south."

Tanyth sat up and pulled her boots on. "I know what's happening in the south, but if I don't find a bush right now, I'll be walkin' with wet pants all day."

Gertie gave a girlish giggle. "I used that one over there." She nodded her head at a nearby stand of juniper bushes.

Tanyth didn't take long and soon rejoined her at the fire. "There's some kinda dig goin' on down there. A tunnel under the waterfall, if I'm any judge."

Gertie raised her eyebrows. "A dig?"

"That's what it looked like." She pulled the pot away from the fire with a stick and popped the lid open. The oatmeal inside steamed a bit in the chill morning air, wafting the scent of nutty grain to mingle with the wood smoke. "A tunnel or something dug into the cliff face."

"You had a dream?"

Tanyth nodded. "An owl I met on the way out from Northport. She wasn't happy where there were so many people, so she headed south. Went all the way to the coast, apparently."

"What do you mean, so many people?" Gertie asked, accepting a portion of the oatmeal in her travel bowl.

"We left Northport without the garrison commandant's

permission. A squad of troopers showed up on our trail. The owl saw them and decided she didn't like 'em."

"How long ago was that?"

Tanyth blinked and tried to count the nights on her fingers. "I'm not sure. Time's been kinda strange lately. Maybe five or six days. I don't really know for sure."

"They didn't follow you, though?"

"After we dropped into Black Rock Canyon, we never saw them again. Penny thought they may have turned south and followed the rim of the canyon on a patrol or somethin'."

"Why would they do that?" Gertie asked. "The garrison's only for local support, not patrollin' out here in the hinterlands."

"No idea, but maybe they was looking for some sign of why a dead guy showed up on the road into town."

Gertie snorted. "That's a pretty common thing, I'm sad to say."

"Not when the corpse was supposed to be lost at sea months before."

Gertie put her spoon down in her bowl and sat up straight. "Lost at sea?"

"Yeah. His ship was reported lost at sea with all hands a few days before Rebecca and I got to Kleesport. That was days before the Call. The ship was supposed to be headed east and south, not north. Anyway, weeks later, the same guy shows up as a fresh corpse on the road into Northport."

Gertie's head started bobbing forward and back. "Of course. Lost at sea."

"Why do you say it like that?"

"The trees have been talkin' about ships lost at sea. I didn't get it before. They're not always the sharpest splinters in the woodpile, trees. I think the winds have something to do with keeping them confused and stirred up."

Tanyth laughed in spite of herself.

Gertie grinned back at her. "Yeah. That sounded wrong, didn't it?"

"I see why we'll need to live alone. Anybody hearin' us talk like this would think we'd gone mad."

"True, but what if they're not lost at sea?"

"Who?"

"The ships. What if some of them actually come ashore?"

"All right." Tanyth closed her eyes. Something lurked on the edge of her memory. "Insurance."

"Insurance?"

"Yeah. Captain Groves kept talkin' about the insurance company sinkin' ships that didn't have insurance to convince more shippers to buy it."

"Well, that explains some of them, but what's that got to do with a hole in the cliff down south?"

"I don't know," Tanyth said. "But one of the crew also said that some of the ships weren't actually sunk but beached somewhere and the cargo stolen. Then the insurance companies would sell the stolen goods for a little extra profit."

Gertie shook her head. "That makes no sense. What about the crews? The ships?"

"Well, they assumed the crew got a long walk off a short pier somewhere, with rocks for water wings." Tanyth stared into the fire. "What if they didn't?"

"You think they're in that hole in the cliff?"

"It would make sense. They'd have to be somewhere and that bay looked pretty remote."

"There's just straight cliff down to the water," Gertie said. "I saw it once. Winters ago now, but there's no place to land. Really. It goes straight down. That's why that bay never got developed. No way up to the top of the cliffs and no way to land at the foot, even if there was."

"You saw it yourself?"

"Yeah. From the top. I took a trip down one summer to see the waterfall. It's really only a couple of days from the valley. Maybe three."

"What about in winter?"

"What about in winter?" Gertie asked.

"I assume it freezes over?"

"All the other bays do, but what good is that?"

"Something the garrison commandant said about Rebecca's father bein' in town until the very last minute. He had to take a sledge out to the ice dock."

Gertie took a spoon full of the oatmeal and then nodded.

"Yeah, that's pretty common in the fall. Stretches the season a bit."

"What if they built an ice dock there? At the bay?"

Gertie frowned. "From the water side?"

"Yeah."

"It'd be dangerous. You can't just sail a ship up to the edge of the ice."

"No, but you could row a small boat."

"Well, sure, but why?"

"If you had an ice dock floating in the open ocean, put a rope on it and tow it to the edge of the ice with a small boat. Install it on the ice and then you can land whatever you want. Supplies, men, stolen merchandise."

Gertie gasped. "Then just use sledges to drag it up the bay."

"Yeah. And use the ice as a beach in the winter. Carve a cave out of the rock down there and you've got a place to land in the summer. Use the tailings from the dig to build up the landing area."

"That's a lot of work for a little stolen property, isn't it?" Gertie asked.

Tanyth frowned. "Yeah, seems like there should be an easier way."

Gertie finished the oatmeal in her bowl and washed it down with a swig of cooling tea. "We'll just have to go take a look, won't we?"

Tanyth looked up at the rapidly brightening sky. "Yeah. I guess we will."

Gertie rolled up bedding while Tanyth rinsed out their dishes in the pond. By the time the sun began shining through the treetops to the east, they'd put a mile behind them.

"One thing bothers me a bit," Tanyth said after a while.

"What's that?"

"What'll we do when we get there?"

Gertie smiled at her over a shoulder. "We'll just have to figger that out when we get there, won't we?"

"Yeah. S'pose so." Tanyth revisited the dream in her mind. The details felt faded and worn, but one thing remained crystal clear. The cave held a lot of men. Whoever ran that operation wouldn't be thrilled by having two meddling busybodies sticking their noses in.

They walked in silence for most of the morning. Just before noon they broke out of the spruces and into an enormous stand of oak and maple. After the closed-in spruce trees, the space between the boles and the clear understory made Tanyth's shoulders itch from the exposure.

A boggy swale at the foot of a blowdown made Gertie stop. "Fiddlehead greens," she said, pointing at the tightly curled baby ferns. "We should stop on the way back and pick some, don't ya think?"

Tanyth huffed a short laugh. "Assumin' we get to come back this way."

Gertie turned her face toward Tanyth, Squeek's tiny black eyes shining like polished onyx in the dappled light from the canopy. "This is the path. Why wouldn't we?"

Tanyth shook her head. "If those people..." She paused and started again. "If they're willin' to hijack ships, kidnap crews, and steal the cargoes, then these pirates aren't gonna quibble over tossin' a couple of old ladies into the drink to keep 'em quiet."

Gertie's head bobbed up and down every so slowly. "Then if they catch us, we'll wanna make sure they keep thinkin' of us as a couple of old ladies, won't we."

Tanyth laughed again and nodded. "Well, old lady, let's get our poor arthritic bones movin'. It's almost noon and I need a sit down and a cuppa tea before we go much farther."

"I like that idea, myself," Gertie said and turned her steps south once more. "This time tomorrow we'll be at the coast."

"That's fast."

"It's not all that far and we're makin' good time."

"I thought you said two or three days."

"Tomorrow would be two days and a bit. It'll take longer goin' back because we'll wanna harvest some of those fiddleheads, and I've seen a bushel of purslane as we've been walkin'."

"Greens?"

"Don't look at me like that. You're the one who brought the subject up."

"Sorry. It just struck me funny."

"You're doing good, dearie. I remember my first week up here and I was a wreck. Course, I didn't have your advantages of travel and all. I just came in from Northport."

Tanyth shook her head and kept walking.

Above her a faint breeze sighed through the spring leaves but the trees offered nothing to dampen Tanyth's anxiety.

Chapter 28
More Lessons

They made camp that night in the rock and mud-caked roots of a blown-down oak. A narrow brook blubbed and chattered nearby. Even before they got their own fire started, Tanyth smelled the tang of smoke and humans drifting in the breeze.

"Sure we should be lightin' a fire this close?" she asked.

"Dearie, you worry enough for both of us." Gertie's voice carried the first hint of exasperation that Tanyth had heard from her during the whole journey.

"Well, if we can smell their fires..."

Gertie turned her face up toward Tanyth's. "We can smell theirs because the wind's onshore and blowin' it into our faces. They're still half, three-quarters of a day south. They're not gonna smell anythin' over the stench they're makin' themselves."

Tanyth accepted the old woman's assurances, but continued to scan the trees around them until the deepening dusk made moving shadows of solid wood.

"You gonna make tea?" Gertie asked.

"What?"

Gertie pointed a stick at the kettle bubbling away in the fire pit, loose drops hissing and sizzling as they escaped onto the hot coals. "Tea?"

"Oh, yeah." Tanyth tossed some leaves into the pot and focused on getting the sticks and twigs out from under her bedroll. She jumped a little when Gertie's hand reached out of the dimness with a piece of bread wrapped around a hunk of sausage.

"That'd be better warmed over the fire, but I'm too hungry to wait," Gertie said, her quiet voice barely louder than the snapping flames in their tiny fire.

Tanyth took the food and settled herself. "Sorry. I been a bit nerved up."

"Trust the All-Mother, dearie. She's stood by me all this time. And you, too, if you think about it."

Tanyth took a bite of the dry, chewy bread and nodded. "Yeah. All true."

A gust of evening wind rattled through the branches over their heads and Tanyth cocked an ear, trying to hear.

"Trees are terrible gossips," Gertie said.

"Did they speak to you?"

"No." She bit off the word and spit it out. "That's what makes 'em terrible. Like I said before, they only speak when you'd just as soon they shut up and seems like they never talk when you need 'em to." She threw a small stick into the fire. "Where's your owl? She might have a better view."

Tanyth shrugged. "Dunno. Could be anywhere. Including back at Black Rock Canyon."

Gertie shook her head and signed. "Not what I meant. See if you can get an image from her. You know. Like you did with the sparrow hawk back at the cottage."

"But I knew where the sparrow hawk was."

"I'll grant you that, but just close your eyes and try. Humor an old lady, for pity's sake."

Tanyth sighed and closed her eyes. "You're gonna play that old lady card once too often," she muttered.

Beside her in the dimness, Gertie chuckled softly. "You started it, dearie. Don't blame me."

Tanyth grinned in the dark. She had the right of it. "Hush. I'm tryin' to concentrate."

Gertie tsked once but didn't speak.

Tanyth stilled her breathing and tried to focus on the feeling of the owl. She drew the memories of her dreams close and pushed herself out, seeking the feisty bird. After several long moments, she sighed and opened her eyes. "I don't have the knack of it yet."

Gertie patted her knee. "You'll get there, dearie. Just you

wait."

Tanyth poured the tea and Gertie shared out another bit of the dried sausage and bread.

"How much of that did you bring, anyway?" Tanyth asked.

"Enough sausage for a few days. The bread'll be gone tomorrow. How much tea we got?"

Tanyth grinned in the dark. "Enough to go and get back and a couple of weeks besides."

"That's all?" The disappointment was clear in Gertie's voice.

"I left some back at the cottage. I thought we'd be traveling light and home again soon."

"As we shall, dearie. You wait and see."

They sipped tea and nibbled their meal, quiet as the mouse in Gertie's hair.

"How's Squeek holdin' up?" Tanyth asked.

"Squeek?"

"Your eyes. How's he holding up? Don't they trade off when you're at the cottage?"

"Oh, yeah. They do. This isn't my Squeek." She waved a hand toward her head. "She's a lovely little forest mouse that joined us this morning."

"You collectin' them as we go?"

Gertie giggled. "I told ya the li'l buggers like me. There's mice everywhere. Surprising what you can see if you know where to look."

"So, why'd you have me lookin' for my owl if you can look with mice?"

"Just to see if you could do it yet."

"Did the mice see anything?"

"Nobody within half a mile of us here." Gertie finished her tea and dug out her canteen. "Little cider for dessert?"

Tanyth drained her own cup and held it out. "Just a splash. Maybe the trees'll be more talkative."

Gertie's smile gleamed in the firelight.

They sat quietly, sipping around the fire as the night wore on. Eventually Gertie rolled into her blanket with a mumbled "G'night."

Tanyth watched the moon through the canopy of new

The Hermit Of Lammas Wood

leaves. The dappled light seemed to fill the forest around them. In moonlight, Tanyth's night vision was enough to fill in some of the gaps. A doe and fawn crossed through the forest downwind of them, silently gliding from moonlit patch to moonlit patch. They disappeared into the undergrowth with no more noise than Gertie's quiet snores.

Above her the trees sighed in the night wind. Tanyth stiffened as they whispered. *Two young women rest comfortably in camp. Several men camp near the coast a day west of the town.* Far away a raven cawed and Tanyth couldn't tell if it was something she heard or a whisper on the wind.

She sighed and rolled into her own blankets, pushing the pot of oatmeal closer to the faint coals. At least they'd have a warm breakfast before they faced whatever the new day brought them.

☽○☾

The cold moonlight splashed across the river and over the field. A faint breeze bobbed last year's seed heads, casting shadows that made hunting difficult. She dropped from her perch and soared a few feet above the grasses, her ears focused on finding a rustling that feet made. The stench from the humans reached her clearly. In her focus on the hunt, she sailed over the cliff's edge and saw the gleaming ocean far, far below. A red glow came from the cave and illuminated the falling water.

A movement on the cliff's edge made her wheel and soar back over land. Two men huddled in a crude nest at the top of the dropoff. Her eyes picked out a line of them around the end of the bay. No wonder the hunting was so bad.

One of the men turned to look up at her, his pale skin shining in the moonlight. She flexed her wings and drove herself almost down to the grasses and skimmed them silently until she was able to glide into the forest yards away from where the men waited and watched.

☽○☾

Tanyth cracked an eyelid and considered the fire. It wasn't low enough to feed or high enough to be seen. With a sigh she rolled over and pulled her blankets up around her ears. "Damn fool bird," she muttered.

Chapter 29
Intruders

Morning crackled with cold. Tanyth's breath blew foggy clouds into the still air. She found a single glowing coal in the bottom of their fire pit and blew a few small flames to life with the help of a twist of dried grass.

"Yer bones didn't hurt last night?" she asked.

Gertie shook her head, blinking her eyes. "They hurt this mornin'. Weather's comin'."

"Weather's here. What's comin' next?"

"Hang on, dearie. My mousies haven't caught up with me yet." Gertie put her arm down and a gray streak zipped out of the leaf litter and around her shoulder. "There we go." She turned her head back and forth, scanning the area.

"I'll have some heat under the tea in a bit," Tanyth said by way of apology.

Gertie fought her way to a full seated position, her bedding draped around her shoulders. "That would be lovely. And your oatmeal. That makes mornin's so much better. You been doin' that for a while."

Tanyth nodded and poked the fire a little more. "Travel rations are good and all, but they get old. Oatmeal's light so I can carry a lot of it in my pack. Only need a little bit to make a full meal that sticks with me. Dependin' on the season I can find apples or berries to put in it. Not like I have to carry a lot of extra with me."

"Cuts down on the amount of time you have to deal with strangers."

Tanyth raised a shoulder in a half shrug. "Yeah. That,

too."

The oatmeal began to bubble so Tanyth pulled the pot away from the fire and began dishing it up.

"I saw the owl last night," she said, not looking at Gertie.

"In a dream?"

"Yeah. She's ahead of us, right on the coast. At least she was."

"What happened?"

"Too crowded for her. Too many people scarin' away her meals."

Gertie spooned the warm mush into her mouth, licking the spoon with each bite. "What d'ya put in this to make it so tasty?"

"Nuthin'. It's just oats, water, and a pinch of salt."

"Hmm. Tonight, let's make it with cider." Gertie grinned. "There's some left, I think."

"All right."

"So why don't you tell me what has you so upset this mornin'." Gertie took another spoonful of oatmeal and kept her face down as if looking into her bowl.

Tanyth saw the bright eyes of the mouse watching her and chuckled a little. "They got men guarding the whole upper edge of the cliff. Two of 'em in little lookout stations all around the top."

"That's good," Gertie said. "That'll make things a lot easier."

The old woman's quiet words interrupted Tanyth's report. "How d'ya figger that?"

"They must have a way up and down." Gertie scraped the last of the oatmeal from the bowl and placed it on the ground in front of her.

"What?"

"If they got lookouts on the top of the cliff, they must have some way for a body to get from the top to the bottom and back again." Gertie shrugged. "They certainly didn't fly."

Tanyth finished her oatmeal in silence, digesting the observation.

"Trees say Penny and Rebecca are almost back to town," Gertie said.

"Yeah, I heard that last night. Who're the men coming west?"

Gertie shook her head. "What men?"

"Trees also said a group of men camped along the shore a day west of Northport."

Gertie's smile lit up the campsite. "They like you."

"Who are they? How do you know they like me?"

Gertie waved her hands in the air. "No, no, dearie. Not the men. The trees. They like you. They tell you things they won't tell me."

"How does that work, exactly?"

Gertie picked up her tea and stuck her nose in the cup before answering. "I wish I knew. Gossipy things. Would be handy to be able to rely on them for findin' stuff out. Sometimes it works. Sometimes it don't. Sometimes who's doin' the listenin' hears nothin'. Sometimes hears more than they care to know." She huffed a final indignant huff and took another pull of her tea.

Tanyth blinked, trying to sort out the threads of whatever tapestry the old woman wove. "So you don't know who they are?"

"I didn't say that. I said the trees like you."

"Who are they?"

"Richard Marong and a bunch of garrison soldiers unless I'm very much mistaken."

"Mice tell you that?"

"No, Miss Tree Listener. The mice didn't tell me that." She sipped her tea. "I've a gull in the harbor. She saw the *Sea Rover* sail into port day before yesterday."

"You can see that far away?"

Gertie sipped her tea and muttered something into the cup.

"Sorry, Gertie. What was that?"

Gertie's lips twisted in a sideways grimace. "Only when I'm asleep."

Tanyth's quiet laughter brightened the chill air.

"Nothin' to be laughin' about. That's a long way to read anything, let alone somethin' as scattered in the head as a seagull."

"No, indeed," Tanyth said, struggling to control her mirth. "That's why you have me practice, I'm sure."

Gertie's face brightened. "Just so, just so. Untrained like you are, why, who knows what skills you might have and how much talent."

Tanyth chuckled all the way through clean-up, and even Gertie giggled once or twice.

When they'd finished packing away their camp and kicked soil over the fire, Gertie started off to the south once more. "We'll be there by midafternoon, I suspect," she said. "Then we'll see what we see."

For a lark, Tanyth closed her eyes and reached out for her owl.

☽O☾

The sun was too bright and the air too cold. The spoils of a good night's hunt filled her belly and she hooted in consternation at being awakened at such an hour. She swiveled her head and scanned the surrounding forest. Nothing looked amiss.

She shifted her weight, testing the branch with her talons, before puffing up her feathers to protect her from the cold and tucked her head under a wing to sleep until dark.

☽O☾

Tanyth tripped on a root and saved herself from a nasty fall only by the grace of a strong grip on her walking staff.

Gertie marched on a dozen paces ahead of her.

Tanyth drew in a deep breath and stepped along sharply to catch up to the old woman. As she closed the gap, Gertie turned to smile back over a shoulder.

"Told ya," she said.

At midmorning, Gertie called a halt. "I need to put this pack down for a minute, I'm afraid."

"Are you all right?"

"Oh, yes. Quite. Just want to sit a bit here and catch my breath. The mice seem a bit restive and I'm not sure the cause." Gertie slipped her pack from her shoulders and plunked it down beside an ancient maple. In a moment she'd joined it on the ground and settled herself among the roots.

Tanyth followed suit and settled against a sturdy oak a few feet away.

"If you can find a bird, dearie? There might be somethin' to see."

Tanyth shrugged and closed her eyes, slipping into the space where sometimes she could see through other eyes. As she sat there, the world slipped away and she became aware of the tree behind her. Its roots anchored it to the soil and rock, the bones of the earth providing a firm foundation. The wood was merely arms reaching into the air. The trunk held tiny rivers carrying the blood of the earth high into the sky and through it all pulsed the fire of life.

☽○☾

Heavy steps rustled last year's leaves and the stink of man sent panicky thrills through her body. She froze, belly to ground and ears down. Her mottled brown coat still winter white on her belly but hidden as long as she remained still. He pushed through the undergrowth without stopping. In a moment he was far enough away that she could make a break for the nearest hole. She stayed frozen for several moments longer. Another man followed the first at some distance—moving slower, quieter.

☽○☾

"Somebody's comin'," Tanyth said.

"Mice say a couple of 'em," Gertie said, heaving herself up off the ground.

Tanyth scrambled to her feet and took up her staff, grinding the iron foot into the leaf litter and soil. She felt the comforting strength of the trees around her and turned to focus on the sound of crunching leaves.

A shadow detached itself from the backdrop of trees and shrubs and lumbered toward them. As he drew nearer, he started growling. Under other circumstances it might have been disconcerting but on the whole, Tanyth had to choke back a laugh. He raised his arms, hands curled into crude claws. When he was only a few yards away, she realized that his clothing—a dark green work shirt and heavy black trousers—were smeared with mud and dirt. Leaves stuck out of his greasy tufts of hair and twigs festooned a bushy beard. He stopped a few feet away and uttered a ridiculous approximation of a roar.

The Hermit Of Lammas Wood

Gertie chuckled. "And what are you supposed ta be? A bear?"

The man's eyes blinked a few times and he brandished one arm as if clawing the air. "Who dares decorate my forest?" he shouted.

Tanyth looked to Gertie who shrugged in return.

"You! Woman!" the man pointed at Tanyth. "Why come you to the Lammas Wood?"

"Seemed a nice day for a walk." She looked to Gertie again. "Ain't that right, Gert?"

"Oh, aye. Chilly start but I must say it got my blood movin'–"

"Silence!" he roared again. "These woods are mine. You will be wise to leave them. Now!"

"'Zat so?" Gertie said. "And who might you be when you're at home and not scragglin' through the forest, then?"

The man raised his arms again and took a few steps forward, his face screwed into what he might have considered a most threatening scowl. "I am the hermit of Lammas Wood. Leave now or suffer my rats."

"Suffer your rats?" Gertie asked. "Are they decoratin' your forest somewhere nearby?"

"Where's your pal?" Tanyth asked. "You got an apprentice lurkin' in the bushes back there?"

A rustling in the undergrowth to their right resolved into an archer, longbow strung and arrow nocked but not yet aimed at them. "Who, me?" he asked.

"Ah, there he is," Gertie said. "Good, now maybe we can get to the bottom of this."

"Lady, the only thing you're getting to the bottom of is a real tall cliff if'n you don't turn tail and git."

"You picked him to impersonate the hermit because he's big and scary lookin'?" Gertie asked jerking a thumb at the big man with his arms still in the air.

The big man roared again—somewhat half-heartedly to Tanyth's thinking.

"Oh, that's quite enough now. Stop being silly," Gertie said. "Put your arms down. They must be tirin' to hold up like that."

With a glance at his companion, he lowered his arms slowly to his sides.

"There, now, I know you're not the hermit, so who are you, exactly?" Gertie asked.

The big man started to speak but the archer interrupted him. "Shut it. We're not here to have tea. You're trespassin' and you're just leavin'."

Gertie made a show of looking around the forest, even though Tanyth knew she was blind as two bats in a bag. "Seems to me this is Lammas Wood, ain't it? King's land unless you've a warrant by his hand, and I ain't heard anybody been granted a warrant since Northport."

The archer raised his bow and drew down. The wicked broadhead gleamed in the late morning sun. "Here's my warrant, lady. You and your traveling biddy here turn your behinds around and git or I'll deliver it in person."

"Oh, goodness. Gettin' so a body can't take a stroll in peace." She turned to the burly man, now shifting his weight back and forth and shuffling his feet. "If you're gonna keep doin' that, at least get it right."

"What?"

"You've got a couple of the words wrong. You should say, 'Who dares desecrate my forest?' not 'decorate'," she said.

"Lady knows we ain't much decoration, come to that," Tanyth said.

"Desecrate?" the man asked.

"Yes. Say the whole thing so you can get the feel of it," Gertie said.

"Who dares des—dessicate—."

"Des-e-crate," Gertie said. "Crate, like a box."

"Des-e-crate," the man repeated.

"Very good. Now in a sentence?"

"Who dares desecrate my forest?" the man said.

"Much better. Don't you think that's better, Tanyth?"

"Lady! Shut it or I'll shut it for ya." A most alarming blotchy red covered the archer's face.

"I'm jus' tryin' to help. If you're gonna chase people off, it would help if you at least used the right threats and all."

"What part of 'arrow through the ribs' is gettin' lost under that gray hair?" he asked.

"Arrow? What arrow?" Gertie asked.

"He's got a bow, Gertie. Drawn with an arrow pointin' roughly in your direction," Tanyth said, feeling a stirring in the ground under her feet. "I'm pretty sure he'd miss if he actually loosed it, but just so ya know."

"What, is she blind?" the archer asked.

"Oh, yeah. Quite blind. Cataracts in both eyes. You can see 'em in the right light," Tanyth said.

The archer frowned in concentration and the point of his arrow dropped a bit.

"How'd she know I had me hands up, then?" the burly man asked.

"Oh, you were payin' attention," Gertie said and clapped her hands in girlish delight.

"She has help seein'," Tanyth said.

"What? Are you her eyes or somepin'?" the man asked.

"Naw. She has a mouse who sees for her."

"A mouse? Really? Where?" the man asked.

Gertie lifted a hand and pushed aside the white hair. "Here. You see her?"

A small brownish shape reared up for a moment on Gertie's head.

"Well, I'll be. Malcolm? Did you see that? She's gotta mouse on her head!" The big man grinned in apparent delight and took a step closer. "You have her there all the time?"

"For pity sake, Arnold. Shut up," the archer growled, his face turning even redder.

"Don't she crap in your hair?" Arnold asked.

Tanyth laughed, caught up in the moment. "I asked her the same thing."

"Last time," the archer said, arrow point rising again and his jaw clenching. "Get out."

Tanyth stepped into his line of fire, stabbing her staff deeper into the ground. "Or what?"

"Or else I put a yard of oak into each of you and leave you for the mice to eat."

The stirring under the ground grew. Tanyth felt it in her staff and focused her mind on the power of the trees around them. Time itself felt soft and stretchy. The light, a golden syrup falling around them. The litter around the archer's boots shifted slightly and pale roots crawled out of the ground and around his ankles while Tanyth stared into his dark eyes.

"Try it," she said.

The archer loosed, his fingers splaying wide behind the bow and the arrow spun toward her. A slight shift of her arm and her oak staff caught the broad head half a foot above her hand.

The big man coughed in surprise. "Did you see that, Malcolm?"

"Impossible," he said, his words a bare whisper, his eyes wide enough to show white all around.

"As impossible as that?" Tanyth asked and jerked her chin in the direction of his feet.

He looked down and twisted his hips. His feet didn't move. "What the—"

"Oaks. Strong roots, eh?" Gertie said. "Don't mess with oaks. Hard wood. Long memories. Terrible gossips." She turned to Tanyth. "Well, I suppose we should be goin' now, don't you?"

"Yeah. I'm rested," Tanyth said although her legs felt rubbery and weak.

Gertie hefted her pack up from the ground, shrugged into it, and turned away to retrace their steps. Tanyth stripped the arrow from her staff and dropped it into the leaf litter. A careless step as she picked up her pack resulted in a brittle cracking sound.

"Wait," the archer said, his voice a strangled gasp. "Wait. What about me?"

Gertie stopped. "What about you?"

"You can't just leave me here."

Gertie turned back to him. "You were gonna leave us here with a yard of oak, as I remember."

"Yeah, but not alive," the man said.

Gertie turned her face to Tanyth before looking back at the man. "What? You want us to kill you?"

The man turned a stricken gaze on them and reached for another arrow. He pulled out a snake that curled around his forearm and raised a fanged head as if to strike. The man screamed and shook his arm, casting the snake aside—and a broadhead arrow landed on the ground.

The big man took a small step forward. "Wait, please, mum," he said.

"Yes?" Gertie asked.

"Who are you, mum? How did you do that?"

Gertie smiled. "I'm the real hermit of Lammas Wood." She glanced at Tanyth. "At least for now."

The big man gulped audibly.

"And I'd appreciate if you two would stop decorating my forest," she smiled at him.

His gaze went back and forth between Gertie and Tanyth a couple of times and then he smiled back.

"Thank ya, mum. Soon's I get Malcolm loose, we'll get out of here. I promise."

"I believe you," Gertie said. "And if not you'll suffer my rats."

The archer huffed in exasperation. "It's wrath, you stupid bitch. Wrath!"

Gertie turned her face toward the man and the smile she gave him was not very friendly.

The leaves across the forest floor rustled as if being struck by rain. The sound grew louder by the second—the whisper becoming a roar—and in moments a grey brown carpet surged around them as thousands and thousands of rats filled the clearing. As suddenly as they came, they froze—ears and whiskers twitching, all facing the archer.

"You say it your way. I'll say it mine," Gertie said. She turned and led Tanyth back down the trail.

They heard the man shouting for quite a long time.

Chapter 30
Strategic Retreat

---※---

Gertie stopped when they got back to their campsite and tossed her pack on the ground. "Any tea left?"

"I was about to ask the same thing about the cider," Tanyth said but shucked out of her pack and knelt to the fire pit. Her peripheral vision wavered as if underwater but focusing helped keep her head clear. She scraped together some of the half-burned stubs and stacked up some dried grass and twigs left over from their earlier fire.

"I think there's cider left. Do you want some?"

Tanyth smiled and shook her head. "I'll wait for tea now."

"I'll go find some more wood."

"You think they'll follow us?" Tanyth called.

"Not right away. They'll go report first, prob'ly." Gertie's voice drifted out of the woods followed by the sharp crack of a breaking stick.

Tanyth fanned the small flame, feeding it twigs as it grew. She took a moment to fill the kettle with water and placed it ready for heating. By the time she was out of twigs, Gertie came back with an armful of sticks. She dropped them unceremoniously beside the ring of stones and plunked herself down across the fire from Tanyth.

Tanyth glanced up to find Gertie cross-legged, her hands folded in her lap, and the mouse leaning forward out of her hair. Staring. Inasmuch as a mouse stares, perhaps, but Tanyth still found the tiny obsidian eyes a bit unnerving.

"What?"

"Roots?" Gertie asked. "That's a neat trick."

The Hermit Of Lammas Wood

Tanyth blinked. "I thought you did that."

"Wasn't me."

"I don't know how to do it. Musta been you."

"You know how to blow out a storm, dearie?"

"Well, no, but—"

"You know how to slow time and catch an arrow on the fly with an inch and a half of oak?"

"Of course, not. I didn't do—"

"Yes, dearie. You did. And unless I miss my guess, you're gonna drop like a dead tree in a high wind unless we get something into you pretty quick."

"I'm fine."

"Yeah, and I'm twenty again. And a virgin." Gertie rummaged in her pack and pulled out the package of sausage. She carved off a chunk with her belt knife and passed it to Tanyth. "Chew on that. It'll help."

Tanyth took the bit of sausage and tucked it into her mouth. It didn't make her feel any better but gave her tongue something to do.

"Now, you wanna talk about roots?"

"Not partic'a'ly."

"Catching arrows on the fly?"

"It wasn't movin' that fast."

"Tell that to the archer."

Tanyth pushed the kettle closer to the fire and looked up to see Gertie smiling at her.

"You're goin' ta be fine, Tanyth Fairport. I'm so proud." A clear tear formed in the old woman's eye and escaped down her cheek.

"What ya mean, I'm gonna be fine?" She sat back on her haunches in alarm. "And why you gettin' all teary-eyed on me?"

Gertie took a deep breath and blew it out. She swiped the offending tear from her cheek with a fingertip and shook her head. "I was worried about ya, that's all. I'm...glad...now."

Tanyth frowned but couldn't find the edge to Gertie's words. "Great. T'riffic. I'm gonna be fine." She shook her head and gazed at the fire for a moment, judging it big enough for the tea kettle. "What about those men?" Her arm shot

194

out and pointed down the trail.

"We knew we'd run into somebody sooner or later," Gertie said. "We learned a great deal, didn't we?"

"What? What did we learn?" Tanyth asked.

"First, they're very well organized."

Tanyth scowled but nodded to grant the point. "We knew that before."

"How?"

"The guards at the top of the cliff. That don't happen without a lot of help and a good organization."

"Yep. And the roving guard?"

"Been enough folks around and they don't want others to get too close."

"Right. If we were the first ones to be around here, we'd have walked right out into the field without bein' stopped in the wood. What else?"

Tanyth lowered her gaze to the fire once more but she didn't see it. "They tried to scare us off before they brought out the killer."

"Zactly," Gertie said.

"Why? If they wanted to be sure, why didn't they just put shafts in us from hiding?"

"Same reason they have their hermit decoratin' the woods to begin with. Too many people just strollin' by. They can't kill 'em all without somebody noticin'."

"Who's out here?"

"You'd be surprised, dearie. Trappers. Lumberjacks. Even hunters."

"And now Richard Marong," Tanyth said, a new idea forming in her head.

"Yeah. Richard spent all season traipsing around the backwoods last summer. What's he lookin' for?"

"Ain't his daughter."

"You sound sure."

"He knew all along where Rebecca was."

"So he's lookin' for somethin' and he don't want the locals to know what," Gertie said.

"I think we figgered that much out."

"I think he's lookin' for this place."

The Hermit Of Lammas Wood

"Make sense," Tanyth said. "If he knew where it was, he'd sail to it. If he knew what it was, he'd sail to it."

"So what's he lookin' for?" Gertie asked again.

"If he don't know where and he don't know what...what's left?"

"Who's he work for?" Gertie asked.

Tanyth raised her shoulders in a shrug. "No idea. I got the impression he works for himself." She busied herself pulling the kettle out of the fire and tossing in some tea to steep.

"What's he do, though? What's his business?"

Tanyth sat back on her heels, trying to remember. "I don't know. Something with shipping. I don't know if he's a broker or an agent. He might own ships, as far as I know."

Gertie chewed her lower lip and stared at the tea kettle. "There's somethin' we're missin'."

Tanyth closed her eyes and tried to remember what Rebecca had said about her father. "He's somebody important in Kleesport. City council? Seems to me Rebecca said that once."

Gertie's head came up as if she were sniffing the air. "That's it."

"What's it?"

"City council in Kleesport. Buncha windy old crusts with delusions of importance."

"Tax grabby, if ya ask me," Tanyth said. "I got the impression they'd tax the pennies on a corpse's eyes."

"They would and do, but that's not the important part."

"What is?"

"They want the city to prosper. They tax ever'thin', it's true, but it's a cheap tax and it's enforced right across the board. If you make money, you give your share to the city."

"City pays the king," Tanyth said.

"Yeah, but the city gets their cut first and I'll bet ya they heard somebody's eatin' into that cut."

"How's that possible?"

Gertie scratched her chin and scowled into the fire. "Whatever they're doin', they're doin' it down there." She nodded her head toward the south.

"So all we gotta do is go tell Richard that his tax cheats

are in the cove and we're home free," Tanyth said.

"He's three days away. We're just a few hours."

"He has garrison troops of the King's Own with him."

"They may be in on it." Gertie shrugged. "Hard to keep this kinda thing secret on your own. Easier with somebody on the inside."

"You just wanna go find out what they're doin' down there," Tanyth said, her mouth twisted in a sideways grin.

"I know what they're doin', dearie. Trees told me. I just don't know who's all in it."

Tanyth felt a stab of pique. "Trees told ya what?"

"They're diggin' under the waterfall."

"Trees told you all that?" Tanyth asked.

"Don't get smart with me, young lady." Gertie's mouth twitched in what looked suspiciously like a grin.

"Look, Gertie. We can go harin' off down there and prob'ly run into more guards the closer we get, or we can do the smart thing and go get help. Richard Marong is only a couple days away. Less unless I miss my guess on the direction he's headin'."

Gertie chewed her lower lip some more and jerked her chin at the tea kettle. "I'm ready for some tea and perhaps a crust of bread to go with it. Lemme think."

Tanyth poured the tea and Gertie shared out some of their rapidly dwindling supply of bread.

"Can I ask you somethin'?" Tanyth asked. She stared down into the cup cradled in her hands.

"Of course, dearie. Ask away any time."

"What'd you do with the snake?"

"Illusion. I just made the arrow look like a snake. When he threw it down, it went back to lookin' like an arrow."

"Where'd all them rats come from?"

Gertie giggled. "They wasn't rats. Just another illusion. I don't think there's that many rats between here and Northport, and I'm sure I'd never be able to call that many even if there were."

Tanyth chuckled a bit, deep in her chest. "Whew. The thought of that many rats starin' at me was a bit nervous."

"Mice," Gertie said.

"What?"

"They was mice. I just made 'em look like rats."

Tanyth felt her eyes go round in surprise.

"What? I told ya. There's mice everywhere and the li'l buggers just like me."

Tanyth closed her eyes and bathed her face in the warm, aromatic steam from her tea. She tried not to think of thousands of mice swarming.

Chapter 31
A Mad Plan

Tanyth tossed the last of her tea back and looked across at Gertie. "You can't be serious."

"I'm not serious all the time," she said. "But this time? Yeah."

"You're sittin' there suggestin' we go down in that cave and see what's goin' on?"

"No, dearie. Don't exaggerate. I jes' think it'd be a good idea to know what we're lookin' at when we go try to tell somebody."

"Well, they got men with bows and arrows and a lot of pointy metal bits, for one."

Gertie stopped and cocked her head to one side. "You didn't mention pointy metal bits before. That nice man pretending to be me certainly had none."

"The archer did. Along with a quiver full of arrows."

"None of which did him any good." Gertie smirked into her cup. "And I bet he thinks twice before he pulls another arrow out of that bunch."

"That was just two of us against two of them, Gertie."

"Yes, we did have them out-numbered and I'm sure the next meetin' will be a tad more challengin'." She frowned into the cup and sighed before patting it dry with a bit of toweling and stuffing it into her pack. "Where's yer spirit of adventure? Leave it in your other trousers?" She winked and climbed to her feet, using her pack as a lever.

Tanyth sighed and got to her feet, kicking dirt over the small fire once more.

"You came to learn, didn't you?" Gertie asked, her voice low and her face turned up to Tanyth's.

For the first time Tanyth realized Gertie only came up to her nose. The gentle smile on her face and the laugh lines around the old, blind eyes asked nothing of her, offering only acceptance.

"That I did," Tanyth said. She pulled in a breath and blew it out her nose. "I just never thought these'd be the lessons."

"Well," Gertie said, bending down to pick up her pack. "You haven't thought you were goin' mad once in the last two days, have you?"

The question caught Tanyth's funny bone and she gave a surprised laugh.

"A week ago you thought talkin' to trees was crazy and now you're miffed because they talk to me and not you. That's progress in my book, dearie." She jostled her pack into place and stood, her face turned to Tanyth, a patient smile plastered on her lips.

Tanyth laughed again and scooped her pack onto her back and took up her staff. "Let's go then."

"You lead. Lemme take your arm," Gertie said.

"Why? You sick?"

"I'm old. That's not a sickness. Somethin' you—of all people—should recognize." She beckoned Tanyth with a wave of her hand and took hold of her upper arm. "You just go slow. I'm managing the mice. They're spread in a ring about a half mile across. We'll get warnin' before we walk into anythin' too surprisin'."

"Lord and Lady, how many mice is that?" Tanyth thought of her difficulty trying to communicate with a single bird. The prospect of what Gertie was doing made her a bit weak in the knees.

"Honestly, Tanyth, I don't know. A bunch. Now move along, and don't let me trip on anything."

They moved through the forest at what felt like a snail's pace. The afternoon sun worked its way down the western sky, casting the forest floor into a deeper gloom as it settled toward evening.

"We gonna walk right over the cliff in the dark?" Tanyth asked, unable to control her tongue any longer.

"Hold up here. The edge of the trees is just at the top of the rise up there." Gertie pointed at a low knoll. "Lemme thank my mousies so they can get back to their holes before dark." She stood still for a moment, her head cocked to the side just a bit. "There. All but one." She hunched down and a gray streak shot up her lowered arm and disappeared into her collar. In a moment whiskers and nose poked out of the wave of hair on Gertie's brow. "There," she said. "All together again."

"Now what? Cold camp and scout them in the morning?"

"Don't be ridiculous. Where's your owl?"

Tanyth felt her eyes roll but she closed them and tried to focus. A few yards away, an owl hooted once in the deepening dusk.

)O(

Day still gripped the land but she shook out her wings. Things to do. Things to see. Food, perhaps. She hooted again and spun her head around to see what dangers lurked near. Two people stood at the foot of her knoll. One looked up in her direction while the other stood, leaning on a pole—head down. The sight made her fluff her feathers and she hooted once more, a warning call just in case.

Nothing answered and the people didn't move.

She launched, dropping from the bough and soaring on silent wings out onto the flat grassland atop the cliff. This would be prime hunting if not for the people—men—in the holes around the edge. She sailed across the plain and between two of the outposts. Silent and gray against the winter bleached grasses, none of them so much as turned a head.

The updraft from the cliff caught her and lifted her high. A twist of her tail and a flicker of primaries turned her path along the cliff, sailing along behind the men who all looked away from the sea. Finally the cliff top was clear of humans. The scent of them left far behind up wind as she made her way along the headlands.

A wind-bent spruce offered shelter and cover near the last of the cleared land. She sailed up into its welcoming branches and folded her wings. The moon would be up soon and then she could hunt. This would be a good place to feed. In the meantime, it was a good place to nap so she fluffed her feathers and curled her head down and slept.

☽○☾

"Nothing's changed," Tanyth said. "The guards are still along the top of the cliff. They're all looking toward the trees."

"Your owl?"

Tanyth nodded. "Yeah. She flew along the top of the cliff behind them until she found a place to hole up and hunt tonight."

"Well, then that's perfect." Gertie started off up the knoll.

"Where are you goin'?"

Gertie kept climbing the hill. "I didn't come all this way to be turned back now."

"But where are you goin'?" Tanyth said, stretching her legs to try to catch the crazy old woman before she broke through the line of trees.

"To see the guards, of course. How else will we get down the cliff?"

"As prisoners?"

"Oh, don't be silly. Of course as prisoners. They're not goin' to jus' welcome us with open arms."

"How's that goin' to help?"

"I don't know yet. Do you have a plan?" She stopped and turned her face toward Tanyth, a wide smile and raised eyebrows painting the perfect picture of eager curiosity.

After a moment Tanyth shook her head. "No."

"All right then. We go with mine."

"What's your plan?"

"First we stash our packs in that hollow tree over there, then we go see the guards. They take us down the cliff. We see what's happening. Then we leave."

"It's the 'then we leave' part that has me most concerned," Tanyth said.

"Me, too, dearie. It's the weakest link, to be sure." With that she turned and marched on into the deepening dark.

Tanyth looked around the darkened forest. "Will we be able to find them again?" she asked.

"The guards? I'm sure they'll find us, dearie."

"No, the packs."

"Oh, certainly. This is the only hollow tree for half a mile in any direction."

Tanyth shook her head and snorted.

"One step at a time, dearie. We may not make it back out again, after all." Gertie stopped at the broken, gray tree and looked back down the slope. "Let's not get ahead of ourselves, shall we?"

The evening breeze started whispering through the tree-tops.

"Don't you start," Tanyth muttered and clambered up the hill after Gertie. "I got enough trouble with what I know already. Don't need any more tales."

Chapter 32
Into The Hole

The full moon rose with the sunset. "Shearing moon," Gertie said. "Solstice is right around the corner now."

"I'll be happy to see it," Tanyth said.

"You'll see it better than I will, dearie."

Tanyth chuckled a little. "You've always got an answer, don't ya?"

"At my age, just getting a good question is reward enough, but I try to answer as many of them as I can."

"What d'ya suppose they're doin' down there?"

"That's a good question," Gertie agreed.

Tanyth laughed.

"Hold it right there." The man's voice seemed to come up from the grasses in front of them.

"Oh, goodness," Gertie said. "Don't be scarin' an old lady like that."

"Shut up."

"Rude, too. Young man, didn't your mother teach you any better?" Gertie tsked. "At least stand up here and greet a body properly. Honestly."

Tanyth reached for Gertie's arm in warning when the grasses gave way and a scowling man stepped up out of a depression in the soil. "There. Better?" He wore the same black trousers and green shirt that the two in the forest had worn.

"Much, thank you," Gertie said. She stuck out a hand. "I'm Gertie Pinecrest. This is my friend, Tanyth Fairport. You are?"

The Hermit Of Lammas Wood

"Morris? What are you doin'?" A second, tired-sounding voice came from the grasses.

"We been watchin' for ya, mum," the first man said. He reached out and shook Gertie's hand. Before he let go, he slipped a loop of rope from his wrist onto hers and snugged it down.

"Watchin' for me?" Gertie said. "With a rope?"

"Malcolm and Arnold came back an hour ago. They had a lot of stories to tell. The boss figgered you two wouldn't take 'go away' for an answer."

"Well he was certainly right, wasn't he, Tanyth?"

"Oh, yeah. He was right."

The man gave Tanyth an odd look. "You the witch with the stick?"

Tanyth looked at her staff. "I never thought of it as a stick, really. More like a walkin' staff."

"You'll have to give that to me, mum."

"Will I?"

"Yes'm."

"How'll I get down the cliff without it? It's a walking stick. It helps me walk."

The man looked down the hole behind him and then back at Tanyth. "Who said anythin' about goin' down the cliff?"

"Just a guess. Ain't your boss in the cave down below?"

"How do you know about the cave down below?" The man's voice all but squeaked in surprise.

"Morris, shut up. If they was guessin' before, you just told 'em."

Morris clamped his lips together in an angry line. "Gimme the stick, mum. You won't need it goin' down."

"S'pose your gonna take it from me?"

"No, mum. They will." His gaze went over Tanyth's shoulder and she saw three archers with bows drawn standing four yards away.

"Gertie, I think they've heard about us," Tanyth said.

"Yes, dearie. You didn't hear them coming?" She nodded back at the archers.

"Nope."

"We'll have to work on your hearin' later. Why don't you

give this nice man your staff. We don't want to hurt him."

Tanyth released the staff, giving it a nudge so that it fell forward and measured its length on the new grass.

"Thank you, mum. Now if you'd stick out your hand?" He held up the other end of the rope with another loop in it.

"You think that's going to stop us?" Tanyth asked.

Gertie sighed. "When I said that about the questions earlier? I didn't mean you should ask so many, Tanyth."

Tanyth looked to Gertie and saw the grin at the corner of her mouth. "Sorry. I still don't see the point, but all right." She stuck out her hand. "There you go. Tie us together."

"Thank you, mum." He slipped the loop over her wrist and snugged it down. The knots were tied to offset each other so that if the women tried to pull apart, the knots would grow tighter.

Gertie held her hand palm up and Tanyth gripped the gnarled hand in her own. "It's your party," Tanyth said. "Now what?"

"Tanyth." The warning sounded clearly in Gertie's tone.

Morris closed his eyes and shook his head a couple of times. "Come on. Let's get this over with."

He turned and followed a faint path in the grasses where many feet had apparently worn the old grass away and prevented the new grass from sprouting. He didn't turn to see if they followed. The archers behind them made sure of that.

They walked along the cliff top toward the river. The roar of falling water grew from a quiet whisper to a dull roar. It made little sound falling over the edge. The roaring came from below, echoing up the cliff walls. Morris led them out to the edge and into a small wooden structure pegged to the rock face. He stepped to the far side of the room and the archers pressed Tanyth and Gertie to follow him.

"Mind the crack," Morris said, pointing to a line across the floor.

As she stepped over it, Tanyth had a chance to look straight down to the sea below.

"Hold onto the rails there," Morris said, pointing to a rough wooden rail at waist height. "And stand still."

"What—?" Before Tanyth could finish her question, Mor-

The Hermit Of Lammas Wood

ris pulled a lever and the floor dropped out from under them.

Gertie's laughter bubbled up and Tanyth turned to look at her as soon as she realized they were not falling to their doom.

"What's so funny?"

"It tickled my belly inside. I'm very ticklish."

Morris gave the old woman a smile. Tanyth thought it looked genuine. "You really the hermit?" he asked.

"Yeah. Been the hermit for so many winters I've lost count."

Morris looked down at his feet and screwed his mouth shut.

"Think nothin' of it, Morris," Gertie said. "I've had a good run and it's almost over."

Morris glanced out of the corner of his eye but only shook his head.

The platform slowed as it neared the bottom. Tanyth was grateful for the railing. It gave her something to focus on beside the seemingly endless descent straight down.

From below she could look up and see the shelf of rock projecting out, letting the full river flow off the edge and down into the bay below. It pounded the surface with a huge, nearly deafening roar.

Finally, the platform slowed and stopped. More archers met them at the bottom. Morris gripped the loop of rope between them and tugged them off the platform and onto a stone and mortar landing.

The bay extended almost due south, the arms of the bay spreading until the mouth must have been a half-mile wide. Below them a floating dock scrubbed against the sheer rock face; a two-masted sailing vessel lay moored at it. The craft itself looked smaller than the ship Tanyth had ridden from Kleesport, but not by a lot.

Morris tugged on the rope and interrupted her reverie. "Come on, ladies," he shouted. "The boss is waitin'."

He led them across the landing and pushed through a wooden door. Two burly men-at-arms, each with a mace and sword, guarded the door and scowled at Morris as he passed between them. Inside, the tool marks left by the miners who must have carved the hole gleamed in flickering torch light. When the door swung closed behind them, the noise from the falling water diminished but was still too loud to speak over. With another tug on the rope, Morris took them deeper into the tunnel and turned right at the first branch. The noise notched back again thanks to the intervening rock, and Tanyth could hear her own footsteps as they trod along this new corridor. Near the end two more guards, both wearing the black and green livery and carrying swords and maces, stood guard outside an iron-bound wooden door.

"This them?" the guard on the left asked, jerking his thumb at Tanyth and Gertie.

"Yeah. They just walked right up and introduced themselves," Morris said with a glance over his shoulder.

The guards looked at each other and then at the two women, shaking their heads. "Pity," the first guard said. "Go on in. He's expectin' ya."

Morris grabbed the handle and pushed the door open with his shoulder. "Boss? They're here," he called as the door swung open. He led them into a carved-out chamber of rock. A rumpled cot stood in an alcove on the right side of the room and a sturdy wooden desk held pride of place in the middle. On the left side, four sets of chains hung from bolts set into the stone of the wall. Tanyth didn't look at the dark stains on the floor very long before the thought occurred to her that Gertie was more than a bit mad.

A tall man, broad at the shoulder and narrow at the waist, stood and leaned on his knuckles over the desk. "Ah, ladies. So glad you could make it. I wondered if I'd have to hunt you down, but here you are."

Tanyth stared at the man. His face seemed familiar. The negligent stance and the darkness about his eyes struck a chord in her memory but she couldn't place where.

"Well, we were in the area. Seemed the least we could do. Stop in and greet our new neighbors," Gertie said, a bright smile on her face.

"How charming!" the man said and with his words, recognition snapped into place.

"Malloy," Tanyth breathed.

The Hermit Of Lammas Wood

"How astute of you, mum. And after only one meeting. I'm flattered you should remember me."

"You made quite an impression," Tanyth said. "Might work on makin' it a good one next time."

His eyelids flickered but his smile never wavered. "I'll take that under advisement, mum, but tell me. How is it I find you here?"

"You mean in this cave?" Tanyth asked.

"No, I mean alive. I thought you were sailing with that fool, Groves."

"Oh, yeah. That. I did. A lovely man and a handsome son. My travelin' companion found the young Mister Groves most attractive."

"That's impossible!" Malloy punched the desk for emphasis.

"Oh, I assure you, it's not. He quite made my heart pitter-pat a few times, I don't mind sayin'."

"Tanyth, you minx," Gertie said. "You never told me about that."

"We been kinda busy since I got to your place."

"True."

Morris cleared his throat and tugged on the rope. "Ladies. The boss is talkin'."

Storm clouds gathered on Malloy's face and Tanyth saw him take a deep breath, his mouth caught in a rictus that might have been a smile if it hadn't looked so strained. "Leave us, Morris. Get back to your post."

"But, Boss..."

"I think I'm safe from two old ladies, Morris. And I've got the boys just outside if I need help."

Morris bowed his head in acknowledgment and muttered, "Of course, sir." He turned on his heel and stood the staff up against the wall before going back through the door.

When the heavy wood bumped closed again, Malloy turned his gaze on Tanyth. "You did not sail with Groves."

"Really?" Tanyth said glancing at Gertie and then back at Malloy. "He said he was Captain Groves. The ship looked very much like *Zypheria's Call*. You saw me in his company the night the wind changed."

"*Zypheria's Call* is at the bottom of the Bight." He bit his words off one at a time before shouting, "How did you get here?"

"Don't be ridiculous. *Zypheria's Call* is prob'ly halfway back to Kleesport by now."

"Halfway back?" His brow beetled even more severely than before. "Halfway back to Kleesport? You mean he's been and gone already?"

"Of course. Once we found the bomb on board and dismantled it—"

"That's impossible!"

"You keep sayin' that, Captain Malloy. It's not only possible. It's history."

"Where's the device now?"

"I'm sure I don't know. I believe Captain Groves turned it over to the garrison commandant."

"Oakhurst has it?"

Ice splashed through Tanyth's veins. "Is that the commandant?"

"Yes, yes. Tiresome lad. Doesn't know his station." Malloy chewed his lips and glowered at the two women. "You? You're the hermit I keep hearin' about?"

"Oh, yeah. That's me. Gertie Pinecrest." She gave him a smile and a truly vacant stare.

Malloy blinked several times and his head cocked sideways just slightly. "And have you been the hermit long?"

"Mercy sakes, yes. Prob'ly longer than you've been a captain. Twenty-five, thirty winters."

Malloy pursed his lips and nodded slowly up and down one time. "I see. That's a very long time to live alone in the wilderness. Aren't you afraid?"

Gertie laughed. "Oh, no. Nothin' to be afraid of. I have my apple cider and my goats. Every few months somebody pays a visit. It's quite peaceful."

Malloy ran one bronzed hand through his hair. The look on his face nearly made Tanyth laugh herself.

He snorted and shook his head. "Never mind that," he muttered and waved a hand toward the wall with the chains on it. "If you two would be so kind? I need to see a man about a bomb, and I can't be havin' you two wanderin' around loose until I get back."

Gertie turned toward the chains. "You're not thinkin' we're gonna wait in them chains against that cold wall, are ya?"

Malloy nodded, a look of pained sadness on his face. "I am sorry, ladies. My hospitality is truly shocking, I know, but..." He made a tsking sound between his teeth. "There it is. Unless you'd like to join the men in the mine?"

Gertie turned back at Malloy. She pursed her lips and raised her face to the ceiling. "Very well. Chains it is," she said and led Tanyth over to the wall by their joined hands.

Malloy's look of exasperated disbelief was almost worth it, but Tanyth wondered what the old lady had in mind. She was a bit concerned that the answer might well be nothing at all.

Chapter 33
Chained

Tanyth looked up at the chain, then over at Gertie. "This is gonna get uncomfortable fast."

"Would if we were gonna be here long," she said.

"What? You got more mice in your pocket?"

Gertie turned her face toward Tanyth. The small black eyes in her hair stared out. "What good would mice be?"

"Oh, I don't know. Maybe scamper over to Malloy's desk and get the keys for the manacles." She rattled the chain for emphasis.

"Don't be silly, dearie. The keys would be much too heavy for a mouse to carry." She looked up at her own chains. "At least I convinced him that one arm would be enough."

"It's that one arm that's already gettin' sore."

"Oh, for Lady's sake. Hold on. I wanna give 'im a chance to get underway before we do anythin' rash."

"Rash? Like escape?"

"Yeah. I can only do this once, and if he comes back because he forgot a change of underwear or something, that wouldn't be good."

Tanyth blinked and looked down at her companion. "You mean you have a plan?"

Gertie shrugged. "Not a plan, as such. No."

"Then what?"

"Can you untie our rope?"

"Sure. Reach up so I can get the knot."

Gertie lifted her arm up. Tanyth pulled the slip knot loose from her wrist, then did the same for Gertie, dropping the rope to the floor. "We're still chained on the opposite hands."

"Grab your staff." Gertie nodded to where Morris had left it standing beside the door.

Gertie lifted her chained hand as high as it would go. "Use the slack in the chain."

Tanyth traced the loop of chain up, through the eye bolt in the rock and down. She edged away from Gertie and spun so that her free arm could reach the familiar oak shaft. Her fingers were just an inch too short.

"Tug the chain a bit," Gertie said. "See if you can get another link through the eye bolt. I'll stand on tiptoe."

Tanyth tugged but the chain wouldn't budge. "You're just too short, Gertie."

"Well, yer gonna be that way about it, come over here an' scootch down."

"What good's that gonna do?"

"Tanyth, I swear on the Lady's lacy knickers that if you keep givin' me grief I'm gonna leave ya here to rot." Her eyes blazed and she stamped her foot.

Tanyth took a deep breath and blew it out. "Sorry, Gertie. I've been workin' alone a long time. It's hard to adjust."

Gertie smiled and gave a shrug. "Same here, but if we're gonna get out of this, you need to trust me."

Tanyth scuttled back along the wall. "What? Hands and knees?"

"That'll work," Gertie said.

Tanyth got down so Gertie could step onto her shoulders. "Sorry about this." In a moment she stood on Tanyth's back, her boots bruising Tanyth's shoulder blades for a moment. Then the pressure was gone. "Quick. Move."

Tanyth slipped out and looked up.

Gertie hung from the eye bolt by her hands. "Pull the chain. Quick. I don't know how long I can hold this."

Tanyth pulled and the chain ran freely through the eye. She reached the staff easily and returned quickly. "Now what?"

"Use the staff. Push some slack back through the eye so I can let go without pullin' my arm out of its socket."

Tanyth used the stout oak as a lever, and in moments

Gertie stood beside her once more.

Gertie shook her arms and hands out. "Don't wanna do that again any time soon."

"Me, either, but what do we do with this?" Tanyth held up the staff.

"What *you* do is use the iron shoe, and what I want you to do is get a good swing and hammer right on the end of the eye bolt. Can you do that?"

"You want me to drive the bolt in farther?"

"Even a fraction of an inch will do it. Yeah."

Tanyth opened her mouth to ask why, but thought better of it. "Right on the end?"

"Yeah. Hit it with the iron, not the wood."

"All right." Tanyth flipped the staff and held it like a bat. She placed the iron shoe against the tip of the eye bolt and pulled back. She put all her focus on the eye bolt and swung with all her might.

The iron missed the eye bolt altogether and cracked against the stone just above it. The shock rattled the staff out of Tanyth's hands and it dropped to the stone floor with a loud clatter.

"What was that?" The guard's voice from outside the door.

His partner gave a muffled reply. Tanyth scrambled to pick up the staff as the door swung inward. When her fingers wrapped around it, she stood and thrust it behind her, pinning it against the wall with her back. Feeling the very top of it behind her head, she leaned back and lifted both arms to hang on the chain.

"What was that?" the guard asked.

"What was what?" Gertie asked.

"That crack."

"What crack?"

"There was some kinda noise in here. Sounded like somebody dropped a plank or something."

Gertie made a show of turning her head to and fro. "I don't see any planks and I didn't hear anything. Did you hear anything, Tanyth?"

"Nope. Just that waterfall out there."

"Don't mention the waterfall, dearie." Gertie pushed her knees together and shifted her weight.

The burly guard's face turned two different shades of red before he scuttled out, slamming the door behind him.

They heard a muffled question and a sharp answer. "Nuthin'. Wasn't nuthin'."

Gertie giggled quietly. "Some men. Honestly." She stepped aside. "Try again. You can do it."

Tanyth took a deep breath and let it out slowly, then thrust a hand behind her to take up the staff again. Once more she lined up her swing. She felt the scrape of iron on iron as the shoe kissed the eye bolt. Letting the weight of the staff pull the long oak shaft back, she held it for a half a heartbeat and then swung again. The momentum of the blow built for a long fraction of a second. The length of the shaft amplified the strength of her arms, and the solid iron shoe struck the iron eye bolt with a clean *thock* no louder than a stamped boot on stone.

Tanyth stared in disbelief at the eye bolt. Her heart sank. "It didn't break."

Gertie snorted. "Of course it didn't break. That's forged iron. It's too soft to break."

"Then what was I hittin' it for?"

Gertie grinned and started backing up, pulling her chain against the eye bolt. "Pull," she said.

Tanyth shook herself into action and pulled on her end of the chain. They put a solid strain on the chains–and nothing happened.

Gertie let up her side, and Tanyth followed suit.

"You really think we're gonna pull that out of the wall?"

"Yep, but we're pullin' at the wrong angle."

"How d'ya figger?"

Gertie grimaced. "I'm too short. We're pulling down, not out."

"We need to pull it straight out of the wall?"

"Yeah. Which means we have to pull from up here."

Tanyth grinned. "I got this one."

She picked up her staff and took a turn of chain around the top, and had Gertie do the same.

"Let the chain run until I get the staff up near the eye bolt."

They worked the loose chain around the staff while Tanyth lifted it up.

"Now snug it up tight and hold on."

Gertie tugged the chain and the links locked around the oak.

With a grin, Tanyth pushed the staff up through the chain until the wood reached the low stone ceiling. She wiggled it around a bit until she found a bit of rough stone, then pushed the oak hard against the roof. With a smile she pulled the foot of the staff away from the wall, drawing the eye bolt straight out of the rock, pulling rock dust with it in a fine cascade, until it dropped with a quiet clank against the staff.

"Perfect," said Gertie.

"How did that happen? I thought you wanted to break the eye out of the bolt."

"I studied rocks. This stuff is relatively soft. Softer than the iron, and worse, it's brittle. A sharp strike breaks it. That's how they were able to carve these caverns. You didn't need to break the iron. You only needed to break the rock between the threads of the bolt." Gertie held up the eye bolt.

Stone filled the threads in places; Gertie brushed it away with a quick twist of her fingers.

"All right then," Tanyth grinned. "What do we do next?"

"Well, next we need to get out of this room without the guards stoppin' us."

"How do we do that?"

"I haven't a clue."

Chapter 34
Some Outside Help

Tanyth sat beside Gertie, their backs against the wall. She fiddled with the lock that held their manacles closed. "We'll wanna get this chain off."

Gertie pursed her lips and studied the links, the manacle, and the lock. "Links are soft iron. So's the manacle. Lock's prob'ly the weak spot. If we can open the lock—or break it off—we're free." She sighed and looked at the door. "We still have the problem of the guards."

"You think they're gonna just leave us here?"

Gertie shrugged. "Hard tellin'. Captain what's-his-name entertains here sometimes, so prob'ly they're used to leavin' his guests just hangin' around."

"He's gonna be gone for days if he's sailin' to Northport to see Robert."

"Robert?"

"Robert Oakhurst. He's the commandant."

"You were only in town for three days? How d'ya know that?"

"Long story. Robert and I go way back. He was just as surprised to see me as I was him."

"So, they leave people to die in here?" Gertie asked, looking around the room. She pointed to the cot. "Sloppy housekeeper. Maybe they do."

"Well, if they come to feed us and we're not on the wall–?" Tanyth shrugged.

"If we can get out of the manacles, we can hang 'em back up."

"If."

Low voices came through the heavy door.

"He didn't leave no orders." The surly guard's voice carried clearly.

They heard more mumbles, two voices.

Gertie jumped up. "Quick," she whispered and rushed over to one of the remaining sets of chains.

Tanyth had little choice but to follow or have her arm yanked out. Gertie reached up with her manacled hand and grabbed one of the two manacles hanging down. She pointed to the other one and Tanyth did the same. They stood close together, hiding the loose chain behind their bodies just as the door opened and the big guard stepped in, giving them the stink eye.

Tanyth stared back.

He pushed the door open wider and stepped out of the way. Another guard wearing black and green walked in carrying a loaf of bread and a jug.

"You make a mess in here, Morris, and the boss is gonna make your life even worse than it is already."

"Yeah, I got it. I'll be careful."

The guard gave them one last scowl and stepped out of the room, closing the door behind him.

"Ladies, I thought...that is...food and water," he said.

"That's very considerate of you, Morris," Gertie said.

"It's the least I can do, mum. It's gonna be a day or so before the boss gets back. He'll be in Northport by morning but won't be able to get back here before tomorrow night at the earliest." He looked down at his boots and shrugged. "Least I can do is make you as comfortable as I can before...before he gets back."

"What happens when he gets back?" Tanyth asked.

Morris's eyes went to the chains. "It won't be pleasant, I'm afraid."

"Can you help us?" Gertie asked.

"Help you do what, mum?"

"Escape, of course. And take all the miners with us."

Morris's eyes grew round and he stared at Gertie. "Mum, you know there's miners?"

"Chipmunks didn't chew these holes in the rock, Morris."

"Oh, yeah." His gaze swept the walls of the room. "Guess it's pretty obvious."

"Your boss gave us a choice of waiting here or in the mines," Tanyth said. "We thought here would be more comfortable. Mines usually have miners."

"Slaves, more like," Morris muttered.

Tanyth nodded. "They're the sailors from the hijacked vessels, aren't they?"

Morris nodded, staring at his shoes. "Captain Malloy hired us from his crews for special duty. Good pay and not a lot of work, he said. We been stuck up here for over a year. I haven't seen home for two winters."

"When will you get to go home?" Gertie asked.

"Oh, my time's almost up. We only have to be here two winters and then he rotates us out. New fish come in every spring. I'll be heading home soon with enough gold in my pocket to leave the sea behind for good."

Tanyth glanced down at Gertie and then back at Morris. "Death comes on white wings," she said.

Gertie stiffened. "Trees talked t'you 'bout that too?"

"Yeah."

"What's that?" Morris asked.

"Think about it, Morris. Captain Malloy's goin' to take a bunch of sailors back to Kleesport and turn you loose with money in your pockets?"

"Oh, not Kleesport. He'll take us down to Runland and we'll go our own ways. Start a new life."

"You're never gonna see home again?"

"Well, that's the plan, yeah."

"Nobody goes home, Morris." Gertie's gentle voice seemed not to reach the man. "Malloy can't afford to have the word get out."

Morris started shaking his head back and forth, slowly at first and then more vigorously.

"You know it's true. There's too much at stake. Think about it," Tanyth said.

"No. That's...It's not possible."

"It makes a sick kinda sense, man. Malloy hijacks the ships

The Hermit Of Lammas Wood

and sells the cargoes. He press-gangs the crew into workin' the mines or taking a long drink of deep water," Tanyth said. "He sells or sinks the ships so nobody's the wiser. Insurance pays off, and everybody's happy except the bereaved families and the slaves in the mines. He hires you and your friends to guard the mines. You're supposed to either scare off or kill anybody who gets too close. Then what's he goin' ta do with you, huh?"

Morris shook his head. "No, that can't be right."

Gertie said, "Morris, you already know it's true. Your head is tellin' ya one thing but your heart's tellin' you somethin' else."

"What about that guy—White? Reggie White?" Tanyth asked.

"Reggie? You know about Reggie?"

"He showed up dead just outside of Northport a few days ago. Lotta his friends miss him back in Kleesport. Lotta people know that his ship couldn'ta' been lost at sea."

"He slipped out of the mines and ran. Nobody thought he'd make it that far."

"Lot more people gonna be looking once that bomb gets back to the magistrates in Kleesport," Tanyth said.

Morris looked up at her. "Bomb?"

"The insurance folks been blowing up ships they don't like. Captains who won't pay the premiums."

"That's what the boss is tryin' to get?"

"Yeah. He thinks it's with the garrison in Northport."

"It's not?"

"Nope. Halfway back to Kleesport by now. Every day he spends lookin' for it in Northport is a day closer to the magistrates."

"He's behind that, too, en't he, Morris?" Gertie asked.

"I don't know. Maybe."

"If he weren't, he'd be a lot less interested in finding the evidence," Tanyth said.

Morris took a deep breath through his nose and held it a moment before blowing it out. "Yeah. Yeah, he would."

"You got a few hours, Morris. Can you get the men out?" Gertie asked.

His head came back up and he looked at her. "What are you askin' me?"

"You and the other guards. All the men in the mines. Get them up and out of here. You got until tomorrow afternoon before he gets back," Gertie said.

"What about you?" he asked.

"Oh, we're just a couple of old ladies. Nobody'll miss us, but you men need to go tell the garrison in Northport. Turn yourselves in. Tell the authorities what's goin' on. They'll take that into consideration, won't they, Tanyth?"

"Yeah. They'll do that. Once Captain Groves gets that bomb back to Kleesport and Richard Marong finds this place, it'll be all over."

"What'll happen to the gold?" Morris asked.

"Every man fill a pocket and run. Marong's only a couple days east down the coast. He's got a dozen garrison troops with him," Tanyth said. "Let Malloy choke on the leavings."

He stared at Tanyth, and then his eyes focused somewhere else. He stood a little straighter. "It's all true, isn't it?"

"Yep," Gertie said.

"What about you?"

"Unless you got the key to these manacles, you got better things to worry about. Get those men out of here. Run east along the coast," Tanyth said. "We'll take our chances here."

"All right. I'll do it." He thrust the bread and water into their free hands. "It's all I got right now. I'll try to bring more later."

"Feed the men, too. They'll need their strength," Gertie said.

He crossed to the door and stopped at the latch, his pale face staring back at them for a long moment. "I'll try to find the key," he said, and slipped out, pulling the door closed behind him with a thud.

They heard low voices outside the door again and the burly guard stuck his head back in, eyeing them up and down with a scowl. Apparently satisfied, he closed the door once more.

Gertie and Tanyth stood together for a long moment without moving.

"Think he'll do it?" Tanyth asked.

"He's scared. He may just scoot on his own. He's got a good chance up there as a guard."

"Better chance if he convinces his buddy."

"His buddy?" Gertie asked.

"I wondered why there were two guards in every position," Tanyth said. "Less chance one man will take it into his head to run. He'd need to convince his buddy to go with him."

"Or kill him," Gertie said.

Tanyth sighed but said nothing.

"Well, let's eat. That bread smells half decent, and it's been a long time since lunch," Gertie said, letting go of the shackle and dropping cross-legged on the floor. "Maybe somethin'll occur to us."

Chapter 35
Punch Press

Gertie lifted her arm and dropped it again, letting the iron chains clack together. "This is gettin' old," she said.

"Yeah," Tanyth said. "Wonder how Morris is doing."

"I wonder if we can break these locks," Gertie said. "They're the most likely point of failure."

Tanyth sighed. "You think we can crush them with my staff or something?" She held up her own wrist to examine the locking mechanism for the hundredth time.

"Well, let's at least see what else is here," Gertie said. "Malloy might have left a spare key in his desk."

Tanyth clambered to her feet. "All right. Let's look again. The first time through his drawers didn't turn up much, but maybe we overlooked something."

Gertie followed in Tanyth's wake, being careful to keep the iron from dragging on the stone floor. "You take the left, I'll take the right this time," she said.

With a shrug, Tanyth traded places and they rifled down the drawers in short order.

"He doesn't keep much in this desk," Tanyth complained. She glanced over at Gertie. "How well does your li'l helper read, anyway?"

Gertie sighed. "Not well. If I make the shapes big enough and clear enough I can make them out, but most of this stuff is just pages with scratches on it as far as I can tell."

"You're not missin' much. Account books, equipment lists. Nothin' we can use to get out of here."

"We're missin' somethin'," Gertie said, standing up and

arching her back in a stretch. "Somethin's not here."

"What?"

"If I knew that, I'd know where to look."

Tanyth straightened up and stretched her own back. "Malloy is a pirate and a thief. He's got kidnapped sailors mining gold out the cliff."

"Where's he keep it?" Gertie asked.

"What? The gold?"

"Yeah. And how's he sellin' it?"

Tanyth stopped and stared at Gertie. "How's he sellin' it?"

"Gold's a metal. Not much use 'cept as jewelry and coins. Turnin' it into spendin' money? How's that work?" Gertie took a deep breath and closed her eyes, her brow furrowed. "There's another thing."

"What's that?"

"Captain Malloy strike you as the trustin' type?"

"Not 'specially."

"So, he has all these slaves and workers he's planning on killin' to keep his secrets. He ain't gonna be sailin' around with all his treasure on the ship."

"It wasn't that big a ship."

"And it might get lost," Gertie said. "Somebody might notice it."

"Where's he gonna keep it?" Tanyth said, her gaze scanning the room again. "It ain't gonna be far away."

"He'll wanna be able to keep his eyes on it," Gertie said. "What's here that's not stone?"

"The desk," Tanyth said. Her gaze raked the room. "The chains. His cot."

Gertie led the way to the alcove. A strong fug of stale sheets hung in the air.

"Guess he don't believe in airin' dirty laundry," Gertie said with a grimace.

Tanyth got down and looked under the cot. "A small iron chest under here." She reached under and grabbed the handle, giving it a tug. It didn't budge. "It's heavy," she said, her breath coming in grunts as she tugged the heavy case out from its hiding place.

Gertie crouched beside her but even with both of them lifting, they couldn't budge it off the floor.

Tanyth stared at the small box in disbelief. "That can't be more'n a foot on a side. How much can it possibly weigh?"

"More'n we can lift. Is there a lock?"

Tanyth looked around the sides and found a simple hasp welded to the iron. "Another one of these locks," she said, rattlin' her manacle.

"Musta bought 'em in bulk," Gertie muttered.

"I still say we could smash 'em with my staff," Tanyth said.

"Prob'ly could, but the noise would have our neighbors knockin' on the door and that would be bad."

Tanyth put her shoulder to the box and shoved it back under the cot. "We know it's there. Best not let anybody else know we know."

"If we don't get out of here soon, it won't matter," Gertie said, her mouth twisted to the side. "Somethin's still missin'."

"What?"

"Gold ain't easy to handle."

"That's why he's got slaves," Tanyth said.

"And his own crew, too, but that's not what I mean." Gertie sat back on her haunches. "Gold in the ground like this? Down here? He's gotta be mining a quartz vein that's back under the cliffside."

"Penny and Rebecca didn't. They just picked it up off the ground."

"Yeah. Nuggets like that happen. Prob'ly how they found it. Somebody picked up a nugget, and they got curious. That's in gravel and along rivers and such. I got a good look at the tunnel mouth–they're diggin' out rock."

"How's that help us?"

"I don't know yet, but he has to have a crushin' mill somewhere down here to break the rock up, and a smelter, too, unless he's shippin' the ore somewhere else."

"He'd need somewhere to land it without the tax men finding him."

"Aye, and those boys have eyes everywhere. I keep expectin' 'em to show up at the cottage some day to tax my cider." Gertie swung her head back and forth. "No, he's got it all here, which means he's also got his blankin' mill and coin press here, too."

"You're talking, but the trees make more sense."

"One of the things that got me interested in rocks was makin' coins. Ya have to find the gold, melt it down to take out the dross. Then you make it into sheets. Gold is soft so it rolls out easy. Makes pretty sheets. Then you use a blankin' mill—it's like a biscuit cutter for metal—to make the li'l disks. Punch out a bunch of them, and then press the king's face onto one side and some pattern on the other. That's a coin."

"Sounds like a lotta work."

"It is and it ain't. You got enough gold to make a sheet, punching it out may be nothin' more than one man with an iron punch and another with a big hammer. Place the punch. Bang the end. Poof! There's yer blank. Pressin' 'em takes a little more care, but not much."

Tanyth's gaze went to the small iron chest under the cot. "So that's prob'ly full of coins?"

"That'd be my guess."

"How's that get us out of here?" Tanyth asked.

"I'm still cogitatin'." Gertie tapped her lips with her fingers. "Once they're coins, they're money. Anybody can spend 'em."

"Sure."

"So our trustin' Captain Malloy ain't gonna let that coin get far from his control. He can have his people make the metal sheets and even punch the blanks. Ya can't spend a blank coin. Show it to the wrong person and you'll have the King's Own in your small clothes faster'n a bedbug in a flop house."

"Is he pressin' the coins himself?"

Gertie shook her head again. "Not likely, but I bet he keeps the press close."

"Where?"

Gertie shrugged. "Maybe he keeps it next door or somethin'."

They sat there in silence for what seemed like a long time. "How many mice down here?" Tanyth asked.

Gertie chuckled. "Darned if I know. Prob'ly hundreds."

"Well?"

"Well, what?" Gertie asked–and then her face lit up with a broad smile. "Why didn't I think o' that?"

"We been kinda preoccupied."

Gertie scrambled to her feet. "Come on. Let's go grab a chain in case somebody looks in while I'm busy."

They crossed the room, and each woman grabbed onto a loose manacle.

"Close enough," Gertie said as she closed her eyes.

Time dragged as Tanyth stood and watched Gertie's eyelids flicker.

"Not as many as I thought," she muttered. "Enough."

"Anything good?"

Gertie shook her head. "Mostly bad."

More time ticked by. Tanyth measured it by the thrumming of blood in her ears.

"Got a mouse in the passage outside. Same guards on duty," Gertie said.

"You'd think they'd change reg'lar."

"Prob'ly do. It just feels like we been in here a week."

"Good point," Tanyth said.

After another moment, Gertie grunted. "Found the coin press. Darkish room. Door."

"Where is it?"

Gertie shrugged. "Can't tell."

Tanyth shifted her weight, and the chain clinked against stone.

"Oh," Gertie said.

"What?"

"Clink again."

Tanyth rattled the chain.

"Yep. Just like I thought. It's nearby. Mousie heard the metal clank."

"Sharp ears," Tanyth said.

"Yeah."

"We just need to know where."

"He's runnin' around the room. Stone floor. Stone walls. Heavy wood door. Smells of machine oil and somethin' else."

Gertie tilted her head to one side. "Corridor lit up outside the door."

"Anything else?"

"Short legs. Give 'im a minute." Gertie's head straightened up. "One wooden wall."

"A wooden wall? Under ground?"

"Yeah. He's got a little squeeze hole in it, and there's light on the other side."

Tanyth glanced across the room and gasped.

"What is it?"

"A wooden wall," Tanyth said.

"What?"

"Behind the cot. It's a wooden wall."

"Oh, my. That's the one," Gertie said.

"What? Can you see it?" Tanyth looked on Gertie's head but saw no mouse.

"No, dearie, but my mousie can see us." She flickered her fingers in a wave.

They crossed to the alcove again, and Gertie leaned down to the floor. A small gray mouse leaped onto her outstretched hand and clambered up her sleeve. "There. This li'l squeek has agreed to be my eyes for now," she said. "Now let's see if we can find the door."

"What makes you think there's a door?" Tanyth said.

"You think Captain Malloy entertains his guests by letting the others see them movin' back and forth down the tunnel?" Gertie jerked a thumb at the chains on the wall.

"Why move 'em at all?"

"Maybe he just likes company," Gertie said. "Besides, why have a wooden wall here if there's not a door in it."

"Kinda obvious hidin' a door in a wooden wall," Tanyth said.

"Not that obvious. We never noticed it. I s'pect his other guests all have somethin' else on their minds, too. Like survival."

Tanyth grunted. "Good point."

"If I was a door latch, where would I hide?" Gertie said, her quiet mutter just barely audible. She pushed and prodded the wooden panel with her gnarled fingers.

Tanyth stepped back to look at the wall. A smudge on the wood next to the stone caught her eye. She walked over to the smudge and stared at it. "Dirty hands," she said. She pressed on the smudge and felt a click in the wood.

"What was that?" Gertie said, turning her face toward Tanyth.

"I think I found it." A crack between two of the vertical planks seemed marginally wider than it had before. She pushed on it, and the door swung into the next room.

"I think you did, too," Gertie said as she stepped through the door.

The scent of machine oil mixed with something else filled the room with a faint musk that made Tanyth's nose itch. "What's that smell?"

"Fear," Gertie said as she walked around the room, holding her head still at various points. "This is the press," she said.

A solid wooden frame stood in the middle of the floor. Two simple uprights held a narrow iron table with a dent in the middle. Tanyth stepped forward and ran her fingers over the dent, feeling the impressions at the bottom. "One side of the coin?" she asked.

"Yeah. Toss a blank in there. Put the top on..." She pointed to a round metal bar hung on a lanyard from the top of the frame. "Then pop it once with a hammer. Instant coin."

Tanyth started to reach for the metal bar but stopped and looked at Gertie. "Hammer?"

"It's gotta be here somewhere." Gertie's grin glowed in the light coming from the other room.

Tanyth looked around the frame. "Has ta be here somewhere. Tied down, prob'ly."

"Got it," Gertie said. "Was in the shadow over here." She hefted what looked like a five-pound hammer on a short handle. "Stout cord on it, too. How'd you know?"

"Malloy wouldn't want his helper to hit him with it."

"Ah," Gertie said. "Of course."

"Now, how do we pound on these locks without bein' heard?"

Gertie's brow furrowed as she looked from the hammer to the manacle on her wrist. "And how do we get a clean hit without crushin' an arm?"

"That part's easy." Tanyth held up the eye bolt, still threaded on the chain between them. "Just need someplace to rest the manacle on. Line up the bolt. Bang! We're done."

"We need two bangs," Gertie said. "That's the problem."

"Act'ally, I think that's the solution," Tanyth said.

Chapter 36
Break Out

Tanyth scanned the room. "I could wish for more light," she said.

"If you can see it, they can," Gertie said with a nod toward the door.

"I need a knife. Somethin' to cut this cord. Morris took mine."

"Mine, too." Gertie fished in her pockets. "But he left my rocks."

"You got a pocket full of rocks?"

"Not full, dearie," Gertie pulled her hand out and held a flat flake of gray stone in her palm. "Just enough to be useful."

"Flint?"

"Yeah."

"We startin' a fire?"

"Nope, gimme a minute." Gertie braced the flint against the wooden frame with just a bit of the edge hanging over. She grabbed the hammer and choked up the handle until the heavy metal head rested on her fist. She took a deep breath and just nudged the edge of the stone with the heavy hammer.

Tanyth heard a quiet click as a piece of the stone fell off onto the floor.

"Get that flake," Gertie said. "I can't see well enough to find it in this light."

Tanyth crouched down and felt around on the dark stone floor. A glint of gray near the foot of the framework drew her notice, and she picked up the small piece of rock.

The Hermit Of Lammas Wood

"Don't cut yourself," Gertie said.

Tanyth pressed the flat piece of stone into her palm and tilted it so the light from the next room illuminated it. "Will it cut the cord?"

"It'll gut a rabbit and skin it, too. Stop askin' questions and get on with cuttin'."

The flint blade made short work of the cord holding the hammer to the frame. She handed the hammer to Gertie. "Hold that."

Gertie took it and glanced out at the other room. "What are you doin' now?"

Tanyth sliced the cord holding the metal rod and rolled it in her palm. "Makin' sure he can't make any more coins."

Gertie took it and slipped into one of her pockets. "Get the other one."

"How?"

Gertie leaned down to look under the table. "Oh, here." Something snapped, and the dent in the table became a hole. Gertie came up with the other die in her hand. "You want it, or should I keep them both?"

"I'll take the hammer. You take the dies. We just need to get my staff from the other room, and we're ready to go."

They scurried out and back, being careful not to scrape the chain as they went.

"Now what?" Gertie asked.

"Now we need to figure out how to see in the dark."

"If we could do that, dearie, we'd be owls." She turned her face toward Tanyth. "I don't suppose there's an owl down here?"

Tanyth snorted. "If there was, I don't have time to find it. We need to move before they change the guard."

"Fire," Gertie said.

"What?"

"We start a fire."

"In here?"

"Yeah, but I was thinkin' more about in there." She pointed back through the door. "If they're all busy puttin' out the fire, they're not gonna see an extra light under the door, are they?"

They went back and Tanyth tried to pull one of the torches out of its wall bracket.

"It won't budge."

"Why didn't he use a lamp?" Gertie said, her mouth puckered. "Short-sighted on his part."

"Get some papers from his desk. We can light 'em on the torch."

"Machine oil," Gertie said.

"We can light it on machine oil?"

"No. Come on." Gertie dragged Tanyth back into the other room and walked around the clutter of goods scattered against the walls and in the corners. Every so often she sniffed. "Here," she said. She reached down and came up with a large clay jug. "Lantern," she said.

"Looks like a jug."

"That's what a lantern looks like." Gertie dragged Tanyth back to the alcove and worked the cork out of the top of the jug. She sloshed it around a little, then announced: "About half full. Plenty. Grab that blanket and cut a piece off with the flint. About that long." She held her hands a foot apart. "Don't need to be too precise."

While Tanyth attacked the blanket, Gertie sprinkled a bit of the oil onto the bedclothes.

Tanyth came up with the strip of cloth.

"Good, now take the cork and cut a notch in it while I make the wick."

Gertie laid the piece of blanket on the bed, spilling oil along its length and getting a fair amount on the bedding as well. She sloshed the jug again and nodded. "Should be enough."

Tanyth handed her the cork.

Gertie stuffed the piece of blanket down into the jug and then wedged the cork in beside it, carved notch aligned with the fabric. She held it up and nodded once. "It'll smoke like crazy, but it'll do for as long as we need it."

Gertie headed for the nearest torch and held up the makeshift wick.

"Wait," Tanyth said as she dragged Gertie to the desk. She pulled open the middle drawer, pulled out an accounting ledger, and grabbed a handful of papers from the desktop. Holding them up to the nearest torch, she smiled grimly as flames licked the edges immediately and began to spread. Then she held the burning papers out to Gertie, who thrust the oil-soaked wick into the flame for a moment. It was a long moment, but at last the wick caught. Tanyth dropped the handful of papers onto the desk.

They scooted back into the alcove, stopping to light the oily bedding with the lantern on the way.

Tanyth pressed the door closed and heard the latch snap. "All right. Let's get these locks off." She dragged Gertie over to the table, where she positioned her manacle over the hole where the die had been and took the hammer. "You hold, I'll strike."

Gertie lined the point of the eye bolt against the lock's hasp. "Don't miss," she said with a grin.

Tanyth lifted the hammer and brought it down on the eye bolt with a loud snap.

"Tough little bugger," Gertie said, looking at the unbroken lock.

"Did you hear that?" The guard's voices in the corridor carried clearly.

"I heard something, but I smell smoke," another voice said. "Look."

They heard the door crash open in the next room. "What the—?"

Shouts rang out up and down the corridor. "Fire! Fire!"

"Well, we missed our chance to get out while they were busy, but..." Tanyth swung the hammer, bashing the lock against the metal flange on the coin press. The lock popped open on the first blow.

Gertie held her own manacle in position, and they broke her lock just as quickly.

Running feet and shouts of "Fire!" echoed in the tunnel outside.

"I don't think they heard that," Gertie said, her grin illuminated from below by the makeshift lamp. "Now, how do we get out of here before that wooden wall goes up?"

"You got a mouse in the tunnel?"

"Not at the moment, but I will."

"If you can get eyes outside the door, I have an idea." Tanyth flung the chain over her shoulders and took up her staff. The weight of it felt good in her hands.

"All right. There's a bunch of them green shirts bein' mostly useless in the tunnel."

"Anybody outside this door?"

Gertie cocked her head to one side. "No. They're all lookin' the other way."

"Time to go." Tanyth cracked the door a bit and peeked out. "Nobody in sight."

Tanyth led the way down the tunnel away from the conflagration. Gertie grabbed the back of Tanyth's trousers and kept watch behind them.

"We're goin' the wrong way," Gertie said after they'd made another turn.

"I know, but there's no branches here and we can't get back through that herd."

Tanyth turned another bend in the tunnel, trying to keep track of where they were, and ran smack into a broad chest covered in green twill fabric.

"Oof," he said, and wrapped heavy arms around her torso.

When Tanyth looked up, she saw a smiling face. "Arnold?"

"I know you, lady." He looked over her shoulder where Gertie still clung to the back of Tanyth's trousers with one hand. "And you're that hermit lady. With the rats!" He smiled at both of them. "You really made Malcolm mad. He hollered and hollered." He released his arms and stepped back, letting Tanyth stand on her own. "What you doin' down here? If Malcolm sees ya, he's gonna be really mad."

"We're tryin' to get out. You should be, too," Tanyth said.

"Why's that?"

"There's a fire in the boss's room. He's gonna be really mad when he gets back. Would you like to come with us?" Gertie said. "We'll keep you safe from Malcolm and the boss."

Something happened in the man's face, the light in his eye went out and his cheerful smile crumpled. "You're tryin' to ex-cape," he said.

The Hermit Of Lammas Wood

"Yes, dearie. We are. If we don't, the boss will kill us," Gertie said, placing a hand on Arnold's arm.

"It's my duty to keep you from ex-capin'."

"He's goin' to kill you, too, Arnold. When he doesn't need you any more, he'll kill all of you," Tanyth said, conscious of the time ticking away. Sooner or later somebody would realize the prisoners weren't in the cage and they'd come looking.

"No. He's gonna take care of us."

"Arnold, we don't have time to argue. Are you going to capture us?" Gertie asked.

"All right. Yeah. I'll capture you and then I'll be a hero."

"Excellent. The boss is waiting up in the field for us. If you take us up there, I'm sure he'll give you a reward," Gertie said.

Tanyth pulled the chain from her shoulders and latched the manacle onto her wrist, twisting the latch and handing the other one to Gertie. "See? You've got us. All you have to do is take us up to the boss."

"I can do that," Arnold said and turned away, walking down the tunnel. "This way is faster."

"Wait!" Tanyth called.

Arnold stopped and looked back. "What?"

"You should take the chain in your hand. That way the boss will know you captured us."

"Oh, yeah." Arnold came back and took the loop of chain that Tanyth held out.

He turned and lumbered away, dragging them behind. For a big man, he moved quickly; they didn't have to pretend he was dragging them along behind. They could barely keep up.

"Think it'll work?" Gertie asked, her voice low.

"Dunno. Better than running blind."

Arnold led them out of the narrow tunnel and into a wider cavern. Tanyth couldn't see the ceiling in the dim light of the flickering torches placed along the way. The stench of unwashed bodies and human waste stung her eyes.

"Wait, Arnold," Tanyth said. "Is this the mine?"

Arnold fetched up and turned to look back into the cavern. "One of 'em. Yeah."

"Are the miners sleepin' now?" Gertie asked.

"Some of them, yeah. They always mine. Sometimes they sleep, but somebody always mines. 'Round the clock."

Tanyth shook her head, and Gertie shrugged.

"Thank you, Arnold. We better get up now."

"All right." He struck off again and soon had them out into the cool night air once more. The roaring water seemed to be falling almost on their heads as they picked their way along the slippery, wet rocks toward the platform that had brought them down. They climbed aboard, and Arnold pulled a lever. His face split in a broad grin as the platform started to rise.

It didn't go up as fast as it had come down. The trip down had been swift. The ride up—with them fearing that their ruse would catch up to them at any moment—seemed interminable. At the top, Arnold led them off and up onto the top of the cliff face once more. The full moon hung almost directly overhead.

"I don't see the boss here," he said.

"He's down at the end, there," Tanyth pointed.

"Will you show me your rats again, Hermit?" Arnold asked as they ambled along.

"Maybe. You been decoratin' my forest again?" Gertie's voice carried that teasing tone most effective with young children.

He laughed. "I know now. Des-e-crate. You taught me."

"That's good, Arnold."

They walked along the trail in the full moon's light. Tanyth saw heads turn as they passed guard stations, but the clanking chain and the lumbering guard stilled any inquiries.

The end of the trail wasn't marked as such. The grass simply grew thicker and thicker as they neared the end of the line of guard posts. Eventually they walked on just salt grass, Arnold placidly leading the way until they neared a wind-blasted spruce that Tanyth recognized.

"That's far enough, Arnold," Tanyth said, her voice fighting the wind.

"The boss isn't here," Gertie said. "We tricked you into helpin' us get away."

Arnold's face split into the huge grin again. "No. You didn't. I tricked you!"

Tanyth looked around, seeing nothing but grasses waving in the wind.

"The boss wasn't never up here," Arnold said. "Only guards come up here."

"How did you trick us?" Tanyth asked.

"Now I can ex-cape with you!"

Tanyth and Gertie shared a glance. "You wanna leave with us?" Gertie asked.

"Well, yeah. Malcolm was always mean to me. They was gonna have me out scarin' travelers again tomorrow. I don't wanna des-e-crate your forest, lady. That just ain't right."

"I thought the boss was gonna take care of you," Tanyth said.

"Naw. I jus' said that. He's meaner'n Malcolm. They call me dumb, but I don't b'lieve a word he says. He jes' wants his gold and he'll take it." Arnold nodded once, as if for emphasis. "So, where do we do this ex-cape?" His eyes gleamed in the moonlight.

Tanyth flipped the latch on her manacle and pushed it off her wrist. Gertie did the same. "We need to get into the trees over there," Tanyth said, pointing to the line of maples and oaks. "Then we'll be almost home free."

"Can I be home free, too?" Arnold asked.

"Of course, dearie. We know a nice man who'd love to meet you. He'll take good care of you."

"He's not mean like the boss, is he?"

Gertie's grin matched Arnold's. "No, dearie. He's a nice man who's been looking for you for over a year."

Tanyth looked at the old woman and felt her own grin growing in the silvery light of the moon.

Chapter 37
Hide And Seek

The moonlight let them move through the forest almost as easily as day. They found the split, gray tree that sheltered their packs in a matter of a few minutes.

"Hey, that's real clever," Arnold said.

"Didn't want one of your patrols to find 'em," Gertie said. "Wasn't no sense takin' 'em in."

With the comforting weight of the pack on her shoulders, Tanyth closed her eyes and sought her owl.

☽○☾

Silvery light cast everything into sharp relief. The days grew warmer and the nights less cold. A fine baby rabbit rested comfortably in her belly. She didn't want to leave her roost, but she dropped from the perch, snapping her wings open to catch the night wind.

She soared close to the ground for a few yards and then caught the updraft from the edge of the cliff. The distinctive shape of the bay slipped under her as she flew east along the coast. There would be men there. She'd spot them, and then she could digest her rabbit in peace.

There, a small fire glowed among the trees and she slipped lower, gliding between the oaks on silent wings. Two men huddled beside the meager blaze, one or the other looking behind him to the forest that surrounded them.

She flipped her tail feathers and, with a single downbeat of her wings, lifted back through the canopy to continue eastward. She settled in for another long glide, nearly overshooting the clearing. A crack between two hills sheltered a banked fire and many men—some standing, others stretched out on the ground.

She dropped onto a tree just under the crest of the hill and looked back at the bay to the west. The moon crawled down toward the horizon. She could sleep here.

☽ ○ ☾

"Looks like Morris convinced his buddy," Tanyth said, opening her eyes. "Marong's about a day, day and a half to the east."

"If we start now, we can prob'ly meet him by tomorrow night," Gertie said. She turned to Arnold. "You ready for a walk in my forest, Arnold?"

"I'd like that, but I don't have a pack to carry. Do you want me to carry yours?"

"No, that's all right, Arnold," Gertie said. "Tanyth and I are fine."

"Malcolm made me carry his, sometimes, when we were out in the forest."

Tanyth sighed. "Malcolm never did impress me much."

"He's sinkin' in my esteem," Gertie said.

"You got a mouse?" Tanyth asked.

Gertie tilted her head down to show the black eyes and nose.

"Let's go, then."

As the moon climbed down the western sky, they trudged steadily eastward. At the first glimmer of dawn's rose on the eastern horizon, Gertie called a halt.

"Dearie? I'm gettin' old. I need to stop and have a bit of tea and perhaps somethin' to eat."

Tanyth's legs and back agreed with Gertie.

They turned and saw Arnold holding an armload of sticks. "You'll wanta fire, yeah?" he said.

"Yeah, that's good, Arnold," Gertie said, patting his arm. "We just need to find a place to settle for a bit."

"I'll keep pickin' up wood then," he said. "That's all right, en't it? That's not desceratin' or nothin', is it?"

"You're doing very well, dearie," Gertie said, and gave the big man another smile.

Tanyth listened to the predawn forest, and her hearing led them to a small creek. An oxbow provided a flat sandy bank on which to set up camp. "Just put the wood there, Arnold." She pointed to a spot in the sand, and Arnold dutifully unloaded his firewood with a clatter.

Without another word he dropped to his knees and scooped out some of the soft sand with his hands, making a shallow fire pit in a matter of a minute or two.

"You're a pretty handy guy to have around, Arnold," Tanyth said.

"I like to be useful, lady."

"Do you like tea?" she asked.

"Sure."

"Give us a few minutes and we'll have some. Then maybe a little nap."

Arnold nodded and proceeded to break up the longer sticks into shorter pieces that would fit in the fire pit. He simply cracked them over his knee and stacked them up.

Gertie shrugged and set about gathering some dried grasses from along the stream bank while Tanyth filled the kettle with water and began arranging the small sticks. Before long they all sat back and relaxed.

Arnold groaned a huge yawn. "We'll be able to sleep soon?"

"A bit of tea and somethin' to eat first," Gertie said. "Then we'll nap a little."

"We should keep a guard in case somebody comes along," Arnold said.

"Oh, we will." Gertie patted his knee. "You remember my rats?"

Arnold laughed, nodding. "Malcolm was so scared, but they didn't do nothin'. Just looked at him for a while and then ran away."

"My rats will look out for us. They'll wake me if somebody comes."

Tanyth pulled the boiling kettle off the fire and added the leaves to steep. "We got any food left in there?" She nodded at Gertie's pack.

"Still have some sausage."

"I've got a few travel rations left. Few days' worth for the three of us."

Gertie pulled out the sausage and reached for the empty sheath of her belt knife. "Morris still has my knife."

Tanyth nodded. "Mine, too."

"I have one." Arnold pulled out his knife and held it up.

Gertie handed him the sausage. "Cut that into pieces for us, would you, dearie?"

"Sure." Arnold focused on the dried meat and hacked a few pieces off, handing them back to Gertie as he did so. "That enough?"

"That's lovely, dearie. Thank you."

Arnold smiled and handed the last piece of sausage back to her.

Gertie pressed it back into his hand. "You eat that, Arnold. You'll need your strength before the day's out, I bet."

Arnold nodded. "Thank you," he said and began gnawing away. The sausage looked pathetically small in his hands.

Tanyth pulled a travel ration out of her pack and tossed it across the fire pit to him. "Eat that, too, if you're hungry."

Gertie shared the sausage pieces with Tanyth, who in turn poured Gertie's tea.

It took them a while to get all the food and tea distributed and consumed. By the time they did, the sun was well up. Arnold's broad face showed his fatigue clearly in eyelids that kept drooping.

"Two hours, sleep," Gertie said.

"All right," Arnold said. He flopped over onto the sand and curled up. Before either of the women had a chance to more than blink, he was snoring.

"Tired boy," Gertie said.

Tanyth chuckled. "He had a busy day."

"You think Marong'll be glad to see him?" Gertie asked.

"Yeah. I think so. He's been lookin' for somethin' since last year. At first I thought it was the gold, but that didn't make sense."

Gertie pulled her bedroll out and laid it out on the sand, lying down even as they chatted. "Why's that?"

"Gold's easy to find up there. He wouldn't be searchin'

the coast for it if that was all. He'd be headin' up to Black Rock Canyon."

"Well, he was up there last summer." Gertie yawned. "Trees were all a-whisper over it."

"So, not gold. Or not gold exactly."

"Makes sense."

"He's looking for the mint."

"Yeah. That's what I think, too."

"You still got them dies?"

Gertie patted one of her deep pockets. "Right here."

"Good." Tanyth stared into the fire for a few more moments before she realized the sun's light was brighter than the flames. Gertie's snores were blending with Arnold's. She tossed another stick on the fire and stretched out, resting her head on her pack.

Gertie's low voice woke her. "Tanyth. Time to go."

Tanyth felt a groan in her chest but stifled it. She blinked across the fire pit to where Arnold–wasn't. "Where'd he go?"

Gertie jerked her head toward the bushes and finished rolling up her bedding. Before she was done, Arnold shambled out of the brush and walked back to their meager camp.

"Breakin' camp, Arnold," Gertie said.

"All right." Arnold stepped into the fire pit, stomping the coals down with his big boots and then kicking sand in on top. "Fire's out," he said. "Sure you don't want me to carry a pack?"

"We're fine, Arnold. Thank you," Gertie said. She turned to Tanyth. "Any idea where Marong is now?"

"He shoulda been movin' this way about the time we laid down," she said. "Don't know what kinda back country hiker he is."

"He's ten miles closer than he was last night, or I'm no judge," Gertie said. "We need to find Morris and his pal."

"Arnold, who stands watch with Morris?" Tanyth asked.

"Danny. They had the watch last night. Bet they're sorry they missed all the excitement."

Tanyth's laugh floated on the midmorning air. "Likely he found a bit of his own."

"Owl's no good this late in the day," Gertie said. "You

The Hermit Of Lammas Wood

got any thing else?"

Tanyth closed her eyes and pressed outward. After a few moments she shook her head and opened her eyes. "Nothing."

A crow cawed three times from the top of a straggly oak across the creek.

Gertie looked at Tanyth and back at the bird in the tree top.

Tanyth sighed and focused on the bird.

☽○☾

Food would be good. Hungry time. She fluffed her feathers and launched from the tree. People walked in the wood. People had food. Sometimes they killed food and left it. She wheeled around the people nearby but they didn't have food. They didn't even smell of food.

She lifted above the treetops and sailed over the canopy. Two people stumbled along. One looked like he might be food soon. She circled and cawed a couple of times but they didn't look up. She kept moving. Food was nearby. It must be.

Movement in the forest drew her attention and she dropped into the forest to fly between the trees. It was not good to be seen. She soon found the line of men walking through the forest. Two men in the front with long shining things, two men behind with the curved sticks. She ducked behind a tree and flew up out of the canopy. Men with curved stucks were a danger. She needed to find food someplace else.

☽○☾

Tanyth opened her eyes to find Arnold staring at her. "I'm all right," she said.

"Morris?"

"He and Danny are that way." She pointed in the direction that the crow had spotted them. "It's either them or two others who smartened up and left."

"Morris and Danny are out here?" Arnold asked, his face alive with excitement. "Will the man we're goin' to meet want to meet them, too?"

"Oh, yeah. I'm sure of it," Tanyth said. She squinted, trying to remember the bearings as she scanned the trees. "Marong is that way. Maybe twenty miles. He's got armed troopers, and they're movin' fast."

"He'll be at the bay by tonight," Gertie said.

"Yeah. That's what I think, too."

"Just in time to meet Malloy," Gertie said.

Tanyth turned to Arnold. "Let's go, Arnold. We got people to meet." She led the way between the trees, the other two following close behind.

Chapter 38
Hunters And Hunted

They heard the two men thrashing through the forest long before they saw them. "I've heard whole herds of elk make less noise than that," Gertie said.

"You got mice out?" Tanyth asked.

"A few. Don't seem to be anybody else around."

"What in the Lady's name are they runnin' from?" Tanyth asked.

"Hunters," Arnold said.

"Hunters? Who'd shoot them?" Gertie asked. "Not like they're gonna be mistaken for game."

"Not hunter hunters. The boss's hunters."

Gertie and Tanyth skidded to a stop in the leaves. "The boss's hunters?"

"Sure. How else would he keep people from ex-capin'. If'n you run, the hunters'll track you down and take ya back." His mouth tightened in a thin line. "Getting taken back is real bad."

"How soon's that happen?" Gertie asked.

"Soon's they find you're gone. Watch changed at sun-up."

Tanyth and Gertie shared a glance. "Lemme see if any more of my li'l friends are out there in the leaves," Gertie said and her face went blank for a few moments.

Tanyth scanned the surrounding forest, looking for anything out of the ordinary. She couldn't hear anything because the two men still made too much noise. "They won't need to be very good trackers," she said. "Just have good ears."

Arnold made a little hee-hee noise. Tanyth had to look at

The Hermit Of Lammas Wood

him to make sure of the source. The amusement danced in his eyes.

"There's two guys comin' in from that direction. Few hundred yards at most." Gertie pointed. "Swords. No bows."

"Only two?"

"That's all I see."

"All right. We'll have to stop them first. Arnold, you take Gertie here over to meet your friends. See if you can get 'em to stop and be quiet. I'll handle these two."

"You sure?" Gertie asked, concern in her eyes. "There's two of them and one of you."

"Yeah, I figger they're outnumbered. They just don't know it. Scoot."

Gertie patted her on the shoulder and beckoned for Arnold to follow as they hurried to catch up with Morris and Danny.

Tanyth stepped into the scuffed trail of leaves the two men had left. She tsked. It would be hard to make a trail more obvious. She scraped the leaf litter away with the side of her boot, grounding her staff in the rich loam. The iron dug in, and the wooden core seemed to vibrate.

A shadow flitted between two trees in the distance. Another in the opposite direction.

"Gentlemen," Tanyth said. "So nice of you to join me this mornin'."

Steel zinged from two sheaths as the pair stepped from behind their respective trees.

"What you doin' here, lady?" the one on the right said, his voice a low growl.

"Oh, strollin' along, Enjoyin' the fine spring weather. You? What brings you two strappin' lads into the wood?"

"We got no time for this," the one on the left said. His mutter barely reached Tanyth over the thrashing in the brush behind her.

Tanyth felt the strength of the trees and the power in their branches. "And I've no time for this either. Here's something you might have time for. There's a garrison patrol headin' this way with one of the Kleesport city council. They'll be here in about an hour. You value your skins? You'll be gone from here."

The two spared a glance for each other. "You're bluffin'," the mouthy one on the right said, spinning his sword along its axis so it flashed in the morning light.

"As you say. We'll have the answer shortly. In the meantime, if you'd like to wait with me? I got nothin' better ta do."

A tree branch creaked overhead, leaves rustling.

The hunter on the left glanced up and squinted.

"Or you could turn around and get back to your base, and tell all the guards there to put down their weapons and surrender. It'll save a lot of people gettin' hurt."

"Lady, the only one's gonna get hurt is you, if you don't get outa here," the one on the right said.

Tanyth closed her eyes and felt for the roots on purpose this time. The ground practically writhed with them, pale worms with silky hairs that drank their meals from the soil and grew food in their leaves. She felt the bones of the world beneath her feet, and as before, the blood of the earth in the tiny rivers in their trunks; the breath of the world stirred their limbs, and they all but burst with life.

"Leave now," she said. "While you can."

"I thought you were in no hurry," the mouthy man said, his eyes challenging her. "Change your mind?"

"I'm not," Tanyth said. "They are." She looked up at the canopy of limbs swaying in the breezes coming in from the ocean a few miles away.

"What? The trees?"

Tanyth looked back down at the two men. "The trees," she said.

They both started laughing but their laughter turned to screams as the storm of pale white roots erupted around their feet, snaring their legs and growing upward, upward.

Tanyth turned and followed the rude trail in pursuit of Gertie, Arnold, and the two escaping guards. "Gettin' to be right crowded out here," she muttered.

The screams cut off just before Tanyth broke through the line of brush to find Gertie waiting with three men in green and black. Arnold, she knew. The other two were strangers who sat on the ground with Arnold standing over them. Their eyes all but bulged from their sockets when Tanyth approached.

"What was that all about?" Gertie asked, with a jerk of her chin.

"Feedin' the trees."

"Ah, spring is the best time for that. They get powerful hungry over the winter." She scratched her chin and pursed her lips.

"Arnold, can you introduce us to your friends?" Tanyth asked.

"Well, this here is Jimmy and that there is Fred," Arnold said. "But they ain't my friends."

Tanyth looked at Fred's legs. One seemed off, somehow. "What's wrong with your foot?"

"Sprained my ankle runnin' across the field," the man said. He scowled at the offending limb.

"Came near to gettin' us killed, too," Jimmy cuffed Fred's shoulder.

"Where's Morris and Danny?" Tanyth asked.

Jimmy snorted. "How'm I s'posed ta know that? Last I seen of them, they was down in the tunnels tryin' to get the fire under control."

"Was there a fire?" Gert asked.

"Yeah. Not sure how it got started, but it burned up the boss's office. He had two prisoners in there, too. They got burned right up. He's gonna be really mad when he gets back from Northport."

"Losing two prisoners? Yeah. I can see where that would ruin his day." Gertie nodded.

"So what're you two doin' out here?" Tanyth asked. "Another quarter hour and those hunters woulda had ya."

Jimmy shook his head. "We ain't stupid. All hell's gonna break loose back there, between the mine and the slaves and the cargoes. That can't just go on and on without somebody findin' out."

Fred nodded and winced as his weight shifted. "Yeah. Signs are all there. Low-level grunts like us always get it in the neck. We figgered the fire was a good distraction, so we beat it out of there soon's the guard got pulled back for fire-fightin'."

Jimmy sighed. "We'd a been miles away if he hadn't stepped in that rabbit hole."

"Coulda been you," Fred said.

"Yeah, but 'twasn't, was it?"

"Easy there, gentlemen," Tanyth said. "The garrison's sent a patrol. They're just over that rise. They'll take good care of ya. Tell them nice stories, and they'll prob'ly let ya go home after a while."

"Garrison?" Freddy spat on the ground, disgust warping his face. "Malloy paid off the garrison first. They're just gonna take us back to the hole."

Tanyth's world focused down to the two men sitting on the ground. "What?"

"You can't operate somethin' this big out here for as long as Malloy's been playin' without payin' off the garrison." Jimmy shook his head. "Half the time it's the garrison bringin' the runaways back."

"They've got one of the Kleesport city council with them," Gertie said.

"Who? That Marong fella?" Jimmy sniffed. "He looked all summer long last year. Never got a twitch. Funny how that works when the garrison's drivin' the cart."

"If he gets too close to the hole, he's gonna find himself swingin' a pick with the rest of 'em and his patrol'll have a sad, sad tale to tell when they get back to town," Fred said.

"Bears, prob'ly," Jimmy said. "Bears don't leave much behind so they take a lot o' blame for folks gettin' lost in the back country."

"That or the hermit," Fred said and laughed.

Arnold stirred himself at that, storm clouds filling his face.

Gertie waved him down before he could speak. "Never mind now, Arnold. We'll deal with that later."

The two men looked up, but other than a stormy-looking Arnold there wasn't much to take in.

"You two don't stray. Arnold here'll keep ya company and make sure ya don't wander off, won't ya, Arnold?" Gertie asked.

"You bet." He nodded his head once for emphasis and

folded his arms across his chest.

His fierce expression nearly made Tanyth giggle as she led Gertie off to the side of their small clearing.

"So, Marong isn't in on it but his garrison patrol is," Gertie said.

"That's what they say. They got no reason to lie about it as I can tell."

Gertie puckered her lips and stared off into the middle distance. "So we gotta get Marong out of the pack without them bein' the wiser."

"And do it soon, before they get too close and make him a slave, too."

"You know the man?" Gertie asked.

Tanyth shook her head. "Only by reputation, and that's prob'ly not accurate."

"Seldom is," Gertie said with a shrug. "I met him once. Winters ago, now."

"How old is he? Rebecca's only in her mid-twenties."

"He's a late bloomer, he is. Didn't have kids until he was nigh on forty. He's older'n you, but not by that much."

"How do we do this?" Tanyth asked.

"The trick is gettin' him alone. Somewhere out of earshot of his escort."

"How d'we do that?"

Gertie's eyes started to sparkle and she glanced over toward the guards across the clearing. "I think they just told us how."

"They did?"

"Yep. Bears."

"Bears?"

"Definitely. Bears."

Chapter 39
Unlikely Ally

Tanyth slipped between the ancient oaks. Behind her, Gertie and the green shirts waited behind a raspberry brake Gertie's mice had told them about. Somewhere not far ahead, the squad of garrison troops approached.

Two dozen yards away, the vanguard stepped into the small clearing. The troopers ambled along like they were on an afternoon's picnic, not noticing Tanyth standing in their path until she spoke.

"There you are. Is Richard Marong with you?" she asked.

The troopers started and reached for hilts as a pair of bowmen followed them into the clearing. The archers walked with strung bows but no arrows nocked. They ambled up to the first two, and one of them leered at Tanyth.

"Well, well, well. What have we here?" he asked. "You're a long way from civilization, mum."

She smiled at him. "You're King's Own, aren't you? Civilization goes where you tread. I need to speak with Richard Marong. You're aiding him in his search, aren't you?"

The soldiers shared a glance among themselves, and one of the bowmen looked back along their trail.

"Our mission is the king's business, mum. None of your own." The bowman's words carried a veneer of politeness, but the steel in his voice made it clear that her questions had no authority with him.

She sighed. "Yes, yes. I know. King's Own. You answer to the king alone and we're all glad for it, but Richard Marong is just around the bend behind you and I need to speak with

The Hermit Of Lammas Wood

him."

The bowman stiffened. "Maybe he is. Maybe he isn't. Who are you, mum? What business have you with the magistrate?"

"That's more like it," she said and raised her voice. "My name is Tanyth Fairport, and I have news about his daughter, Rebecca." Her words all but echoed through the forest, ringing in the afternoon air.

A tallish man sporting a salt and pepper beard of black and white strode into the clearing between the soldiers. Several more soldiers tagged his heels, half-running to keep up with his long, rapid strides. "What news have you of Rebecca?"

"Ah, Richard, I'm so glad I caught you." Tanyth approached the group of men, ignoring the soldiers as she made her way along the forest path. "Rebecca asked me to give you news if I saw you before she did."

His brow furrowed and his eyes searched her face. "You have the advantage, mum. Do I know you?"

"Well, of course. We met last Yule in Kleesport. The Mapletons' party?" She continued moving toward him, threading her way through the soldiers as if strolling through passers-by and giving them no more notice. "I'm Tanyth—Tanyth Fairport?"

He frowned at her and shook his head. "The Mapletons' party? You were there?"

"Well, of course." She laid a hand on his arm. "I'm not surprised you don't remember. Forgive me. You must meet so many people, one old woman must seem much like another."

He smiled then and waved a hand at the men crowding his coattails, signaling they should back away. "Of course, but you have news of Rebecca? Is she all right?"

"Fine, fine..." Tanyth glanced around at all the soldiers. "The news is of rather a personal nature. Perhaps we might...?" She drew him by the sleeve and stepped away from the crowd, leaning into him to whisper. "Rebecca is in Northport and fine, but these troops are not in your employ."

"What?" His voice rose in alarm.

"Please. You must listen. I know what you're really looking for. These soldiers have orders to kill you if you get too close. In a moment, a bear is going to come down that path. You need to order these men to retreat. Gertie and I will take you to the counterfitters."

"Why should I trust you?" He scowled at her, but he kept his voice down.

"You have no reason at all, but Rebecca always spoke highly of you."

"Now I know you're lying," he said. "What did she really say? The truth or I'll have these soldiers take you into custody."

"You're a close-minded, pig-headed man who thinks he has the right to tell her how to live her life," Tanyth said. "You complained bitterly when she moved out to Mapleton's settlement, and you've been after her for years to give it up and take up a respectable life."

Marong's eyes went wide in surprise and then he laughed. "That's her," he said. "Now what's going on?"

"Bear. Draw your sword and tell the troops to run."

The words had no sooner left her lips than a huge brown bear shambled out of the forest. Rearing onto its hind legs, it roared a challenge at the soldiers.

"Now, before the bowmen draw," Tanyth said, her voice a hiss against his ear.

Marong stepped forward, drawing a meter of gleaming steel and pushing Tanyth behind him. "Run, men! Get safe! Go!"

The bear roared again and staggered forward one step.

The soldiers scattered, running back through the forest as fast as their legs would carry them.

The bear roared a third time and fell down on all fours. It turned its broad head and glared at Marong, baring yellowed fangs.

"All right, Arnold. That's very good. You can stop now," Tanyth said.

The bear bobbed its head and shambled back around the raspberry brake.

"What in the Lady's name—" Marong said.

"No time. Quick, before they realize it's a ruse," Tanyth

The Hermit Of Lammas Wood

took Marong's arm and half led, half dragged him after the bear.

On the back side of the raspberry patch, they found Gertie and Arnold hunkered down out of sight.

"Where's the bear?" Marong asked.

Arnold raised his hand. "That was me, sir."

"We need to scoot," Gertie said. "Them soldiers will regroup in a minute and we need to be gone."

"What's this about?" Marong asked, pulling his arm out of Tanyth's grip. "Do you people know who I am?"

Gertie snorted and settled her pack on her back. "If we didn't, we wouldn't be riskin' our lives to save yours. Now get a move on, yer lordship, or yer gonna be the late Richard Marong, Magistrate-at-Large, when them boys get back here and fill you full of arrows." She turned and marched away with Arnold on her heels.

"Come on, Mr. Marong. We've got the dies. Malloy is goin' to be back in the mine shortly and when he is, these woods are gonna be full of people who'd like nuthin' better'n to skin you, me, Gertie, and anybody else they find skulkin' about."

"The dies? The dies for what?" Richard asked.

"For the coins that Malloy is pressin'. Come on. We can hash this all out later." She pointed down the trail where Arnold and Gertie waited, waving their hands. "You gotta go so I can cover our back trail, and we're runnin' out of time."

"Gertie? Gertie Pinecrest?" he asked.

"That's her." Tanyth pointed. "Go talk to her about it, would ya?"

Richard started off down the path, his steps growing longer with each stride until he finally got out of the way. Tanyth followed him a short distance and then stopped, waiting for them to move off a bit more before grounding her staff. "Mother help me here," she said, her eyes closed and her words barely louder than the breezes in the tree tops.

The earth around her seemed to boil for a moment, leaves and small twigs rustling and shifting, the soil itself seeming to shake itself clear like a fresh sheet of snow. When the movement stopped, the ground looked untrammeled for yards in any direction except for the very obvious scuffle in the leaves that led into a boggy hollow in the forest, but didn't come out the other side.

With a satisfied nod, Tanyth picked her way through the leaf litter until she found the real trail. In moments she'd caught up to Gertie and her band.

"Now what?" Marong asked.

"We bought some time, but Fred here has a sprained ankle and can't move fast," Gertie said. "Arnold and Jimmy, carry the litter. We need to get as far away from here as we can get before Malloy's men start tearin' the woods apart."

"With any luck, the garrison's troops will find them," Marong said.

Gertie snorted. "That's not gonna help us."

"Malloy owns the garrison," Tanyth said. "That's why they dragged you all over the back country last summer. They figgered you'd give it up and go away."

"There's too much at stake," Marong said. "Somebody's been hijacking ships, stealing the cargo, and reselling it. That can't be allowed to stand."

Gertie laughed. "If you only knew."

"What?" He squinted at Gertie. "You're Gertie Pinecrest?"

"Yeah. Most days. And you're Richard Marong. We got a lot to say to each other, but we gotta live first. If you can see your way clear to move your posterior? I'd really like to survive til mornin'."

Marong seemed to come to some decision. "Let's go, then."

"'Bout time," Gertie said and struck off down the trail into the forest.

Arnold and Jimmy grabbed the ends of a crude litter and hefted Fred off the ground. They wasted no time following Gertie. Richard glanced at Tanyth and followed, leaving Tanyth to watch the back trail as she followed along behind.

Chapter 40
Bad News

Gertie led the party steadily northward through the day. They made a cold camp for food at midday but otherwise kept walking. As the sun began turning the treetops red, she called a halt in a narrow valley between two ridges. An eroded bank on one side gave them a modicum of shelter. A ring of white stones around an ash pit marked the spot as recently visited. "We camp here tonight," she said, slipping her pack from her shoulders and standing it next to the bank.

Arnold and Jimmy lowered the litter to the ground and Fred eased himself off it so he could lean against the grassy bank.

"How you doin'?" Gertie asked.

"Hurtin', and bein' carried all day made me dizzy, but that's a small price to pay for livin'," he said. "Thanks. All of you." He looked from face to face and then down to his hands, clasped together in his lap.

"We got any food left?" Tanyth asked.

"I'm hopin' you got travel rations for all of us for tonight," Gertie said, a smile on her lips. "If not, we're gonna go hungry til mornin'."

"Yeah. I got some, but we gotta either stop addin' people or recruit a hunter," Tanyth said. She plopped her pack down beside Gertie's and rummaged out six travel rations, handing them around.

"I'll get some wood," Arnold said and turned to walk up the ravine.

"Don't go far," Gertie said. "We'll need to keep a close

The Hermit Of Lammas Wood

watch tonight and make sure Malloy's men don't stumble on us."

"I'll help him," Jimmy said and struck off after Arnold.

"So, can we talk now?" Marong asked, hunkering down beside the fire ring.

"Yeah. We can talk now," Gertie said.

"What's all this about Malloy? Who's Malloy?" he asked.

"Malloy's the man you're lookin' for," she responded. "He's the one behind all this."

"All what?" Marong asked. "He's the pirate hijackin' the ships?"

Fred laughed, a single, bitter bark in the deepening gloom. "Yeah. Ya might say that."

Arnold and Jimmy came back, each with an armload of wood, which they deposited beside the fire ring.

Tanyth pulled a few twigs out of the grass beside her and started a small fire. She filled her tea kettle with water and shoved it next to the coals. Nobody spoke while she worked, the long day following the longer night catching up with all of them except Marong, who looked from face to face around the fire.

"Mr. Marong, we lied to ya," Tanyth said. "Those men weren't s'posed to kill ya."

"What? Then why—?"

"They were gonna make you a slave in Malloy's gold mine," Gertie said.

"Never waste a good slave," Fred said, his face shadowed by his hair. "That's what they told us. Don't kill anybody unless you can't capture 'em."

Marong's face went blank, his eyes unmoving as he stared into the middle distance at nothing at all. "I've got a lot of catching up to do," he said. "Gertie? Care to start?"

"What are ya really' lookin' for? Ain't yer daughter. You knew where she was last year," Gertie said.

"The council sent me up here to find out where the hijacked goods were being landed. We knew somebody was stealing the cargoes—just didn't know how they were bringing the goods ashore. Or where."

"Why up here? Lotsa places handier," Gertie said.

"The council heard rumors about ships being hijacked as long as five years ago. At the time it was only rumor, but more and more ships never arrived in port. Some of them carried insurance, some didn't. Insurance payouts were pennies on the pound. We watched and waited, but for the longest time we only had rumors."

"What changed yer mind?" Tanyth asked.

"Stephen Mapleton convinced the council that it was in their best interest to make sure the insurance cartel's fingers were not in the pie."

"William's brother?" Tanyth asked.

"You know William Mapleton?" he asked and then shook his head. "Of course you do. You're the healer. You wintered there last year, didn't you?"

"Yeah. That's me."

"That's how you know Rebecca," he grinned at her, the firelight casting shadows across his weathered face.

"Yeah."

"Anyway, the council took Stephen seriously and three winters ago started shipping goods all over. Small, relatively expensive items, but marked. We know where they left from, who took them, and where they were supposed to be going." He shrugged. "Almost at once a ship carrying one of our cargoes was lost at sea. Never arrived in port. Over that summer we lost four shipments—some were insured, some weren't."

"Not much to go on," Gertie said.

"No, but by fall one of the marked items showed up in Northport and a second one back in Kleesport itself." He shrugged. "By spring we'd found a third one, and I was dispatched north to try to find the smuggling operation along the coast."

"Why didn't you sail instead of trampin' all over?" Tanyth asked.

"The council's cutters sailed up and down for weeks and never spotted a thing," he said. "My masters on the council decided that boots on dirt might give better results. There's still a cutter out there on patrol."

"You know who the captain is?" Gertie asked.

Marong shook his head. "No idea. Somebody the council

hired."

"Well, Mr. Marong, you're in luck. These fine gentlemen worked for the smuggler, and now they just want to get away without bein' killed."

Marong eyed them up and down. "What were your jobs?"

Fred looked up from his hands and stared at Marong. "Guards. We kept the hunters and trappers out and the slaves in."

"Slaves," Marong said. "What's this about slaves?"

"Malloy didn't just steal the cargoes, Mr. Marong. He stole the whole ship—keel to top, crew included," Fred said.

"How do you know that?"

"I was on the *Esmerelda*–deck hand when Malloy came alongside and the skipper turned the ship over."

"What happened to Captain Harris?" Marong asked, leaning forward over the fire.

"Malloy tossed him over the side. He went down like a ten-ton anchor." Fred paused and looked into the fire. "That's when he asked for volunteers to join his guards."

Only the sound of the fire crackling filled the silence for several long moments.

Marong looked to the other men. "Same story?"

"More or less," Jimmy said.

"Yeah," Arnold said.

"Malloy," Marong said. "That's not the same Malloy who used to skipper the *Sea Rover*?"

"That's him," Jimmy said.

"Used to?" Fred asked.

"I came up on the *Rover* a week ago. Malloy's first mate made skipper over the winter. He's captain now."

"Malloy's had his hands full here most of the winter," Jimmy said. "He went south just before the Call."

"How's that possible?" Marong asked.

"Dunno, but he was in and outta the hole half a dozen times this winter." Jimmy said. "Kept an ice boat in the cove, and he'd run out in that."

"He had an ice dock," Arnold said. "Log booms."

All eyes turned to the big man huddled close to the fire.

He shifted his weight and glanced around. "Some of the

guards talked about it. They talked about a lot of things when I was around 'cause they said I couldn't understand 'em."

Marong's brow furrowed as he stared into the fire. "Nobody'd expect he'd come up here because everybody knows you can't get in or out in the winter."

Tanyth pulled the kettle back from the fire and measured out a handful of tea. "We'll have to take turns. We only got two cups."

The evening breeze stirred the treetops above them on the ridge. *Change is coming.*

"Yeah, yeah," Gertie said. "Change is comin'."

Tanyth snickered.

"What's that?" Marong asked.

"Them fool trees. Always with 'the change is comin'.' Change is always comin'. If they're gonna gossip, least they could do is tell me somethin' interestin'."

"The trees," Marong said.

"Terrible gossips," Tanyth said.

"I see," Marong said and glanced around at the other men.

"So, anyway. Malloy has his slaves diggin' gold out from under the cliff," Tanyth said. "We just need to figger out how to get them out of there."

Marong blinked several times and stared at Tanyth. "He what?"

"That's what we been tryin' to tell ya," Gertie said. "All them sailors? Them that didn't choose to be guards? They're miners now."

Fred nodded. "She's tellin' true. I have no idea how long the operation's been goin' on, but it was well underway when I got here last fall."

"I been here just over two winters now," Arnold said. "The boss said he was gonna take care of us and we had nothin' to worry about, but I didn't believe him. My time's almost up and I don't want him to take care of me. When these ladies ex-caped, I tricked 'em into lettin' me come, too."

Jimmy snorted. "Smartest one of the bunch of us, ya ask me."

The starch drained out of Marong, and he slumped down

The Hermit Of Lammas Wood

by the fire. "Gold mine? What's he do with the gold? The council would have heard if there was a lot of new gold around."

"He stamps it into coins. Takes the coins to town and spends 'em."

Marong frowned and shook his head. "Are you sure? Making gold coins is an exacting process. He'd need—"

Gertie reached into her pocket and pulled out two metal rods. "A coin press?" she asked and handed them across the fire to Marong. "He'll need a new set of dies, now."

Tanyth almost laughed at the expression on Marong's face when he tilted the dies to look at the impressions. "We thought you were here lookin' for the counterfitters, Mr. Marong. Sorry for the confusion."

The wind sighed through the treetops again. *Change is coming. Snow falls in the high country.*

Gertie glanced up with a disgusted look on her face. "I tell ya, Tanyth. It's like that all the time." She raised her voice and shouted at the trees. "Tell me somethin' I don't know, you vertical stack of firewood!"

He has the girl.

Tanyth looked up at the treetops, her heart making so much noise in her chest she wasn't sure she heard correctly.

He has the girl.

Gertie sighed and closed her eyes.

"What?" Marong said. "What's wrong?"

"The trees. They're terrible gossips," Tanyth said.

Gertie nodded. "Sometimes they tell ya stuff you don't wanna hear."

Marong scanned the faces around the fire. "Is this a joke or something? The trees are gossips? A back-country thing to tease the city folk?"

Gertie shook her head. "Wish it were."

Arnold shrugged. "You better believe her, or you'll suffer her rats."

"You mean wrath?" Marong asked.

"No, he means rats," Gertie said.

Tanyth poured tea into her cup and slurped off a mouthful, letting the hot liquid roll down her throat. She handed the

266

cup to Marong. "Drink up. We've gotta go back."

He took the cup from her and sipped. "Back? Back where?"

"Back to the hole," Gertie said. "How far away are we, Tanyth?"

Tanyth closed her eyes and centered herself, seeking her owl.

☽○☾

The last glow of the sun faded as she blinked and stretched. It had been a good sleep. The hunting was good here, away from the men. She ruffled her feathers and preened a bit, giving her primaries a good oiling. The night called her, and she dropped from the branch to soar between the trees.

She lifted above the canopy, circling once to get her bearings. The pointed bay lay to the southwest, and she soared north, looking for a fire in the trees. Shadows moved in the forest and she dropped down to see men moving, some rapidly with much noise. Some very quiet.

A twist of her tail and she soared above the treetops once more. It took her several long minutes of gliding through the chill night air before she found the glow of a fire half hidden in a ravine. She turned and sailed back toward the pointed bay and the fields where hunting would be sparse this night.

The moon, just past full, peeked above the eastern horizon as the sun's final glow gave way to darkness and stars.

☽○☾

Tanyth opened her eyes and looked to Gertie.

The old woman smiled. "Welcome back."

"Thanks. We're about eight or ten miles from the bay, but the woods are crawling with green shirts."

"I don't understand," Marong said. "We know where this place is. All we need to do is get back to Northport and get help."

"Who you gonna ask for help?" Gertie asked. "The garrison works for Malloy."

"I'll take the next boat back to Kleesport and get the council's support. Malloy and his men haven't bought that, or I wouldn't be here."

The Hermit Of Lammas Wood

"Ya. You can do that. Take these guys with ya," Gertie said, waving a hand at the green shirted ex-guards. "We gotta go back. Right now."

"I don't understand. Why?" Marong asked.

"Because Malloy has Rebecca," Tanyth said.

Marong sat up like he'd been hit with a stick. "What? How can that be? She's out at Mapleton's little clay mine."

Tanyth shook her head. "She came north with me."

"She's here?"

"She was in Northport. When Malloy found out that Robert didn't have the bomb, he prob'ly grabbed her as leverage to try to get me to talk," Tanyth said. "He's gonna be surprised to find I'm not waitin' for him."

"He's gonna be mad you burned his office," Arnold said.

Marong looked at the two metal rods in his hand, hefting them as if judging their weight. "That's not the half of it," he said. He shook his head and looked at Tanyth. "What bomb?"

"Oh, we found a bomb on *Zypheria's Call* on the voyage north. The insurance cartel wanted to make an example of Saul Groves by sinkin' his ship on the way out. Malloy knows about it. When he found out that the *Call* wasn't sunk, he lit out like a scared cat."

Marong opened his eyes wide and stretched his face. "Under any other circumstance I'd think I was dreaming." He stared at Tanyth. "This is all true? All of it?"

"Yeah. Wish it wasn't."

Marong handed the dies back to Gertie. "You keep these for now."

Gertie shook her head and jerked a thumb at Arnold. "Give 'em to him. We're goin' back in the hole, and I ain't takin' them back in with me."

Marong looked at the big man and held out the dies. "Keep 'em safe."

"I will, sir," Arnold said. He took the metal rods and slipped one into each of his front trouser pockets.

Marong stood and dusted off the seat of his pants. "For all I know, I'm going to wake up in my bed in the morning, but for now let's play this nightmare out."

Gertie and Tanyth scrambled to their feet as well.

Gertie turned to Jimmy. "You three stay here tonight. Get some sleep. At first light, follow the ravine north. It'll take you almost to Black Rock Canyon. You should get there by sundown tomorrow if you move along. Even carryin' Fred. If you can get to Black Rock, you'll prob'ly be safe. Just don't talk to any garrison troops while you're wearin' black and green."

Tanyth looked to Marong. "I hope you're right about wakin' up in your bed tomorrow morning, but I'll settle for wakin' up alive."

Marong's lips tightened into a line above his beard. "You're sure he's got her?"

Tanyth looked to the trees at the top of the ridge. "Terrible gossips, trees," she said. "Most of the time they tell ya stuff you already know, and the rest of the time they tell ya stuff you don't wanna hear."

Gertie nodded. "Sorry you had to learn that lesson, dearie."

Marong glanced at the trees above them. "Let's go get my daughter back," he said.

Chapter 41
Back Down

Tanyth, Gertie, and Marong moved fast. They left their packs behind after they distributed the food to the remaining men. By midnight, they stood just inside the tree line, looking out at the cliff top.

"I thought—" Marong began, but Gertie shushed him with a scowl and a wave of her hand.

"I thought," Marong whispered, with a glance at Gertie, "that the forest was full of guards. We haven't seen one."

"You haven't," Gertie said.

"Gertie uses the forest mice as scouts. We've been sneakin' between 'em. We came past twelve or so in the last five miles." Tanyth said. "There's guards in holes along the top of the cliff."

"No there ain't," Gertie said, her eyes unfocused. "More'n half them posts got nobody in 'em."

"Huh. Wonder where they went?" Tanyth muttered low.

"Given the number of men in the woods, I'd guess at least some o' them took a lesson from Fred and Jimmy," the old woman said.

"Where are the rest, though?"

Gertie sighed. "You gotta stop askin' questions we can't answer. Wastes time. They're either down in the hole or out in the woods. Ain't much difference which, as long as we can get to the platform and get down to the hole."

Tanyth shot Gertie a smile. "How do we get across the field?"

"Shoulda put Richard in Arnold's shirt. He could walk us

in," Gertie said.

Tanyth eyed Richard's gray beard and the white hair peeking from under his cap. "Yeah. That'd work. How many fifty-year-old men you think guard the hole?"

"Ladies? Any chance we could have this conversation later?" Marong asked.

"Yeah," Gertie said. "Mousies say there's nobody on the ends. Prob'ly be able to get around the line and then walk along the cliff top. Walk right by 'em."

"Won't they see us when we walk by?" Marong asked.

"Might," Tanyth said. "Mos' likely they're gonna keep their eyes front and hope who ever's walkin' behind 'em ain't the boss."

Marong chuckled softly. "Fair point."

Gertie led the way back along the familiar path, and they circled the open land just inside the tree line.

Tanyth swallowed a yawn. The day was getting too long for the amount of sleep they'd gotten. One way or another, it would soon be over.

A stray breeze whispered through the tree tops. *Change is coming.*

In the lead, Gertie snorted, but kept going.

It took them more than an hour to skirt the open grassland; the waning moon hung nearly overhead.

"What do we say if they challenge us?" Richard asked, his voice a raspy whisper on the onshore breeze.

"Say nothin' and keep movin'," Gertie said. "It's not like they're gonna chase us and leave their posts."

"You sound pretty certain."

"Three more pairs have crossed the field while we were workin' our way around," Gertie said. "They're gittin' while the gittin's good, and I don't blame 'em."

Marong took a deep breath and started to lead the way along the cliff.

Tanyth planted her staff in front of him. "Unless you know the way, one of us should go first."

"She's my daughter."

"So stop bein' a hero, and keep yer head down." With that Tanyth led the way. They soon found themselves striding along the bare soil path that ran behind the guard posts. Tanyth didn't try to see which ones were manned. She just kept her eyes straight ahead and kept moving. In a matter of minutes they stepped down to the wooden platform on the side of the cliff.

"I knew it was goin' too easy," Gertie said, staring at the hole where the moving platform should have been.

Marong leaned over and looked down. The look on his face when he stepped back made Tanyth grin.

"Has to be a way to bring it up again," Tanyth said. "Some kinda lever or signal or something."

"This is prob'ly it," Gertie said. She pointed to a handle at the side of the platform, a simple stick of wood with a dirt-smeared top.

Marong reached for it and pulled, but nothing happened. The stick didn't move. He pushed and it moved forward half a foot, then stopped with a loud *ka-chunk* that Tanyth felt through her boots.

"You're lucky that weren't the trap door," Gertie said and peeked over the edge. "It's comin' up."

"What'll we find at the bottom?" Marong asked.

"Falling water so loud you can't hear yourself think," Tanyth said. "Prob'ly a couple o' guards."

"A couple of guards?"

"Yeah. Big guys with swords and maces, if I remember right."

"What do we do about them?"

"Dunno. We got a couple minutes yet to come up with somethin' if you're feeling adventurous," Gertie said.

The platform rose into place and stopped with shudder. Gertie and Tanyth stepped aboard and grabbed the railing. Marong eyed the contraption.

"You comin'?" Gertie said.

"Is it safe?"

"Prob'ly safer goin' down than gettin' off at the bottom." She grinned at him.

He grinned back and stepped aboard.

Gertie bumped the lever that she'd seen Morris pull, and the floor began to sink under them.

"You trust two old ladies who listen to trees gossip and go harin' off across the countryside in the dark of night, but quibble over this?" Tanyth asked, waving a hand at the machinery.

Marong blinked several times and cocked his head sideways. "It does seem odd."

"How d'you know we're not takin' ya down to be slaves ourselves?" Gertie asked.

"I don't," he said. "If you're who you say and if what you say has happened, my daughter needs me. If not, then I'll probably die knowing I would have been there had she needed me."

Tanyth patted his arm. "Hold that thought."

"What? Die knowing I would have been there?"

"No, the one about your daughter needin' ya." Tanyth had to shout over the sound of the water falling from above.

The platform bumped against the stone landing and stopped. The big door leading into the tunnels stood open, the pair of burly guards nowhere in sight. With a shrug, Gertie led the way up the wet stone steps into the tunnel.

The stench of wood smoke and something less appealing assaulted them immediately. They stopped just inside the door. Half the torches were missing, and the few that remained guttered and threatened to go out. Odd bits of charred material littered the floor.

Tanyth stepped over to Gertie to speak directly into her ear. "Mice?"

Gertie nodded once and led the way into the tunnels. Her steps halted now and again, and she trailed a hand along the wall as if keeping her balance. In spite of their slow pace, only minutes passed before they were in Malloy's office once more. The smoke still lingered in a blue-gray haze. The cot lay in smoldering ruin, the frame kicked aside and the mattress tossed against the wall. Malloy's desk had survived more or less intact, with a large scorch mark in the center and wisps of smoke rising from the back side.

"Father?" The weak voice drew their eyes to the manacles on the wall. "Tanyth!"

"Rebecca!" Marong rushed to his daughter's side, pulling

at the chain to no good effect. "Are you hurt?"

The young woman grimaced and shook her manacles, rattling the chains. "These aren't exactly silver bracelets and I can't remember the last time I ate, but otherwise still whole."

"Where's Malloy?" Tanyth asked.

Rebecca shook her head. "He stopped long enough to chain me up here, kick the cot apart, and get a couple of his guards to drag that box out. They're supposed to put it on the ship."

"Then what?"

"He pulled out the drawers in the desk, fumbled around inside, and cursed a lot. He went through there"–Rebecca jerked her chin at the hidden door–"and came out almost immediately. He didn't look pleased."

"I dare say he wasn't," Marong said. "We've come to get you out of here."

"What, you didn't just stop by for a visit?" Rebecca's eyes sparkled in the light of the ruined torches.

"Mr. Marong? If you'd get out of the way, we'll get her off the wall," Gertie said.

Marong stepped aside just as Tanyth swung her staff, iron end foremost, at the eye bolt. The bolt jumped, and in a few moments they pulled it out of the rock, just like before.

Marong's surprised look made Gertie laugh. "Practice pays off," she said. "He locked us in here the same way yesterday."

"Too bad we left that hammer with Arnold," Tanyth said. "We'll have to find another way to break those locks."

"Drape the chain over your shoulders for now, dearie," Gertie said. "We'll deal with them once we're out of here."

"What? Leaving so soon?" Malloy's voice made them spin. He lounged in the door with two archers backing him up. "You'll miss the fireworks."

Marong's hand went to the hilt of his sword.

Malloy raised a hand and one of the archers drew down on Rebecca. "Tut, tut, Richard. Let's not be hasty."

"I scarcely believed it when they said it was you behind all this, Charles."

"We all have our secrets, don't we? Even you." Malloy's

The Hermit Of Lammas Wood

smile made Tanyth's stomach roil. "I confess I never expected that you'd actually make it in here. The garrison troops were supposed to keep you busy elsewhere."

"They did a good job of it," Marong said. "They had me running hither and yon through the back country for weeks. How much did you pay them?"

"Not much at all," Malloy said. "A gold or two here and there, a large tab paid at the tavern. It was easy to buy myself the loyalty of a whole squad for the price of a decent sword."

"You didn't bribe the commandant, then?" Tanyth asked.

"Robert Bloody Oakhurst? You obviously don't know the man," Marong said and spat on the stone. "There was no need to, at any rate. I only needed to buy enough of his troopers to keep Richard here chasing his shadow through Lammas Wood."

"How did you know I was coming?"

"Ah, that would be telling, wouldn't it? I don't think so." He shook his head, a playful smile on his lips.

"You'll never get away with this, Charles."

Malloy's face lost its smile. "I already have, Marong. Oh, yes, this little enterprise is about to close its doors, but I've enough gold stashed on the ship to buy the kingdom twice over. That's more than enough to set myself up in business elsewhere—say, the Eastern Islands?"

"What did you mean, fireworks?" Gertie asked.

"Oh? Did I say fireworks?"

A series of sharp reports shook the air and dust filtered down from the rocks over head. The distant roaring from the waterfall changed pitch and disappeared.

The two archers shared a glance with each other but a sharp look from Malloy steadied them.

"Well, I think that wraps up my business here," Malloy said.

"What was that?" Marong asked.

"That, dear Richard, was the door closing on my little enterprise here, as I said before."

"You collapsed the mine," Gertie said, her eyes narrowing and her voice a harsh rasp.

"Oh, don't be melodramatic, dear girl. I did no such

thing."

"He collapsed the shelf," Tanyth said. "He blocked the entrance."

"Ah, a woman who understands!" Malloy's oily approval did nothing for Tanyth's feeling of dread.

Marong looked around at the faces. "Blocked the entrance?"

"Yeah. And I bet all those slaves are still inside, aren't they," Gertie said.

"Well, of course. Extra mouths to feed and all that. An overhead I couldn't afford, you see." Malloy's cheerful mein shifted to dark anger, and he scowled at Gertie and Tanyth. "It's your fault. If you busybodies hadn't come snooping around, we'd still be in business and those men would still be alive."

"What about all your guards?" Tanyth asked, her eyes on the archers behind Malloy. "Did they all get out first?"

Malloy opened his mouth to speak but a quick glance in the archers' direction made him close it.

"They didn't, did they?" Tanyth said.

"Yes, of course they did. What few are left."

"Left? Did you kill them all already?" Tanyth asked.

"Don't be ridiculous. They're out chasing down deserters." Malloy spit the words out casually. "Another thing I have you two to thank for."

"How many of them will go with you?" Tanyth asked.

He scowled at her. "That's none of your business. It's time for me to go, anyway." He turned to the archers. "Give me ten minutes to get aboard the ship. Then kill them." He grinned at them, but his expression contained no humor. "Oh, and those miners you're so concerned about? They'll outlive you by at least an hour, maybe two." He raised a hand and fluttered his fingers in their direction. "Good-bye. Sorry to be an ungracious host and run out, but the tide's with me and I need to be off." He pushed away from the door frame and disappeared down the tunnel.

"He's gonna kill you, you know," Tanyth said to the archers.

They glanced at each other but kept their bows at the ready.

The Hermit Of Lammas Wood

"What did he mean by saying the miners will outlive us?" Rebecca asked.

Tanyth kept her gaze on the archers. "He collapsed the entrance. All the miners and their guards were well back from the entrance, I bet."

Gertie nodded, her gaze far away. "There's mice in there. There's a lot of confusion, but so far nobody's been hurt."

"You boys know the back way into the mine?" Tanyth asked. "Arnold took us out that way earlier. It might still be open."

Gertie nodded. "I haven't found a mouse there yet, but don't mean there ain't any."

"What you wanna bet he blows this tunnel, too?" Tanyth asked Gertie, looking away from the archers.

"Naw," Gertie said, shaking her head. "He's prob'ly already sailing down the bay. No need to blow the tunnel, there's nothing left here that matters." Gertie turned her face toward the archers. "One of you wanna go take a peek? See for yourselves?"

"What?" one of the archers said.

"I said he's prob'ly already sailing down the bay. If you run, you might still catch him."

The two shared a look, and the taller one nodded. The shorter one released the tension on his bowstring and trotted off down the tunnel, his boots clattering in the quiet. Moments later a distant shout echoed down the corridor, and the bowman came clattering back. "She's right. He's already casting off."

A sharp bang nearby interrupted them, and dust fell from the ceiling once more. A heavy cloud of it billowed down the tunnel, leaving the archers blinking against its sting and waving it away from their faces, their bows forgotten.

"Looks like I was wrong about collapsin' the tunnel," Gertie said.

Chapter 42
Trapped

Marong looked at the guards. "Well, we're all in the same boat now. You can kill us, or you can help us get out."

The archers threw down their bows and ran off down the tunnel, stripping off their quivers and dropping them with rattly clatters as they ran.

"They're prob'ly goin' to see if the cave mouth is blocked," Tanyth said. "That's a big hole, and all the labor is that way."

"If we can get out of here before Malloy gets too far, I can stop him," Rebecca said.

All eyes turned to her.

"How?" Marong asked.

"Fire arrow." She pointed to the bow. "A few rags wrapped around the head of one of their arrows should make a mess of their canvas."

"Gertie? Any mice that can see?" Tanyth asked.

Gertie's eyes focused on the middle distance for a moment, and she shook her head. "Too much noise and runnin' about. They're all tucked in holes."

"So are we," Marong said, his mouth twisted in a grin. "But we need to get out."

"So do they," Gertie said. "They just don't know it."

Tanyth picked up her staff and pointed at the ruined bedding. "Rebecca, see if there's enough rag there to make a couple of fire arrows. There's a jug of oil in the next room you can soak them in."

Rebecca set to work while Tanyth led the rest of them back toward the tunnel mouth.

The Hermit Of Lammas Wood

"Why this way?" Marong asked.

"He was surprised to come back and find us gone. He wouldn't have brought Rebecca back to use as leverage otherwise. Blowin' up the mine? He prob'ly had that planned. Blowin' up his bolt-hole? I'm hopin' that was a rush job," Tanyth said as they turned the corner and shuffled through the fallen rock and dust to where the tunnel entrance had been.

A fall of black rock blocked the opening, cascading into a rubble field in the tunnel.

"So much for that," Marong said and turned to walk away.

"Maybe not," Gertie said. "It's dark out there and lighter in here. Hard to see any light shining through, but there might be a way out. We just gotta find it." Nimble as one of her goats, Gertie clambered up the rock fall and started pushing and pulling rocks. She looked over the shoulder at Marong. "You comin'? Or you just gonna supervise?"

With a shrug and a glance at Tanyth, Marong followed Gertie up the rubble. Between them they rolled a couple of the topmost rocks down to grind onto the stone flooring.

"This looks hopeless," Marong said after the third block fell.

Gertie sat back on her haunches and chewed the corner of her lip. "You might be right. This rock is old and brittle. It's why we could pull the eye bolts out. The blast musta shattered rock halfway up the cliff face."

Running steps echoed down the tunnel, and Rebecca skidded to a halt a few feet from the turn. She clutched three arrows in one fist. The smell of machine oil overwhelmed the stench of black powder and rock dust.

"Malloy musta gotten underway by now," Marong said.

"We need to get out of here fast," Tanyth said. "If we don't, he'll disappear into the east and we'll never make him pay for what he's done."

Gertie tilted her head down and Tanyth saw one of the mice looking in her direction. The old woman had a playful expression on her face. "You're the one with the strength to do it, if anybody can, dearie. Feelin' up to the challenge?"

"What are you thinkin'?"

"A little shake on this pile might spread it out enough Rebecca can put an arrow or two in the air."

"A little shake?" Marong asked.

"Yeah," Rebecca said. "You could say one of your prayers, mum. Smack that pile and watch it collapse."

Tanyth looked from face to face: Rebecca's filled with hope and confidence, Marong's clouded with confusion. Gertie's made her pause.

"What's the problem, Gertie?" she asked.

"It'll take a lot of strength. Remember that storm?" She raised her shoulders and let them fall. "Dunno if you got enough to move the pile without killin' yourself."

"If we don't move it, Malloy gets away and we're trapped in here to die," Tanyth said.

"Yeah. Prob'ly sums it up."

"Wait a minute," Marong said. "What are you suggesting?"

"Father, Mother Fairport has...a talent."

"Besides talking to trees?" he asked.

"I don't talk. I just listen," Tanyth said, leaning her weight on her staff, feeling the iron bite into the tunnel floor.

"Yes, Father. Besides communing with nature." The young woman cast a glance in Gertie's direction. "Mother Pinecrest was supposed to be her teacher, so I'm guessin' she has a talent or two of her own."

"I've seen that one," Marong said. "She talks to mice. I don't see how mice can help."

"Your mother was right," Gertie said. "You're pig-headed."

"You knew my mother?" Marong asked, his jaw dropping.

"He is, and he's got the focus of a squirrel," Rebecca said.

Tanyth heard their words, but they seemed far away as she centered her entire being on the staff. Around her she felt the slow ebb and flow of the earth, heard the distant splash of wave against rock.

"I'll do it," Tanyth said, eyes closed, head bowed. "Get away from the rocks. Get back into Malloy's office where it's safe."

"Safe? Safe from what?" Marong asked.

"Sonny, you ask more stupid questions than Tanyth does,"

Gertie said, scrambling down the pile as nimbly as she'd climbed it. "If this goes wrong, she may pull down the tunnel roof on top of everything. Herself included."

Tanyth focused on the staff and the power rising under her feet.

"That's preposterous," Marong said.

"Well, you stand there, then. I'm getting' out of the way. When the rocks start flying, this is gonna be a poor place to be."

"What about her?" Marong asked, pointing at Tanyth.

"You let her worry about herself, Father," Rebecca said. "I've seen that woman do more amazin' things than rattle a few rocks. We need to do what she says." She hooked her bow over her shoulder and grabbed her father's hand. "Come, Father. Let her work. She'll need us after."

"Need us?"

"Yeah," Gertie said. "If the rocks don't kill her, the power she'll need might. We need to make sure that we stop Malloy if she manages to open the cave."

"Wait? She's going to die?"

"Shut up, Father. We don't have time for this." Rebecca looped her arm around one of Marong's, and Gertie grabbed the other.

"Come on. She might die if she tries this. She *will* die if we don't get out. I'll bet on the woman with the stick over the stick in the mud. Now move it."

Between them they pulled him away, and the trio disappeared down the side tunnel, their voices receding fast as Tanyth focused.

She raised her closed eyes and felt for north, pivoting her body around the grounded staff. "I call upon the Guardian of the North, Keeper of the Stone, Bones of the Earth, to aid and protect me this day," she said, her voice sounding muffled and small in the still cave. The taste of rock dust filled her mouth, and she tried to swallow it away as she turned to the east.

"I call on the Guardian of the East, Keeper of Wind, Breath of the Earth, to aid and protect me this day."

She turned to face the south, her staff grinding against

the powdered rock on the tunnel floor.

"I call on the Guardian of the South, Keeper of Fire, Soul of the Earth, to aid and protect me this day."

She turned to face the west, hearing her own blood pounding in her ears, louder than anything else in the tunnel.

"I call on the Guardian of the West, Keeper of Water, Blood of the Earth, to aid and protect me this day."

She completed her circle, facing north once more as the silence filled her ears.

"In the name of the All-Mother, Keeper of Life, Sower of Seed, and in the name of the All-Father, Keeper of Void, Gatherer of Fruit, I ask your aid and protection this day. Lend the strength of stone, the power of wind, the passion of fire, and the clean presence of water to my purpose. So mote it be."

She raised her staff and tapped the floor.

A hollow boom shuddered down the stone passage. Tanyth felt the vibrations through the soles of her boots and opened her eyes.

She raised her staff once more and thrust the iron shoe against the pile of stones, striking a spark from one of the larger ones at the bottom.

The pile shuddered with her strike, and the sound of grinding rock filled the tunnel. A tiny crack of light shone between the rocks at the top of the pile. The silver glow of moonlight gleamed a promise.

She raised her staff again and again struck the stones at the bottom of the pile.

The pile shifted and shook, rocks grinding against rocks and flowing downward and outward around her. The sliver of moonlight grew until Tanyth saw nearly a finger's width of the moon sailing high in the sky.

She also felt her arms growing leaden and her chest barely pulling air into her lungs. Gertie was right. She thrust the thought aside and raised her staff for what had to be the last time. It quivered in her hands, the moonlight glinting off the stone-scarred iron at the foot. With all her might, she struck the rock a final time–

And watched as the staff slipped off the rock, striking the

stone floor of the tunnel and shattering in her hand.

The hollow boom shook the floor and rattled the rocks, which fell away, rolling downhill away from the tunnel mouth in an avalanche of sharp-edged stones. The earth itself quaked, dropping more stones from the cliff face above. Tanyth saw rocks split away from the cliff face opposite. The rumbling, grinding roar spread like the sound of thunder on a summer's eve.

Her strength faded and her knees folded, dropping her to the rock-strewn floor. Her balance failing, she fell sideways, a small rock stabbing her shoulder as she did so. She rolled onto her back, the air refusing to enter her lungs and the light fading from her eyes. She saw the waning moon sailing above the cliff opposite, completing another voyage across the face of night.

Then she saw no more.

Chapter 43
New Plans

The taste of rock dust filled her mouth, but the scent of sea air filled her nose. Tanyth pried her eyes open and saw Gertie's wrinkled face smiling down on her.

"If yer done lazin' about, dearie, you might wanna get up and come see what you've done."

Tanyth's gaze went to the sky outside, still dark with a smattering of bright stars. The friendly moon had disappeared, but ruddy light flickered against the cliffs opposite. She heard shouts echoing against the stone but couldn't make out what they said.

She rolled over, trying to avoid the sharpest edges, and got her knees under her. "We shoulda brought your canteen," she said.

"A little cider would taste good, wouldn't it?" Gertie said by way of agreement. "Let's see if we can get you up and out of the rocks, at any rate."

With the old woman's help—and feeling rather aged herself—Tanyth pulled herself to her feet but found she needed to lean on Gertie far more than she wanted to.

"Ah, I've got a few days left, dearie. You just lean on me, and we'll be out in the air in a jiffy."

They shuffled their way through the shattered rock and dirt until Tanyth made out the source of the ruddy light. A schooner lay mostly engulfed in flames, crew bobbing in the water or swimming toward the banks where men in torn and filthy garb waited with hands outstretched to pull them up onto the rocks.

Tanyth gave a weak laugh.

What's so funny?" Gertie asked.

"Them. They gonna help the men who kept them slaves?"

Gertie took in the scene. "Sailors are sailors. I don't think many of 'em would wish death by fire or water on any other."

They watched for a time, Tanyth picking out the tall figure of Richard Marong, his white hair shining in the darkness, hat lost somewhere in the melee. Behind him, standing on a rock with bow in hand and arrow nocked, Rebecca kept watch.

"So her fire arrows worked," Tanyth said.

"Yep. First one took the main sail, second one took the aft."

"Malloy?"

"Third one took him straight in the chest. He was prob'ly dead before he hit the deck."

"How'd they get out?" Tanyth waved a hand at the men in tatters.

"Well, when the ground stopped shakin', they was able to make a hole big enough to squeeze through at the mouth of the cave. Funny how fast men with picks and shovels and a will to live can move a bit of stone about."

Tanyth turned to survey the end of the bay for the first time. What had been a majestic cascade of water falling from the cliff's edge now flowed in splashing ribbons down an incline of tumbled stones and soil.

"Did I do that?" she asked.

Gertie cackled. "Not hardly," she said. "At least not all of it. Malloy's charges did most of it. I won't say you didn't help it along, but I wasn't out here to see, so I don't really know."

Figures moved among the rocks and water. "Who's up there?"

Gertie shrugged. "Mouse isn't much use that far away," she said. "Normally I'd suggest you ask your owl, but that's prob'ly a bad idea until you've had some rest and some food."

Tanyth gave another low laugh. "Rest would be good. Water would be good. Food would be good." She ran a hand over her face, brushing away rock dust and spitting it out of her mouth. "The question I'm strugglin' with is why I ain't dead."

Gertie grinned. "I'm askin' the same question. I s'pect the powers that be ain't done with ya yet."

"You have these adventures all the time?" Tanyth waved her hand at the chaos around her.

"Well, bein' the hermit has mostly been borin'," she said. "Cider, goats, playin' with rocks. Keepin' my journal up. This is the most excitement I've had so far, if you don't count the blizzard five winters ago when I had eight goats, three trappers, and a mule all stayin' in the cottage."

Tanyth glanced at the old woman and found her grinning back.

"Took till spring to get the stink out, and it's not something I'd like ta repeat."

"An' this is?" Tanyth asked, finding her sense of humor appeared to be intact even if very little else seemed quite where it should be.

"No," Gertie said. "I'd be happy if this was a once-in-a-lifetime adventure, too."

Tanyth looked back up the bay and saw the figures were much closer. "I believe that's Arnold," she said, spotting the hulking, green-shirted figure picking his way down the slope. "Yeah, Fred's hobbling on a crutch, and Jimmy's helpin'."

"They was supposed to be goin' the other direction at sunup," Gertie said. She grimaced and her forehead wrinkled in a frown. Her apparent pique evaporated a moment later. "Look like they have the packs with 'em?"

"Arnold has at least one of them. Hard to tell in this light."

"If they brought the canteens, I'll forgive 'em."

Tanyth chuckled and slumped back against the stone. "We still have to hike back to the cottage," she said.

"Prob'ly wait 'til we've had some food and sleep. I don't know about you, but I'm draggin'. Good thing I'm an old lady and don't need much sleep."

"Please. Don't talk about sleep. My eyes keep tryin' to close. The only thing keepin' me awake is the sharp rock I'm sittin' on."

Most of the crew had climbed up onto the rocks; Marong

had them sitting in a row with their hands folded behind their necks. Rebecca kept an eye on them from a distance. A few stragglers heaved themselves over the wet and glistening stone to join their fellows. None of them seemed inclined to put up much of a struggle.

"S'pose that ship's gonna sink?" Gertie asked.

"She's ridin' kinda low in the water." Tanyth said. "I can feel the heat from here."

"Wonder how much gold is on it."

Above the cliffs, the sky turned pale and translucent in the pre-dawn while the ship continued to burn. As the day grew lighter, the morning breezes started blowing on-shore. The cliffs acted as a funnel, and in no time at all the faint onshore winds began shoving the flaming hulk back toward shore at the head of the bay. A yardarm gave way and crashed to the deck, scattering sparks and ashes into the air. The wind fanned the flames, and the fire's roaring grew.

"Hermit lady!" Arnold waved a hand in greeting as he approached.

"Arnold, you're s'posed to be heading north. What're you doin' back here?" Gertie asked.

"Didn't seem right to leave you to pick up the mess by yourself, mum. I tol' Fred and Jimmy we should come help."

"I see they're comin' along, too," Tanyth said.

"They didn't wanna," Arnold said. "They said we was s'posed ta go north and so that's what we should do. I told 'em I was comin' and they could go north without me, or they could come with me and help."

"What changed their minds?" Tanyth asked.

Arnold turned around and displayed his back. "I took the packs and headed this way. I figgered you'd need 'em, and with out 'em they couldn't get very far."

Tanyth looked to where the two men still picked their way down the slope. "I see that worked."

"Yep. It did."

Gertie waved him over. "If there's anything left in that canteen...?"

"Oh, yes'm. Should be." Arnold pulled the straps from his wide shoulders and dropped the packs on the stone. "We ate some of the food and drank some of the water, but there's plenty left in the canteen."

Gertie grabbed her canteen and took a slow swallow of the cider before handing it to Tanyth. "That'll put spring in your step again."

Tanyth sipped the sweet tang from the canteen and let it roll around her mouth a bit, washing the rock grit from between her teeth and moistening the parched tissues. "Oh, that's delightful," she said, handing the canteen back to Gertie. "I can only handle a little bit right now or I'll be keelin' over again."

Gertie laughed and patted her knee. "You earned it, dearie."

"What, the keelin' over?" she asked.

"Well, yeah, but I was thinkin' more like restin' up."

The crackling hull drifted deeper into the cove as the morning wind picked up. They watched it bump into the cliffs on the far side, the wind spinning the hull so the bow pointed at the pile of collapsed stone at the end of the cove. Fire had burned almost all the superstructure and licked the rails nearly to the waterline. As the wind gave the hulk more speed, the main deck collapsed into the hull, sending sheets of sparks and ash into the air.

Fred hobbled over to them, Jimmy in tow. "That looks like Malloy's ship," he said.

"It was," Gertie said.

"Was?"

"He's dead."

"So it's over?" Jimmy asked.

Richard Marong walked up the landing toward them, his steps measured and exhaustion writ on his sagging face. "All but the sweeping up."

"What's goin' ta happen to us, sir?" Fred asked.

He took in a deep breath and looked around at the men on the landing, some in green shirts and black pants, others in the tattered remnants of whatever they'd been wearing when captured.

"There's probably going to be a hearing, but I'll use my influence with the council to convene it in Northport."

Fred's mouth tightened up and he sighed. "Can't be helped, I s'pose."

"I'll recommend that all of you get full pardons and immunity for whatever happened here," Marong said. "The men who were made slaves were no less victims than you. The evil in this died on that ship." He nodded at the burning hulk just now drifting up into shallow water. "There's probably plenty of bloody-mindedness to go around. Any one who wants passage back to Kleesport, or anywhere else that might be home, I think I can arrange that."

A muffled *krump* sounded deep in the hull, and a blossom of black smoke bloomed just aft of the mainmast. The hull started heeling over almost immediately, the burning wood hissing as the cold water touched it. They watched as the hull rolled partway over and sank onto the rocky bottom. The small waves driven by the morning's breeze crested where the curve of the hull lay just below the surface.

"There should be enough we can recover from that wreck to pay reparations to the victims," Marong said. "I suspect the council will convince the king to annex this cove to Kleesport. There'll be jobs here for any who want one."

"A job, sir?" Fred asked. "Mining?"

"Malloy was many things, but stupid wasn't one of them," Marong said. "I suspect he saw this cove as the perfect place to land stolen goods and sell them back. When they stumbled on the gold, he was quick to take advantage of the extra bodies that otherwise would have been fish bait. I think we can do better as administrators. I believe we can turn this tragedy into something positive."

"What about the garrison troops?" Tanyth asked.

"That's a matter for the King's Own to decide. I suspect many of the men involved are trying to gain passage to somewhere far away right now."

"So what're ya gonna do with them?" Gertie asked, jerking her chin in the direction of the soggy sailors shivering on the rocks.

Marong cast them a long look and sighed. "Offer 'em the same deal, I suppose. Nobody's going to gain from hanging a bunch of men who were as much prisoners as any slaves.

Maybe we can salvage something from this, too."

"Well, if you're not gonna kill 'em on purpose, might wanna let 'em get some shelter and dry clothes before you kill 'em by accident," Gertie said.

Marong started and stared at her for a moment. "Yes," he said after a moment. "Of course, you're right."

"There's plenty of food and uniforms in the mine, sir," Arnold said. "We should get the cooks movin' on makin' breakfast, too."

Marong smiled at the big man, who grinned back and looked down to his shoes at the attention. "Good suggestion. You wanna round everybody up and get them assembled in there. I assume there's some kind of dining hall?"

"Yes, sir," Arnold said.

"Excellent. Get everybody there. Ask the cooks to make breakfast, and we'll hash out some arrangements. I suppose we need somebody who can write to record all this." He looked to Fred, who shook his head.

Jimmy spoke up. "I'd be happy to, sir. I learned my letters and numbers afore I went to sea. If we can find somethin' to write on and somethin' to write with."

"There's plenty of ledger books and quills in the manager's office, Jimmy. I can show ya where," Arnold said.

"Very good then," Marong said. "Arnold, if you and Jimmy would get everybody sheltered and the cooks working?"

"Yes, sir," they said and ran down the landing, Jimmy shouting orders and Arnold just looking big.

Marong laughed. "Nobody'll give them much guff, I wager."

Fred smiled. "No, sir, they won't."

Marong looked Fred. "How's the ankle?"

"Still sore, sir, but it's healin' pretty quick."

"You seem to know your way around here pretty well. Fancy being my second in command?"

"Me, sir? There's lots o' men senior to me."

"I'm sure there are, but you're here. You came back when you didn't need to. We're going to have to work together to make this happen. Right now we've got a mess to clean up,

291

The Hermit Of Lammas Wood

people to feed and shelter, and a gold mine to inventory. You know most of these guards, don't you?"

"Oh, aye, sir. There never was many green shirts. I know most of 'em. Not sure how many survived or how many might still be headin' for greener pastures."

"Well, you want the job?"

"Yes, sir. Thank you, sir."

"You don't wanna give it to her?" Tanyth asked, nodding her head at Rebecca.

The young woman stood leaning on her long bow, arrows in the quiver on her back, watching Arnold and Jimmy forming up the shivering, frightened men.

"She looks right at home, don't she?" Gertie asked.

"Aye, she does," Tanyth said.

"I would but for two things," Marong said. "First, I don't believe in nepotism. She deserves better. Second, she's got another path to follow. I see that now."

Tanyth saw the look in his eye and offered a smile. "You might wanna tell her that before you forget or she starts down that path without ya."

He cast a glance at Tanyth, and his lips curled up in a wan smile. "Mother Fairport, that's very good advice. If you ladies will excuse me?"

Tanyth and Gertie both nodded. Marong strolled down the landing, stepping aside to let the guards and ex-slaves pass. He took his daughter aside, the pride in his face shining bright in the dim light of dawn.

"Any loose ends here?" Tanyth asked, glancing at Gertie.

"Oh, prob'ly. Marong's a good man. He'll see to 'em."

"What about Rebecca?"

"What about her?" Gertie asked.

"She needs to get back to Northport, don't she?"

"Yeah, prob'ly. There's a bit of time before that Groves boy gets back."

Tanyth turned to stare at Gertie. "That Groves boy?"

"Yeah, Saul's son. Benjamin?"

"For a hermit you sure know a lot of people."

Gertie shrugged. "Trees. Terrible gossips."

Tanyth snickered.

"'Sides, that one's got more to do, I expect. Lots more."

"More hermit magic?" Tanyth asked.

"Well, if you count common sense as hermit magic, I s'pose so."

"How'd ya figger that?"

Gertie turned her face toward Tanyth. "Easy. Bein' around you for a year. You don't know the effect you have on people."

Tanyth snorted. "Right now the effect I'd have on most people is disgust. I've been wearing the same clothes for a week, and I would happily wrestle a bear for a hot bath."

Gertie laughed. "Most o' these men been wearing the same clothes for a year. I s'pect you smell just fine to them."

Tanyth watched the ex-slaves march back into the mine. "Could you do it?" she asked.

"Do what, dearie?"

"March back in. After what they been through? To get outside at last, only to turn around and go back?"

Gertie nodded. "Oh, sure. It's shelter and food. There's hope. Nobody's swinging whips or clubs. The green shirts look more shaken than the men who were slaves, I reckon."

Tanyth noticed it then. The tentative stances, the uneasy smiles. "There'll be some repercussions. Dark tunnels. Late night visits."

Gertie sighed. "Prob'ly. Richard'll have to deal with it."

"Richard'll have to deal with what?" Marong asked striding back along the stones, Rebecca walking along side.

"The retribution some of them guards are gonna be on the wrong end of," Gertie said.

Marong's mouth twisted like he smelled something vile and he sighed. "Probably." He shook his head and sighed again, suddenly fascinated by the toe of his boot. "Can't say I'd blame 'em."

Tanyth pursed her lips and glanced up at the sky. "I s'pect most o' the guards who'd be most deservin' have already left. There was an awful lot of green shirts movin' through the forest last night. I don't imagine many of 'em will be back to bother."

Richard scratched his beard and nodded. "I'll hope you're right, mum, but I'll plan for the worst, too."

Rebecca stepped forward. "What'll you do now, mum?"

"Gertie and me'll head back to the cottage, I s'pect. A good place for two old ladies to stay out o' trouble."

Gertie laughed. "Just you wait, dearie. I still haven't showed ya the hot springs."

Tanyth groaned. The thought of sluicing off a week's worth of grime and about forty pounds of rock dust sounded heavenly. "How far is it? Can we be there tonight?"

Gertie shook her head. "Sorry, dearie. We ain't leavin' here until you and me get a good night's sleep and maybe some hot food."

Tanyth's stomach rumbled loud enough for them all to hear, even over the burbling of the new river at the end of the cove.

"Let's go see what's for breakfast, shall we?" Marong said, waving his arm in invitation as if to a palace instead of a half-collapsed hole in the ground.

"Thought you'd never ask, Richard," Gertie said. She rose and took his arm. They trailed the men along the slick rocks toward the cave.

"You need a hand, mum?" Rebecca said, offering her arm for support.

Tanyth looked at the young woman, at her soot-streaked face, hair tied back out of the way. Her eyes had seen too much, perhaps, but they were a woman's eyes now. Tanyth reached for her arm and levered herself off the rock. She held on to Rebecca with both hands and tottered along on legs that held more rubber than bone.

"Thank you, my dear."

"You're welcome, mum. Can I ask you a question?"

They ambled well behind Gertie and Marong.

"Long's it doesn't need a lot of answer. I'm still a bit wobbly."

Rebecca patted Tanyth's hand where it rested on her forearm. "Mum, after that, I'm s'prised you're vertical at all. You were out for three days after that storm, comin' out here."

Tanyth grunted. "Yeah, well. What's your question, my dear?"

"What now?" she asked. "You and Gertie can't be just

goin' back to the cottage, can you?"

Tanyth looked up at her earnest face, Rebecca's gaze searching hers as if trying to read the future in the lines there. "I learned a lot already, my dear. Trees gossip, you know, and they have cruel roots."

"I didn't know that, mum." Rebecca's careful tone made Tanyth laugh loud enough to make Gertie and Marong look back over their shoulders.

"I got a lot more to do. I think I'd like to stay with Gertie for a bit. Through next winter anyway. Should be plenty o' time to get my notes together and write down all the herb lore I've collected."

"That sounds like a good plan, mum."

"You've got another road to travel, my dear," Tanyth said, leaning in to speak quietly. "And if you're willin', I'd like ya to help me out a bit before you go."

"Of course, mum, how can I help?"

"You and Penny seem to hit it off right well."

"Oh, aye. She's a pip, Penny is. We had a good time traveling together. Even though I was kinda sad to be leavin' ya, it was still fun to be with her."

"Did you find any gold nuggets on the way back?"

"Oh, yeah. Penny said I was lucky. We found a small bag full. Maybe half a pound of it. Penny sent it off to Kleesport to be sold."

"You'll be set up and quite independent, then, won't ya?"

"I will. Penny said I can stay with her, but Perry and Amanda want me to stay with them and help with the dining room in the evenings."

"What do you want to do, my dear?"

Rebecca fingered the bow string that ran across her chest. "I think I'd like to spend more time in the woods. It's almost like magic out here. Before, down in Ravenwood, it was nice, but here the mountains are huge and they're right close. The woods are full of game. The rivers have more fish than I've ever seen. Including at the fishmongers'."

"What'll you do out there in the forest?"

"I don't know, mum. Do I need to do anything?"

"Might be. Maybe not."

The Hermit Of Lammas Wood

"Well, there's always looking for more gold. I s'pect there'll be a lot more people up here once word of the gold mine gets back to Kleesport."

"I s'pect you're right."

"Why do ya ask, mum?"

"Well, I'd take it as a kindness if you'd plan to ramble between town and the cottage a couple times a month." Tanyth looked into Rebecca's eyes. "I'd like ta stock up on tea for the winter, and I don't know how much paper and ink Gertie has squirreled away. Seems like the woman has everything somewhere."

"Except tea."

"Yeah." Tanyth sighed, "And I miss my teapot."

"The white china one you left in Ravenwood?"

"Yeah. Left it on the mantel in Mother Alderton's hut. Didn't expect Gertie wouldn't have one."

"You know that's Mother Fairport's hut now, don't ya?" Rebecca said, the lilt of humor tinting her voice.

Tanyth laughed and leaned on the young woman's strong arm. "Prob'ly."

"So, you're askin' if I'll be a courier for ya for the summer? Izzat it?" Rebecca asked.

"Yeah. Maybe you and Penny can come out when she's got a break between births or somethin'."

"I think I'd like that. I can check up on ya."

"Scamp, and here I was planning to use it to check up on you."

Rebecca patted her hand again. "We'll check up on each other, mum."

Tanyth hugged Rebecca's arm. "That we will, my dear. That we will."

They finally made it to the entrance to the cave and made their way underground, leaving the cascading river bubbling happily in its new channel.

Chapter 44
More Gossip

---※---

Tanyth found a peace in the tiny garden that fed a part of her she hadn't known was hungry. The long trail back from the south took nearly a week of slow travel. Gertie seemed in no hurry to return to her goats, and Rebecca delighted in each new vista. Tanyth's strength returned a little more each day. They even cut a length of oak from the thick stands to the south to replace the staff that she had lost. The closer they drew to the Valley of a Thousand Smokes, the greater the sense of peace filling her.

Gertie kept her promise and showed Tanyth the hot spring, fed by a trickle of cold water inside the mountain. The hot water and quiet peace drew the last of the pain from Tanyth's exhausted body, and restored her.

Three days after returning, Tanyth felt strong enough to take up a spade and turn several small plots of soil beside the cottage to plant her carefully gathered seeds. She surveyed her handiwork daily and drew a quiet pleasure as the seedlings thrived under the high country sun. As the solstice approached, she began making notes about what other seeds she needed to round out the collection.

A breeze rustled the leaves in the ancient trees. *Change is coming.*

Tanyth laughed quietly and plucked a fledgling weed from the new chives. The wind always said change was coming.

A swirl in the wind sent a chill down her back, and she looked up to the snow-capped massifs that surrounded the head of the valley. The winds dropping down from the heights often brought the icy reminders, even on the warmest days.

Good-bye.

The chill wind rattled the branches in the sudden gust. Tanyth blinked back a sudden fear even as she scrambled to her feet. The treetops shook and bobbed and the sighing leaves repeated the message.

Good-bye.

"No," she said and scrambled to her feet. "No."

A few steps found her in the snug cottage, Gertie's journal on the polished tabletop, her heavy mug beside it.

Good-bye.

She turned to see the old woman stretched out on her cot, fully dressed.

"No!" Tanyth knelt on the hard stone floor beside the cot, holding the gnarled fingers of the last of the old witch woman as they grew cold. "No," she said, her tear-choked whisper barely louder than the wind in the trees.

Good-bye. Good-bye. Good-bye.

The gust blew itself out after a time. Tanyth levered herself up from the floor, groaning as her knees straightened painfully after kneeling on hard, cold stone.

She crossed to the table and ran a finger across the page where Gertie had made her last entry—the letters overly large, and the ink sometimes blotted.

With these words my tale comes to an end, but as in so many things, each end sows the seeds of a new beginning. My journey draws to its final destination as all must. This body grows tired and heavy. I join my cold sisters in the sure belief that my time here leaves the world better than when I came and that the solstice will see a new hermit to keep the old knowledge.

I call on the Guardian of the North to lend her the strength of the stones that surround us and keep her safe.

I call on the Guardian of the East to give her the gift of the winds that bring the freshness of spring, the fullness of summer, the ripe harvest of fall, and the clean renewal of winter each in their turns.

I call on the Guardian of the South to bless her with the fire of life, to keep her passion alive even as she enters the autumn of her days.

I call on the Guardian of the West to wash her in the waters of renewal, that her sense of wonder might never leave her.

I ask in the names of the All-Mother and the All-Father, guard and protect, nurture and support the Hermit of Lammas Wood.

So mote it be.

Tanyth sat in Gertie's chair and let the tears flow down her cheeks unheeded until the clatter of hooves on the stones outside drew her back to the world. The delicate bleats of the goats reminded her that she had things to do, that the world still pulsed with life. She closed Gertie's journal and rose from the table.

She glanced once more at the still figure on the cot and stepped out into the afternoon sun. She'd have to honor her friend, but first she needed to see about getting the milk out of the goats and into the bucket.

The does nuzzled her hands and butted her gently. "Patience, ladies. Been a long time since I've been under a goat." She grabbed the stool from beside the door and placed it on a solid looking bit of rock. "Hope I remember how this works."

The does didn't seem to mind her lack of expertise one whit.

Tanyth straightened from her labors and stretched her back, glancing into the bucket at the warm, frothy milk and smiling. She'd never be able to see the goats without remembering the feisty old woman who'd gentled them to her touch. As she gazed around the small yard and out into the orchard beyond, she saw evidence of Gertie's hand and heard her voice in her heart.

Her eyes started to tear up again, but she fought back as figures stepped from the shadows on the path and into the sunlight.

"Rebecca!" Tanyth said, her voice echoing from the stony faces around her. "I didn't expect you back so soon."

"I've brought company," she said. "I hope you don't

mind."

A gust shook the tree tops. *Change is coming.*

Tanyth laughed. "Some things never change," she muttered.

"What's that, mum?" Rebecca asked.

"Who'd you bring?" Tanyth asked in return.

A tall man wearing a leather vest and a broad-brimmed hat stepped out of the trees. Tanyth's voice caught in her throat.

"Howdy," Frank said. "Thought I'd come see how you was doin'."

"Frank." It was the only word she could think of to say. "Frank."

Rebecca laughed, her merry peals echoing around the mountains. "First time I ever seen you speechless, mum."

A moment later Tanyth hugged him as if her life might pound out of her chest if she didn't. She reveled in the strong arms that wrapped her in return, and for long moments nothing else mattered.

"I brought you something," Frank said.

She pushed back and looked up into his rugged face. She traced his cheekbone with fingertips. "Indeed you did."

"No, I mean something else," he said. He shucked off his pack and pulled a bunched sweater off the top of it. He held it out to her.

"A sweater? You came all this way to bring me a sweater?" The absurdity of it threatened to send her off in giggles.

"Take it," he said, thrusting it into her hands.

The bundle was solid in the center. Hard, even, under the wool. She parted the fabric, and the gleaming white of china sparkled in the high-country sunlight. She pulled her teapot from its cozy nest and hugged it to her chest.

Tears streamed down her face again, and she gazed into the eyes of perhaps the only man who ever loved her.

The wind swirled and gusted around them.

Tanyth looked up at the treetops.

Change has come.

Nathan Lowell

The Golden Age of the Solar Clipper

Quarter Share

Half Share

Full Share

Double Share

Captains Share

Owners Share

South Coast

Tanyth Fairport Adventures

Ravenwood

Zypherias Call

Hermit Of Lammas Wood

Awards

2011 Parsec Award Winner for Best Speculative Fiction (Long Form) for *Owners Share*

2010 Parsec Award Winner for Best Speculative Fiction (Long Form) for *Captains Share*

2009 Podiobooks Founders Choice Award for Captains Share

2009 Parsec Award Finalist for Best Speculative Fiction (Long Form) for *Double Share*

2008 Podiobooks Founders Choice Award for *Double Share*

2008 Parsec Award Finalist for Best Speculative Fiction (Long Form) for *Full Share*

2008 Parsec Award Finalist for Best Speculative Fiction (Long Form) for *South Coast*

Contact

Website: nathanlowell.com
Twitter: twitter.com/nlowell
Email: nathan.lowell@gmail.com

About The Author

Nathan Lowell first entered the literary world by podcasting his novels. The Golden Age of the Solar Clipper grew from his life-long fascination with space opera and his own experiences shipboard in the United States Coast Guard. Unlike most works which focus on a larger-than-life hero, Nathan centers on the people behind the scenes—ordinary men and women trying to make a living in the depths of interstellar space. In his novels, there are no bug-eyed monsters, or galactic space battles, instead he paints a richly vivid and realistic world where the hero uses hard work and his own innate talents to improve his station and the lives of those of his community.

Dr. Nathan Lowell holds a Ph.D. in Educational Technology with specializations in Distance Education and Instructional Design. He also holds an M.A. in Educational Technology and a BS in Business Administration. He grew up on the south coast of Maine and is strongly rooted in the maritime heritage of the sea-farer. He served in the USCG from 1970 to 1975, seeing duty aboard a cutter on hurricane patrol in the North Atlantic and at a communications station in Kodiak, Alaska. He currently lives on the plains east of the Rocky Mountains with his wife and two daughters.

Printed in Great Britain
by Amazon